All of the fictions in this character are real,
and any resemblance to the rest of you lemmings is strictly intentional.
This said, the author wishes to forewarn all readers that the really big questions,
e.g. What is the "meaning" of life? Is there a God?
What happens to us after we die? How did everything "begin?" etc.
will be addressed, perhaps for the very first time with absolute truthfulness, herein.
None of these answers will make you "feel good,"
therefore, you will feel, they cannot be "true."
This feeling (because it's being processed by your brain)
you will assume is a thought.

NOTHING WILL SHAKE YOU FROM THIS ASSUMPTION!

Since you won't *like* what the author is imparting here,
and since it runs contrary to all you've been taught to think,
the author "must" therefore be "wrong."
Now, as it stands, there's a plethora of standard, positive responses you can get
from any number of informed sources with cute little degrees
proving their owners can authoritatively repeat what *they've* been taught to think.
So why should you pay attention to this author? You shouldn't!
Simply continue to wallow in propagannda and put on a happy face.
And don't believe the author when he tells you there's really no such thing
as happiness after all, that it's an invention, a concept, and,
albeit well-meant, an obfuscation.
God bless the beguiled.
Better yet, ignore this work completely. Pick up a Harlequin Romance instead.
Just don't touch yourself or you'll go blind.

# Carnival

Also by this author:

Microcosmia

Freak

Signature

Moth In The Fist

The Deep End

Legerdemainia

Hero

*ronsandersatwork.com*

"Kevin, I'm convinced mankind's true evolution will commence when this whole aboriginal God trip is junked!"

—Eddie

"It's just that honesty takes all the fun out of a witch hunt."

—Lance

"Shit, I seen eunuchs got more balls than you got."

—Nefertiti

"I tell you, life's a gag, man, a joke; a silly little diversion in the endless labor of creation. And I'm not saying it's not a good joke. I bust a gut every time I think about it. But it's like this is a *running* joke, you dig? It just goes *on and on and on!* Okay, so maybe I'm not smart enough to see the glorious purpose of this living hell, and maybe I'm not deep enough to know whether it's a deity or demon running the show, but before I go, man, *before I go*, I've simply *got* to get my hands on whatever's in charge and say, 'Hey, Sucker! I'm hip to sick jokes, okay? And I'll take the fall as lamely as the next second-billionth banana. But don't leave me hanging! Man oh man oh *man*, just what the hell's the punch line?"

—Sahib

"Too trippy," Kevin said, slowly shaking his head, "much too trippy."

# PART ONE

## BLEAK NEWS FROM THE GENE POOL

It's a riot, it's a romp, it's a ride. It's a roller coaster of a revolution that jangles to this day.

Actually, it's 1967, and the place is Haight-Ashbury, a district of a few square blocks just outside downtown San Francisco.

The occasion? A spontaneous gathering of revelers, all set to erupt into lawlessness, licentiousness, and madness—that roller coaster's mind-blowing feature plunge.

And it's the intent of this document to accurately describe not only the event but the times—to, in so doing, fairly portray a philosophical dichotomy that pitted American against American with a bitterness not seen since the War Between the States. The work does not mean to defend one side against the other; it strives to be an account, rather than an argument. The following introduction attempts a brief history of the political climate and social turmoil leading to that emotional maelstrom known as *The Summer of Love*.

*For Lucian*

# Chapter 1

# The Itch Of Being

*In the beginning there was a burst of energy.*

To the disillusioned it was the sweet flowering of the human spirit, the blossoming of man.

*We were shell-shocked—a charismatic young president was in the ground. Smog was in our lungs, mercury in our fish, acid in our rain. And every night the tube laid it out straight for us: the sky was falling, ghettos were ablaze, drought-stricken countries were somehow producing starving children even faster than their desperately concerned parents could frantically copulate. Amazing. And, still playing King of the Mountain, the goliaths were scrapping over some festering wound in Southeast Asia. But that was all just news and nonsense—more emphatically than all these crises combined, the Bomb made it plain. We were doomed.*

*The blossom emerged Underground, with roots in British rock, Mexican hemp, Indian mysticism, American pharmaceuticals. Suddenly there was a beat in the air. We became light-headed and gender-fuzzy, politically hip and vagabond-chic. Rather than bear arms, we bore daisies. Instead of seeking enlistment, we sought to bedevil our senses. It was our world now, and we were going to fix it; with smiles, with slogans, with symbols and songs. At the very brink of perdition we stood, synchronizing our auras to chant the Devil down.*

*It would take time. But we were young and strong and many. We had all this energy.*

*Enough to galvanize even the witless and despondent. Enough to give the staunchest of doomsayers pause. Enough to, for a stutter in time, make a difference.*

*And that burgeoning energy was Love, flinging its seeds and budding anew, fitting piece by piece each anomalous member of the stubborn human puzzle.*

*To our fathers, however, the choreographer's hand was unmistakable. All this business about peace and love could only be the usual commie line, designed to seduce and regiment the usual parade of whining followers. And the parade grated. After Normandy, after Inch'on, after all the lost lives and limbs—that we hairy young hedonists should spew a single syllable concerning policy riled even the most moderate of conservatives. We'd turned their Beaver Cleaver streets into psychedelic playgrounds, muddied the mat of every Judeo-Christian ethic—but pacifism under fire was the final straw. They raged and appealed, threatened and condemned, hurled accusations of everything from homosexuality to treason. Almost overnight "peace" became a dirty word, and any mention of spiritual flowering made palms itch for the rough kiss of a trusty scythe.*

*Eventually the blossom shriveled. We grew bored with it all, became pragmatic, and, to our everlasting and unforgivable shame, adopted typically pedestrian lives of dollar-based drudgery, bald-faced brown-nosing, and soulless confrontation.*

*Now the Revolution is little more than a doddering irrelevancy. Yet there are those who still believe the corpse can be resuscitated, the rush reproduced. They'll bend your ear if you let them. They'll hound you with tales of an age gone by, when freedom grew wild in the Pollyanna Spring. Be gentle with them, and never broach that lesson every generation learns way too late: that all that energy—all that optimism, enthusiasm, and potential—was vested in, of course, the impetuous hands of youth.*

joon 28 1967
jime
wuts hapunen
man hav i gawt nooz 4 yoo
dig this i <u>finule</u> tawkd mi old man in2 ltn me rid up 2 frisko
with ed an mik
4 rel
i thenk i wood hav split newa evn if he kp saen no bcuz i kant
~~stumak~~ ~~stommuk~~ <u>stan</u> thu thawt uv hangen urown this dump
awl sumr
4 1 theng mi mawmz rele bin awn thu rag L8Le she keps
thrtnen 2 grown me or snd me 2 sumr skool so its u good thng
im gtn owt yl thu gtnz good
4 unuthr theng thu vibz mi old man poots owt wood kut throo
stil
sumtimz he triz 2 ak lik he kaerz but i bt hez ltn me go jus 2 gt
rid uv me
thu giz u rel dinusor jime awl he duz iz sit urown hawlren an
gripn an guzlen ber lik thaerz no 2mro
he wont lt me gt uwa with <u>nethen</u>
but thats kool he duzn no it but 4 3 wex now iv bin shaken
kwrtrz owt uv that sprklts bawtl he throz hiz chanj in iv gawt
ovr 20 bux 4 thu trip
stil b4 i go id lik 2 tl him hez jus u wrthlus old frt drenken hiz
lif uwa
but i thenk hed kil me
newa i lookd in thu fre prs an fown owt thu big goldn g8 prk
konsrts stil awn
thaerz goen 2 b so mne fr owt bichn sooprhv groops it jus bloz
mi min 2 thenk ubowt it jfrsun aerplan kand het an thu gr8fl dd
4 shr
wut u gas
2 bad yoo had 2 go an bus yr lag but il b ritn an il lt yoo no wuts
hapunen ech groov stond mil uv thu wa
wl i gs thats awl 4 now im rd 2 jam
jime im so xsitd i cood flip owt <u>thenk uv it</u> thu hol sumr awf an
her im awn mi wa 2 thu sit

mab il ml yoo sum pawt bkuz i no wel b gtn hi up thaer
wl thats awl iv gawt 2 rit 4 now im awn mi wa
bi thu tim yoo gt this ltr il prawble b gtn it awn with sum groopz
or rapn with hendrix az we pas u joent
don b srprizd if i gt 2 yootopu an dsid 2 nvr cum bak thaerz
nuthen down her evn wrth remmbren
xsp 4 awl mi sooprtit frnz uv kors
wl i gs thats awl jime so b kool an sta hi
kevin


     Kevin ran his eyes down the letter lustily, nodding with savage glee. The thing was a bombshell, all right; just the kind of brutally crafted, carefully polished communication he needed. A sprinkle of subtle allusions, a dash of trenchant wit. Something to play cat and mouse with the imagination. Jimmy's frustration would be calamitous, and this missive would lodge, hopefully, at the very root of the hobbled boy's misery, remaining to fester all summer long while Kevin, hundreds of miles up the coast, tapped salt in the wound with further letters exaggerating his own good fortune.

     Now Kevin dropped the sheet of paper and wrung his hands, visualizing Jimmy, confined to his room in Long Beach, receiving an endless stream of mail postmarked an instant before arrival. This letter would be the first irritation—the first indication of the itch that couldn't be scratched. Kevin could just picture Jimmy's face contorting, the paper in his trembling hands smoldering with tales of high adventure and lush conquest. Kevin clenched his fists with the image, pounded his big paws together and nodded harder. For the briefest moment—so brief he wasn't sure it had really occurred—the boy's mind went utterly blank, like the switching-off and immediate switching-on of a hall lamp. This instant of blackness was accompanied by a sick pain behind the eyes, of such brief duration it, too, was questionable.

     Strange.

     That had been happening a lot lately. Or had it? He felt anxiety coil in his chest and pass. Stranger still. There wasn't any reason to be anxious, was there? Things couldn't be more bitchen.

Outside his bedroom rose a thundering, heart-stopping bellow of absolutely mindless passion, finally punctuated by a tremendous two-footed stamping that rattled the windows and shook the door. A string of black obscenities, another bellow, and a long groan followed by a truncated curse. Kevin, so accustomed to these outbursts he hardly noticed, folded the letter and slid it into an envelope. Before repetition could sour the image of Jimmy's frustration, he licked the envelope's gummed edge and sealed it, trapping the image inside. But while laboriously centering Jimmy's address in thick block print he felt his enthusiasm slip away, almost as if it were leaking out the pen's felt tip. It was an old problem, this relentless sinking of spirit, connected, in some way, to the effort expended in concentration.

At least he was pretty sure it was an old problem.

Hadn't he just, only seconds before, been thrilled, awed, or expectant about some notion, conviction, or gambit related in some way to some plan or other? He wished he could put his finger on it, and wished, too, that he could include in his letter some reference to this problem—if there really was a problem—and maybe get his friend Jimmy's advice. But it was too late, the envelope was sealed, and besides, Jimmy really wasn't that close a friend. In fact, Jimmy wasn't much of a friend at all, the prick. When he had moved to Long Beach there had been no goodbye for Kevin, no acknowledging the big shy boy as a human being worth remembering. Kevin had procured Jimmy's new address from an acquaintance in common, and had continued the charade of having a pen pal (even though he'd never received a note in return) only because he so desperately needed friends. His emotional turmoil had not diminished with time. But Jimmy would be sorry now. He sure as hell would. Kevin looked around for some assurance, for some kind of tangible evidence to support his excitement, and saw nothing but the dirty, cracker-thin walls of his bedroom, coldly returning his stare. He tore through the clutter on his desk, found a clipping scissored from the *Free Press*, held it up to his eyes as if it were pornography:

HAIGHT-ASHBURY—Now that the long-awaited and much-ballyhooed Summer Solstice Festival is history, the Hashbury flower children are clamoring for more. And apparently their very vocal reactions to the Festival, a disappointing assemblage of less than 5,000 on Golden Gate Park's Speedway Meadows, have inspired several hip organizers to rally freaks statewide for a comeback which, in concert promoter Bill Graham's opinion, will be a tribal gathering to dwarf even January's highly-publicized Human Be-in. And *so*—in effect—this new festival will simply be an extension of the big July 6 concert announced in the *Freep*'s May 7 issue. Since the date for the festival coincides with what is expected to be the peak of Hashbury's Summer of Love invasion, San Franciscan official-dom is doing some pretty tough talking. By now, however, it must be obvious even to the hard-hearted civic council that any effort to halt an enterprise involving such a multitude of freaks would only exacerbate the situation. After endless bullying and cajoling, the *Freep* was granted an interview with Mayor John Shelley Himself, whose outlook on the  festival was something less than positive.

"*It's a disgrace,*" the mayor stated. "*It's an outrage! You people think you can exploit the common goodwill…*"

(and here Kevin skipped down the column impatiently)

"*…latent communists…swinish habits…hotbed of drug users and runaways…Haight Ashbury district…reputation as a haven…rebellious types…indications of this cancer spreading to the park proper…over three hundred men covering the park, and drugs will not, repeat* will not *be tolerated!*"

Then some obviously inflated figures dealing with current Park Station manpower, followed by one of Shelley's stock got-it-covered speeches. Kevin frowned smugly and read on:

The mayor's precautions, however, are bound to prove embar-rassing. Reports from The Berkeley Barb—and rumors sub-stantiated by reliable underground sources—indicate an expect-

6

ed crowd of some 30,000 freaks from Marin, San Mateo, Contra, and Alameda counties, and a possible influx of up to 20,000 from other parts of the state.

Kevin dropped his arm and let the lost smile slowly reform. Although he'd read the clipping a hundred times, the joy he now felt came as something new and refreshing. Oddly, the repeated readings hadn't improved his spelling and punctuation comprehension a whit. He was one of those essentially lazy individuals who absorb the world selectively. If it required any work, any *application* that did not result in instant gratification, it was far too abstruse for Kevin. But he carefully folded the clipping and filed it in one of the flimsy plastic windows in his wallet, where he could always reach it and, like a fresh convert riffling Bible pages, search it for those familiar words so vital to his ambition: *flower children, Summer of Love, drug users, runaways. A haven. A hotbed. Freaks, underground sources.*

It was way too good to be real.

Just emancipated from high school and one week into a promising summer—a summer that had, only two weeks ago, presented all the horrors-to-be of a long and depressing three months divided into neat halves:  six weeks of summer classes, followed by six weeks of stewing around the house dreading each confrontation with his parents. That this prospect was no less unappealing to the parents had been revealed by the father's uncharacteristically quick compliance. Big, tough, irascible Joe—who wouldn't let no goddamn punk kid of *his* get away with doing any goddamn thing he wanted t'do, and just who the hell d'you think wears the goddamn pants in this goddamn family—big, booming, diehard Joe had, for some obscure reason, readily acquiesced to his son's desperate request. And Kevin, always forced to remain in the neighborhood, had felt new wind under rusty wings. Unaccustomed to independent thought, his mind was suddenly teeming with plans. And slowly an idea had taken shape, at last solidifying to become The Secret:  Kevin had no intention of returning to this zoo—ever. But The Secret had to remain a secret. If Big Joe found out his son had pulled one over on him he would kill the boy, slowly

and exquisitely, with his bare hands. Even Eddie, who had initi-
ated Kevin into marijuana smoking and to the vague principles
of the youth revolution that cold rainy night last November—
even loyal revolutionary Eddie could not know The Secret. Not
yet.

From the front room came muffled television sounds, a
whine from his mother, another bellowed curse from his father.
Joe was in a particularly bad mood, and getting out of the house
without facing him would be impossible. Still, Kevin wasn't a-
bout to be intimidated by the old man, not today. He tucked the
letter into the pocket of his checked Pendleton shirt, stood and
crossed the room determinedly. But he made sure to open his
bedroom door quietly, and to close it with care.

In the hall the composite blast of television and squab-
bling parents was overwhelming. Kevin slipped into the bathroom and eased shut the door.

The bathroom (ceiling sagging with the weight of the
avocado's boughs, floor tilted by the tree's humongous roots)
was forever in gloom, the air thick and sour. The ghetto-like
clutter and heavy stench had always dispirited Kevin, and today
his conviction firmed as he disgustedly looked around.

Nobody deserved this hell.

Paint was peeling from the walls in limp sticky leaves,
damp and discolored. On the bathtub's rusted curtain rod hung a
dismal still life: the enormous, billowed balloons of his father's
jockey shorts, the ancient drooping cups of his mother's
brassieres, an old throw rug spotted with blood and grease. This
whole side of the room stank the musty stench of broom closets.
The sink's drain was clogged, its basin filled to the brim with
dark filmy water for long as Kevin could remember, corpses of
cockroaches and flies blemishing the surface like tiny tankers at
anchor. Empty and near-empty prescription bottles were
scattered behind the faucet handles and atop the commode tank,
with labels reading *mysolin, chloromycetin, compazine, metho-
trexate, lasix.* The steel-reinforced toilet's extra large bowl was
streaked with black, the throne's high-impact custom seat
veined with cracks.

Now, Kevin had spent a good deal of his young life
creating fantasies to blot out the assorted horrors of living in

this house, and so it was that, paradoxically, he could at times dredge glamour from unutterable foulness. This bathroom could be a Shanghai back alley or a tenement in Delhi, and he a dark secret agent, or a nameless footsore Hero of the Common People on some unclear mission of goodness and selflessness.

Standing in front of the sink, his back to the mirror, Kevin assumed an expression of coolness and sensitive macho charm. He abruptly whirled to face this tough, virile paladin.

A fat, brooding boy of sixteen blinked back from behind the glass, the eyes dejected, the lips moping. He wore, because his parents insisted he wear, large, conspicuous horn-rimmed spectacles that were forever sagging on his nose. Almost every part of Kevin sagged. He stood just over a ponderous six feet, sulking and hulking, his slumping shoulders burdened by a cumbersome adolescent despondency. His face bore out this slumping; the expression hangdog, the flesh drooping at the cheeks and underchin. Only the great tumbleweed of uncontrollable frizzy brown hair countered this overall collapsed effect, radiating from his scalp like a frayed clump of fine wires. There was nothing you could do with this rowdy growth. You couldn't part it or style it in any way. Those hairs were tensile as steel wool.

The tough, virile paladin dissolved as Kevin stared, exited sneering at his inquietude. For the thousandth time the boy tugged irritably at random clumps of hair with a huge stubby hand, as though to inspire straighter growth. He could almost hear the clumps scream in protest as they were released to bunch closer to the scalp.

Wagging his head, he stepped aside to confront the commode. All was quiet for a while. With eyes squeezed shut and forehead resting against the wall, Kevin was at last granted a trickling emission. San Francisco, he thought, grunting. Frisco. A whole city run by refugees from the plastic whirlpool; by liberated souls tuning in to life and reality, turning on to faith and love. And the chicks! Free Love. The trill of his waning stream churning water in the toilet bowl accompanied him now, as he for the thousandth time visualized himself grandly arriving in the legendary city on his derailleur, all his fat turned to lean muscle from the exertion of riding. He saw his torso sun-baked a golden brown, saw his hair streaming down straight with sweat. There would be a virginal covey lined up to greet him, attired in the scantiest of scanties, or (according to some of the juicier rumors) in the altogether.

The excitement welled up again, grew intense and uncomfortable. He shook his head to clear it. Again that instant of blankness, again that sense of having just been robbed of a second's thought. He zipped up quickly, remembered to flush the goddamn toilet, and snuck back to his bedroom.

This room was Kevin's sanctum, and the one thing he'd never be able to replace. Within these four stained, ratty walls cowered all the sanity the house could claim: there were posters and colored lights, record albums and comic books, piles of collected junk—all to be abandoned, he reminded himself, as the debris of a former incarnation. Most of the junk was of a psychedelic nature—mind toys and smoking contraptions mass-produced by enterprising young companies making a killing off the hippie phenomenon. Kevin had worried sorely over his property. He knew he couldn't take it with him, although he'd entertained various ideas and alternatives—even, in one desperate moment, a mad notion of building a trailer to haul it all nearly four hundred miles up the coast. Lacking money and specific destination, he couldn't have it shipped by air or rail, and he couldn't trust his parents to ship it after he'd arrived. And there was something about giving it away to his few ungrateful "friends" that caused him to swell with a fierce sense of ownership. Selling it all would somehow be just as bad; like prostituting his personality. In the end the only thing to do was leave it. His parents would hopefully expect him to return if they saw his treasures still piled high. Leave it. That was it. Leave it and let his memory haunt them evermore.

And, leaning gracefully against the wall opposite the door, was Kevin's pride and joy: his sleek Peugeot ten-speed derailleur. The bicycle was only half a year old, bought by Joe to keep his son busy and elsewhere, an arrangement which suited them both. The custom paint job was Kevin's own; an enthusiastic work of smeared greens and oranges, with current "camp" slogans painted in mustard yellow and dayglo purple. The pedals were swathed in pile carpet for barefoot riding, and strategic spokes had been blacked to make huge peace symbols of the wheels. Scrawled on the beige plastic tape covering the handlebars rode the words **PEDAL POWER** in India ink. Kevin's khaki-colored double sleeping bag, strapped to the rack behind the bike's seat, was lined with an authentic, if soiled, American flag.

The boy said his farewells to the room with feelings of regret and relief. He quietly walked his bicycle into the front room, his breath held.

Once again that suffocating depression took him, and Kevin had to slow at the sight of grimy carpet, of piled-up magazines and starved, cringing houseplants. The room was dusty and shaded, ransacked of cheer and the fragile, priceless personal touches that make a house a home. There were no memorabilia nostalgically preserved, no grinning family portraits proudly displayed. A petty neurosis lurked in every corner, ready to pounce the instant the thundering, throbbing television was switched off. Tears were perfunctory here, and laughter, when it came, was a nerve-shredding howl that teetered on the verge of hysteria. Kevin despised the room as he despised the two absurd, self-destructive people responsible for its oppressiveness. The fact that these two rude people just happened to be his parents didn't dampen his hatred a bit.

His father—seven hundred and ninety-six pounds of ill-tempered, foul-mouthed, intractable Pole—sat stuffed into a split, legless loveseat, guzzling beer and muttering obscenities at the picture tube. The man was *immense*; a harrowing, towering mountain heaped with layer upon layer of drooping glaciers of fat. On even the coolest days he perspired around the clock, wheezing and hollering, verbally abusing anything that would hold still long enough to receive the withering brunt of his wrath, sucking down six-pack after six-pack of Eastside beer in the eye of his own progressively darkening storm. An ex-trucker forced to retire due to gross obesity, frequent roaring tantrums, and an absolutely stupefying flatulence condition, he remained indoors day and night, seldom leaving the terribly distended loveseat. Utterly unabashed, he was never to be seen wearing other than discolored jockey shorts and a moth-eaten T-shirt, both marinated in his own sweat and worn like a sticky

11

thin second skin.

Jozef Mikolajczyk, vile and tyrannical, was given to flaring, unprovoked fits of murderous fury. He'd proven himself both provider and protector, but in Kevin's eyes only a malicious Fate would have kept Big Joe from his coffin all these years. By all rights he had it coming; an opinion confirmed frankly by each consulted, insulted, revolted professional. Each had mentally written Joe off, and each had stringently warned him to control his purple rages. It's said that your heart is about as big as your fist—if that's so, Joe's heart was the size of an overripe honeydew.

Footage of January's Rose Bowl game was being aired for the daily *Sports On The Line* feature, commentary by one of the receivers blaring from the set's single, ruptured speaker. The film clip was half a year old, yet Joe had every sense—every pleading, hating, raging bit of his attention—bent on wracking his brain for a winning countermove in a game he already knew had been lost.

"I was lookin' to be tagged on this one," the set blasted, rattling the windows, "an' I figgered he'd be lookin' fer me." The explosive roar of a crowd, an avalanche chuckle from the receiver. "But I gotta hand it to that line. They got on him so fast he didn't know what hit him."

Kevin watched his father lean forward as the quarterback arced back his arm for a pass. The boy snuck a peek at the set, saw the quarterback get mauled.

His father lurched to his feet. *"GODDAMN YOU STUPID SON OF A BITCH!* Throw the fucking ball! Don't *hold* it, *throw* it!"* He hurled the empty beer can across the room to illustrate. Deeply red in the face, he collapsed with a gravelly gasp on the loveseat. Fresh lines of sweat broke out on his cheeks and forehead, his heart bucking almost audibly. "Jesus," he rumbled, sucking down quarts of dusty air. "*Jesus*, what a ball team."

Kevin's mother, stout, stunted and curlered, waddled in from the kitchen, clucking and feebly reprimanding in her raspy, warbling voice; wearing a limp terrycloth bathrobe, her chipped rhinestone spectacles, and an expression of weary, bewildered hypochondria. She was a wretched creature; squat and chicken-skinned at forty-five, forever cowering indoors. Hair sparse and fried, forehead deeply pinched and wizened. Rotting teeth, dumpy legs intricately marbled by purplish varicose veins. Her eyes were *buggy* with hyperthyroidism, her nerves shot to pieces by a lifetime of harried ineptitude.

The woman's list of ailments was staggering: rheumatoid arthritis, bronchial asthma, hyperalgesic whatchamacosis, indigenous culture shock, acute choreatic distress syndrome. Heart failure twice, cirrhosis, glaucoma, gout. She suffered the painful swelling of hemorrhoids, the heartbreak of psoriasis, the drip, drip, drip of acid indigestion. Heat prostration in summer, pneumonia come winter. Insomnia year round. Cancer of the uterus, the larynx, the breasts, and, through a freak of either nature or radiology, the prostate. The poor woman had been abducted, analyzed, ridiculed, and released by too many uppity extraterrestrials to remember, lost countless nonexistent relatives in tragedies too horrific to convey, had been cheated of stardom by shortsighted talent agencies, of riches by the Mob, and somehow lost at least three Gothic masterpieces in the mail. Self-pity and overexposure to the corrosive vehemence of Big Joe's pointless rages had mottled her perception of reality, and now disenchantment was evident in her every move as she bent grotesquely to pick up the can her husband had thrown and, straightening arthritically, froze in a paleoanthropic stoop when she noticed her son standing sheepishly across the room. Her harassed expression quickly changed to one of harsh reproval.

"Kevin! How many times do I have to tell you to *carry* your bike out? You *know* your tires dirty the carpet."

"Don't shout!" his father shouted. He turned and scowled at his son. *"Keep the goddamn tires off the carpet!"*

Kevin cleared his throat. "I'm—I'm going now."

They stared at him with glassy eyes and slack barracuda jaws. From the television came a strafing of cheers.

Joe grunted. "Ellie, turn down the TV." When she began to object he grimaced and said, "Just *turn* down the goddamn *TV*," gesticulating downward with his huge arm. The room plunged into an eerie, electric silence. Joe looked wetly at Kevin, smiled. "C'm'ere, son."

Kevin leaned the bicycle on its kickstand. He walked

over warily, stood grudgingly before his father, tensed. "Sir?"

Joe beamed over his shoulder. "I like that. My son respects his old man, calls him '*sir*'." He looked back at Kevin and sighed fondly, gently nodding his small, nearly spherical head. Kevin, irritated by this sham of paternal pride, wondered what his father was getting at. As Joe seemed reluctant to elaborate, the boy repeated himself.

"Sir?"

"Son," said his father, "I know you must think your Pa is just a worthless old fart drinking his life away, and that neither one of us gives a good long crap about anybody but ourselves. But the truth is, well, your goddamn mother and me, we care a hell of a lot for you around here, boy."

Kevin clenched his fists, his palms suddenly moist. "No sir," he said cautiously. "I don't think that at all."

His father chuckled. "Well, the point is, son, we want you to have a good time, but we want you to *take care* of yourself." Now the muscles holding the great masses of fat in an insincere sunburst smile collapsed. Big Joe's expression underwent an instantaneous inversion: from relaxed and chummy to righteously stern. The huge saddlebag jowls trembled. Fat drops of perspiration popped from his pores and rolled ponderously over his cheeks. "*Now you listen to your old man.* I hear a lot about all them hippies up in San Francisco. You think your Pa don't know shit about what's going on in the world; you dumb kids think you know everything nowadays, but *me*," and he poked a thumb the size of a mango at his chest, "*I* know. *I* watch the TV. I seen about all them goddamn protestors taking all their goddamn dope and I seen the goddamn cops busting their goddamn frigging heads in. Now you hear me, boy. I want you to steer clear of them freaks, right?"

"Yes sir," Kevin lied.

His mother squinted in his face, smiling hideously. "Your father knows what's best, dear. You just do what he says and have a good time." She winced and forced a hand to the back of her neck.

"Yes ma'am. Well, can I go now?"

"Hang on a sec'," Joe said. "I know you been shaking quarters outta my change bottle for three weeks now, kid, but I figger it's already been spent on whatnot. You don't gotta pull that crap. You *ask*." Grunting and groaning, he reached to the floor, picked up his trousers, found the left rear pocket and pulled out a patent leather billfold flattened and molded to the curvature of his elephantine behind. "Joe Mikolajczyk takes care of his son," he wheezed, and began thumbing through the bills. "Now, here's three hundred dollars for your trip, and I don't want you spending it on no dope, hear?"

Kevin's jaw dropped. This sudden, unaccountable generosity astonished him; it was radically out of character. He looked at his mother, smiling kindly—also very much out of character. She gave her face an extra crinkle, said, "Go ahead, dear. *Take* it."

Kevin held out his hand. As Joe placed the money on the boy's palm he gripped it firmly, almost painfully. "What I said I meant, Kevin. You keep your ass out of trouble." He belched. "Now go on, get the hell out of here. And have a good time."

His mother clamped his head in her hands and gave him a sloppy hyperopic kiss. "Now don't forget to write, dear. I would've packed you a nice lunch of cheese and salami sandwiches, but my back is so sore and I can't get around like I used to." Her expression became resentful. "And *you know* salami makes me break out!" She showed him a trembling claw, the digits twisted and rigid. "See my hand, how it shakes? That's because we're worried about you, dear. You don't think we worry about you, sweetheart, but if you only knew of the migraines your poor mother's developed from worrying about you. All the time. Night and day I worry and I worry and I worry *until I think it's going to kill me!"*

"Aw, g'wan, leave him alone," Joe mumbled. He grunted and shifted with a strong blast of rectal wind. "Get out of here, kid. Beat it."

Kevin's mother pawed at his hair, trying to put it in order, but he pulled away. "Have a good time, dear!" she called, though he was standing right next to her. "Send us a postcard!"

Kevin nodded, walked to the front door and opened it gratefully. "Thanks," he said. "I will." He carried his bike out. As he gripped the doorknob a jangling thrill raced up his arm. With the closing of this door he would be shutting away all the pressures, all the domestic minutiae that made his life unbearable. He closed the door firmly, and the electricity stopped. From inside, muted by the door, came the sound of a long gargling belch, followed by a sour, drawn-out report from Joe's posterior. There was an explosion of raging exclamations, a whimpered objection from his mother, then Joe's voice, booming like God Almighty, "Goddamn it woman! Just *turn* up the goddamn *TV!*" Immediately a crowd roared and the windows shook. The madness was drowned out. Kevin trembled and stuffed the bills in his wallet. There was no getting around it now: he was gone. One hundred percent officially free.

He mounted and rode down the walkway as fast as he could. For a moment he was certain he heard his mother open the door and call after him, but he closed his mind to it, veered onto the sidewalk and thence into the street. He tossed the letter into the first mailbox he encountered.

According to plan, Kevin and Eddie were to rendezvous at Mike's house, and Kevin was preparing to turn onto a street that would lead him there when he remembered the money he'd crammed in his cheap plastic wallet. He pulled to the curb and stopped, shook his head unbelievingly. Three *hundred* dollars! That was a great deal more money than he'd ever dreamed of possessing at one time. He wanted to pull the bills out and count them over and over, but that would be foolish in broad daylight. The world was crawling with people who would cut your throat without hesitation for such a sum. Three hundred dollars…

And suddenly, disgustedly, he thought of one crucial item overlooked in the haste of preparation: unless he was severely mistaken, he and his buddies didn't have a single joint between them. Kevin shook his head, marveling his own absentmindedness. What was the point of their pilgrimage, if not to keep their minds defiantly fogged in the name of the Revolution? The problem had always been one of money, but with his new small fortune Kevin could easily afford an ounce of the best marijuana around and hardly dent his capital. And hadn't Perky, a senior at Kevin's high school, told him in the hall to come by if he wanted any grass? That had been a week ago, just before school let out, and Kevin had seen Perky—who had been on his way to the principal's office to be expelled for lewd and rowdy conduct—only in passing, Perky giving his message without slowing his insolent gait. Kevin didn't know him well; Perky was way too hip to publicly acknowledge the existence of a boy as shy and uncool as Kevin, and, if it hadn't been for the slight elevation in popularity Kevin had gained by turning-on with Eddie that cold November night in the Mikolajczyks' garage loft, his status might well have remained a miserable zero. As it stood, he now knew a few students previously scornful of his society, and, by extension, of Perky's trafficking in marijuana. Of course, in a week's time it was entirely possible Perky was already dry. That gamble would just have to be taken. Kevin knew no other dealers. But he knew where Perky's house was, as did anybody in school who was anybody, or aspired to be Somebody. Perky was the only kid from Santa Monica High to have attained the supreme status of tenant. His parents—one chronic whore and one terminal alcoholic—shared the school board's disgust of their incorrigible son, and were more than glad to let him move out on his own. Legend had it that Perky, obstreperous insider that he was, had traveled and partied with some of the most outrageous freaks imaginable, and could actually knock back a whole pint of tequila without barfing.

So Kevin found himself pedaling hard, up and down the little maddeningly neat avenues, till at last he stood panting across the street from Perky's house.

It was an old, decrepit structure, all rotted lath and crumbling plaster. The yard was in an agony of neglect; overgrown with weeds, choking with refuse. Very little of the original paint remained at the time of Perky's occupancy, so he and his wild friends had (according to legend) thrown a terrific three-day party; a party replete with every drug known, with fell motorcyclists and hot-blooded girls.

There on the opposing sidewalk, Kevin stood and admired their handiwork; the fruit of three days' mind-blown labor.

Each windowsill was painted a different hideous color, and on most Kevin could see how the paint had oozed from the sills to dry on the walls or wretched hedges beneath. The tongue-and-groove sides of the house were a continuous painted mural; some portions ridiculously childish, some not so bad. Each side of the sharply angled roof bore a huge peace symbol in off-white paint, presumably for view by air. Kevin's father, who had read about Perky's house in the offended local newspaper in a famous article dealing with bizarre lifestyles, had often wondered aloud why the goddamn police didn't come and raid the goddamn place, why the Air Force didn't bomb it all to hell. Apparently the owner, who lived in Nevada and received his ill-gotten rent by money order, didn't know or just didn't care.

Kevin, having waited for a break in traffic, now pedaled across the street, up the drive's curb outlet and along the oil-marred driveway to the front porch. An amazingly old Airedale drew itself up on spindly legs at his approach, disturbing a cloud of flies. The dog woofed a half-hearted, perfunctory warning, gave it up and crumpled back down, the cloud descending with him. "Nice doggie," Kevin said, looping his lock and chain through the bike's spokes and around the frame. He snapped shut the combination lock, turned and confronted the front door. The door's window was smashed; a tie-dyed rag of a curtain fluttered behind the knives of splintered glass. This would be the door leading into the famed anteroom, the purported scene of so many lecherous parties. The house proper was built back of this narrow anteroom, so that the room itself poked out like an add-on, which it probably was.

Kevin could hear familiar music blasting inside the house. Moving his lips to the lyrics he realized it was The Doors, and that that was Morrison barking out *Back Door Man*. The music emboldened him. Kevin, front door man, stepped up and rapped three times on the scarred, splintering wood.

At once there was a sound of stumbling, of a scrambling body knocking over a piece of light furniture. Then an abrupt tapering in volume as the music ground to a halt. The house seemed to grow cold in the new silence, seemed to draw into itself. Kevin heard what might have been voices in distant parts of the house, but with all the air and street traffic he couldn't be sure. Then came a quick pattering of bare feet on creaking floorboards. More silence. Kevin had, after half a minute of this silence, an odd feeling he was being watched. He turned his head and could have sworn he'd peripherally glimpsed a dark, intense face watching him from between parted newspaper curtains. But the newspaper curtains were closed. There was no face. He turned back to the door, thought for sure the corner of a curtain behind another window had just ruffled shut. The house was obviously occupied; why wouldn't he/they answer? He knocked again, harder, small chips of the door's smashed window tinkling at his feet. This time there was the sound of heavy furniture crashing on the floor, followed by a quickly muffled breaking of, perhaps, crockery. Thumping footsteps. Quick whispering. The music wound up to its former ear-splitting volume like an air raid siren. Clearly the plug had been pulled at his first knock, and just now reinserted. Uneasily, Kevin locked on the footsteps booming to the door.

The door was wrenched open and Perky squinted out, long tufts of dirty black hair disturbed by his quick movements. From the heavy footfalls, one would have expected a person at least the height and weight of Kevin, but Perky was a little guy, who couldn't have weighed more than a hundred pounds. Though Perky's startling face inevitably brought on unintended stares, any initial interest was quickly replaced by a kind of morbid thanksgiving. Perky had lived a rough, cheap life on the streets. At some time during his violent childhood some rival or other had secured the weapon and opportunity to smash little Perky's nose so badly as to make it, in profile, virtually un-recognizable as a nose at all. Perky's forehead was quite broad, which in a way bore out the flattened nose and lent his face some congruity. But the bones making up the lower half of his face were thin and brittle and looked, except for a haze of black stubble and patchy acne, almost effeminate. A fractional harelip gave his mouth a permanent snarl, and when he spoke one couldn't help but notice that all his front teeth, save a lonely incisor on the bottom gum, were missing. The consequential awkwardness with consonants caused him to snap and grimace when he spoke, which only made him seem meaner than the frightened and frustrated survivor he was. His skin was the color of tallow, his eyes—with whites visible all around—the color of lead. Of course he was a most touchy and cynical young man, yet, in all Santa Monica, his reputation as generous host was without parallel. His alarming eyes narrowed now as they looked straight into the eyes of Kevin, two steps down. He edged out, partly closing the door to block the music roaring out like floodwater.

Kevin smiled crookedly. "What's happening, Perky? 'Member me? Kevin Mikolajczyk. You told me last week at school you had lids for sale. Hope I'm not too late."

Perky sneered. "Hate to have to bum you out, man, but I sold all that pot the same night. I got some more yesterday but it was a burn; all full of parsley and crap. That's all right, though; partner of mine's got a sawed-off .44. Tonight we're gonna pay the dude who ripped me off a visit, blow off his balls and screw his old lady."

"Wow!" Kevin said, jolted by the graphic mental image of Perky and his friends kicking in the door of a rip-off's pad and exacting their rough street justice. Then he remembered his own tough luck and frowned wryly.

"Sorry to hear about you getting burned, Perky. I was really hoping you had some lids for sale, 'cause me and a coupla partners are jamming up to the City to catch the big concert, and it would sure be a drag to go dry. Do you," he wondered unwisely, "know anywhere else I can score?"

Perky considered. "Yeah, well maybe I *can* do you right. Buddy of mine couple streets over's got some lids. Really righteous shit. I gotta go rap with him about something anyway. Come on in."

Kevin stepped up and inside. As Perky slammed the door there came another smash and stumbling of feet. They were now standing in the well of the anteroom. An old gravy-spattered tablecloth concealed most of the room, while to their left upon entering were three wood steps leading up, then the doorway into the front room, which, though narrow, extended the width of the house. Kevin followed Perky up the steps and his pupils quickly dilated. The front room was all in gloom; scarcely a ray of light could squeeze beneath the mangled curtains or through interstices in the grime on the windows. All the furniture and appliances looked like junk thrown out of Salvation Army shops as beyond repair, or pilfered from Goodwill boxes in the dead of night. The carpet was a mishmash of oily, jagged scraps, nailed indiscriminately wherever most convenient for the drunken decorators. Walls were riddled with holes and smudged with the acne of puerile graffiti. Wherever possible those holes had been covered with loud and outrageous posters depicting feverish rock stars. There were coffee tables scarred by cigarette burns, broken lamps with boxer shorts for shades. On the floor a child's phonograph, hooked up to a bulky amplifier and public address loudspeaker, shrieked, crackled, skipped and sputtered through a very scratchy copy of The Doors' first album. Perky knelt and turned the volume down to a tolerable level as Kevin shook his head in fascinated approval, a thin smile on his fat lips. This place was a revolutionary's dream; the atmosphere positively reeked of freedom and good times—of drugs, booze, and wild parties unhampered by the gross, antiquated antics of embarrassingly naïve parents. Kevin's eyes, wide with wonder, continued their sweeping appraisal. Several brassieres were nailed triumphantly to the ceiling, their straps hanging in yellow withered surrender, like crepe streamers. A few badly-torn easy chairs hugged the walls, each with a single rusty spring poking up as a bitter unidigital comment on the state of its surroundings. It didn't take much imagination to visualize those chairs occupied by bearded revolutionaries and sneering motorcycle outlaws, all engaged in the wholly laudable business of headlong whoopee-making.

Then the boy's eyes grew wide and his smile crumbled. For he saw—thanks to the dull glint of a brass earring—a strange little man standing tensely in the corner. The man was lamentably scrawny and small, wearing a gray cut-off sweatshirt and baggy Levis, grungy sneakers. His hair was a riot of long black tangles shot with white, and amid that mess his tiny eyes were in constant flashing motion: from Kevin to Perky to the anteroom doorway, from Kevin to Perky and back to Kevin. He was apparently frozen with apprehension, and this motionlessness, the poor visibility, and the stranger's congruity with the gaudy and wasted face of the room, had initially fooled Kevin into believing he was alone with Perky. Now the guy glared rabidly at Kevin, radiating an instantly infectious paranoia. He looked starved and punished, dogged and discombobulated by some utterly absurd vision.

"Hey, man, it's cool," Perky said, metronomically rocking an arm back and forth before the wildman, whose irises appeared to follow the motion while the orbs remained fixed. "This guy's a friend," Perky went on hypnotically, "a *friend*." He turned to Kevin, indicating the quiet guy approvingly with a thumb, "He's been stoked on speed for three days now without crashing. He can get you and your partners some righteous crystal for your trip if you want."

Kevin looked at the quiet guy, feeling haunted, and shook his head.

"Whatever," Perky said.

"How is this pot?" Kevin asked, feeling the quiet guy's eyes scrambling across the back of his neck like tiny tarantulas.

"Like I said, man, it's really good shit. That's why it goes for fifteen dollars. It's from Lebanon, man, way over by China. Lebanese Lavender. *You* know."

"Sure," Kevin said. "Right." He'd never heard of any such strain of marijuana, was reasonably certain this would be just so-so local stuff. But Perky's transparent assurance was not entirely unexpected. In the groggy dawn of the age of Aquarius it was rare to score without complications or deception. He was also sure that this ounce didn't really sell for fifteen dollars, that Perky would pocket the extra five. That, too, was to be expected, was part of the game.

"Here," Perky said, reaching into his shirt pocket, "I've got a joint you can sample." He fished out a thin marijuana cigarette and lit it with a showy gesture of cordial indulgence, took a long draw and passed it to Kevin.

Kevin sucked on the joint and could tell by its harsh tongue and wishy-washy bouquet that the weed was local, though of fairly good quality. A seed popped at the cherry as the joint began to spider, fell to smolder on the carpet.

Perky was straining to hold the smoke in, taking small quick gulps of air to force it deeper, his face growing red and contorted with the effort. "Whaddaya think?" he wheezed, letting the smoke out slowly.

Kevin exhaled, took another hit. He nodded, let the smoke out with a whoosh.

"Yeah," he croaked, as the boo's effects crept up on

22

him. "Yeah." He took another deep hit.

"Well c'mon then, man…gimme the money. *C'mon!*" Perky was suddenly all impatience, and didn't seem to know what to do with his hands.

Kevin looked at him uncertainly, pondering the mystery of Perky's words. And what was the reason he was… money. Why money? *Because!* A holdup? Kevin's expression clouded progressively toward absolute blankness. He didn't remember owing Perky any money.

"Well, *c'mon,*" Perky said exasperatedly. "You want a lid or not?"

Of *course! That's* why Perky wanted money. Kevin could have kicked himself. He chuckled. This grass was better than he'd thought.

"What's so funny?" Perky demanded.

"Sorry," Kevin said. "This pot's really good." He pulled out his wallet and froze. There were all kinds of bills in the wallet; fives, tens, twenties. He was suddenly and unaccountably rich! Then he remembered Big Joe giving him the money and imagined himself slapping a palm on his forehead. He drew twice more on the cigarette. It burned his fingers and he gamely ate the butt.

"Yeah," Perky was saying, nodding. "What'd I tell you?" He took a ten and a five from the fan Kevin had made of the bills. "That's a lot of bread, man. I can do you a really good deal on a pound of this stuff."

"That's okay," Kevin quacked, his voice seeming to originate in his nose. "I need the bucks."

"Whatever. Back in a flash."

"Oh, Perky," Kevin postscripted, not thinking, "you won't let any of it get away?"

Perky stopped dead and glared. "Fuck no," he said with quiet acidity. "I got enough stash I don't gotta go pinching any lid I get for *you.*"

Kevin colored. "I was only kidding."

"Yeah. So was *I.*"

He slammed the door in Kevin's face and left him alone with the quiet guy. Following the slam, the record player's stylus hopscotched across a particularly warped section of *The*

*End,* ripped through the final grooves, and settled into a rhythmic bobbing at the label's perimeter. Kevin knelt and lifted the arm, turned down the volume, started the record over. It was the only album around. Shrieking laughter blew out of one of the bedrooms, but right now all he wanted was solitude. He'd put his foot in it with Perky all right, no doubt about it, and maybe stiffed his one and only big opportunity to step up the social ladder on the off-chance he, a seasoned traveler, should ever return from his pilgrimage. It was that joint. Grass, grand old herb, had made his tongue stumble again. And now he was beginning to feel self-conscious; hulking and silly-looking. With Perky offended, the logical move was to try to build some sort of casual, cynical rapport with the quiet guy, who knew Perky and was therefore, most likely, something of a celebrity around town. But before he could approach a conversation the quiet guy jumped up and began peeking between the curtains, his head darting side to side. Temporarily satisfied, he cocked his head as if listening intently, repeatedly flexed his fingers, turned his head. Stared crazily at Kevin.

Kevin cleared his throat. "Big jam in Frisco," he managed.

At last the quiet guy spoke:

"*Man,*" he said, and something behind his eyes shot past so quick Kevin got a kink in his neck trying to follow, "there's *always* something heavy going down in Frisco, y'know?" The quiet guy's jaw worked back and forth and round and round as his face fought to find a center. "People be going there getting *wasted,* man, y'know? Yeah man, anything, *everybody,* y'know? Heavy sounds, man, yeah heavy people getting stoned, y'know? *Everybody!*" Kevin could have sworn the man's head had just spun around. Now the quiet guy shrank into himself like a rattler backing into its hole. From that imaginary hole two tiny coals peered guiltily at Kevin. "Did some crystal," the quiet guy hissed, punching the side of his fist into the wasted crook of his arm. "*Jeez!* That's my thing, y'know; if nobody digs it, well, that's *their* thing, y'know?"

"Yeah," Kevin said uncomfortably. "I know."

The quiet guy came out of his crouch, smiling and gently shaking his head like a man suddenly made aware of some mild irony. "Yeah, man, dudes be amping out in The Haight, y'know? Twenty cats to one spike, man, hairy, let me tell you, a super rush, y'know? All of us, man, *everybody*, man! Getting jacked-up, y'know?" The quiet guy pressed his face up to Kevin's in a pose of confrontation. "Some dudes me mainlining skag," he whispered threateningly, "*y'know*? Heavy man, very heavy." He cocked his head, nodding. "*Very* heavy, man, very. Heavy." His eyes rolled like coins. "Getting *wasted*, man, y'know? To the *max*, man! *Man*," he concluded, "man, there's *always* something heavy going down in Frisco, y'know man? *Always*. Y'know?"

"Right," Kevin said. "Right on, man." But something was nagging him. "The Haight," he mumbled, almost inaudibly. "I…I guess you mean the City." He asked incredulously, "Guys are shooting up? But that's not…right…that's not what Eddie said…" He demanded in a voice thick with urgency, "But what're the people like? I mean, it's all peace and love, right?"

The quiet guy's eyes went foggy at the word *people*. His stare did not seem to register Kevin before him, but was rather focused inward, as if the boy's question were a real poser. He spun around and darted to the newspaper curtains, then systematically moved along the wall, carefully separating pages to peek outside.

"Who—who are you looking for?" Kevin asked, worrying that perhaps the quiet guy knew something that he, Kevin, didn't.

The quiet guy whirled, blinking. A fevered look of warped understanding made his eyes appear to sink deeper into their caves. He edged along the wall until he was as far from Kevin as the room's confines allowed. He looked frantically to the front door as if debating dashing out into the arms of a lurking gendarmerie, then quickly back to Kevin. His mouth fell open, a string of saliva joining the lips. Pressing his palms flat against the wall, he froze in the white-hot glare of an imaginary spotlight.

"Um…I have to use the head," Kevin mumbled. "I'll catch you later." He turned and pushed past the soiled bedspread separating front room and dining room. "What a trip," he breathed, and realized he was trembling. After a moment he gently pulled back an edge of the bedspread to peek into the front room. The quiet guy was back at the windows, inching aside the classifieds, carefully looking out. Kevin let go the bedspread and turned to contemplate the small dining room.

Garbage all over the place. The room stank of three-days-old refried beans and of cigarettes doused in beer. One leg of the dining table had collapsed; plates and utensils, crusty with the molding residue of meals long forgotten, were scattered on the dusty, tattered carpet. True; Perky's place was rumored to be a mess, but not like *this*.

Now, instead of awaiting Perky's return where they'd parted, Kevin was stuck with having to make a choice. He could go, a stranger treading private premises, through either of two doorways he was facing. Retracing his steps into the front room was out of the question. He stood there a good while, twisting a lip with forefinger and thumb; his mind, murky from the grass, interpreting sounds as a kind of mixed track of music and sound effects. To his left was an improvised door of stringed ceramic beads. From behind this partition came the orchestral braying of a television, with choral accompaniment of soprano giggling and baritone guffaws. To his right was a hanging American flag. From behind this flag came the sounds of more voices from the kitchen; voices gurgling like streams, rumbling like quakes. Kevin listened closely, and was unsurprised to discover he couldn't identify a single voice in either room. The marijuana's addling effects had subtly grown more pronounced with this steady bombardment of curious impressions, and his mind was so busy merrily making mud pies out of each new thought that the simplest problem automatically became a crisis. He stood stock-still, dreading the likely outcome of any confrontation. But his choices were simple. He could confront the strangers in the kitchen. He could confront the strangers in the television room. He could stand here, confronted by his own cowardice, until Hell froze over.

Kevin impulsively pushed past the flag into the kitchen, where the worst conceivable thing happened: all movement and conversation ceased abruptly as everybody turned to stare at him. Out of all nine or ten people he knew only Gary, the sycophantic, squat little Jewish informer who had ratted on him for having marijuana in his gym locker last month. There were three girls in the room; the teasing, coquettish type, each with slender limbs and seductive eyes. As in an advertisement for hair dye, the hair shade from girl to girl varied to the extreme: an ashy blonde, a fiery redhead, and a brunette whose long waves were a glossy raven black. The blonde was perched on the lap of a guy wearing wrap-around sunglasses and mechanic's overalls, a paisley-pattern headband keeping his long hair out of his face. He zoned out on Kevin, grinning stupidly. The redhead, interrupted while drawing little heart shapes on the kitchen wall in bright vermilion lipstick, stared at Kevin drunkenly before yawning widely. The raven-haired girl—a young woman, really—had apparently been flirting with three strangers sitting on the sink counter. Kevin cursed his intrusion. Two of the guys were campus honor boys, wearing the blue and gold letterman jackets with the school's insignia on the front. The guy in the middle looked tough and dangerous; dark hair combed to cover the tops of his ears, a cruel jet-black moustache. Weekend hippie, Kevin thought. He avoided the guy's unwavering stare, felt instinctively that he was a bully; maybe some punk on leave from the Marines. Christ, the way he looked he could even be a narc. The three other boys in the room were about Kevin's age, and were gathered in a tight circle on the floor, like aborigines around a campfire. One made an obscene noise at him, bugging out his eyes and puffing his cheeks in a mocking caricature. Now Kevin could see the object of the boys' concentration. Two were shaking a cracked aquarium back and forth on the floor. Inside the aquarium was a small, terrified brown rat recently fished from the garbage. The third boy was using a slender steak knife to playfully poke the scrabbling creature. This boy now looked at Kevin and grinned ear to ear, plunged the blade into the rat, held it up bloody and squirming for Kevin's revolted inspection…

*…but the raven-haired girl had the loveliest red,* red *lips, the* brightest*, bright green cat eyes Kevin had ever seen…*

Oh, she easily outrivaled the other girls, with her skin *so creamy and white* it seemed almost translucent. Her jaw line was a fine, sweeping cut, her neck slender and gracefully elongated—like the rest of her figure tapering and so…*very supple.*

But what really blew him away was the LARGEST AND FIRMEST PAIR OF BREASTS he'd ever witnessed on a figure...*so* slender. They were—were—*barely concealed* by the lapels of her *unbuttoned!* beige cotton shirt, which was casually tucked into the waistband of a pair of *skintight* snow-white slacks. This tucked bit of shirt promised to *pop*...FREE! at any moment, as each breath or shifting of weight worried at the waistband's hold. Kevin, instantly in love, supposed correctly that she was an enchantress much sought after. But in reply to his stare of longing she giggled, then buried her face in the lap of one of the honor boys and laughed uncontrollably. Despite her sparkling eyes she'd plainly had a lot to drink.

"Debbie," said the dangerous-looking guy, patting the girl on her *fantastic behind* and nodding toward Kevin, "kiss this dude and see if he turns into a prince."

Gary laughed. It was a hollow, underhanded laugh. "Hey, man. Hey, hey; what's happening, Irving? What's on your mind, man?"

Kevin's flabby cheeks turned crimson. These people were making a fool of him.

"Just tripped in to say 'hi'." His voice was a hoarse rattle. He straightened, said with businesslike demeanor, "I'm waiting for Perky to get back. He went to score me a lid."

"Why don't you just trip out?" suggested the guy with the moustache.

Kevin cleared his throat. His mouth was suddenly very dry. "I was talking to Gary," he said weakly.

"You're talking to me." The guy lowered himself from the counter with catlike grace. He looked as powerful and obstinate as a rhinoceros.

"Oh Christ," Gary said. "I mean, look you guys, don't go starting no fights in here, okay? Perky told me to watch the pad and keep things cool if he leaves. So if you wanna hassle, do it, like, do it out *back*." He shrugged and dropped his arms; body language meant to convey a simple message to everybody present: he wanted absolutely no part.

All eyes turned to Kevin expectantly.

"Look, I don't even know this guy—"

"My name's Dave. Your name's Shit."

28

"—and I didn't come here to hassle anybody. You know. Peace is my bag."

"Oh my God," said the raven-haired girl. "Peace is his *bag.*"

The big guy shoved Kevin hard, sent him crashing into the kitchen wall. The redhead inadvertently drew a line across her hearts motif and moved out of the way. The talking and joking had ceased. Someone in the adjacent bedroom thumped playfully on the wall in response to the thud of Kevin's poor head.

"Listen, creep," Kevin's antagonizer said viciously, "if you want trouble, you're fucking with the right guy." He grabbed Kevin's shirt at the lapels and lifted the boy a good foot and a half off the floor. As big and as heavy as Kevin was, the dark-haired bully had hauled him up with what seemed a minimum of effort.

"No man," Kevin gasped. "No sir. I don't want any trouble."

Now the raven-haired girl tugged at the punk's sleeve, looking annoyed.

"Oh, come *on*, David. You're not impressing anybody."

Kevin, sputtering in a miasma of beer breath, squirmed against the wall, completely helpless. His glasses hung over his mouth, his face steadily grew darker as his assailant's knuckles pressed into the soft wedge of flesh over his windpipe. He intermittently heard arguing voices, then a very direct challenge as Dave looked back up, grimacing. "You want trouble?"

"No sir," Kevin croaked.

"Then split."

"Yes sir."

He let go of Kevin's shirt and the boy dropped in a heap, retching, at last lurching to his feet to stagger into the dining room. Kevin was half-conscious of voices in the kitchen, but the words bounced around in his skull like caroming billiard balls.

"You're quite a man, aren't you? A real tiger."

"Yeah, yeah. And who're you supposed to be, Pocahontas?"

"Oh, when are you gonna grow up, David? That poor kid couldn't be more than fifteen."

"Listen, slut. This is my fist, see? I want you to repeat what you just said, real slow this time so I don't miss a word."

Kevin plowed through the bedspread, whacked his toe on the doorjamb, and stumbled into the front room waving his arms like a drowning man. The quiet guy, running the gamut of his wildest nightmares, almost climbed the wall as Kevin blundered by; choking on his own saliva, using one hand to knead his throat and the other to guard his head against any obstacle he might encounter.

Through the front room doorway, past the gravy-stained tablecloth, into the trashy anteroom. Kevin plopped down on a badly lacerated couch and a cloud of dust enveloped him. He coughed.

Someone was tiptoeing through the front room. There was a hell of a racket as the quiet guy stepped squarely on the record's turning face, a moment passed, and the tablecloth was pulled aside as the raven-haired girl looked in. One side of her lovely face was bright red. The sparkle had left her eyes and rolled down her cheeks, to be wiped away like eyeliner. She sniffled, smiled weakly and sat, with a springy settling of breasts, next to him, snapping open a glossy black handbag embossed with turquoise and silver wildflowers. From this she exhumed two silky hankies, her compact, a filterless Camel, a disposable lighter. In the compact's little round mirror she watched herself light the cigarette, dabbing at her subdued green tigress eyes, speaking to her reflection:

"Look, I'm sorry about David. He's always like that after a few beers."

Kevin grunted noncommittally. "He your boyfriend?"

"Oh, he's not my old man or anything like that, if that's what you mean, and I'm not his old lady. We've shacked up a few times, but we've never felt, like, all that serious about each other. I don't think I've ever felt *really* serious about anybody." She paused to peel a tobacco fiber off her lip. "Anyway, it was sweet of you to take it so well, and please don't hold it against David. He can't help it when he gets drunk. I mean, nobody is *really* responsible for what they do or say when they get drunk. Why else would you drink, if not to have a good time and forget your responsibilities? So it's not really his fault, is it? Oh, it's

30

not *your* fault either, don't get me wrong. Just bad timing. You had as much right to be there as anybody." She switched her gaze from the little mirror for a moment to look at him with a transitory curiosity. "Just what *are* you doing here, anyway?"

Kevin yanked himself back together. His attention had of course been focused on the gentle gyrations, vivacious vibrations, and miscellaneous mind-bending movements of the raven-haired girl's magnificent, mouth-watering mammaries. Now he looked at his hands defensively, afraid to meet her eyes lest she read the guilt cringing behind the black ports of his pupils. But he was certain—certain she had seen.

"I'm wait—I'm waiting for Perky," he said gropingly, his voice damp and hot in his throat. "He went to score me a lid."

"Oh, I really *am* a mess. Crying like a little girl. Over nothing, am I right? Here," she commanded, handing him the compact, "you hold this." She then handed him her half-smoked cigarette. This left her hands free to finger shiny tufts of hair into place while exhaling twin streams of smoke from her exquisitely chiseled nostrils. And he sat there, his own hands wretchedly full, helplessly staring from one marvelous melon to the other while they dipped and rose, as if puppeteered by the fingers arranging those long waving tufts of hair. He'd already forgotten the incident with Dave. She finished with the hair and, to make matters worse, plucked a lipstick tube from her handbag and began, occasionally licking her lips with a slender red tongue, to paint her lips a moist, vulval pink. Kevin squirmed in gnashing misery, wanting desperately to bury his head in the hot valley between those impossibly buoyant mounds.

He had his inhibitions.

In the first place, he was too inexperienced to find the courage—he was certain such an ungentlemanly response would fill the raven-haired girl with rage and disgust. Second, he was becoming aroused to the point of giddiness. He felt sweaty and faint. And he was spellbound, hypnotically affixed to the bewitching quivering of those barely concealed love loaves. But most important, and most perturbing, was his own numb realization that he was already in the grip of a need so powerful it was making him physically ill.

"I know it's just *sickening*," the raven-haired girl was saying, "to see a guy act like that. But he's not really like that, he's really sweet, really. No really, David's like that, really, and I wouldn't want him, or any other guy, any other way. Really. Honey, I'm really sorry about the whole thing. Sometimes I think he *likes* trouble, but that's just the way guys are, I guess. I mean, I don't need to tell *you* what guys are like, am I right? Haha. Not that I give a damn what he does. He can play up to that little bleached-blonde bitch all he wants; it's none of my business. It's his business, not mine. Am I right?"

She paused to consider him again, her expression, Kevin felt, not unlike pity. Then she leaned close, wraithlike, seemingly without the slightest shift in weight. Kevin trembled little tremors of panic, perspiring in the heady fog of her breath, all beer and nicotine and cosmeticized femininity. Very near, she tickled his eardrum with that manipular breath, her tiny voice whispering, "I just don't *give* a damn."

Kevin recoiled from the intended peck of moist painted lips on hot puffy cheek, his ears burning bright red. She drew back in mild offense.

He tore his heart from her eyes; his own eyes, being the furtive and traitorous telltale red of a pot smoker, certain to reveal his agony. All the glib lines and knowing looks he'd cooked up over thousands of lonely hours were instantly dissolved in the aching reality of her loveliness; and now, in the shadow of that loveliness, his own body seemed to grow clammy and foul. Sick with embarrassment, he turned his head to face the still life of dusty objects in the anteroom's corner: a poster reading LOVE THE ONE YOU'RE WITH, the paper peeling and discolored, as was the wallpaper, by last January's rain; a ruptured beanbag chair, its innards scattered all about the room; a half-collapsed mahogany end table—perhaps once a fine piece—shoved in the corner and bearing: a dozen empty beer cans; ashtrays overflowing with mashed butts, ashes, and peach pits; an ice cream cone turned end-up, the ice cream itself having dried trailing down the table's legs; a small portable television with coat hanger antenna, its dark picture tube miraculously intact. Captured on that dark convex surface was a fisheye image of Kevin, his head and shoulders flattened and expanded comically. The image of the raven-haired girl was very tiny behind his flat mountainous face, and as she drew back she grew tinier, minute, vanished.

"Oh, Christ, I didn't mean it like that," she said wearily, having caught the agitation in his eyes before he turned his head. "Really." She placed a reassuring hand on his thigh and squeezed, to let him know, and to remind herself, that she was a real, live, flesh-and-blood woman with thoughts and feelings of her own, and not just another mindless, flirtatious fleshpot. "Really I didn't. Why is it that whenever I'm upset I think roses and talk crap?"

Kevin tried to correct his posture, but there was a weird energy keeping his body crimped unnaturally, bent away from the raven-haired girl's sultry radiation. He'd never been this close to a real, live, flesh-and-blood woman before, let alone one with a slim ivory hand on his leg. The hand seemed to be passing some sort of current through his body, and, so close to the hand, Kevin's chubby little pecker was beginning to respond. If she didn't remove her hand soon, he knew, there would be a violent internal upheaval; he would erupt and ooze off the couch into a silly-looking puddle on the floor.

"Listen," she said, "I really *am* sorry about David making such as ass of himself." She removed her hand and rose to her feet, embarrassed.

"No sweat," Kevin whispered hoarsely. "He was just stoned, like you said."

Out of sympathy, more for herself than for Kevin, the girl now experimented with tact, saying, "You take it just like a man," fully knowing how important those words could be to a boy at his stage of development. "Really."

Kevin blushed furiously.

The girl paused in the doorway, looking back over her shoulder, holding the old tablecloth away and presenting a captivating view of her backside.

Her snow-white slacks stretched gracefully over her beautifully rounded cheeks, clinging with heart-pounding precision to every perfect curve. Her stance was statuesque; weight on the right leg, one hand resting assertively on the left hip— just the way nudes posed in the photographs Kevin had hungrily, secretly studied. Her hair fell loosely to her shoulders, an apostrophe-lock dangling in front of her eye as she looked back.

She was, Kevin thought, far more beautiful than any of the glossy, margined girlies he'd ever admired. The look on that face should have been erotic: oily, sexy, turned-on. But she was only gazing sadly, and he was gripped by the terrible realization that she was looking right through him, not seeing him at all.

The girl smiled sweetly, her eyes sparkling. She cupped and shook her right hand at waist level, blew him a kiss and whispered, "Peace is my bag," before letting the curtain fall. The incredible image dissolved. But the *vision*—that one grief-triggering, mind-rending exaggeration of reality that can make or break a personality—remained onstage, and Kevin swore to himself right then and there, even as its author passed out of his life forever, that he would never lose it.

He stared bleakly at the tablecloth. Then at the wall. Standing, he tore the cloth aside and peered out. Kevin stepped anxiously into the front room, but the raven-haired girl was nowhere to be seen.

She was gone.

The front door flew open and Perky blew in. He plucked a rolled wax sandwich bag from under his belt, handed it to Kevin.

"Here, fucknut."

The quiet guy, his hands clenched into pathetic bony fists, wailed horribly and half-crossed the room. *"Man!"* he cried, with maniacal indignation, "don't *ever* do that! I thought you were the pigs."

Kevin tucked the bag into his shirt pocket. It felt like a good-sized ounce. "Thanks," he said.

"Yeah, yeah, yeah. And look at the fucking tape. I never even opened it. Did you hold down the fort? Have any hassles?"

"No...yes and no. Everything's cool." Kevin stepped outside, plodded down the steps and stood on the walk, knowing his heart was heading for hell in a hurry. It was as though all his gingerly-embraced, sluggishly-entertained reasons for keeping on were being left behind in that house, his soul scampering puppywise at the raven-haired girl's nerd-damning heels, or hovering plaintively to now and again be caught as a silly-looking reflection in her compact's all-seeing mirror. "Later," he said. "And thanks again, Perky. Really."

Perky was about to close the door when his jolted features softened. He cocked his head quizzically and studied the look of absence on Kevin's face, as though he too could feel the power humming like a well-tuned engine inside the house. There was a long and somber silence. "Have a good trip," he said quietly. "Watch out for our Boys in Blue." A thought struck him and he smiled. He closed the door gently.

Alone, Kevin automatically genuflected at his bicycle's rear wheel and began, with thick nerveless fingers, to work the tumblers of the combination lock. The raven-haired girl's face, lips puckered for casual near-kiss, swam into focus on the truncated knob on the lock's round, numbered face. The face drew nearer, and, as in the reflection on a Christmas tree's bulb, the smooching lips enlarged until they became the whole image; the lips parting as they grew closer and larger, then only the black hole leading into her mouth, which grew larger and larger until it completely filled his senses. A sharp pain stabbed behind his eyes, grew intense and passed, left him staring at the lock in his hand. The lock was open. Perspiration was thick in his eyebrows. He stood weightlessly, took off the lock and chain and secured them under the bike's seat. The world revolved giddily and a metallic taste came to his palate as he mounted. He coasted across the flat driveway to the sidewalk and veered blindly on the pavement. There was a jarring thump as his bicycle lurched off the curb. The jarring wrenched him back in time to avoid spilling, and then he was coasting clumsily alongside parked cars.

A man with close-cropped hair and a very red face leaned his head out the passenger-side window of a passing car. "You stupid-ass hippie! Watch where the fuck you're going!"

*Up yours*, Kevin thought.

With another jolt he remembered Mike and Eddie, and was just pulling into a gas station to make a call when he saw them riding his way.

Eddie turned his snubby, freckled face and pointed.

Eddie had reddish-brown hair brushed down all around,

to make it look long as possible. He was tiny and intelligent, bashful and thin, with large brown doll eyes wide with winsome enthusiasm.

Mike, a spry, testy boy with very white skin and very black hair, was wearing cutoffs and his big brother's Army shirt. Mike was so scrawny that, shirtless, the veins of his arms and chest showed clearly. He looked up darkly and waved. Then they were both pedaling hard.

"We figured you were at your house," Eddie said breathlessly, "but your mom said you left already, so we looked all over for you. We're ready to go."

"Yeah," Mike said, "let's go. Let's get the fuck out of here."

Kevin grinned conspiratorially and pulled out the fat sandwich bag.

Eddie's eyes opened even wider. "Far out!" He rubbed his hands together in anticipation.

"Hey, put it away!" Mike hissed. "Goddamn you Kevin, you're gonna get us *busted!*"

Kevin tucked the contraband in his sleeping roll. "Well then," he said, surprised to hear his voice so steady, "all we need is some rolling papers and we can get going."

"I brung plenty," Mike said proudly, his voice ringing as in anthem: "Banana-flavored and wheat straw!" He tamped it down a tad. "And I got two roach clips and swiped my old man's pipe."

"And I've got all the pots and pans and a bunch of canned food," Eddie panted.

They looked at one another nervously. Mike raised his arms and Kevin saw that the middle finger of each of Mike's hands was erect in the flip-off sign. Suddenly Mike cried out, with rude loudness and all the sincerity he could muster, "Fuck you, you goddamned cocksucking son of a bitch of a town!" Eddie gave a war whoop and they all began riding to the corner. The light was against them, and as they were waiting for it to change Kevin turned and looked back to where the roof of Perky's house jutted sharply above the others.

His vision returned, only this time it was not the numbing, unforgettably curvaceous pose. The raven-haired girl was on her knees in this scene, wearing only a few strategically draped scraps of silky fabric; fragments as flimsy and tattered as her recent hauteur. She was looking up repentantly; bruised, bemused, and belittled—all hair and bosom and tender femininity—and her *DEFEATED BUT FOR YOU, MY LOVE* eyes were rapidly scanning the cold, hard features Kevin's generous imagination had ascribed to his face.

Don't go, the girl's eyes begged.
*Please.*
"I'll be back," Kevin said aloud.
His friends turned and stared.
The light changed to green.
The girl in Kevin's vision trembled.
"I'll be waiting," she said.

# Chapter 2

# Good Dogs, Inc.

It was less than three miles to Highway 1—along this stretch known as Pacific Coast Highway, or, locally, as PCH. Soon the boys could see palm fronds dotting the overlooking cliff, and in no time were yahooing and dodging senior citizens out soaking up the day in the long verdant swath of Palisades Park. They stopped and leaned against the cement railing to savor the moment. Far below stretched the highway, and a bit to their left the colorful spine of Santa Monica Municipal Pier, straddling on barnacled pillars one lovely slice of the sweet Pacific. That vast blue prairie would be their westerly panorama for most of the journey.

"Hot damn!" Mike shouted. "Hello ocean, goodbye hometown blues!"

"Forever," Kevin breathed.

Eddie looked up sharply, one thin eyebrow arched inquisitively.

"For the summer anyway," Mike said. He spat over the railing, trying, unreasonably, to hit the matchbox cars crawling along the highway. After a minute he turned to Kevin, who'd been inappropriately down over the past couple of miles. "So what's eating you, toadpuss?"

"Huh?" Kevin grunted. In his mind the raven-haired girl's undulating udders ballooned inches from his burning orbs. But even in his imagination he lacked the courage to meet her eyes. Much as he'd looked forward to this journey, he was half-prepared to slink back to Perky's.

"I said *what's bugging you*, deafboy? I thought you were the one who was supposed to be all jazzed about ditching this burg."

"Nothing's bugging me, *man*. I just tripped out for a minute, that's all. If you'd hit on this stash you'd be spaced-out too."

"Well then," Eddie offered, still studying Kevin's face. "Don't be such a bogart. Roll one up."

Mike tossed a book of rolling papers *just* as Kevin produced his stash, almost causing a spill. They propped their bikes on kickstands.

Kevin looked around warily. Sun worshippers from all walks of life laughed, jogged, gossiped, and panhandled about them. "You sure this is cool, right out in the open?"

Eddie nudged him. "Listen to Mr. Paranoid! We're *free* now, Kevin! If any of these people don't dig our trip, well, they know what they can do with it. They won't be seeing us again for a long, long time."

"Right," Mike said gruffly. He swiped his papers off Kevin's palm. "So if you're too chicken, I'll do it myself."

"*Not* chicken!" Kevin snapped, and grabbed the papers right back. He glared at Mike, a boy he hadn't known long and was just this side of despising. Mike had come along as part of the package in acquiring Eddie's friendship, and had never warmed to Kevin, who'd done his level best to be at least tolerant. Mike was for sure the darkest presence of the three, the wildest and hottest, always suspicious of nonexistent conspiracies between Kevin and Eddie. His hatred and jealousy had simmered over the past few months, as he'd noticed Eddie confiding more and more in the big clumsy intruder. In fact, Eddie really *was* interested—almost fanatically so—in the great mushrooming of color and energy firing his generation. While Kevin, who was genuinely intent on learning to be a good little hippie, provided a pliant sounding board for Eddie's lectures and musings, Mike really didn't give a damn about the politics of the Movement. What Mike wanted, and what the Movement's flexible parameters provided, was an excuse to raise hell and have a good time. And now, thanks to Kevin's discussion-goading intervention, Mike would always be just on the other side of an impenetrable membrane: an interrupter, a bother, a stranger.

"Not...*chicken*," Kevin repeated in an undertone, licking a paper's gummed edge while staring fiercely at Mike. He slowly rolled a large cigarette from the aromatic crushed leaves packed in the sandwich bag, occasionally picking out random stems. To prove his fearlessness he rolled four more, taking his time, then dropped these four into his shirt's pocket. He boldly fired the joint for all to see. A few passersby smiled or sniffed knowingly, but the boys passed it around thrice without a single offended look cast their way.

"Wow," Mike said, his eyes a dull red and half-closed. His voice sounded hollow to him, as though his ears were stuffed with cotton. "Wow," he repeated doubtfully, tripping on the primitivity of the expression.

"This is good pot," Eddie muttered. He tried again: "This *is* good pot." He blinked at Mike and then at Kevin, wondering if his words made sense, hearing the crowd sounds as through headphones. His own voice sounded soft and distant. His round teddy bear eyes were bloodshot and glazed. He looked at Kevin. "This is *good* pot," he said. "*This* is." He looked back at Mike but Mike was embarrassed, and avoiding his friends' eyes. Eddie grew absorbed in a study of the dirt under his fingernails. "You got this from Perky?" he asked his hands.

"That's right," Kevin said, basking in the impression of being a local Somebody's chum. The marijuana hadn't hit him quite as hard as it had hit his friends, thanks to the bracer joint he'd smoked earlier with Perky. "It's a special blend from Germany and the Far East. I only got it because me and Perky are such tight friends."

*"Wow!"* said Eddie.

Mike looked at him hard. "I didn't know you and Perky were partners."

"Well...now you know. So's everybody got their heads tight? Let's get going."

And then they were rolling down the road-to-highway on-ramp, digging the feel of warm air on their ears, alive to being alive. They jockeyed for lead position happily, indifferent to dangerously-close northbound traffic.

In a matter of minutes the boys were riding hard and fast alongside Will Rogers Beach. But by the time they were into the curve that would eventually lead them to Malibu, Kevin was experiencing the toll of rigorous exercise. The three were accustomed to wheeling leisurely along the city's tame avenues, not to going all-out on the highway. Kevin's legs were already sore from the job of driving his bulk hard enough to keep up with his lighter friends, and now even keeping up had become a nightmare. His breath was rasping in his ears, his heart racing. He couldn't afford to appear weak in his friends' eyes, not after he'd boasted of matchless stamina and resourcefulness, but he was falling farther and farther behind.

"*Hey!*" he called out desperately. "Slow down, for Pete's sake!"

Mike and Eddie, still passionately vying to be leader, didn't hear or didn't care. Kevin put down his head and forced himself on.

"*Wait up!*" he snarled. But they wouldn't slow, and didn't stop until they'd reached a gas station at Sunset Boulevard. There they stood, panting, watching a small crowd milling round a roped-off display at the lot's far end. The object on display was a blood-red Corvette Stingray, gleaming like a burnished ruby in the summer sun. Mike and Eddie, inconsequential specks in the ruby's halo, were too dazzled to hear Kevin slowly grinding up behind them, head down and eyes closed, grunting, "wait *up*," with each searing exhalation. His pace slackened to that of a drunken march, then to a wobbly crawl, and finally he chugged to a halt almost at their heels. He dismounted gingerly and doubled over, beads of sweat the size of polliwogs falling from his nose and chin.

"Now *that*," Mike was saying, "is what I want for Christmas, Eddie." He vigorously rubbed his palms. "Who wouldn't give his left nut just to be *seen* in that baby!"

But Eddie seemed distracted. "I guess..." he said absently.

Mike's eyes narrowed. "What do you mean, you *guess*? Look at that and tell me what you see."

"I already looked. It's a car."

"A car? A *car?* A Volkswagen's a car. You mean all you see's a Volkswagen?"

Eddie shrugged.

Mike threw out his arms. *"What a weenie!"* He began walking circles around Eddie, scowling and shaking his head like a man fuming over some obscene and immovable object dumped on his front lawn as a prank. Finally he stopped and just glared, hands on hips, waiting. But Eddie had known Mike far too long to be impressed by his histrionics. So Mike now found himself in the extraordinary position of actually having to appeal to Kevin, a totally out-of-it and altogether untogether load he considered the lowest form of company imaginable, and the last person in the world he'd want on his side—especially when it came down to agreement on a symbol of virility. "How's about you, Kevin?" he asked, turning toward the Corvette and spreading his arms to simulate the gesture of a man on a hill overwhelmed by the abundance of his valley. "Can you dig that or not?"

Kevin smiled goofily. "For sure," he panted, still getting his wind back. "Once you got behind a honey like that everything else'd just fall in place. I'd spend my nights cruising the boulevards with a blonde and a brew. What more could a guy want out of life?"

"Maybe some self-respect," Eddie mumbled.

"Well, what do you call *that?*" Mike sputtered, pointing at the ruby. "Something to be ashamed of? Oh! I forgot. It's just another Volkswagen. Kee-rist Almighty, Eddie! You're starting to let this Movement stuff screw up your head for real."

Something made Kevin watch Eddie closely. Mike was being careless now, as the Movement was not a matter Eddie took lightly. It was his guiding star.

Eddie seemed to shiver in the sun. He said not a word, but looked out to sea. For a wild instant Kevin saw his friend as a kind of Moses figure, somehow all the taller for his diminutiveness, something behind his eyes burning with a radiance that easily surpassed the feeble luster of golden calves and ruby Corvettes. There was an absolutely wrenching suspension of communication, of camaraderie, of that indefinable force that can make seemingly incompatible souls fast, and bind its subjects with a sense of brotherhood deeper even than the imposition of blood. The surf boomed like cannon fire, and a pair of gulls fought vociferously over some nondescript Angeleno's naked garbage.

"…Yeah…" Mike managed. "Well, I'm gonna go check it out anyway. No offense, Eddie." He glared at Kevin, as though Eddie's mood shift was all the fat boy's fault, and walked his bike over to join the crowd.

"When I said I dug the car," Kevin said quickly, "I wasn't saying I worshipped it, Eddie. I mean, when you're hip to the Movement, you're totally hip, right? I was just saying that, as far as cars go, you gotta admit that's a *nice* car."

Eddie shrugged again.

"I don't mean you *gotta* admit it," Kevin amended awkwardly, "and I didn't mean *you* when I said 'you.' I just meant…well, you know, what's good is good, and what isn't…isn't."

"And what's right is right?" Eddie probed. "And what's wrong is wrong?"

"Sure."

"So it's wrong to treat something wrong right, right? And it's right to treat something wrong wrong?"

Kevin blinked. Something…

All else notwithstanding, Eddie was a dyed-in-the-wool philosopher. "And don't you wrong right when wrong isn't right wrong? Or is there a right wrong and a wrong wrong, a wrong right and a right right?"

Kevin's jaw dropped.

Eddie emphasized his point by rhythmically stabbing his right forefinger into his left palm. "And if there *is*, is the *right* wrong right *right* wrong, and the *wrong* wrong right *wrong* wrong?"

Glasshopper's eyeballs seemed to spin in their sockets. His brain became a simple sensory organ for sniffing out mastodons and competing troglodytes. Slowly his speech-center recovered. "Ugh," he said. "Big rock in stinkbush."

*"What?"*

Kevin's eyes refocused. Eddie was studying him with an

odd expression. A sharp pain sprang up somewhere behind Kevin's eyes, and his fingertips began to tingle weirdly. But the pain and tingle passed almost immediately, left him staring stupidly at his friend. Sweat trickled around his eyes. Gonna be a hot one, he thought, or thought he thought.

*"Well?"* Eddie demanded. "Can somebody just arbitrarily do whatever he likes, or do his principles guide his actions regardless of gain or loss? Are you gonna hang with what you believe in, or cop out?"

"That's easy," Kevin parried. His heart added a flam to its regular beat. He gulped. "I don't cop out."

"Then there's no compromising the Movement," Eddie said firmly. "You can't suck up to the glamour and garbage of this society and still be free. It's one or the other, Kevin. We've got to turn our backs on all the plastic crap before it eats us alive. The Movement isn't a part-time experience. We've got to forget about cars and money and status, permanently, or we're right back where we started before we know it."

"But," Kevin objected, feeling better now, "we can't throw out the baby with the birth water, can we? I mean, certain things are just too important to give up on."

"You said it, Kevin: 'just too important.' Nobody's ever satisfied with the basics, because having anything only whets the appetite. Soon as they get it they lose interest. It's the *wanting* that's in control. Only now they want better, and they want more. It starts to snowball, and you end up with a world of greedy adult children."

"But what about money, Eddie? You can't do anything without money, and if you've got the money it doesn't make any sense to not spend it, does it? And if you're gonna spend it, you're gonna spend it on what you like, right? And unless you like junk you're gonna need lots of money; so you're either gonna have to love money or love being poor."

Eddie sighed. "You mean you *still* don't see why it's wrong to take the real world seriously? You can't see what's *wrong* with having a cushy career and a bank account? Or why it's such a bummer to be all turned-on by a bunch of shiny stuff everybody else is drooling over, or the reason it's a hang-up to have wants in the first place? And doesn't it bug you knowing what you'll have to sacrifice for the sake of all that prestige you're trying to accumulate? You're gonna *buy* self-respect? *Can't you see* that dignity, even though it doesn't have a price tag on it, is worth more than all the materialistic bullshit in the world put together?"

Kevin struggled to come up with a succinct response, sensitive enough to Eddie's commitment to know the boy's challenge was in earnest, but uncomfortable with the way it seemed to be blinding him to everything else in life. "Wrong?" he muttered. He looked at the car—futuristic, sexy, powerful, poised...the thing was reflecting the sun so dynamically it appeared ready to burst into flames. There wasn't a human being alive who could fail to appreciate it, and, since Eddie was human, Kevin felt he wasn't getting the whole picture here; that he'd missed something simple but vital in Eddie's argument. Either that or the grass...but, ever since that damp November night of their first meeting, the friendship had proved an uneasy alliance when conversation got into the deep end. Eddie could turn the simplest issue inside-out.

*"Wrong?"* Kevin sputtered. Abstracta had always eluded him. He had a sneaking suspicion that any query regarding that which was intangible—such as whether something was *wrong* or *right*—had to be a trick question, a verbal ambush designed to confuse the listener by making him think. This whole jive thing about *values* was just some phony Government head trip contrived to keep people bored and in line, and the fact that Eddie had been seduced so thoroughly sometimes made Kevin wonder just what kind of stuff his friend was made of. So for a moment he found himself entertaining a vindictive-but-constructive urge to tell Eddie to grow up, or to put him in his place by coolly countering with the one macho response any red-blooded, All-American Guy would make; namely, a half-attentive look of utter disdain, followed by a pointed turning of the head to proclaim complete dissociation. Because the All-American Guy doesn't require intelligence. What he utilizes is far more valuable in the real world than something as ineffectual as a mind. It's a license to bluff; unspoken, unchallenged—but understood, by every gonad in every garage from puberty on, to be the prime postulate of the streetwise: *what's*

wrong *is what I don't like, and what's* right *is what turns me on. And if I can't spend it, drive it, flaunt it, or fuck it, then hey, what good is it?* Men killed for the sake of principles like that. But *knowledge* existed, Kevin was sure, just to make ordinary people feel really dumb about all the things they didn't know; in exactly the way churches existed solely to make people feel guilty about...*everything.* Yet Kevin genuinely *liked* Eddie, even though Eddie had a dangerous habit of asking useless questions, and of caring about things that didn't matter to anybody who did matter. Intelligence was obviously the boy's Achilles' heel; a prissy quality which probably came from being short and indifferent to football, or from wasting his time at school burying his nose in books instead of checking out the babes. He was hopelessly out of touch. And now Kevin found that having to defend the self-evident could be a real test of friendship.

"Wrong?" he repeated. "Eddie, what's *wrong* with wanting to own good things? What's *wrong* with wanting to be somebody? I mean, I know it's uncool to be greedy and selfish and all that, and to make money into some kind of god or something, but how can it be bad to want lots of money and all the neat stuff you can get with it, and then honestly do your thing to earn it? What's so great about having nothing?"

"Because it's not *your* thing you're doing. It's *their* thing. Don't you get it?"

"*No*, Eddie. I really, honestly, totally, truly, absolutely-positively-super-seriously *don't*. If *I'm* earning it, why's it *their* thing?"

Eddie puffed out his cheeks and stared at the gas pumps. He squinted and grimaced, rolled his eyes heavenward. Finally he exhaled.

"Look, let me explain it with an analogy. You know what I mean by analogy?"

Now Kevin was getting pissed. "Eddie, who the heck's gonna be allergic to money?"

"No, Kevin, not an allergy. Analogy. A way to explain a certain quality using an example where it's obvious."

"You mean like a story or picture where you use different stuff to show what you're trying to get across?"

"That's close enough. In this analogy I'll use dogs, okay? Okay. So here we've all these dogs in this house, and the dogs' master comes up like he does every day, with a big box of Liver Snaps in his hand. And he says to the first dog, 'Speak!' The first dog goes 'yap! yap! yap!' and his master gives him a Liver Snap. The master says to the next dog, 'Play dead!' Down goes the second dog like he's been shot. Then he jumps back up to get his goodie. The master moves down the line of dogs, going, 'Fetch! Heel! Roll over!' and each dog obeys and gets a Liver Snap. Finally he comes to the last dog and he says, 'Shake hands!' But this dog just looks at him as if to say, 'Go shake your own fucking hand.' The master freaks out. 'Bad dog!' he says. 'Bad, bad, *ba-a-a-ad* dog! No Liver Snaps for you until you behave!' And he walks away shaking his head and wondering just what the heck's *wrong* with that dog anyway, and trying to figure out some kind of punishment that'll straighten him out. Now, all the other dogs are tripping on this dog who won't behave, and laughing at him. They think he's too stupid to perform simple tricks. Anyways, they're all fat and happy, and have more important things to think about, like when the next Liver Snap's coming. So time goes by and the good dogs get better at their tricks, and hang around snoozing on their cozy circumstances, knowing how choice it can be for a good dog, and how the meaning of life is just a Liver Snap away. But the bad dog refuses to perform, and he gets scrawny and isolated. Eventually he dies, with only his dignity for company, and the house breathes a sigh of relief. More time passes. The good dogs have puppies, and the puppies grow up learning the same tricks by imitating their parents, who are now slow and clumsy and can't compete with the young dogs. But the master doesn't care about the old dogs anymore. The old dogs are bad dogs because they don't perform with the en-thusiasm of the young ones, and anyway Liver Snaps don't grow on trees. The old dogs begin to feel the pinch. So what do they do? They tell the young dogs a story about this wise old dog who wasn't greedy, but instead had the self-respect to not jump up and down making a fool out of himself on account of a lousy Liver Snap, for Christ's sake. The young dogs are made to feel guilty, so out of a kind of peer pressure they try to not make a big thing out of performing, but secretly they dream of pigging out on Liver Snaps, and wish the old dogs would just hurry up and die." Eddie paused, all the frustration gone from his expression now, his winsome features made even more so by that rare gratification that can only come from giving the priceless gift of insight. "So *now* do you see what I mean about dignity, and about not taking the real world seriously?"

Kevin, chewing his lip sadly, tried to not sound condescending. "I...*guess* so, Eddie. You're trying to tell me I should feel sorry for skinny dogs, shake hands instead of being a real prick, and never listen to my parents if I don't wanna die on an empty stomach."

Eddie's jaw fell.

Kevin had to look down, feeling he'd overextended himself by encapsulating in one breath what Eddie found moving enough to spin into some weird speech about dreaming dogs. And, goddamn it, that was *precisely* why smart people always ended up looking like such fools, and why they had to be ditched in public if you didn't want your reputation ruined: they always alienated themselves by talking about things that would bring down the happiest party in no time flat. Like rapping about if we were justified in going to war, one of Eddie's favorite sermons. Now, it's no big secret that war can be a real bummer, and the kind of trip any happening cat doesn't want to get into if he doesn't have to. But...when somebody's fucking with your country and all that, it's like what's the use of talking? The guy you're up against is rowdy because his country's rowdy, and if he doesn't dig apple pie nobody's saying he has to open his big mouth in the first place. If you love peace, if you care about your fellow man, then you gotta be ready to kick his ass to prove it. Everybody knows that, whether they want to make speeches about it or not. Sitting on your thumb *discussing* your differences is like John Wayne playing Confucius to Genghis Khan. A couple of pithy maxims and *slash:* no more John Wayne. Or like babes: what the hell good are books and speeches when you're dealing with a hefty pair of knockers in a fuzzy pink sweater? The very thought caused Kevin's palms to perspire, and he wondered if Eddie, finding himself alone with a hot and long-legged bunny, would respond with a sermon about sex being *wrong*. All *real* men know intelligence is a turn-off to chicks, and like a total insult to what it means to be a Guy in the first place. And that's why the smart kids in school hang out in the library instead of joining the crowd: it's a way to avoid getting your ass kicked for being intelligent. But Kevin *liked* Eddie, and respected him despite his flaws. In the end, Kevin realized, *you simply can* not *argue with intelligent people!* You can only feel sorry for them. Furthermore, Kevin was painfully dependent on a reciprocal relationship with Eddie, the only friend he'd ever had. So, in the name of friendship, he now compromised himself, blushed credibly and said,

"Am I warm?"

Eddie stared straight ahead without replying. After a minute he said, "You're cooking, Kevin. But maybe I shouldn't have been so elaborate. Too many images. Look, what I was trying to say is...a good pet isn't a good dog. A good pet is a dog who's sold out. And when I say *wrong* I don't mean unprofitable or stupid. A 'winner' is a man who's sold out. And the Mephistopheles in this picture is appetite. Anybody whose motivation in life is profit, or pleasure, or any kind of gratification not stemming from the heart, will do or say anything to *get* what he or she *wants*. It's their instinct. They've totally fucked up the whole world since Day One, and they're the enemy. *Because* they *want* they *take*. That's all the justification they need. It's not, you'll notice, in their nature to contribute. But at least they're not hard to spot. In fact, they're impossible to miss, because they *want* you to notice them. They wear their appetites like badges. So listen, Kevin. Any time you see somebody wearing expensive clothes, or driving a sharp car, or displaying any signs of prosperity, that guy's *telling* you what his priorities are, and if he says anything like he cares about the Movement, or about people or positive values, well, you know he's just handing you a line of bullshit. He wants to impress you about how wealthy and successful he is, and in the same way he wants to convince you he's basically a really deep person. See? Since he *wants* you to believe him, there's nothing *wrong* with lying to you, and to him you'll be *wrong* if you tell him he's a liar, because that's not what he *wants!* So you've got to *mean it* when you believe in something, and use your life to help make this world a better place for everybody who lives on it. Otherwise you'd might as well walk around wearing a sign that reads: ME NO KNOW. ME DUMB FUCKING HIPPIE. And you don't want to be a public creep, do you? Of course you don't. You see, Kevin, human beings are hung up on being mammals. That means they instinctively join the crowd and imitate everybody else. And that's why almost all the people in this story are caricatures. They don't, for the most part, have the balls to develop independent identities, because it pays to be a clone among clones. What really blows me away is that it works! I mean, it's okay for monkeys to see and do. They're just monkeys. But what about this marvelous advance, this human brain we're all so proud of? Nobody uses it. Instead our heroes are…what? Athletes? Why? Are we trying to outjump kangaroos, outrun horses, outswing chimpanzees…run and catch the ball, little human! Attaboy! Good human! And let's not forget…*actors*. Yeah! Let's all worship some dink for pretending to be somebody he isn't: somebody with character. And just look how big he is up there on the screen! Boy, am I impressed! And on and on—*Homo sapiens*: Man of Wisdom. Ha! Try taking wisdom to the bank!"

"But Eddie," Kevin interjected, "if what you say's true, then what are we but a bunch of monkeys for joining the Movement? We're just a different brand of clone."

"Uh-uh, Kevin. You're being over-literal. We're not taking the Movement to the bank. A guy can be a head and still be an individual, still have merit. You can use your mind to be a follower, if what you're following is worthy of being followed. That requires judgment with a proper bias, which is a requisite of wisdom. Anyway," Eddie closed, watching a pair of apparent twins coasting exhausted to one of the gas islands on their bicycles, "I've got lotsa faith in you, Kevin. I'm pretty good at gauging people, and I can tell you've got what it takes to be a totally together flower child."

Kevin grinned and pulled out his baggie of grass, held it up in display. "I sure do," he extemporized. It was a throwaway gesture, meant to disguise his discomfort. Kevin knew, in his balls, that he was unworthy of Eddie's confidence, unworthy of the world's analysis, unworthy of his own strut and swagger. He rolled a cigarette carefully, watching the cyclists collapse at the gas island. Mike eyeballed the newcomers thoroughly while slowly walking his bike toward his friends, feigning nonchalance all the way.

Kevin couldn't remember ever having seen two people so done in. By wordless consent he and Eddie sidled over, kidding around until the three boys met at the gas island. It was now evident the cyclists weren't twins after all; that immediate impression was due to their similarly gaunt frames and identical apparel: white T-shirts and shorts with black trim, red and blue-striped Adidas athletic shoes and matching socks, a foot-wide band of gauze wrapped round the left knee of each, and a nylon-and-plastic crown of webbed headgear. The only noticeable difference: one man had the number 19 stenciled on the back of his headgear, while the other sported the number 137.

Now Kevin bent down to see if he could help 19 up, as the man appeared delirious. He was muttering something while pawing at Kevin's shin. "Lucy Ann?" he gasped, "Lucy Ann?" Kevin stared at his friends, shrugged uncertainly, and looked back down. "Sorry," he said. "No Lucy Anns here. I'm Kevin, this is Eddie, and that's Mike. What's your name?"

"No...no" 19 croaked, wagging his head in frustration. "Izyloo..." he gagged. "Loozian...izyanna...is...is this Louisiana?"

"Oh, heck no," Eddie piped. "You guys are way off. This is still Los Angeles."

This announcement caused 137 to heave himself to his hands and knees. "God *damn* it, man! I *told* you it wasn't the Gulf of Mexico."

19 shuddered, coughing and wheezing. He angrily grabbed the water hose's neck and soaked himself head to foot before hosing down his companion.

"Say!" Mike burst out. "I'll bet you guys are marathoners. Right?"

"Were..." 19 muttered. "Right now we're a couple of jackasses." He struggled to his feet and, incredibly, commenced a set of deep knee-bends. 137 watched for a few seconds, then reluctantly began a set of pushups.

"From where to where?" Kevin asked, becoming exhausted just watching the two men exercise.

"Seattle to New Orleans," 19 puffed. "Only we lost our lead car somewhere back in Arizona." He ratcheted his aching neck until he was facing his partner. *"Only four hundred freaking miles ago!"* He dropped his head with a snarl. "It's okay, though," he managed after a minute. "We can make it up if we ride double-time."

"You mean *you*," 137 gasped, "can make it up."

This didn't faze 19 a bit. "Discipline," he panted. "The mind's will over the body's denial."

"Did...did you guys go through San Francisco?" Eddie asked, throwing a fascinated glance at Kevin.

"Yeah. What a mistake. Nothing but hills."

"But what about the people?" Kevin pressed. "I mean, how's the Revolution coming along up there? Like, is everybody grooving?"

This stopped both exercisers. 137 glared at Kevin and Eddie. 19 appeared about to spit on them. Mike, standing behind his companions, shrugged disdainfully to indicate his own lack of involvement while copying 19's sneering expression.

"You mean all that love and peace bullcrap?" 19 demanded. "I *thought* you guys looked like hippies." Mike eyed his partners with contempt from behind their backs as 19 and 137 resumed their exercising.

"Go on up there with your own kind," 137 panted, "and wallow in their crap if you want. That place is the commode of the country. Bunch of faggots!" Mike, sneering behind the boys, mouthed the word *yeah* while looking from one to the other in private triumph.

The three moved a few feet away. "Did you hear that?" Eddie said blinking. "That guy talks about the City like it's a pit."

"Makes me want to puke," Kevin responded. "He talks just like my dad. Sometimes I get the feeling these pricks don't even *know* there's a revolution going on."

"Fuck 'em," Mike said, with a sly toss of his head. "Those jocks don't know what they're missing. They're a disgrace to bikes."

"I'm hip," Kevin said firmly. He fired up the joint he'd been holding, took a hit and passed it to Eddie. "To the Revolution!" He likened 19's stripped, well-machined twenty-speed racer to his own colorful, Mickey Mouse'd bike. There was simply no comparison. Kevin tenderly ran his hand over the top multicolored bar of his bicycle's frame. "Fuck 'em," he echoed under his breath.

The two cyclists had completed their aerobics and were straddling their machines, preparing to push off. A stoned Kevin sauntered up to 19 and said, motioning toward the displayed Corvette, "By the way, what do you think of that?"

19 shrugged, said, "It's a car," and rode away with his partner struggling alongside.

Kevin rejoined his friends, shaking his head. He accepted the joint from Eddie and took the deepest draw he could.

"What'd you just say to those jocks?" Mike demanded.

Kevin exhaled. "I told 'em to lighten up on the Movement, and to not take the real world seriously."

"Right on," Eddie said warmly, no less sincere for his intoxication. "Told you I was a good judge of character."

"Character," Mike growled, his jealousy getting the better of him, "*hell!*" He tore the glowing joint right out of Kevin's mouth, hit on it repeatedly and flicked the roach away.

There came an answering growl from Kevin, but he hadn't opened his mouth; he was still holding the smoke. His stomach rumbled again, longer this time.

Eddie pretended he hadn't noticed Mike's hostility. "So let's get going, you guys! If those clowns can make it from Seattle, I *know* we can get to Frisco!"

"Wait!" Kevin erupted. His stomach was growling and writhing continually, his mouth salivating. "I've got the munchies all of a sudden."

Mike immediately spat out: *"You've always gotta slow us down!"* But marijuana can make the smoker extremely suggestible, and it was plain that THC (the active intoxicant, tetrahydrocannabinol) was playing tricks with Mike's appetite, too.

Eddie licked his lips and peered at Kevin from the crimson caves of his eyes. "What're you gonna get?"

Kevin's stomach roared and gurgled, cursed and beseeched. The imagined taste of strawberry shortcake seeped into his mouth. The tendency of marijuana to exaggerate the symptoms of appetite has an unfortunate twist: the craving—especially in youngsters—is generally for junk food instead of wholesome sustenance. "I don't know," he said, chewing his lip, images of tasty snacks jumbling in his mind like the fruit symbols on a slot machine. "Maybe some potato chips and a candy bar or two."

Now Eddie was repeatedly clenching his fingers. His eyes, though still a dull red, were wide and staring.

"C'mon you guys," Mike urged half-heartedly, "if we stop to scarf up we'll never get under way." He grabbed Eddie's shoulder. "We can eat later, Eddie. Maybe get a cheeseburger for lunch."

Eddie winced at the word *cheeseburger*. His head turned slowly, an inch at a time, like an old door on rusted hinges. He stared unseeing at Mike out of those fixed, haunted eyes, his lax lips joined by strings of saliva. "Cheeseburger," he muttered.

"Come on!" Kevin said. "There's just gotta be a hamburger stand or *something* around here."

So they began pedaling earnestly up Sunset Boulevard, searching for a fast food-stop. Now Kevin, riding feverishly in the lead, fancied he could hear Eddie's stomach growling behind him like a suspicious watchdog.

"Nothing!" Mike cried. "Nothing but hotels and motels and motels and hotels!" It was true. The boulevard was increasingly desolate—only small motels and an occasional house tucked between the weltered trees and dry scrub so typical of the great California coastal desert.

Kevin pulled another joint from his shirt pocket as they came to a halt. His fingers fumbled for a match. "What we've got to do," he heard himself rattling, "is get *higher*. We've got to get our heads together and figure something out. If I don't eat something fast I'll go crazy." He lit the cigarette and drew on it deeply, passed it to Mike.

"Maybe we could sneak around behind one of these hotels and motels and rip 'em off," Mike suggested, smoke seeping from his nostrils. His eyes were almost closed. "Me and

Billy used to do that. They've got little rooms behind them where they keep eggs and steaks and stuff."

"Eggs!" Eddie breathed. Kevin and Mike turned to stare at him. *"Steaks!"* he hissed.

Eddie broke, went tearing up the boulevard like a madman, his friends calling and straining after him.

Mike had handed the joint back before they mounted, and Kevin puffed on it unthinking as he labored, falling farther and farther behind.

"Wait up!" he called, coughing. "Wait up, wait up, *wait up!*"

Eddie and Mike disappeared round a bend in the road. Kevin dismounted sloppily and fell on his butt with a jarring of his tailbone, tears squeezing between his eyelids. Every few gasps he automatically and unconsciously took another hit off the joint until it burned his fingertips. Cursing his gnawing stomach and inconsiderate friends, he remounted and forced himself sobbing up the grade.

Finally he made out a cluster of buildings a hundred yards distant. At the cluster's far end was a liquor store with his friends' bicycles thrown down hurriedly in front. As he rode toward the store he saw Mike and Eddie emerge with their hands and mouths full. He coasted up, braked cleanly, stood his bike on its kickstand with care and pride. Kevin sauntered past his companions without acknowledgment, entered the store with the civility it was due.

Once inside he made a dash for the pastries, grabbed a package containing two chocolate-frosted cupcakes and a package of orange-frosted. His eyes fell on a third, untried flavor: wild cherry! Three packages was going way overboard. But Kevin, through Eddie's New World tutelage, had learned to be disdainful of prejudicial behavior, and could therefore summon the inner strength to avoid favoritism in matters regarding race, creed, or artificial flavor. As he scooped up the wild cherry-frosted, retaining all three flavors, he peripherally noticed something unbelievable: *banana-frosted!* With freaking *sprinkles*, for Christ's sake! Kevin didn't hesitate. He snatched it in trade for the wild cherry-frosted and made his way crabwise down the aisle, seizing a package of cheese puffs, a package of corn chips, and a large bag of cashews, piling all the articles in the crook of his left arm. Another customer stood in his way, but Kevin, wholly preoccupied, shuffled right into him. The man, struck from behind, turned and was about to give vent to his indignation when he saw the saliva at the corners of the boy's mouth, the blood-gorged eyes, the slack face. He meekly stepped aside. "Pardon *me*."

Kevin looked over the deli section excitedly, picked out a ham and cheese sandwich and a cold Fat Boy sandwich. From the freezer he plucked a drumstick and an ice cream sandwich, tasting each item in his mind. He would need something to wash all this down, so he snapped up, in a munchies mini-seizure, a quart carton of chocolate-flavored milk. For dessert he grabbed a large box of chocolate chip cookies. At last he realized he was getting carried away, and turned back by an effort of will. On his way to the counter he guiltily reclaimed the forsaken package of wild cherry-frosted cupcakes. He laid it all on the counter and stepped to the candies rack, selected six candy bars for quick energy, and returned to the counter, where he obtained two sticks of beef jerky for the stamina he'd need on the road. And suddenly he was riveted, gawking at a jar of plump dill pickles floating in vinegar, like the bloated arms and legs of creatures in the formaldehyde of science class. That took care of his willpower. Kevin ordered three from the clerk. When the man had rung it all up he gave the boy only a few small coins in exchange for a twenty dollar bill. Kevin swiped his sackful of goodies and immediately stalked out, his tongue orgasming, his hand already digging in the bag.

Mike and Eddie were involved in a belching contest, sitting happily propped against the store's wall. Eddie turned his head to belch in Kevin's ear as Kevin sat, ripping the cellophane cover off the ham and cheese sandwich with his teeth. Eddie's grinning face was a mass of yellowish whipped cream from the nose down.

Kevin very nearly got the entire sandwich in his mouth with one bite, leaving only a corner between fingertips and thumb. He quickly champed the mouthful, his face impossibly contorted. As soon as he could make room he crammed in the neglected corner, then ripped open the milk carton with his right hand while his left tore free the banana-frosted cupcakes. Kevin swallowed with a huge sigh, just as Mike belched in his other ear. Paying no attention, he tilted back his head and poured down a third of the quart carton of chocolate-flavored milk. Kevin set the carton between his knees and sat like a feasting king, a banana-frosted cupcake pinched in his poised left paw, a dill pickle gripped obscenely in his right. After a huge gulp of air, he savagely chomped off half the pickle and darted his head cobra-wise to the waiting cupcake. When these were swallowed he shoved in the other half of the pickle, gnashed it dribbling, and tossed back his head to gulp a second third of the chocolate milk. With another great sigh he set the milk down, popped the other cupcake in his mouth, and feverishly tore open the ice cream sandwich wrapper. He got half in one bite, but the damned thing was cold and hurt his teeth, so he set the uneaten half down and grabbed the drumstick. That was cold and hurt his teeth too, but he devoured it gamely and followed with the other half of the ice cream sandwich, the cashews, and the chocolate chip cookies. Heaving another sigh, he started on the chocolate-frosted cupcakes.

Mike and Eddie had been watching all this with amazement and cheering camaraderie, and now accompanied his efforts with elongated stereo belches and raspberries. Kevin shoved down the chocolate-frosted cupcakes and began on the Fat Boy sandwich. He was slowing a bit now, and sweat was crawling on his cheeks and forehead. Somehow he got the whole sandwich down. Chest heaving, he started on a second pickle. He wasn't at all hungry anymore, but the marijuana and his companions continued to urge him on. With difficulty he crammed down a candy bar, the orange-frosted cupcakes, and his last dill pickle. He let his head fall back sluggishly, and with cheers and belches in his ears carefully sipped the last of the milk.

"Hoo...*ray!*" Mike's voice was a spike in his brain. "Well done, Kevin old chump."

"Yea!" Eddie cried. "Well, now that everybody's done, let's get going."

"Wait!" Kevin managed. Gimme a break, willya?"

"Aw, why do you always gotta slow us down?"

"Yeah, Kevin, you got what you wanted, so what're you griping about now?"

Kevin turned his heavy head in Eddie's direction. "I—I feel kinda sick."

"Serves you right," Mike sneered, "piggy."

Kevin whirled on him. Before he could rebuke the boy he felt his gut react. In a minute he whispered, "Don't call me 'piggy'."

"Okay, fatso. Let's get going, darn it!"

"Right on!" They picked up their bikes.

"Wait!"

"We waited!"

"Let's smoke—" Kevin blurped, "let's smoke a—let's smoke a joint first."

*"C'mon, porkface!"* Mike said hotly, still trying to provoke Kevin. "How long's your stash gonna last at this rate?"

"Yeah, Kevin. We already smoked three."

"Let him sit there feeling sorry for himself. He can catch up with us later."

"No! Wait!" Too late, they were already riding away. Gasping, Kevin forced himself to his feet, grabbed his bag of goodies and followed. Each inhalation was a sob, each exhalation a moan. He had to walk his bike back to Sunset, but it was quite an improvement coasting down the boulevard. Right away he began to feel better, so he wolfed down a couple of candy bars and the wild cherry-frosted cupcakes to make the bag more manageable. His friends were far ahead, but weren't riding so hard now, occasionally looking back to make sure he was still behind.

Once they were on the highway, Kevin, for some reason feeling almost well again, made steady progress in narrowing the gap. Hating himself, he gobbled down the beef jerky and candy bars he'd planned on saving. The corn chips and cheese puffs quickly followed course, and at long last he was gripping an empty bag. As if cued, thirst descended with a terrible intensity. He shed his heavy plaid Pendleton shirt and left his back naked to the sun.

Try as he would, he always found himself lagging. Mike and Eddie seemed to be equipped with boundless zeal, and were forever calling back, scoffing at his efforts. Kevin didn't admire them for their energy; he despised them for it, and wished they could for but a moment share his aching weariness. Time and again they would wait for him to catch up, and just when he thought it was time for a blessed break they would ride off in renewed spurts of joyful abandon.

Exhaustion wasn't Kevin's only gripe: his stomach was freaking out over the sugary feast. The periods of calm grew less frequent, the discomfort more intense. The pain was very real, and could only be relieved by short, dangerously vehement bursts of posterior wind. On the verge of tears, he threw himself into the Herculean task of barely dragging along.

What Kevin wanted now was a roughly straight road with some measure of consistency, but the highway snaked nauseatingly. Veer to the left, veer to the right, veer to the left, veer to the right. The caution signs alongside the highway didn't help any. ROUGH ROAD. FALLING ROCK. SLIDE AREA. And veer to the left, veer to the right…the ordeal through Malibu seemed to take forever. And after Malibu the highway cut inland, with miles and miles of virtually featureless road. He'd lost all track of time and distance. Surely they had covered a hundred miles, in what must have been hours. But there was no appreciable change in the road, and the sun was still high in the breathtaking June sky. He had to struggle back into his shirt when the rays became too painful. At last the highway cut back to the beach.

After a few more miles the coastline became ragged, the pretty beaches swiftly giving way to a world of growing desolation. Not far offshore, great mounds of rock rose amid the gentle wavelets like humpbacked whales, colonies of seaweed drifted listlessly. But the haunting beauty only added to his misery. What he wanted was a soft clean beach peppered with deck chairs and restrooms.

Perhaps half a mile ahead, Mike and Eddie had stopped to patronize a catering truck serving motorists at a popular scenic turnout. They were thirsty. With a paroxysm of intent, Kevin forced himself to speed to a crawl, realizing the break had at last arrived.

When he pulled up his friends were engaged in a lighthearted battle, using the crushed ice from their soft drinks for ammunition. They pelted Kevin as he wobbled up. He cursed feebly and dropped his bike, collapsed on his sunburned back with a shudder. New waves of nausea shook him like a dog. He closed his eyes at a sudden furious stab of intestinal pain, carefully counted to ten, then to a hundred. Gradually the pain diminished.

"Hey, Kevin!" Mike called. "Wake up! Whatcha say we smoke a joint?"

Kevin sat up slowly, swallowed, felt better. He gave the bag of marijuana to Mike.

"Here. You roll one."

"Whatsamatter? I thought you were the one all gung-ho about getting out and roughing it."

"Yeah," Eddie piped, "we barely get under way and first thing you do is lay down and pass out."

"I wasn't crashed," Kevin rejoined sourly, "I was trying to meditate." And again came the stab of pain, this time really ferocious. His heart skipped a beat, the world went black. When he opened his eyes the pain had vanished quickly as it came, and there was sweat or tears rolling down the sides of his nose. He peeled off his heavy shirt and stuffed it inside his sleeping roll. Mike roared with laughter at Kevin's pink corpulence, but the stout boy took it with clenched teeth and wincing calm. When he was sleek and tanned he was going to make Mike regret his laughter.

Mike swiftly rolled and lit a joint. Kevin held in each draw long as he could, wanting to get as high as possible. When his thoughts were reeling he commended the remedy, feeling an elevation in spirit. But his mouth was dry as the moon.

"What're you guys drinking?"

"So-so Soda," Eddie said with an impish grin, his eyes red and pinched.

"Sounds good. Think I'll get one." He stood up stiffly.

"Don't eat the truck," Mike said, "tubby." He snickered.

Mike's snickering made Eddie titter, and this seemed to touch off a fit of giggling between them.

"*I* don't think it's so funny!" Kevin shot back, causing an upsurge of laughter. The storm mounted and mounted until both boys were rolling with uncontrollable mirth.

"Fuck you guys!" Kevin spat. "I'm not smoking any more pot with you if you can't hold it, dig? Only *kids* get the giggles!" But this only served to redouble their laughter, and Kevin turned away from their roaring, tear-streaked faces with absolute contempt. As he walked to the truck he chuckled, shaking his head. A laugh forced itself up like a belch, but he closed his mouth to contain it. The laugh found its way out his nostrils with a burning explosion.

"What's the joke? Let me in on it."

Kevin looked up to see an Italian couple looking down lugubriously from inside the huge catering truck. His grin dissolved. What joke where?

The man sighed. "Can I help you?"

"Let me have a So-so Soda," Kevin mumbled, certain he was the butt of the couple's private jest. He drew himself erect. "*Just,*" he said assertively, "just let me have a So-so Soda. *Large.*"

"Sorry. Never heard of it. We carry cola, orange, and root beer only."

Kevin darkened. Okay. If they were going to have fun at his expense, he'd just play along and frustrate their little joke with an air of unflappability.

"All right. A large *cola* then."

"Anything to eat?"

A nasty taste welled under his tongue at the mention of food, his stomach lining shimmied. The marijuana muse leaned close to whisper in his ear, and the boy's eyes went blank. Immediately his salivary glands got to work. His eyes re-focused.

"How's..." he croaked, trying to sound nonchalant, "how's the chow here, anyway?"

The man shrugged. "So-so." He yawned, revealing a mouthful of silver-capped ivory posts. "There's a menu to your left."

Kevin ran his eyes down the list with escalating unrest. He stepped back under the morosely yawning man and his grease-spattered wife.

"Let me just get a steak sandwich on rye, with plenty of

kraut, onions, dill, and mustard. And an order of chili fries." His stomach stabbed warningly, but he hushed it with promises of slow ingestion. He threw a glance back at the menu.

"And a hot frosted blueberry turnover with cheese, a frozen chocolate banana, and a couple of those sugarberry fruit 'n' nut crème-filled twists. Make that three. And a caramel-swirl apple, please, and a double marshmallow malt."

When he'd paid he rejoined his friends with a nagging conscience and pounding heart. Kevin angrily squelched his guilt. This trip was turning out to be a real chore and a drag, and, damn it, he'd might as well dredge what creature comforts he could from it.

Closing his mind to it all, he sat down and began to stuff his face.

# Chapter 3

## Suffering Synapses

"Hang on!" Kevin bleated, doubling over in agony on the toilet seat. "For Pete's sake, *hang on!*" His gut was a raging fumarole, heaving violently, swelling with gas. The pressure built up in his lower intestine until he thought he'd die. He gritted his teeth, whined, *"Mom!"* and let the tears breach his eyelids. The utterance was instinctive; he wouldn't have wished his mother's intrusion on his worst enemy. Speaking of whom, he now heard Mike outside, calling,

"You've always gotta slow us down!"

"Hang on," he whimpered. "Oh, *hang on!*" The phrase was repeated in a gasping decrescendo, as much to himself as to Mike, as Kevin fought to marshal his stammering consciousness. His rectum swelled and shriveled like a balloon at the lips of a colossus, gas flared in his colon as the pressure skyrocketed, plunged, rose again. With each attack his mind went blank, his eyes rolled, his heart hammered so hard it seemed to be located in his skull. Just when he was sure the awful pressure would claim him, he spurted a long vile stream of stinking lava, which splashed back up to spatter the twin straining moons of his sunken rump.

"Oh *my God*," he cried, and caught his breath for the next wave. There were giant hands in there, squeezing, punching; punishing his colon with the brutal precision of an enraged masseur.

At last came the acme of all possible agonies. Those

hands twisted Kevin's poor gut until he nearly fainted with the strain. Sweat trickled from every pore, the walls of the tiny outhouse approached and receded. For a terrifying instant he was certain his heart had stopped. And then the screaming began.

Kevin sat with his head buried between his knees and his hands clasped behind his neck, sobbing as wave after wave of fuming excrement spewed from the mouth of hell.

*"Would you hurry up!"* Mike shrieked.

Mike's only answer was a string of splats and plops and gurgles and squirts, sounds he took as clever lips-repartee. Mike stooped and grabbed a large pebble off the sand, hurled it with accuracy at ear-level on the outhouse. Warming to this activity, he began firing anything he could find—Coke bottles, driftwood, shells—until Eddie asked him to stop.

Inside, Kevin sat with head on knees, breathing slowly as his body went about the business of repairs, his mind rolling (little white corpuscle plumbers with hardhats and wrenches speeding to the rescue) in slow fever. He wished, not for the last time, that Mike and Eddie—especially Mike—could share in the rotten breaks. But maybe their numbers were just waiting to come up. Maybe the worm would turn. A tremor rattled his frame and he wondered—but no; the damage was reparable. Yet it felt really bad down there, no getting around it, like he'd been ravished by a hot poker, and the least movement instantly created a wild prominence. So he sat. He moaned over his rashness, and for the first time seriously considered the energy and grit required in covering almost four hundred miles in what looked to be the hottest part of this summer. San Francisco had lost much of its appeal already, and so had the Movement. All these bum trips and bad vibes hadn't been included in the trek's master plan; it was supposed to be nothing but fun and games, smooth sailing all the way. Well, it was a lesson learned well. He nodded ruefully and swallowed. No more munchies orgies; it was that simple. He didn't for a second blame the grass in any way. Right now, as he gazed vacuously at the door's equestrian Teamsters logo, he was thinking about how a good fat joint would do wonders to numb the pain. And not only the physical pain. If the embarrassment he was suffering here—in a tiny outhouse just south of Camarillo—was indicative of things to come, perhaps it was time to begin downgrading his expectations.

These outhouses are not renowned for their fragrance, and with the added pall of Kevin's performance the little pocket of stench had become unbearable. Kevin groaned and got to his feet, cursing feebly as he dabbed at his bespattered cheeks with the rough industrial tissue. Cleaning between them was a very dainty and agonizing operation, involving a grimacing tap dance with breath held. Sensitivity was so great the tissue felt like the coarsest of sandpapers.

When at last the ordeal was over he slouched and listened to his vital processes. He could still breathe, albeit with revulsion in this malodorous cell. He wiped the tears from his face, pulled up his Levis carefully, unlatched the door and moved outside with the tiny feeler-steps of an invalid.

His friends recoiled as he approached.

"Whew!" Eddie laughed, making a sour face and fanning the air in front of his nose. "You smell like a cesspool."

"What'd you do," Mike pushed, "wipe with your shirt?"

"It's not funny," Kevin whispered. "I've never been so sick."

"Serves you right, scarfhound," Mike said nastily.

Kevin tried to take the hard words in stride; he was too weak to retaliate. Someday he would give Mike a lesson in manners, but right now it was all he could do to say, "Be cool, man. It was worse than you think. I could've died in there."

*"Yeah!"* Mike said, grinning. "And we could've donated your body to science fiction."

Eddie laughed and glanced at his friend's hindquarters meaningfully. "It doesn't look like you ran fast enough, Kevin."

*"Where?"* Kevin tried to turn around far enough to search his pants' seat for stains.

They roared with laughter at his gullibility and ran off whooping. Kevin chased them with clenched fists.

"Okay," he puffed, "okay." He held up a hand and stood panting, drained. The fat boy grinned, butt of the joke. "You win."

His friends hopped on their bikes like eager little frogs.

"So let's *go!*" Eddie shouted.

"Wait! I mean, *really*. Gimme a minute, willya? Look at me, man; I'm in no condition to just jump up and take off. How d'you expect me to ride after what I just went through?"

*"Quit your bitching!"* Mike said with venom; the boy on the dark steed. "We've waited long enough!" And they were pedaling away just as fast as they could. Kevin followed grudgingly, muttering as he rode, but it was a long while and many a mile before he ventured to make use of his bicycle's seat. Soon his back and shoulders were smarting with sunburn. He put his shirt on, and the scratchiness was added misery. He took it off and mopped his brow with one of the sleeves. He had to think of other things than his pain or he'd go mad. But the moment he allowed his mind to dwell on the day his thoughts zoomed onto the young woman at Perky's house, zeroing in on her cleavage like a homing pigeon. He was ashamed to think of her this way, but it couldn't be helped. He could only visualize her from the neck down, hearing her voice rambling in dreamy, indecipherable tones from just above the image. He figured she was yet at Perky's, lonely and hurt, perhaps this very moment thinking of him and wishing he would fly to her side.

A heavy gloom absorbed him as he relived the sequence of events leading to their meeting on the anteroom couch. Kevin wished to God he could do it all over again, this time with a bit of foresight. And so several fantasies entertained him as the miles passed and the sun dipped to the horizon. In one of these daydreams he coolly and expertly trounced the mustached bully while the raven-haired girl watched limply, at last collapsing into Kevin's magnificently muscled arms with a sigh of yearning. But when time came for his reward the fantasy stumbled on nerveless feet. He could not visualize taking the girl, for thinking of heaving bodies and lusty breathing somehow only desecrated the fabricated altar. He prayed it wasn't some personal "sexual failing", and began to feel this imagined inadequacy was letting down his fantasy and, by extension, letting down the raven-haired girl. He fought to overcome the flaccidity of his psyche; tried to stir up swashbuckling, libidinous images of her conquest. The images came with a vividness he hadn't expected. He saw himself sinking with her on the couch, the casually tucked hem of her cheap cotton shirt popping free, the shirt peeling away from her chest to reveal— but *no*, the reward was simply too boggling: those awesome headlights bursting forth with jack-in-the-box resilience, their firm round peaks, as on a mannequin, mysteriously devoid of nipples, *jiggling* and *oscillating*, growing up round his ears and snaring his head to draw it deeper into ecstasy. Kevin's breathing grew shallower as his entire attention focused inward. His legs pumped harder, and he was soon caught up with his friends.

"Hey!" Mike shouted as the heavy boy hurtled by. He and Eddie struggled to catch up.

Kevin slowed and looked back with an embarrassed half-smile, his thoughts still damp and sticky.

"If you wanted to race," Eddie said with a grin, "why didn't you say so?" He poked his skinny haunches high, ready to jackrabbit away. "Betcha I can beatcha round that bend."

"Boy, are you *fast*," Mike said sarcastically, meaning: if low man was ready to make his move, then just maybe it was time for top dog to show some teeth. "I guess you're a lot lighter with all that shit out of you."

"Sometimes," Kevin said lamely, "I like to really haul-ass." He abruptly changed the subject, reaching back a hand to tenderly consult his back. It felt like he'd been flogged.

"You'll cool off pretty quick," Eddie remarked sympathetically. "The sun's going down." He peeked at his watch. "Must be around seven o'clock. Gee, look, Point Mugu. *Do you guys realize we've gone almost fifty miles?*"

"Wow."

"Wow."

Getting through Ventura meant negotiating miles of freeway-like road that left the ocean cut off from view by hills and alfalfa fields. Whenever possible the boys followed the scenic drives provided for motorists with romance on their minds and time on their hands. In such situations it was Mike who prevented his companions from lagging, and thus falling behind schedule. "C'mon, you pussies!" he would scream. "We've got to *ride!* What are you guys, anyway—people, or tourists?" Kevin and Eddie would gladly have stopped every few miles to admire the beauty of the coastline as the warm summer breeze blew through their hearts, just as it must have stirred the first Franciscan missionaries to discover salt air could be so sweet. They found the San Buenaventura scenic drive particularly enchanting. It's easy to forget your gripes around such loveliness.

After another hour of riding, the velvety beach degenerated to heaped rocks of all sizes, and only occasional dabs of sand. The scene took on a primitive, lost look, like the savage coastline of another planet. The swells writhed with reflected light. Shadows grew solid and grim. The sun, a furious red ball, was truncated, was composed, by the sea.

And, from out of nowhere, the fog came rolling in. Like a vast preying fungus it was suddenly everywhere, dampening their clothes and blotting the dying sun. It was incredibly swift and thorough, and it surprised the boys and made them a bit uneasy. One moment they had been following the coast in warm late afternoon sunshine, and all at once the world was a dreary, dismal place, the waves had grown choppy, and a buoy, somewhere out in that soggy blight, was lonesomely clanging its funereal bell.

"Kee-rist!" Mike said. "What *is* this? The end of the world?"

"Might as well be," Kevin mumbled, shivering of a sudden. "I don't know about you guys, but I'm not riding in this bullshit."

Mike scowled and thrust forward his torso in the ages-old posture of challenge. "Oh, you were just praying for an excuse to stop, man, so why don't you just face it and quit blaming it on the weather? You're just lazy; no wonder you're so fat."

"Not either!" Kevin retorted, incensed at being called fat and lazy, snarling at the look of vicious delight darkening Mike's face. "I'm just cold. You would be too, if you had the brains to know better...*faggot*."

"Who's a faggot!" Mike cried, and slapped Kevin on the sorest part of his sunburn. He rode off laughing, with Kevin in hot cursing pursuit.

There was a narrow, longish spit of beach between the

piles of rock Mike was making for, laughing over his shoulder. Kevin, who was laughing too by now, forsook the chase when Mike picked up his bicycle and clambered over the rocks to the sand. Kevin waited breathlessly for Eddie. The two picked their way down carefully.

"Hey, guys!" Mike called up. "This is a neat place to camp. There's nobody here!" The fog was now so dense they could hardly see him.

"Yeah," Kevin disagreed, "if the tide doesn't come in and drown us in our sleep."

"Don't worry," Eddie said, "you can see the high tide marks on the sand. If we crash right up next to the rocks we're cool."

"Well, far out then." Kevin rubbed his palms together. "Let's cook up some roast beef hash and some beans and some cocoa." He shivered again, gingerly pulled on the scratchy shirt. "It's getting cold anyway. A fire would be right-on."

They split up to find firewood and met back by their bikes in ten minutes. Mike had discovered a salt-eaten apple crate and some not-too-damp newspaper. Kevin and Eddie each contributed armloads of small branches from the stunted bushes on the highway's other side. And Mike had made an exciting discovery: about sixty yards down, just a darker haze within the fog, an odd-looking man was sitting solo.

"He's just *sitting* there," Mike sputtered, "looking out to sea. He's not dead, 'cause I seen him scratching his self."

"Where'd he come from?" Kevin wondered. "What's he doing there?"

"How should I know?" Mike snapped, looking as though he would spit on Kevin. "Crawled outta the rocks for all I know. Why don't you go ask him?"

Kevin shook his head vigorously. "Uh-uh."

"You, Eddie?"

"Not me!"

"You're both a bunch of chickenshits, man! And you guys always talking so rowdy about what great adventurers you are."

"Well then *you* go ask him," Eddie retorted, "bigmouth."

"Let's eat first," Kevin suggested, desperately.

Eddie, who was nearly as apprehensive, said, "I'm hip to that idea."

It was rapidly darkening. All Kevin wanted to do was eat and clear out of here quietly as possible. The stranger—if Mike wasn't making this all up—was clearly a mental case.

And then they were lost in the thrill of starting and feeding the fire, and Mike's Crazy Man was gradually filtered from their conversation. But Kevin's eyes, as he ate his cold beans and warmed hash, were ever and again surveying the beach, and now he was sure he could see a skinny man sitting motionlessly on the sand. Kevin felt a chill. In the fog the skinny man looked like a huge famished wharf rat, regarding the boys with sunken eyes and whiskers tensed. Kevin thought he caught one brief, fuzzy impression of the man with his head cocked, as if listening, calculating. He almost choked on his beans when he saw the campfire's light reflected off the stranger's questing eye.

It seemed the meal lasted but a minute, and already they were talking about him again.

"Let's go rap with that guy. Maybe he's hungry."

Eddie spread his hands. "We only had the hash and the beans. Remember?"

"That's right," Kevin groaned, hoping to change the subject. "No breakfast tomorrow."

"Tough shit all around," Mike said. "Come *on*, let's go check out that guy." He and Eddie stood.

"Wait!" Kevin said.

Mike sneered. "You really *are* chicken."

"No, I just wanna get high first. Let's smoke a joint."

"Yeah," Eddie said with relief, "that sounds cool to me."

Outvoted again, Mike consented grumblingly. He muttered on about sissies and slowpokes, but sucked deeply on the smoke.

Again, it seemed to take only a moment for the joint to pass round thrice.

"That was dynamite," Mike said. "Now...*let's*...go... *check*...out...that...*guy!*"

"Wait!" Kevin said. He was really high now. Sounds were oddly muffled, absorbing. The waves exploded in B flat,

70

were sucked back in F minor; the wind whisked and whoosked; the noise of the occasional passing car was like that of a huge cruising wasp, the headlight beams like systematic searchlights.

*"Now what?"* Mike screamed.

"Just one more joint," Kevin said, his voice sounding, to him, alarmingly like his mother's. "I already got it rolled."

"That's an offer I can't refuse," Eddie gabbled. "Fire 'er up!" An asinine grin was smeared across his face. His eyes were crimson slits, his hair tousled. He hugged himself and shivered with cold and anticipation.

This cigarette took longer, and Kevin had to hang through a lengthy fit of hacking and gasping. When the smoke was finished his eyes were even redder than Eddie's, and tears covered his cheeks. His mind went blank, the night caved in, and then he was somehow walking dazedly with his friends, and they were approaching the fogbound stranger like travelers from another dimension, materializing out of nothingness onto the haunted coast of a parallel world. They wouldn't have been surprised to see the long neck of a sea monster appear dripping at water's edge.

"What's happening?" Mike called in tentative greeting.

The sitting figure turned his head and smiled approvingly, as if all four were accustomed to meeting here each night, sipping hot cocoa and throwing morsels of sweet Danish for bashful sea serpents. The rodent features were now in hideous focus: a dark body practically covered with coarse brown hair, thin claw-like hands and feet, large blank eyes, a wiry beard and frayed moustache. The mouth was starved and thin-lipped, the nose long and sharp. He was wearing only cutoff blue jeans, and his body was so wasted, with its chicken breast and distended stomach, that Kevin's fears vanished immediately. This guy looked like he lived off sea anemones and slow sparrows. So where there was physical repulsion at least there was no threat of physical danger.

"Sit down, sit down," said the stranger, patting the sand to his left. A few rags of clothing were in a pile behind him. The boys sat, feigning relaxation.

"You sure we're not disturbing you?" Kevin asked.

"We're going to Frisco," Eddie burst out from sheer

nervousness. "To Haight-Ashbury. On our bikes. To join the Movement. I mean we're already in the Movement, but we're moving. From Santa Monica, I mean. To Frisco."

"There's only one movement in San Francisco," the stranger said excitedly. "I've seen it on the piers, I've seen it downtown, I've seen it in the Panhandle. And that's the movement of Blessed Jesus the Holy Spirit."

The boys froze, staring at one another uncertainly.

"Well," said Mike, "got to get back and keep the fire up. Nice to meet you and so forth."

"Yeah, catch you later," said Eddie. He sniggered. "Don't catch cold."

But Kevin said, "I think I'll stay here a bit and rap." The Panhandle, as they all knew, was an extension of Golden Gate Park, and here was a chance for first-hand news. His friends gawked at him. Mike smirked with unconcealed hostility. They walked off laughing, the foggy darkness soaking up their retreating forms like a sponge.

"God bless you!" the stranger called after them. "Jesus loves you, Jesus loves you, Jesus loves you!" He whirled on Kevin. "Jesus can save you. Jesus can show you the way."

"Right," Kevin said quickly. "But I just wanted to ask you about the city. Like, how's the Movement, you know, the hippie movement, working out?"

The stranger shook his head, and for a moment sobered. "Just a word, brother. Don't be calling the Haight 'the City'. People up there don't go in for neology, they go in for theology. And they don't like being called hippies. That's like 'nigger'."

Kevin cocked an eyebrow. "The Haight," he mumbled. "The Haight." He was learning fast. "And it's Utopia," he prompted, "right?"

"Utopia? It's Heaven, brother, Heaven! God's kingdom on Earth, the Lord's—"

"But what I mean is," Kevin broke in, "I mean besides all that religious stuff, how are the people? Everybody's turned on, right? Everybody gets high?"

"Everybody's turned on to Jesus, brother, to Jesus! To the one and only Son. Everybody gets high on Christ the Lord Jesus. Glory in Christ, and hallelujah! Hallelujah!"

"Okay. Okay. But what about dope? What about drugs, I mean."

"Nobody needs narcotics, man. God's children weren't placed on the world to put impurities in their bodies. There's only one drug, and that's Sweet Jesus Himself. I was like you: I was young and confused and hung up on all my problems, problems too great for me to bear."

"I'm not confused."

"But Sweet Jesus of Nazareth lifted my burden and lightened my heart with Divine Light. The light of God! I said, 'I can't go on! I've had it!' and Jesus came down to help me with my load. Praise Jesus! Praise Jesus! Praise Jesus! Man, it was in*tense*. His eyes were blue as the sky, and filled with tears as he looked down on me. Read your Bible: *For the wages of sin is death; but the gift of God is eternal life through Jesus Christ our Lord.* There! What does that tell you? It tells you if you deny the one true God—not the god of the pagans, not the god of craven images, but the one and only Savior Himself—it means you're a sinner, and it means Almighty Jesus will laugh as your eternal soul fries and rots in Hell!"

Kevin frowned at this. It's no great trick to see through these people; they're obviously all willing dupes, extras on the ever-evolving set of mankind's most elaborately contrived fantasy. The point it, as anybody should be able to see: these Jesus freaks, these born-again just-converted amateur holy rollers, are losers from the word *GO*. Christianity, to those with nowhere left to turn, is irresistible. Free security and direction and society for those too paranoid, aimless, or boring to satisfy these deep human needs any other way. Religion was an issue Kevin religiously avoided, but when it was being stuffed down his throat he couldn't help taking a stand. So now he squared his shoulders, cocked back his head, and boldly said:

"Anybody who would make some guy who's all cut up carry his shit around for him has no right to tell me I'm a sinner!"

The stranger stared, shaking his head incredulously. "Lookit me, man!" He thrust out his wasted arms. "For six years I lived in a scummy tenement with nine other speed freaks, fighting over syringes, sleeping on the trash pile in the boiler room. The Feds were on my ass, my old lady was pregnant, and the both of us had hepatitis, crabs, and the clap. There wasn't nothing left to live for and no way out of that hole. And then one day, one day when I was slumped across the shitter with my outfit in my hand, man, and trying to get a register from that collapsed old vein, I said one day brother, when it looked like I was heading for the Big Flush—brother, I looked up at that leaky ceiling and I saw God Almighty *Himself*. God who wasn't too high and mighty to take the time to try to save a poor burnt-out pissant like me. And He said to me, '*My child, do you repent of your sins and accept the Lord Jesus Christ as your savior? Do you hold any gods sacred above the one and only True God?*' And I said, 'Man, I'm freaking out. I gotta be over-amped. This is it!' Like you, I didn't believe it at first. I thought I was rushing to the max. And He told me I wasn't hearing things, and that if I wanted to save myself I'd better get my ass down on the floor PDQ and let Him know I meant it. And brother, that's just what I did. I got down on my knees at the base of that commode and accepted Jesus Christ as my savior. And I threw away my works right then and there, and Jesus came down and held my hand and told me He loved me. Man, it blew my mind! I changed my whole scene just like *that!* I went out to spread the Word of Love to all my brothers."

"Love," Kevin echoed. "That's what I'm looking for in San Francisco. A different kind of love. A love that has everybody grooving together, stoking their heads on hashish and trying to win the world back from the Government. Y'know, 1984 isn't so far away. You can't win a revolution with religious love; it takes *passive resistance*."

"Oh, *man*. It makes me so *sad* to hear that! God *is* love! God is my sunshine, God is my lifeline. God is my guru and my goaltender. God is my helicopter, man, and God is my tele-prompter. All you gotta do is *admit* you're a sinner and accept the Lord Jesus Christ as your healer."

"I'm not a sinner."

"You're *sinning* if you're living without *Christ*. We're all born in sin."

"And you—you're not a sinner, huh? You're special?"

"*Born* in sin. *Born* in sin. I said we're all *born sinners*, man, but we can be saved. Look at me. God has lighted my life!" He gave Kevin a used car salesman's smile full of teeth like stalactites before pounding a gnarly fist on his palm. "I was a sinner in God's eyes and a loser in my own! Jesus showed me the way! *Jesus showed me the way!* Jesus gave me His breath, His faith, and His body. He gave me His *life*, man!"

"Super!" Kevin snorted. "That's all just really bitch-en...*for you*. But it's like I gotta get it on in the real world, you dig? Look—"

"No, *you* look! You think I'm just making idle conversation here? This is first-class wisdom you're getting, buddy, and you oughta be grateful. You want some real-world advice, is that it? Okay then, man; okay, you got it." He placed one hand over his eyes and the other over his heart. "Beware of men with moustaches," he droned. "A moustache is a proof of vanity, and vanity is woman's province. Therefore, if you're ever in the same gym showers with a guy wearing a moustache and you happen to drop the soap, never retrieve it in a bent-at-the-waist posture while facing away. You've been warned. And," he said bitterly, "*never* smile for a photographer! If you're ever accused of, oh, say...ripping off parishioners while posing as a minister, and the newspaper features a picture of you smiling it'll look like you enjoy bamboozling people. Then again, if you don't smile people'll think you're really a prick, and therefore likely guilty. Always pose beatifically, with your eyes raised heavenward and an expression of grudgeless suffering. Remember, innocence is a word coined by the guilty. What else? Oh yeah, don't eat stuff out of a dumpster if the seal's broken on the package. And watch out for that guy who lives in the storm drain over on Seventh and Cranberry. He bites." The stranger now placed his palms together. "So there you go. Now you got all you need to get through the real world. But what you *really* need, man, is *wisdom*. What you *need* is *Christ*."

"Listen," Kevin said patiently, "I mean, no offense or anything, but everybody to his own trip, right? Me, my thing's the Revolution, and you, your thing's religion. Okay. All I wanted to know was, like, how are the chicks up in the... Haight, and are they into the Movement and Free Love, and are they as friendly as the rumors say they are? What I mean is, you know, do they put out?"

"They put out for *Jesus*, man, for Jesus! I'm not making myself clear? I'm not speaking loud enough? For *Jesus*. They are Sacred Sisters and are *one* under Christ."

"That's not—"

"For *Jesus*, man. *Jesus*. J-E-S-U-*S!* Jesus the Son. Jesus the Christ. Jesus! Jesus Christ!"

"Well I...I guess I'd better be getting back. My partners'll be wondering."

"Jesus died for you, brother! He *died* for you."

"Anyway, it's getting cold."

"Read your Bible: *Doth the wild ass bray when he hath grass?* Think about it."

"*I,*" Kevin said contemptuously, a parting thrust, "don't *need* a Bible."

Quick as a flash the stranger whipped out a worn old coverless dog-eared Bible from his pile of clothes. His left hand snatched Kevin's right wrist. The boy froze.

"Look, I really have to get back," he chattered. The hand was an iron talon.

"When you have the warmth of Jesus in you...when you have the warmth."

"You know, time to roll up, time to hit the hay."

The stranger dropped the book onto his lap, flipped it open with his free hand. He tore at the leaves until he came to page one of Genesis. "*In the beginning,*" he quoted, and a wild pride came into his eyes, "*God created the heaven and the Earth!*"

Kevin groaned piteously. By the look of things, he was about to be read the entire Old Testament. But the harder he tried to pull away, the fiercer the stranger's grip became. "You're *hurt*ing me!" Although it should have been readily within Kevin's power to break free of this scrawny man, the boy found himself suddenly paralyzed, and unable to think assertively. The steely fingers seemed to be siphoning blood from his brain, down his numbing arm to the relentless bite of those five inflexible leeches. His pulse hammered in protest.

Now the stranger slapped shut the book and duplicated

the hold on Kevin's other wrist. "Do you accept the Lord Jesus Christ as your healer and admit you're a sinner?" He squeezed.

"No, I just—ow*wW!* You're hurting me!"

"Do you forgive men their trespasses? *Do you accept the Lord Jesus Christ as your savior?*" He squeezed harder.

"No!" Kevin howled. "I mean, yes! Yes, yes! But leggo my—*yes!* Eddie! Mike!"

"Are you gonna remember the Sabbath Day? And keep it holy?"

"*Yes!* Mike! *Eddie!*" Kevin's hands were half-filled water balloons. He looked around wildly.

"Do you beg mercy," the stranger panted, "of the Lord your God in His infinite wisdom?" He clamped Kevin's hands together and squeezed with all his strength, his teeth bared in a ferocious snarl, his head lolling feverishly.

"Yes!" Kevin screamed. "Oh God, oh God, yes, yes!"

*"Blessed are the poor in spirit!"* the stranger cried, his eyes rolling in their sockets. "Merciful Lord, bathe us in eternal light! Take this poor damned sinner in your heart that he may witness You also! Show him your *Son!* Show him…*forgive his sins!* Yes! Forgive his sins! Show him…show…show him— *sweet*…*JE*-sus!" On the penultimate syllable his head fell forward, his shriek fluttered down to a rasping sigh. After a minute he looked vaguely at Kevin, who was green, and released the boy's wrists. He stared down at his own hands, then back at Kevin. "This—all this—everything's cool. What I mean is, like, nothing *personal*, okay? No offense, man." He searched through his pile of clothes and dug out a plain white business card with type in thick black italics covering most of its face. "I want you to come to our church. The address is down in the corner." He scooped up his clothes, rose stiffly, and vanished in the fog. Kevin heard his bare feet slapping on the rocks as he climbed to the road.

The boy stood and stumbled across the sand. He stopped and looked back, but all was foggy darkness. For a moment he felt it had all been a dream or hallucination; perhaps an effect produced by the eerily shifting curtains of mist during a particularly poignant pot high. And, if a dream, he must now be passing through the portal separating sleep and wakefulness.

But things were getting darker and colder instead of lighter and warmer. Then positively black. After a while his mind cleared and he stood looking back, sluggishly trying to recapture the night. His face was bathed in sweat, he was wobbly at the knees. He grew aware of the soreness in his wrists, massaged them, rubbed his moist palms down his legs. He shuddered and listened. Nothing but the breaking of small waves.

He used the sound of surf to find his way back to their campsite. The fire was out. Mike and Eddie lay shivering, a-sleep in their bags. Kevin sat on his sleeping roll and stared at nothing. Pensively, he pulled his notepad and a pen from an odds-and-ends sack he kept tucked in the roll. He looked out toward the sound of breakers, and after a minute began to write:

jime
wl hr i am up pas vnchru awn thu bch sumwaer jus groovn awn thu nit
2nit we gawt stond an i had u rap sshn with this gi hoo jus kam awl thu wa down frum sanfrans—

To hell with it, he thought, and crumpled the page. He climbed in his sleeping bag, tucked in his head, clasped his knees. Into the abyss of slumber he dropped like a stone.

# Chapter 4

## Beach Blanket Bozo

joon 29 1967
jime
im sndn this frum u mlbawx in krpntreu
if yoo look awn u map yool c thats olmos 70 milz nawt bad 4 u
da an u hafs rid
spnt thu nit awn thu bch gawt stond an prtd wut u trip
howz thu lag btr i hop don fel 2 bad iv gawt u sunbrn an mix
gawt kaf kramps an ed kawt u kold but thats kool iv rele tufnd
up u lawt jime an thu sunbrn duznt bawthr me u bit im gunu hav
u sooprtan bi thu tim we mak thu h8
did yoo dig that
the h8
thats wut we kawl it up her
nuthen much 2 rit ubowt rele its jus bin u konstunt prt good ppl
good xrsiz good dop an ech pasen da brengz us that much klosr
2 paerudis
wish yoo wr her
wl thats awl 4 now jime tim 2 go rol unuthr joent
trublz trublz
tak it ez
kevin

   Kevin opened the mailbox hatch carefully, slowly raised
his other hand, released the letter. He let the hatch slam shut and
took a deep breath before lowering his rigid arms an inch at a
time. For a full minute he stood like a man of stone, eyes

closed, sweat trickling down the back of his neck.

The label on the salve's container had promised cooling relief, but this hadn't been the case for Kevin. He winced when his shirt, sticky with the stuff, clung to his chest and shoulders as he gently turned on his heel.

Eddie, sitting slumped against the diner's wall, called Kevin by name with the gasping decrescendo of delirium. The fat boy slowly opened his eyes.

They'd made excellent time this morning, having quickly abandoned their chilly little beach for the warming exertions of the road. The previous day's sickness left Kevin empty and irresolute, irritable and ill. But he was obsessed by sunburn. All morning he'd been silent and moody, answering Mike's painfully abbreviated gibes with grunts and mono-syllables. Having looked forward to this adventure as a gift from whatever gods watched over ambitious young revolution-aries, Kevin now saw those same gods deriving mischievous delight from rubbing his mortal nose in his enthusiasm. Yet this morning he'd never once allowed himself to lag. His bitterness had provided maleworthy, but very temporary, balls, pushing him all the way to this perpetually summery little community barely ten miles south of Santa Barbara.

Eddie's eyes were swollen, his jaw slack. Every few seconds he would sniffle and moan. Kevin, walking over stiffly, wondered again if Eddie had an allergy unknown to any of them. He was in pretty bad shape for a boy suffering a simple exposure cold.

"Bike says your badgakes are ready," Eddie said miser-ably, placing a hand over his eyes. When he removed the hand his fingers were wet with tears. "I ca'd ead eddythig righd dow."

Kevin nodded. "Thanks, Eddie. I wrote Jimmy you said Hi."

Eddie dropped his head in acknowledgment, but lacked the strength to haul it back up.

"Why don't you stay out here in the sun for a while, Eddie. It'll do wonders for your cold." Eddie, managing to half-raise his head, immediately let it fall backward and roll side to side against the diner's wall, looking like a man undergoing intense interrogation. His entire body went limp. Kevin walked inside to join Mike at a window booth, asking heartily, "How's the legs?" while seating himself with care.

"Not so hot," Mike grumbled. "Every time I walk it feels like my calves are tearing apart, and when I sit down they cramp." An untouched bowl of cornflakes was on his side of the table. On Kevin's side was a big plate of steaming buttermilk hotcakes with elderberries and chocolate whipped cream, a side dish of bacon and scrambled eggs smothered in tobasco, a plate of hash browns with chopped onion and chives, butter-drenched french toast topped by praline sprinkles and orange-mint marmalade, and a large glass of iced prune juice with lemon slices and maraschinos.

"How about you?" Mike asked indifferently.

"Ha!" Kevin barked. "A little sunburn. But you don't see me bitching about it, do you? What'd you guys expect, a pleasure cruise? Figures I'd be stuck with a couple of cry-babies." It felt good to say that. Real good. He rubbed his hands vigorously, elbows held tightly against his ribs. "Well! This outdoor life sure brings out the appetite in a guy!"

Mike glared, good and hard. "It sure brings out the bull-shitter in a guy, too. Just you wait, hop-along. Next time you're stuck crapping out your brains somewhere...just you wait."

Kevin chuckled lustily, but forced himself to eat slowly. When he'd finished he belched for effect, only half-satisfied. Mike still hadn't touched his cereal.

Kevin smiled tightly. "Don't pout, sonny boy. Papa's gonna burn one bad-ass doobie and fix you right up."

Mike wobbled to his feet like a newborn colt. Kevin tipped the waitress lavishly, then paid for both their meals. Mike wasn't impressed; he knew a fool when he saw one.

The boys rejoined Eddie, who hadn't moved a muscle since Kevin's departure. Only an occasional moan verified he was alive at all. Kevin's mock gaiety grew oddly real as he considered the extent of Eddie's and Mike's compound misery.

"A fine bunch of revolutionaries we are! Only one day gone and we're all ready to throw in the towel!" He flashed a joint, cried, "To the Movement!" and fired it up with a flourish. "To Love and Peace and Good Dope and Heavy Sounds forever and ever and ever!" He took an enormous draw, handed it to Eddie.

Eddie allowed his head to roll in Kevin's direction. He peered at the reefer doubtfully, his eyes so watery and puffy he had to tilt back his head to see. The flesh around his nostrils was red and inflamed from constant furious sniffling; his lips rubbery and limp. He couldn't decide whether a toke was worth the effort, so he just sat there; looking gloomily at the rising smoke, and at Kevin frozen in the awkward pose of leaning down with arm extended; eyes growing redder and redder as he held in the hit, comradely grin gradually dissolving to a tortured grimace, smoke escaping from his nostrils in tiny spurts. Finally Eddie poked out a trembling hand, accepted the cigarette and drew on it weakly. He held in the smoke for half a second before going all to pieces, hacking and retching and sneezing and drooling.

Kevin simultaneously exhaled with an explosion nearly matching Eddie's in fury. After a minute, when he'd caught his breath, he realized that the one elongated hit was all he'd need—he was already tripping. He looked at his friends dully, at a loss for words or action. Mike was hitting the joint now, and Kevin suddenly saw Mike as a frustrated enemy masquerading as a revolutionary for cheap thrills and the exploitation of their friendship. The insight passed instantly, and Mike became a scrawny boy getting high with his buddies; a third comrade, albeit an annoying one, on a journey that was to become a turning point in their lives. The background and boy became a cartoon, again became real. Kevin swiveled his gaze to the street. Cars were zipping around like ants. Doll-like humans were dotting a backdrop of cardboard houses painted in watercolors. He felt his eyes throbbing like twin hearts, realized his breath was held. He let it out with a sigh, felt a hundred years old, then forty, then an awkward sixteen again. Kevin found he couldn't face the clockwork reality of the street, so he turned back to his friends, his eyes finally resting on Eddie simply because they had to rest somewhere. After a moment Eddie seemed to feel Kevin's eyes on him, and slowly turned his head to return the stare as best he could. Embarrassed, Kevin looked away and mounted his bicycle. Eddie followed suit sniffling, Mike introspectively, still sucking on the joint.

They rode on through the morning almost like strangers. By one o'clock the day had peaked at 86 degrees, and their private gripes were being dissolved by the remarkable recuperative powers of sunshine and unrestricted liberty. By three Eddie's cold or allergic reaction had vanished without a trace. They shot through Santa Barbara, stopping only to drop water balloons on cars from an overpass. A long refreshing swim at Goleta Beach did wonders for Mike's cramps, and even Kevin's sunburn was forgotten in the exhilaration of the day. A vendor at Naples provided kraut dogs, pretzels, and tall cups of Fresca. They raced on the open highway and Mike won hands down. At fancy swerves it was Eddie all the way. But at 'chicken' Kevin came on like an eighteen-wheeler. They smoked another joint and zinged pebbles at petrified spider crabs on the rocks past El Capitan Beach. And the sun crept down and turned everything lemon, then amber, then tawny gold. And up from the sea came cooling salt breezes, smelling of algae and things submarine.

And Kevin was lying flat on his back looking up at Eddie's tiny face, which seemed miles away, and wishing Eddie would quit calling his name over and over and over. Why couldn't Eddie see that he was right here, right in front of him, and how many times did Kevin have to tell him that he was right here and could hear him loud and clear?

"Right here," Kevin said thickly, the words ringing in his skull. He forced his eyes open wide. "Right here!" he said, loud and clear.

"Wow," Eddie said. "You okay now, Kevin?"

Mike looked in over Eddie's shoulder. "Told you he was faking."

Kevin sat up. His face was wet with tears. His left shoulder hurt like hell.

Now Eddie brought a fuzzy pair of glasses into view, precariously guided the arms to straddle Kevin's brow. The world swam into focus. Kevin raised his heavy hands and took over from Eddie, setting the crooks of his spectacles in place behind his ears. One of the plastic arms was twisted and gouged. "What happened?" he asked, because it seemed the appropriate thing to say.

"Shit," Mike said. "Crybaby."

"You don't remember?" goggled Eddie. "We were all just coasting along having a good old time. You said something that didn't make any sense—something about hairs in the air. I slowed down like you were and said, *'What?'* and you just kind of looked past me for a second. Then you went face-first over your handlebars and did a nose-dive onto the road. I couldn't figure you out."

"Hairs in his head is more like it," Mike said.

"So I got off my bike and bent down to check you out. I thought you might've been hurt. Then I saw: you were having a fit of some kind. Your eyeballs were rolled way up in your head like that Incredible X-ray Man guy, and your mouth was working real funny, and you were squeaking and burping."

"Spastic," Mike whispered nastily, his eyes gleaming over Eddie's shoulder. "*Spazz-o.*"

"Then I remembered this film we watched in Miss Phugitall's class, and they had this guy in it—only he was faking—and he was behaving just like you were." Eddie said reasonably, "They stuck a wooden spoon in his mouth, so he wouldn't chew up his tongue, I guess," and then, with profound frustration, *"but I didn't have a wooden spoon!"* He blinked at Kevin and shook his head compassionately. "All I could find to use was the arms on your glasses, which were right next to me on the ground. So I stuck in one of the arms and you really gobbled it up. But I guess it stopped you from biting your tongue; you're not bleeding."

"Scarfhound," Mike said. "Eats anything."

Kevin nursed his shoulder with heavy electric fingers. His toes had the same numb-tingle, but the scary feeling passed as he stood and walked around. Eddie had to convince him a dozen times that he and Mike weren't just pulling his leg and waiting for the right moment to let him in on it—he couldn't, for the life of him, remember a thing other than riding along feeling splendid in the late afternoon sun. It made no real sense, but even as he paced he began to sense a connection with that chilly wet November night, when he and Eddie had huddled in the Mikolajczyks' boxlike garage loft and Eddie had gone on and on about the Movement. Kevin had been a fascinated, avid listener, and had pumped Eddie—who had been only too thrilled to provide—for all the juicy details about Free Love, psychedelia, communal living, an under-thirty society, and open nudity. And Eddie had played guru, lighting an enormous marijuana cigarette and passing it to his new friend, and Kevin had taken his first puff. Many people don't feel the effects of THC the first time; some never do at all. Perhaps they simply refuse to relax and enjoy, fearing they'll expose their secrets and weaknesses to any persons who just might be checking them out, never suspecting that those persons might also be feigning nonchalance for fear of exposing their own secrets and weaknesses to any persons who just might be checking them out while actually feigning nonchalance. But Kevin wasn't one of these social combatants, forever inspecting their armor for chinks. His secrets, at that time, weren't worth shielding, and his weaknesses, he felt, were already exposed for all to see. After three draws he was sucked away from all the silly, self-promoting games continuously played by the insecure when dealing with others. He froze in a gawking stupor, unable to say a word, staring at Eddie. Eddie, who was just as high, had also been rendered mute by the drug, and in their embarrassment they had fought eye contact, turning aside to study either of the two rectangular doors of the loft. The awkward silence, broken only by the forlorn pinging of rainwater hitting the aluminum downspout, had grown and grown, and both boys had continued to look fixedly at a different door as if awaiting a revelation, too self-conscious to even clear their throats. Just when the silence had become deafening, and the pretense of composure too painful to support, both doors had been yanked open to reveal the awesome bulk of Big Joe, filling up all the space like a hairless King Kong, a snarl of simian wrath squinching his sweaty, purpling face. At last Joe had found an outlet for his rage.

"You're sure you're okay now?" Eddie asked as they rode along.

"Yeah, Eddie. Yeah...I guess I'm fine. I don't feel any worse, but it sure is spooky. I think it might have something to do with these little blackouts I've been having lately."

"The heat," Eddie said. "That must have been heat-stroke."

"Some kind of stroke."

"We won't ride so hard tomorrow," Eddie offered considerately. "We're really making good time, anyway. Look," he said, pointing at a cluster of palms sprouting idyllically alongside the flat, flat highway. "There's Refugio State Beach. We could camp here. Gee, look at the sun go down."

The boys, slowing, gradually coasted to a halt.

The sunset was breathtaking, so gorgeous it was painful to watch for long; just another superb example of those wonderful westerly light shows displayed summerlong on the Southern California coast. The boys watched the day shutting down, until the bloody hub of the spectacle succumbed, swallowed by the sea. As twilight deepened, the flat wet sides of certain rocks on the jetty lit up like the facets of crudely cut gems; the creaming waves retreated from the sand to leave brief, ever-changing swirls of sapphire-emerald dust. The ocean became a broad highway of shimmering crests, of bobbing patterns growing ever subtler as night drew on.

There were still small bands of merrymakers scattered over the sand, and while the boys were wheeling round the parking lot a young man broke from one of these groups to run up waving. "Hey! Any of you guys got a match or a lighter? We're fixing to get a fire going, and out of half a dozen people not a one of us has a light. I mean, is that unreal, or what?" He had long brown hair and an enormously thick moustache, a round face and a jolly round belly. He seemed genuinely friendly.

They stopped. Mike was first to offer a book of matches. "Here you go. What's cooking?"

"Hot dogs and marshmallows. You guys hungry? Come on over. We've got some wine we're gonna pass around."

"Far out," said Kevin. "And we've got some dynamite pot."

"All *right!*" The young man danced a little jig. The boys dismounted, shouldered their bikes, and followed him over to his group.

There were three girls throwing twigs on a teepee of slightly larger branches, two young men strumming battered guitars, a third playing a harmonica, and a fourth clapping his hands in time. Three fat gallon bottles of a cheap red wine were shoved in the sand. The young man with the thick moustache offered his name as Smokey, and introduced the girls as Cathy, Stephanie, and Michelle.

Cathy was a vivacious brunette of nineteen, a trim girl forever chatting and gesturing, doing her best to inject inane merriment into the little party. She was full of bubbly cheer and girlish affection, and when she shook hands she smiled at Kevin in a way that made his palms perspire. From the clavicle up there was a disturbing similarity between her and the raven-haired girl; and also in the way she carried herself, and smiled without real humor. She wore indigo slacks and a man's work shirt, open modestly at the throat.

Stephanie was a tense little braided blonde in a faded beige granny dress. She was constantly grinding her teeth and clenching her fingers—the gymnastics of amphetamine tripping. She would listen with undivided attention, passionately, as if sucking energy and spirit from the speaker, nodding constantly and vigorously. She was both leech and radiator; when the speaker had been bled to exhaustion, the leech would turn. Stephanie would speak with rapid-fire, urgent enthusiasm, running her words and sentences together and rarely pausing for breath. The stuff of her conversation was absolutely meaningless to Kevin; simply the downhill prattle of a silly girl in the grasp of stimulants.

Michelle was the laconic one; a big, chunky girl in her early twenties. She had short dishwater-blond hair and a pasty, rotund face. Since she didn't talk all that much, she was perfect prey for the longwinded passages of Stephanie. Kevin fell in love with them all, but ever and again his eyes would fall on dark Cathy with a kind of catatonic angst.

It turned out the boys were in illustrious company. Once the fire was leaping and the wine circulating, they discovered that the three musicians had played in a number of L.A. clubs and had hopes of a recording contract. They were named William, Steve, and Koko Joe. They were hitchhikers, as were Smokey and Guy (the young man who had been clapping in time to the trio's music). They had all been picked up by the three girls in Michelle's chartreuse and carmine Volkswagen van.

"I'll let you in on a secret," Smokey informed Kevin when it had grown fully dark and they were comfortably positioned round the fire. He looked around furtively. The beach was practically deserted. *"Me and Guy's,"* he said under his breath, *"ditching the draft.* I think I can trust you, brother; you got an honest face. But it's like a big, *big* secret, so just don't go blurting it all over the place, okay? Nobody likes a blabber-mouth."

"Wow," Kevin said. He'd already rolled three cigarettes from his stash, and was in the process of lighting one. He dropped the match and extended an appreciative hand, repeating, *"Wow.* I mean, more power to you! But where are you guys gonna hide out? They'll be after you with cops and trigger-happy soldiers."

Smokey clapped his hands with delight. *"Saskatchewan!"*

Guy looked up sharply. "Jesus Shmesus, Smokey! Tell the fucking *world*, why don't you?" Guy was a somber, shapeless fellow, with a bushy brown beard and an electric mane of curly brown hair reaching nearly to the small of his back. He wore rimless spectacles, and was dressed entirely in leather, fancying himself a powerful advocate of the American Indian. The rights of the American Indian, Kevin knew, was a major issue of the Revolution, and he respected Guy's brave visual participation. Ultra-liberal Guy somehow equated the United States' involvement in Viet Nam with the grievances of Native Americans who, though miserable enough stuck on shrinking reservations, had better sense than to head up to Canada.

Smokey put a hand to his mouth, embarrassed and chagrined by this latest in a long line of indiscretions.

"Hey, it's cool," said little Eddie, in the fire's flicker looking half his age. "We're all revolutionaries nowadays. You guys don't have to worry about us blowing it for you."

Guy grumbled, uncertain.

"That's right," Kevin said, supporting his friend. He remembered his lessons. "And when my time comes I'll be right behind you. Nobody's gonna make me fight a war that's none of our business. I mean, the whole thing's a joke! The fatcats are just keeping it alive because they're afraid to back out now that they've made such a big deal about how high and mighty we are. Well, they shouldn't have committed us in the first place!" He smiled and winked at Eddie, hefted a jug and began to guzzle.

And suddenly, by spontaneous, tacit agreement, everyone around the fire was a full-blown and highly opinionated participant. The guitarists stilled their picking and leaned forward. Cathy's airy chatter tapered to murmurs and cooing. Michelle turned her morose, dejected eyes to Kevin and Guy. Stephanie sat cross-legged and tense, nodding her head rapidly from Kevin to Guy and back, desperate for one to begin.

"That's just about it, brother," Guy said at last, apparently satisfied. "Viet Nam's an embarrassment to the government pigs. This country had to go stick its bully-nose where it didn't belong, and now the shit's so deep we can't step out of it without leaving big holes. So we send more Army Issue children to fill those holes. And what happens—the poor sons of bitches go crazy over there. Who wouldn't? After you've been satisfactorily dehumanized you're sent out into the jungle with froth on your lips, chanting some vicious doggerel about righteous GIs and rotten gooks. And once you've seen a quartered child, or a mother hugging a garbage bag full of hamburger that was her husband...once you've seen enough of your buddies walking around with some peasant's ear for a medallion and brainwashed gleams in their wild eyes, well, you just flip out. You got no choice. You can adjust to it and kill your quota, or cringe in the bushes and smoke dope and hope the war'll go away. It's no wonder guys are deserting like never before."

"Those poor boys," Cathy mumbled wistfully, realizing any efforts to stir up a cheerful party would now be in vain. "But what's going to happen in the long run? If the President and his cronies are out to make trouble, what's to stop them from spreading the war in Viet Nam until all Asia, and then the whole world, gets sucked into it?"

Guy put his palms on his knees and leaned forward pointedly, the fire's light dancing on the lenses of his spectacles. "Just this: the Movement's in full swing now. Everybody's deserting or dodging. Pretty soon there won't be anybody left but those poor brainwashed bastards overseas, and if they don't get blown away by the Viet Cong first they'll shoot each other like dogs. One of these days Uncle Sam's going to point his Great Greedy Finger and say I...*Want...YOU*, and there just won't *be* anybody. Everybody's gonna be in Canada. A new free society north of the border, and nothing but a bunch of sick, malicious old fogies down here. We'll call Canada 'New America', and our children will grow up to be peaceful and strong. No more of this rowdy bullshit."

Kevin nodded and nodded. He lowered the jug and passed it to Smokey, lit all three marijuana cigarettes and passed them round.

"Hey, man," Koko Joe said to the group in general, "we got a song about The War. It's an original." Koko Joe was a thin, excitable type, with a long peaked nose and eyebrows that ran together. His face and neck were ravaged by a hardy acne condition which, by the looks of it, extended well below the collar of his blue serge shirt.

"Lay it on us," Mike said happily. "Wail on."

"Okay, okay," Koko Joe muttered nervously, rubbing his palms together. "I know you're all gonna dig this. It's like I wrote the lyrics *myself*, man; a lot of time and thought went into it. This song...this song shows just where our generation's at." He looked to William with his harmonica, then to Steve. He held his own guitar in a clumsy embrace. There was an awkward silence as they studied one another, synchronizing their movements. Suddenly Koko Joe nodded. His friends began to play, harmonizing on backing vocals, as he sang in a coarse, wobbly voice:

> *"Oh, baby, baby, what's comin' down?*
> *Life's such a bummer, man, I can't hang around."*
> (Can't hang around)
> *"Oh, baby, baby, what does it mean?*
> *The War is a drag, man, I can't dig that scene."*
> (Can't dig that scene)
> *"Don't wanna fight! Don't wanna die!*
> *Just wanna hang out, get laid and get high."*
> (Why?)

*"'Cause baby, baby, The War isn't cool.*
*I may be a freak, but I'm nobody's fool.*
*Baby, yeah."*
    (Yeah!)
*"Baby, ooh."*
    (Ow!)
*"Baby baby baby, 'cause hey man, I dig you."*

Kevin joined loudly in the applause. He'd been steadily imbibing wine for fifteen minutes now, and his movements were sloppy, his voice slurred.

"Right on!" he roared repeatedly, long after the applause had died. He lifted the jug again, pouring down his throat and over his chin onto his shirt. Kevin set the jug back down with a lopsided grin, pulled out his baggie of grass. He spilled a lot trying to roll another cigarette.

"Let *me* roll one," Eddie offered. "You're losing it, Kevin."

Kevin turned his head and squinted. "Fuck you!" he snarled, his head lolling. "You don't think I can roll, huh?" He shrieked with indignant laughter and blacked out. Eddie gently disengaged the baggie. "Sorry," Kevin mumbled. "Go ahead and roll, Mike."

"Sounds good to me, Mike!" Mike called out devilishly, half-hidden by leaping flames.

Eddie laughed. "How much you want me to roll, Mike?"

Kevin recklessly threw out his arms, accidentally smacking the side of Eddie's face. "Whoopee! I don't give a fuck, Mike! Roll up the whole fucking thing for all I fucking care!" He grabbed the jug and chug-a-lugged. On the back of his eyelids swam a radiant image of Cathy, wholly naked and almost dripping with desire, her arms spread in beckoning heat. He lowered the jug, but upon opening his eyes was looking at big morose Michelle. Kevin tried a knowing, sexy smirk. Her expression didn't change. "Me shell:" he croaked, in perhaps the world's worst McCartney impression, "Ma Bell." The laughter and chatter ceased abruptly as the young men and women all turned to stare. Kevin sniggered, hefted the jug and staggered around the fire to plop down with the three girls, his knee resting against Stephanie's, on his right. He looked to his left at Michelle and grinned hideously, his intention being to win Cathy's affection by making her jealous.

"Hey, what's happening, Mike?" he said. Michelle stared for a long hard moment, her dejected eyes burning in the campfire's glare. When the slap came Kevin was so drunk he didn't see or feel it. He only knew he was now facing Stephanie, and that one side of his face was having a delayed reaction to yesterday's sunburn. "She's playing—" he drooled, "she's playing hard to get." Stephanie nodded rapidly, urging him on. When he continued to grin stupidly she commenced an endless barrage of undulating chatter, a barrage he was way too frustrated to follow.

Kevin offered occasional affirmative grunts in return, quickly becoming depressed by the incessant banter. He took increasingly long swallows from the jug, astonished to find he'd already guzzled well over half the contents.

And now Cathy seemed to notice little Eddie for the first time. He had come over to return Kevin's grass, and Kevin heard her cry out, "Ooh! Isn't he just *darling?*" Kevin sluggishly swung his head until he was facing in the direction of her voice, squinting to focus his lazy vision. He saw Eddie standing with his head down and his hands thrust into his pockets, blushing terribly, a silly grin on his elfin face. Cathy was exclaiming melodiously and making a great fuss over him, smoothing his collar and playing with his hair. Eddie took it all like a puppy being scratched behind the ears, eyes half-closed and tail tucked under.

Kevin swelled with rage, certain he'd been outmaneuvered. He began chugging wine with furious tension.

"He's so *cute*. Just *look* at him!"

Kevin simmered, only dimly aware of Stephanie still gibbering at his elbow. He angrily raised the jug and threw back his head. The glass mouth rang hard against his front teeth, but he paid no attention, swallowing with vindictive haste. The alcohol had a nasty warning taste now, but continued to flow down his throat with little resistance.

"Look at those *adorable* freckles! Oh, he's *so* sweet!"

The blood was roaring in Kevin's ears, his teeth were

grinding together. His fingers clenched with murderous energy, his trembling face flooded with blood. His whole frame grew tense.

So he didn't hear Eddie approach, and wasn't aware of his close presence until Eddie had repeated himself.

"Hey, Mike! I brought you your grass back!"

Kevin looked up with a black, ugly snarl. "You fucking son of a bitch."

*"What?"*

"That's right," he said, standing and weaving. "You heard me, prick." He hiccoughed, poured wine down his throat and over his face. He tore the baggie out of Eddie's hand and stuffed it in his own shirt pocket.

"Kevin, you're drunk. You don't know what you're saying."

"Sure I do, you little bastard." Eddie's blurry figure kept disintegrating and reforming, replicating and throbbing back into focus. Kevin addressed all the sneaky little regimented bastard Eddies with vicious sprays of contempt. "I know *just* what I'm talking about, you little pansies, you traitorous turds."

Eddie was aghast. "What did—what did *I* do?"

Kevin took a slug to steady his vision, the jug much lighter in his hand. It was like drinking diluted kerosene now, but the fact that he'd managed to nearly finish off the jug only bolstered his ego. He swayed, steadied himself, lifted the jug and swallowed. He dropped his arm and belched fire on unstable Eddie, then raised his voice two octaves, mimicking a girl's.

"Oh, what did *I* do? What did sweetsy-weetsy li'l Eddie-weddie do?" He lowered his voice to a guttural, sputtering rumble, spacing his words out menacingly. "I'm gonna kick… your…*ass*, punk."

"Look, Kevin, whatever I did, I'm sorry. But let's talk about it in the morning, okay? You're really making a scene, and everybody's getting uptight. So why don't you just crash out in your bag here. Everything's cool."

"Fuck 'em!" Kevin bellowed. "Fuck 'em if they don't like it!" He took a swallow and pivoted awkwardly, ready to quash all comers. The fire blazed out at him, dazzling, backed by what seemed an army of shadowy gargoyles. "Fuck you all!" he raged, then pivoted in reverse to re-confront that conniving little prissy bastard Eddie. He had trouble finding him, so he took another long swallow. A cataract poured off either side of his chin and at last the jug was empty. He gave a huge manly groan of satiety and carelessly flung the jug away. There was a ringing thud and a sharp cry. Kevin wobbled his head in the direction of the cry. Someone didn't like him throwing the jug? Well, he would deal with he/she/it/them later. But first of all these little pansies here. He rolled his head back to face Eddie.

"Okay, punks. You wanna hassle, we'll settle this right here and now."

"I'm not hassling you, Kevin. You're my friend, my blood brother. What about peace, and love? We're revolutionaries together, Kevin. We're *friends*. Let's talk about it tomorrow when you're sober."

"*Right here and now*," Kevin roared. And the roar kept right on roaring, filling his ears with Fourth of July reverberations, imploding his skull with mad dreams of whirling faces and leaping flames. His pulse shot off in jackhammer rage at the whole conspiring world as he lunged forward, threw a haymaker at Eddie and felt the planet screech to a halt. Kevin plowed vengefully into the sand and was out like a light.

# Chapter 5

## All Things Must Piss

It was pale morning when Kevin's crusted eyelids, through no desire of his own, peeled apart to admit the day. His face was half-buried in chill morning sand, his nostrils clogged with the stuff.

A flurry of intense sensations woke his silly ass in a hurry.

Chief among these was a sense of desperate, soul-shaking thirst. His mouth was so dry it felt glued shut. It was this terrible, all-consuming thirst which had so urgently roused him from his near-coma.

Or was it?

Right after the thirst came a knotting of the gut, followed by an overwhelming impression of freefall. The early morning light crashed against his retinae. Kevin's eyelids slammed shut, and the light's aftermath went cartwheeling through his brain. He shuddered violently. The shudder preceded a sick, scary pain in his skull. Everything went blood-red.

Nausea came hurtling up his spine like a runaway locomotive, broke into his brain with a screaming *clang-a-lang-a-lang* of alarm, shook him to his knees. He trembled there, on all fours on the sand, absolutely overcome, a half-squashed cockroach struggling to crawl. His jowls were quaking, his face purpling, his eyes rolled up in their orbits.

A sputtering relay on the cerebral control panel caused him to jerk forward his right hand, then to advance his left knee.

Arm followed leg as the smashed cockroach made its way to the ocean's foaming edge.

Kevin's diaphragm reared, hauling up his belly and arching his back, preparing his body for the ejective motion of lurching forward to puke his guts out. But his esophagus remained constricted. Nothing was evacuated, and Kevin was treated to a mad, suffocating vision; seeing, in his imagination, a tiny spark of fight abandoning the control tower in his splitting skull. All was chaos in there, the punch-drunk operator laughing hysterically amid a hellish scene of billowing smoke and pinwheeling jets of flame.

The reaction to heaving is to gasp desperately, accompanied by a rocking motion on the supporting arms in the opposite direction of the heave—but air met the same impediment. When Kevin's ravenous cells received no oxygen his body arched up again, his eyes went sightless. Once more he lurched forward; every aching cell, every agonized, quivering nerve called to arms in a last-ditch, all-out attempt to *hurl* onto an area of a few square inches of sand. Kevin's black, fluttering face was drawn magnetically, irresistibly to the spot.

But the heave was a bust. Nothing was ejected, and no air burst into his lungs as ecstatic shrieking razors. When his body rocked back this time, it was with the sluggish tremor of submission. Red firefly sparks leapt convulsively in his consciousness, while the senseless, rocketing film of his life played over and over, half an inch high on the fuzzy silver screen of his mind. All engines shut down for Kevin, and darkness stormed his brain like warrant-brandishing cops bursting through the door to his soul. It was lights out.

Yet he slumped with a horrible croak, gagged, and barfed out mouth and nose for all he was worth. As the gasping reaction drew him back he still received no air. Kevin's flapping face immediately took on the rictus of unrelieved vomiting. Pulling back from the fifth or sixth heave he did manage to draw some air, maybe a teaspoonful, but his throat at once cruelly seized shut.

Kevin hurled once more, his stomach bursting. He went briefly insensible; choking, gagging, swooning. Finally air flooded his lungs. Gradually he got into a broken rhythm of gasping, until the hands got to work in his gut again, twisting and compressing. He vomited twice more, but less forcefully.

When he was finished he remained hunched, glutting air with great stabbing hiccoughs. Violet light began to swirl against his retinae, grew red, composed itself.

Kevin was a sobbing wreck, trembling head to toe. After a minute he managed to crawl away from the piteous mess he'd made. His arms buckled and he pitched face-first into the sand, where he lay in a rapturous fever of cool, nectarous air. He wanted to lay there and luxuriate in it, to drink it to his heart's content. He wanted to weep himself dry, but before anything he simply had to get rid of the disgusting taste in his mouth, the burning residue in his nostrils.

He pushed himself to his feet, stumbled off to the rest-room, pounded despairingly against the locked door until his streaming eyes fell on a water faucet. The boy gargled and spat, ducked his head under the water's thin arcing column, filled his mouth and swallowed. It was a mistake. He quickly flashed the water, hacked some more. He rinsed his mouth, spat carefully, stood and controlled his breathing, let his thumping heart gradually slow.

It was over. Kevin dragged his feet through the sand.

Eddie was sitting up in his bag, rubbing his eyes. Mike was still asleep, only the top of his head visible. Eddie grinned when he saw Kevin shambling up.

"So you finally came out of it! How's your head?"

"Terrible," Kevin admitted, slumping. He sat on his tousled sleeping bag and massaged his temples. It felt like there was a big aching bruise in there, lividly etched on the living walls of his cerebrum.

"I held onto your glasses for you," Eddie said, and handed them over.

"Thanks, Eddie. You're really a pal. Did I make a scene last night?"

"Boy, did you ever! Don't you remember?"

"I—I guess I drew a blank."

"You don't remember grabbing the girls and getting all pissed off about something? Or hitting Cathy in the face with your wine bottle? What a shiner she got! Don't you remember taking a swing at me?"

Kevin swallowed. There *were* vague impressions of just such scenes shuffling in his mind, but he had tried to suppress these thoughts, afraid to dwell on them and possibly form incriminating chains of association, chains which might reveal further ugly misdemeanors lurking like whores in the shadows of his memory. So now he said, "Sort of. But not really. I think I remember taking a swing at you. Gosh, I'm sorry, Eddie. I just didn't know what I was doing."

"Oh, heck, Kevin, that's all right. I knew you were wasted. You missed me by ten feet and passed right out."

When he'd gathered the nerve, Kevin asked, "And that was it? I just crashed?"

"Yeah, for a while there. But then you woke up about two hours later. We were all still partying away when you came staggering into the middle of our circle and pulled out your dick."

Kevin jerked from the butt up. "I did *what?*"

"Yeah, man, you just stood there holding your pecker for everybody to see. Nobody said a word. It was weird. You were rocking back and forth like one of those plastic punching clowns, and we knew if you let go there'd be a fountain out of control. But nothing came out. I guess you must've thought you'd done your thing, though, 'cause you put it back in and zipped up." Eddie's face squinched with merriment. "So then you got your pecker caught in the zipper and started howling. By this time we were all cracking up. Finally you zipped up your pants and just stood there swaying. All of a sudden we saw one leg of your Levis turning dark. I couldn't believe it—*you were pissing your pants!* I laughed so hard I cried."

"Oh no..." Kevin's head rolled in his hands. "No!" But suddenly he could see it as Eddie had described it, vividly, as if it was happening now before his eyes. The fire and their astonished faces lit like jack-o-lanterns. Their laughter. His brain began to throb anew.

"*Yeah,*" Eddie said, enjoying himself. "And then you started raving."

"Raving?"

"You were yelling about how everybody was trying to

screw you around, even your friends. That shows how drunk you were. Me and Mike never did nothing to wrong you, Kevin. Anyway, you started calling the girls names—"

"Oh, come on!"

"Really! Every dirty name in the book. You said they were all full of shit and had these like super-snotty complexes. Then you started calling them a herd of two-bit sluts and cock-sucking whores. You kept *shouting* about what complexes we all had. You were starting to get, I mean, *super* loud and rowdy, so one of those draft dodgers—I guess he was kind of para-noid—suggested that maybe you should just shut the fuck up and go to sleep. Well, that got you *really* pissed off. You started yelling that the girls were sluts and bitches again, about how you wouldn't fuck them with *my* dick. Then you kicked sand all over the fire and that was pretty much the end of the party. All those people packed their stuff up in their van and split."

"Oh, Jesus," Kevin groaned. "Oh my God."

"And then you had this big crying jag."

"Crying jag!"

"Yeah. You started bawling about how sorry you were, over and over. Mike asked you if we could maybe roll a joint and smoke it with you. We thought some pot might help your head. You looked up and just stared at us for a minute with tears all over your face. Then you took your stash out of your pocket and said, '*Sure*, you cocksuckers. *Take* my pot, just take it *all*', and shook your whole stash in the air, laughing like a lunatic. Then you started hitting the sides of your head with your fists and bawling about how sorry you were again. You got to rap-ping about killing yourself, and we were getting kinda worried there. Me and Mike never saw anybody freak out on wine before. But finally you just cried yourself to sleep."

Kevin languidly wagged his aching head. "Don't tell me any more. Please. I can't take any more."

"There wasn't any more. Like I said, you did the big boo-hoo scene and crashed right out. There wasn't anything left *to* do after that; we three were the only ones left on the beach. So we rolled you up in your bag and went to sleep. I'll say this much: you wasted a lot of pot, but you sure had a swell time. I should've drank more of that wine."

Kevin looked at him then, convinced Eddie wasn't making this all up. If only his head would quit pounding. But the more he thought about it, the surer he was he could remember most of the scenes almost exactly as Eddie had described them. The raving and name-calling…hadn't he had a dream like that? And the crying—that was plausible; weren't his eyelids stuck together this morning? No sin in crying when you're plastered out of your mind. But wetting his pants! Kevin placed his hands on his thighs, as if to wipe his palms. The material on his right leg was dry, but the left side was damp and crusted with sand. He hung his head.

Mike squirmed in his bag and sat up sleepy-eyed. He threw out his arms, yawned cavernously, blinked at Kevin.

"G'morning, shitface. And how are our complexes today?"

Kevin turned away. "Lay off. I already paid for it."

Mike yawned even wider. "Man, do I ever have a hard-on. There's nothing like sleeping on sand."

"Well, don't go back to sleep," Eddie said. "I'm hungry."

Mike scratched his legs while peering irritably at Eddie. "So *tell* me, boy genius. You just *tell* me where you plan on eating. From the looks of things this beach is the hot spot of the whole coast, and the only building on it's the bathroom."

"We won't get any breakfast just sitting here," Eddie said, with the practicality of a tramp.

Mike nodded sullenly, rolled his neck, stepped out of his bag. As he shook out the sand he stared hard at Kevin. "Well we might have got a ride in that chick's van if *somebody* didn't have to go call her a claphound."

"Shove it," Kevin whispered, and struggled to his feet. He waited for the pounding in his head to soften with eyes squeezed shut, breath shallow and controlled. "Let's get going." He dragged his bike and sleeping bag toward the parking lot with small painful steps.

Mike, rolling up his own bag, grunted, "All right, hold your horses! But you better not eat too much, man. I mean it. I don't wanna spend half the day outside an outhouse again."

"Don't worry," Kevin whispered, swallowing a combination of stomach acid and vomit residue diluted with phlegm and saliva, "I'm not hungry."

They rode for half an hour before finding a place to eat, and by then the sun had turned away the stiff morning cold. Kevin sat outside while his friends ate their breakfasts, his mind all in gloom. Even after his pals had eaten and they were again pedaling up the highway he found he couldn't shake it. His mood continued to darken.

Surely there were lessons to be learned on this trip if he were to enjoy it, or even survive it. The lessons should have been obvious.

But it seemed he was being attacked almost exclusively by the things he cherished and stood by, and this made the hurt harder to bear. To enjoy eating was to wind up sick as a dog. To drink was not the happy, comradely excursion of the old days, but a nightmare of distrust and distortion. Good old pot didn't seem to be helping his head at all, and the sun was no longer his friend, but a wicked, searing overlord.

Kevin reconsidered the price of morphing his embarrassing girth into dignified golden muscle. The greatest pains were in the expected spots: triceps, calves, thighs; but unexpected aches lurked in the back of his neck when he raised his head, his chest seemed about to rip down the middle whenever he inhaled too deeply. He computed the extent of torture yet to be faced against the impossible distance yet to be covered, and concluded he would one day arrive arthritic and hunched, a hopeless cripple.

Nodding as he pedaled, Kevin barely managed to pay attention to the road. An unsuccessfully interred memory came back to haunt him: he as a chubby, graceless child at his uncle's funeral, boxed in between the wheezing mountain of Joe Mikolajczyk and his squat sniffling wife as they ponderously filed along. Kevin had been ridiculously dressed in knee-length pumpkin-colored stockings and shiny Buster Brown specials, in navy blue shorts, a pink ruffled shirt with lemon-and-lime striped tie, and a tiny plum vest that must have originally been worn by an organ grinder's monkey. And the somberness of the occasion had done a number on the boy's bowels. Kevin now remembered with horror his pleading, in frantic whispers, to be taken to the restroom, and his mother shushing him at first, and then covertly smacking him on his bottom as he grew insistent. The boy had hopped and danced in wailing agony, and the mourners had turned swollen annoyed eyes on the mother and son. And Joe had swatted him hard on the back of his head and lifted him and shook him. And try as he would the boy had lost all control, crapping wildly on his brand new "special bought" clothes as his father bellowed in his face and shook him and shook him and shook him.

"*And,*" Mike was saying, in a just-loud-enough aside to Eddie, who was now riding between Mike and Kevin, "we could be toking on some pot if it wasn't for fatso over there. It's just been one fuckup after another."

Kevin looked at Mike's sneering, harshly-cut face. What was it about Mike, besides his rude words and hostile manner, that had been eating away at Kevin's brittle camaraderie for as long as the heavyset boy could remember? There was something rotten, almost *evil*, about the way Mike always took the negative view; about how he would push you just to the point of a fight and then desist, laughing at your heat. Seeing the wicked twist to Mike's lips, Kevin was suddenly aware that he'd never once seen the boy wearing a good old, winning, sincere smile. *Someday*, Kevin thought, his eyes burning directly into Mike's, whose own eyes narrowed and gleamed at the look, *sooner or later, buddy, you and I are gonna get into it, and when we do, motherfucker, I'm gonna kick your ass so bad it'll take a surgeon to get my boot out of your asshole.* Mike's eyes seemed to shine brighter. His sneer grew broader.

"Look, beagle breath," Kevin said hotly, while his stare still had the advantage over Mike's, "you wouldn't have smoked any pot *at all* if it wasn't for my generosity, dig? And I'll do any darn thing I wanna do with my pot, hear? If I wanna throw it away, then I'll throw it away, whether *you* like it or not. And I don't dig being called fatso, man, 'cause it's not fat, punk, it's muscle, which you'd know if you weren't all skin and bones."

Mike's sneaky, pouncing grin didn't falter a bit. "Oh, *yeah*, fatso? Well, fatso, I'll fucking call you fatso any fat fucking time I want to, *fatso!*"

Kevin saw red, his eyes straining in their sockets. He turned his wheel sharply toward Mike, intending to leap on him as cowboys did when fighting steed-to-steed in spaghetti westerns. But in his unblinking rage he had discounted Eddie's presence between them, and all three went sprawling in a crazy tangle of arms, legs, and spinning wheels. Kevin found himself on his butt, wearing his bike's frame like a yoke. When he got to his feet Mike was cussing and spitting from behind Eddie, who was doing his best to hold the little bully back. Then a station wagon was bearing down on them, sounding its horn and swerving wildly. They all sprawled shouting to the side of the road. When Kevin picked himself up this time he was out of breath. Mike began laughing at him, which was worse than name-calling, then remounted his bike and slowly rode away. He chuckled viciously as Kevin feigned pursuit, too exhausted to give chase.

"Come back here," Kevin gasped, "and fight like a man, you chicken."

"Fuck you, fatso!" Mike called back, still laughing. "Fatso, fatso, fatso!" he sang. "Come over *here* and call me chicken!"

Kevin was too worn out to do anything but hang his head. When Mike realized Kevin was not going to play his game he returned gradually to rough formation, not saying anything, but snickering nastily and victoriously.

"Why?" Eddie wondered. "Why do you guys keep chipping away at each other? We're all friends, right? What kind of impression are we making for all the straights? We've got to live in *peace*, you guys. What are they going to think of L.A. in Frisco if we get up there and start brawling?"

"Oh, bullshit," Mike sneered. "When are you gonna grow up?"

"No, really," Eddie said reasonably. "That's what this trip is all about, Mike. We want to go up to the City and see our people. If we're fighting between ourselves we don't really deserve to be there, and I wouldn't be surprised if they wouldn't have us."

"Oh, *Christ!* You can't even have fun any more. Not around *you* guys."

A knowing look passed between Eddie and Kevin. The look was not lost on Mike, who tensed and considered them rabidly, ready to burst into tears. "So that's it!" he cried. "Fuck you *both* then!" Mike put down his head and pedaled hard. He maintained his distance fifty yards ahead, refusing to look back.

After an interval of silence Kevin offered, "I agree with you, Eddie. You know that. I think what you said just now was really together, and I guess I looked pretty bad all ready to fight like that, and last night, too, when I got rowdy. But I was drunk last night, so I figger I've got an excuse for *that* bum trip, and believe me, I learned my lesson. But just now...I don't know, Eddie—you saw how he was pushing me. I don't think Mike's a real brother at all. I don't want to fight, but, *darn it,* I don't like being *pushed!* I wish we could've come without that guy."

Eddie nodded emphatically, relishing his role as mediator. "I'm not blaming you, Kevin. That was obviously all Mike's fault, and you reacted like anybody. But now dig this— and I'm not trying to preach to you; I just want to say it before I lose my thread. I've been doing a lot of reading; stuff by Leary, Huxley, Kesey, Hesse. And the whole trip is that we can't let other people's hangups get to us. So you take a guy like Mike. Okay, I've known him forever; ever since we were kids together in Pasadena. Now Mike is a prick with a capital p, right? I don't know *why* he's like that, but he *is*. He's got his good side, but the point is he's the kind of guy who likes to pick fights and start trouble. All right. I've learned from my reading that a dude like Mike *wants* you to retaliate, see? He needs to justify his rowdy nature, so he tries to make someone else throw the first punch, and then he figures he's defending himself, fighting against the bogeys that've been haunting him all his life. That's *his* hangup, but *we* make it *ours* by getting pissed in return. If you let his attitude get to you, well, then you've got *two* people who're rowdy. You see? Mike's so messed up he thinks I'm taking your side, so he'll need somebody else on his side to even the odds. Then you've got *four* people involved. When this action goes down between whole countries you get the mess we've got in Viet Nam. But now we've got guys who *refuse* to get involved, and who just plain *won't* fight. That's the only way to deal with it, and that's what the Movement's all about.

Like, when Mike gets hot, you just smile and flash him the peace sign. Pretty soon he picks up on the idea that nobody's out to get him after all, and he starts to groove. It's that simple."

Kevin grunted and smiled sheepishly. "Yeah. I oughta know better. Thanks for talking me down, Eddie."

"No thanks necessary," Eddie said, gobbling down Kevin's gratitude. "It's not my thought. Like I said, I read it."

"Well, if you look at it like that—you know, like Mike's sick—then I can't really hold his crummy attitude against him, can I?"

"Right."

Kevin braked and took a deep breath. "You know what I'm gonna do, Eddie? Just to prove I'm hip to the Movement and all, I'm gonna go tell him no hard feelings. Right to his ugly face." He pushed off, and after a minute had almost caught up. "Hey, Mike!"

Mike tensed. He turned his head only partly round, just far enough to keep an eye on Kevin. "Yeah? What do *you* want?"

Kevin drew even, smiled. "I just wanted to say that everything's cool. No hard feelings."

"Oh yeah? What have you and your good buddy been rapping about all this time? Gonna ditch me, is that it? Well go right fucking ahead, fatso. I can make it without your shit."

Kevin's smile grew taut. He spoke through his clenched teeth, only his lips moving. "No, really, man. We haven't been ganging up on you or anything like that. I just want to drop the whole thing and be friends. Let's keep it cool."

Mike stared suspiciously, unmoved. *"Why?"* he jabbed. "So you say you just wanna pretend nothing never happened, huh, fatso? Okay, fatso; that's fine with me. We'll let it go and stay friends…*fatso!"*

Kevin's eyes blazed. "No offense, see? It's not your fault when you get nasty or rowdy."

"Oh, yeah? It's *not*, huh?"

"No, man, it's like you're *sick* and you just can't freaking *help* it. *That's* why I'm willing to let it drop. I figure you're going through some bad head trips, is all, and it's like the duty of us *true* revolutionaries to keep cool when you get uptight, so that maybe someday you'll catch on and get your stupid act together like the rest of us."

"Is that *so?*" Mike spat, mouth twisted out of shape, teeth bared in a ferocious snarl. "Well maybe I don't *want* your help, dig? I mean, did you *hear* anybody asking for your *fat* help? *I didn't!* And if I ever *do* need help, *four-eyes*, you can rest assured you'll be the *last* fat creep I look up!"

"Now *look*, man. I'm *trying* to be friendly, *right? So don't blow it!* Like I said, you're *sick*, punk, and don't know what you're *saying*, so I'm not holding it against you! Why can't we just be *friends*, cocksucker, and let the whole thing drop before I lose my fucking temper and *kick* the holy reaming *shit* out of you? Can't you see, God fucking *damn* you all to hell, *that you're screwing up the whole revolution?"*

Mike snaked back his head and aimed, lunged and spat a thick gob of snotty saliva directly onto the lens covering Kevin's furious red eye. He kicked out hard, connecting with Kevin's thigh. Kevin flew off his bike sideways and went hollering and cartwheeling through the dirt.

By the time Eddie pulled up, his best friend was wiping his glasses and cheek with a shirt sleeve. Kevin got to his feet wordlessly, rubbed his scraped rump and looked to his bicycle. One pedal was bent, its carpet sleeve thrashed. The chain was fouled.

"I tried," he told Eddie. "You saw how I tried."

"Don't lose your head," Eddie pleaded.

"Oh, I won't. Funny, but I don't feel mad anymore. Only tired." He winced. "And hungover." He looked up the road. Mike stood in the spare shade of an equally scrawny spruce, blinking at them hatefully. "The guy's sick all right. You saw how he acted when I tried to make up."

Eddie shrugged helplessly. "He'll come around, eventually. If you show him you're still not upset he'll have to see how wrong he is."

"I—I'm not sure I can talk to him. Not right now."

Eddie licked his lips. "I'll go tell him you're not mad. You ride back here."

Kevin nodded. "Okay, go ahead and give it a try. Like I said, I'm perfectly willing to meet him halfway. But I'm telling you, Eddie, one of these days I'm gonna kill him."

Eddie grimaced. He pushed off. After counting to ten Kevin followed slowly. He watched them riding ahead, Mike gesticulating heatedly while Eddie tried to get a word in edgewise. As they pulled close together, the action was transferred one to the other; Eddie making explanatory gestures while Mike glowered. Suddenly Mike pulled back his arm and socked Eddie hard on the ear. Eddie dragged himself to the curb and collapsed. After a minute he forced himself into a sitting position, buried his head in his arms, and began bawling like a broad. Mike sat down on the other side of the road, looking paranoid and bitter.

Kevin sighed. His heart went way out to Eddie, who was just too ingenuous, just too innocent to survive a world of bullies, jackals, and perverts. He needed someone like Kevin to protect him from the callous hordes ranging worldwide, their senses perked for gracious prey to trample. Poor little Eddie would die a burn victim—he'd be persuaded and swindled, seduced and abandoned, enlisted and betrayed. He'd wind up penniless, homeless, helpless, friendless—suckered and set up and suckered again. And, having been royally screwed by every person he'd ever trusted, he'd speak eloquently from his deathbed of his unbending faith in the ultimate goodness of humankind. Now Kevin glared at Mike. It would be the last time Eddie was punched. He made sure Mike saw his look of exaggerated spite, then dismounted next to Eddie.

Eddie looked up at Kevin, then past him at Mike, who was slowly coasting across the road.

"Whatcha doin'?" Mike asked ominously, a hateful sneer on his face, his fists ready to go at the first wrong move. "You guys talking about me behind my back? I thought we all agreed before we left there wasn't gonna be no secrets."

Eddie looked away.

Kevin said, "You can think what you want, *man*. We were minding our own business, so why don't you just mind yours?"

Mike ground his teeth together, blinking rapidly. Finally he exploded. "Why don't you mind *yours*, you fat fucking Polak! Why don't you crawl back in your hole where you belong! Everything was just bitchen before you showed up and started taking sides. Me and Eddie used to have a real good time until you got him all hot on this 'Revolution' bullshit. *Love!"* he spat, his whole face trembling. *"Couple of faggots, that's what you are!"* He avoided looking at Eddie when he made this accusation. He stabbed a forefinger at Kevin's nose. "And it's all because of *you!"*

Kevin's fists rose halfway to jabbing position. But then he saw, out of the corner of his eye, Eddie looking up and watching him intently. It came to Kevin in a flash that this instance was, clearly, a kind of test. Eddie's words were still fresh in his mind: *"But now we've got guys who* refuse *to get involved, and who just plain* won't *fight. That's the only way to deal with it, and that's what the Movement's all about."* His ten-speed had been left leaning against his flank, and, in a surprise move, Mike deftly grabbed the handlebars of Kevin's bike and pushed off before the fat boy could snatch it back.

Kevin ran in hot pursuit while Mike roared with malicious hilarity. Mike skillfully steered Kevin's bicycle for a few hundred feet before allowing it to drop with a crash. He kicked and kicked at the spokes with his heels, then used the front wheel of his own bike to wreak further damage.

Kevin screamed out a string of loose obscenities, fell to his knees. Suddenly his eyes were welling with tears. Mike rode off guffawing.

There was little damage; only a few bent spokes, an ugly scrape on the leather seat. Kevin straightened the spokes, breaking two, and mounted with the weariness of depleted rage.

"Don't let it bum you," Eddie said soothingly as they wobbled away together. "I know just how you feel." He laughed. "Look at us, crying like a couple of kids. Only three days on the road, and here we are, blubbering away like the world's gonna end."

Kevin looked at him glumly, sniffed away his tears and swallowed. He knew how important this trip was to Eddie, and in gratitude for the friendship he'd done his royal best to keep Eddie's enthusiasm hyped up over the months. But now he was beginning to treat his serious doubts seriously. At last he made his confession.

"You're right, Eddie. It's just that I wasn't ready for all these bad vibes. I thought this was going to be a giant joyride, and everybody would be cool. But ever since we left things've been getting worse. For me anyway. It's been one big disappointment after another. Eddie, I don't know how to say this …but I think we've been fooling ourselves. So far everybody I've met from Frisco has been a gazillion percent different than what I expected." He sniffed again, chucked Eddie lightly on the arm. "Well, partner, it's good to know I've got at least *one* true friend."

Eddie colored. "You can always count on me, Kevin."

Kevin regarded little Eddie affectionately. "But we've *still* got to score us a lid. That was pretty dumb of me to throw it all away last night." He darkened. "And when I get some more I'm not gonna smoke any with Mike."

Eddie's delicate brows arched. "Oh, no! We can't be like that at all. That's not fair."

"You mean you *still* feel that way, even after he punched you for no reason?"

"Mike's our brother," Eddie said with conviction. "We can't ever forget that, no matter how he acts. Elsewise we'd might as well just turn around right here and head back home."

"Wow. You really *are* a heavy revolutionary…now I feel guilty as all heck, Eddie. How can I ever clean up my act?"

"I'm telling you," Eddie told him, "that things are going to imrove *naturally*. The nearer we get to the City, the cleaner our heads will be. We'll be like angels, Kevin—everybody who comes within a thirty-mile radius of the City *instantly* becomes turned-on. These people we've run into are on their bum trips because they're away from the City. ¿Si comprendo? They're going through Love Withdrawals."

"The *Haight*," Kevin corrected him gently. "That lousy Jesus freak told me they don't like it called 'the City' up there. Disrespectful and unhip."

*"Really!"* Eddie's eyes lit up and his jaw dropped (Eddie really loved extending his hip vocabulary and adding odd facts to his private storehouse of informational tidbits concerning the Revolution. Back at Santa Monica High he'd been well-known as an authority on the subject. His shy nature had pre-

vented his vaulting to campus prominence, but he was one of the few boys popular with almost everyone. It was Eddie who had introduced Kevin to marijuana that rainy night last November, and Eddie who had fired Kevin's imagination about San Francisco, and molded their relationship of eager teacher and faithful pupil. Although Kevin was willing to let Eddie tutor him, he really dug the chance to catch him off guard; to pay his friend back with a trippy morsel and look cool in the process).

"And they don't like the word 'hippie' up in the Haight," Kevin added pointedly. "They think it's a real put-down."

*"No kidding!"*

Kevin could see Eddie tucking the information away.

*"Thanks*, Kevin! 'Hippie' *does* sound sort of plastic, I guess. We'll just have to call each other 'freaks'. Nothing plastic about that." Eddie was silent for a minute. He then looked defiantly into Kevin's eyes, as though he didn't expect to be taken seriously. "I—I've been thinking, Kevin. You know how important this trip is to me. Look...what I'm trying to say is...I think this is the biggest thing to *ever* happen to me. To you too. I didn't tell you before we left because I sure as heck didn't want to freak out your head, but, what I'm trying to say is...ism...uh...ism...is...*this is just too heavy!* Kevin, this is the Big Ditch. Damn it, it's the Ultimate Run!"

Kevin nodded hiply, knowing he'd really scored some major points here. "I can dig what you're rapping, man," he said, "and it's all like totally groovy. I'm tripping too. My head is, you know, like *truly* happening."

"No, you *don't* know what I mean! Kevin, this trip's for real! What I mean is...is...*I'm not coming back!* There. I've said it."

Kevin gawked. Tears came peeking from his eyes. When he could get his mouth together he managed, "Eddie! This is crazy! What a mindblower!"

"What is?"

"Eddie, I planned to run away, too! I didn't tell you for the same reason."

Eddie's whole body locked up.

They turned and shared something ineffable. After a few

seconds the tears were squeezing between Eddie's eyelids. He did his best to suppress them, but it was too late. The boys hugged and sobbed and laughed, pounded one another on the back.

"Revolutionaries together!" Eddie cried. "All for one, and one for all!"

"Forever!" Kevin said. But something was nagging him. A cloud passed over his joy. The Big Ditch? "Eddie…you aren't planning on ditching me up there and sticking me with Mike, are you?"

"Of course not," Eddie said, and sobered considerably. "What ever gave you that idea?"

"Oh, I don't know. Nothing, I guess. I'd just hate to get separated, that's all. I knew this trip was important to you, Eddie, but I never thought you'd want to leave your mom and dad for good. Me, there's nothing that could make me happier than to never see my folks again."

"*Kevin*," Eddie said with solemn finality, "*nothing in the world* means more to me than getting to San Francisco and living there for the rest of my life. Nothing! The worst thing anybody could do to me would be to stop me from getting up there. He'd might as well cut out my heart. I'm determined!"

Kevin set his jaw. With a whole mouthful of soul he said, "Eddie, you can count on me. As long as I'm with you I guarantee nobody will screw up your plan. I guaran-*tee* it! We'll be the heaviest flower children the Haight ever saw."

"And you'll change your feelings about Mike?"

Kevin squeezed his hand brakes. "And I'll even change my feelings about Mike. But it's gonna be *hard*."

"Just you wait," Eddie promised. "If we're cool to Mike, *constantly*, his whole trip'll change. We'll be proud of him."

And sure enough, Eddie's prophecy proved correct. Several hours later, while Kevin and Eddie were shoveling hamburgers at a Gaviota food stand, Mike slunk over and said with an embarrassed smile, "Hey, you guys. I was rapping with this cat who says he knows where we can score some pot."

"Far out," Kevin spewed. It was the first time they'd spoken since the quarrel.

Mike looked over his shoulder and beckoned. A small

Filipino boy, with round pleading eyes and glistening coal-black shoulder-length hair fastened at the back, walked over shyly, avoiding their eyes. He looked about sixteen, and wore baggy slacks, rope sandals, a floral-patterned short-sleeved shirt.

"Guys," Mike announced, "this is Mitchell. Mitchell, this is Eddie and...*that's* Kevin."

The Filipino boy shook hands, coloring deeper. "I can score grass," he fumbled, speaking quietly, "but have to go ways get. Friend of mine works head shop. Has lids. For sale good pot."

"That's cool of you," Kevin said. "And I'll give you a nice pinch for going to the hassle."

Mitchell blushed again. As they followed him down the sidewalk, Eddie couldn't resist nudging Kevin.

"See?" he whispered. "What'd I tell you? Mike's sorry, so he's helping you score. He feels bad about acting tough, and now he's doing his best to make it up to you."

Kevin grinned awkwardly. "I guess you're right, Eddie. It's like everybody's got love in their hearts. They just gotta be shown they're not alone."

"Now you're grooving."

The grin remained on Kevin's face, but the scene in his mind belied it. Eddie might be right about a lot of things, but he was just too guileless to see beyond the surface. So for now, in Eddie's company, Mike was okay, Mike was safe. But the clock was running against him. He'd become, in Kevin's eyes, Pure Evil. Pretty soon, when the time was right, Kevin vowed, in the name of the Revolution, to kick the holy crap out of him.

# Chapter 6

## Hooked

The head shop was a tiny, parti-colored store sand-wiched between a florist's and a jeweler's. The shop's interior was dark, but, thanks to the lighting arrangement, never for too long in any one place. A backlit plastic disk, its clear surface splashed with colors, revolved on a slow arbor above the doorway, scattering brief bursts of colored light about the room, over the boys' heads, across shelves stacked with hookah pipes and mind toys. A huge surrealistic painting of Alice's Cheshire Cat grinned mischievously from the far wall, blue smoke spurting from its nostrils in ever-widening rings. A strobe light pulsed over the cat's head, distorting time and space within the shop, rendering motionless the thick smoke trails of jasmine-scented incense wafting from every corner.

Now Mitchell, asking Eddie and Mike to wait outside, led Kevin around a purple velour curtain draping a doorway below the Cheshire Cat's tail. They emerged in a tiny storeroom. Seated at a card table, a fat, bald little man perspired heavily before the rapidly revolving blades of a small electric fan while nervously watching the goings-on in his establishment via closed-circuit TV. Head shops were Meccas for shoplifters. The store's owner knew he needed to blend in, and, at the same time, advertise. So for the sake of his business he was dressed exclusively in his own merchandise: a synthetic alpaca greatcoat with copper zodiacal charms dangling from the cuffs, draped by a loud, heavy zarape with braided fringe and the legend *LOVE IS WHERE IT'S AT* lettered boldly on the back and front; a thick and highly polished nickel swastika medallion hanging almost to his lap; an "Indian" belt of tiny strung yellow beads and fake turquoise, with erratically spaced profiles of a teepee, horse, and the standard bonneted chief in red beads; patriotically striped-and-starred trousers with snaps down the sides and bordering the pockets; Liverpool-style black patent leather ankle-high boots with oversized heels and a replica of Dave Clark's signature stitched in white on the toes. Kevin felt this man, despite his outlandish appearance, was the straightest and most uptight person he'd ever encountered in a head shop. The man's bare skull shone like a cue ball, with only a sparse fringe of brown curls about the ears and nape. He was forever squinting worriedly at the monitor, drawing deeply on a cigarette, tapping the ashes in the general direction of an amber glass ashtray overflowing with neurotically mashed butts. The only interruptions to the ash-tapping were frequent pauses to roll his neck, and a compulsive tugging at the front of the coat as he pulled it free of his sweaty chest. The room was as thick with tobacco smoke as the shop had been thick with incense fumes.

"Yeah, whatcha want, Mitch?" he asked in a tough voice, reluctant to avert his eyes from the screen. Before Mitchell could reply the little man spun in his seat, hollered, *"Mark!"* and whirled back around, spilling ash on his striped pants, then furiously rubbing that ash into the material with a wide stubby hand.

Immediately another curtain was pulled aside and a thin, long-haired man of thirty peered out over the top of blue-tinted, square-rimmed granny glasses. A single streak of his banded brown hair was dyed iridescent green. "Yeah, dad?" The granny glasses swung to Mitchell. The longhair motioned him inside. Kevin was ignorant of store protocol, but he wasn't about to remain with the edgy little owner. He shoved through the second curtain behind Mitchell.

This room was scarcely larger than a medium-sized bathroom, illuminated only by a single dusty bulb dangling from a frayed and twisted cord. Tier upon tier of large cardboard boxes left barely enough room to squeeze in sideways.

The three spoke in whispers. The long-haired man's attire was, in Kevin's eyes, as inspired as the father's. This Mark wore a tan leather vest with long strips of beaded fringe, slick black leather trousers, platform shoes spangled with brass buttons. Cheap turquoise jewelry dangled from his wrists and neck. An armband on each skinny bicep had the words OFF THE PIG embroidered in red, white, and blue. Now Mark opened a nondescript cardboard box tucked behind one of the tiers to display at least thirty bagged ounces. Kevin chose the thickest, and, after smoking a joint and fingering the contents, gave the benignly smiling and nodding man a ten dollar bill. The entire transaction had taken a mere five minutes; no fuss, no muss. As promised, Kevin gave the Filipino boy a generous pinch from his stash. Still whispering, he bade adieu to Mark and to the obsequiously smiling Mitchell, who had business to discuss in broken English. Kevin strode through the stockroom, past the nervous little owner now almost hidden in a tobacco fog, and out through the purple curtain. He leaned against the mural.

A hat rack stood adjacent to the purple velour curtain. Dozens of different styles of caps, fedoras, derbies—even one rhinestone-studded turban—dangled from pegs on the rack. But Kevin was taken by a floppy brown hillbilly affair, which he pulled low on his ears and admired in a small rectangular mirror affixed to the rack for that purpose. The hat's crown reined in his wild hair, while the great nether brim created a frizzy shape resembling a broad puffy collar. Suddenly Kevin was too cool for words.

He looked around for his friends, saw them, froze. Mike and Eddie—especially Eddie—were being entertained by two bikinied girls in the center aisle, next to a large cylindrical postcard rack. Both girls were bronzed, brunette, and slender. They were such an even match that Kevin first supposed they were twins, but as he approached and hesitated he noticed one girl bore a slightly Oriental cast, while the other was certainly a Jewess. He hesitated because he was high from the grass, and because the two girls and his friends had hit it off so well— giggling and poking and pinching—that he was at a complete loss for action. He certainly didn't feel like giggling or poking or pinching. He felt like bashing Mike's and Eddie's heads together, for his pot-rationale found something selfish and down-right unfriendly about his pals enjoying the goodies while he was away on an errand for their mutual benefit. Testosterone worked the fingers of Kevin's right hand into a fist. The boy took a deep breath and relaxed.

He forced a saunter as he approached Eddie, now being teased by the Jewish girl, and asserted himself with the robust announcement of his purchase. Eddie either didn't hear or ignored him completely, responding to the girl's tickling with nervous, slavering giggles. Kevin had never seen his friend so beside himself. Eddie's eyes were wild and rolling with agitated bashful lust. His oddly contorted body was hunched in what could only be described as a standing fetal position. He was absolutely electrified by the girl's probing fingers. Flecks of foamy saliva showed at the corners of his mouth. His giggles were spastic, rattling deep in his throat. Every now and then he would convulsively paw her shoulder or arm, his idiotic giggles ascending in frenzy.

Mike slapped the girl hard on her bottom. As she spun round laughing, Eddie grasped her arm and stroked it with rigid, crooked fingers. She backed straight into Kevin, who could only grin vacuously.

"Excuse me," the girl said with complete indifference, and pursued the passionate tickling of Eddie, who continued to wheeze and titter moronically. Now the other girl joined her friend in the exquisite tickling torture. A string of saliva rolled from Eddie's lower lip. Furious, Kevin ground his teeth, wanting to passionately fondle either rude, shameless girl; showing them how a self-assured man behaved, and revealing what a fool Eddie was making of himself. Then the other girl, swinging around to tickle Eddie from behind, spooned right into Kevin.

*"Excuse me!"* she snapped, with a look of profound distaste. In an instant he was forgotten. She squeezed right back between Eddie and the postcard rack.

His cheeks and ears burning, Kevin stepped around the rack, which occasionally clattered counterclockwise from the disturbance on the other side. He stared blindly at a colorful postcard, wanting to slam his fist into anyone, anything. Slowly the blood drained from his face, and he saw that the postcard was a glossy photograph of San Francisco Peninsula, taken from across the bay. He removed the card for a closer inspection. This created a view space, revealing the trespasses on the rack's other side. Helpless to avert his gaze, he looked on with icy ire.

Eddie was pretty far gone. A grimacing grin was frozen on his face, shudders were racking his body. He was bent like an old, old man. His arms and hands were white as death, but his face was so red Kevin fancied he could feel its heat. Little hiccoughing yelps of frantic arousal burst sporadically from Eddie's nostrils. Now Mike reached around and pinched the Jewish girl on her derriere. She laughed and turned half-around, her bikinied breast thrust almost into flabbergasted Eddie's bulging, throbbing eyeball. Kevin could just about feel the primitive impulses shrieking through Eddie's overheated brain, as the boy stared transfixed at this taunting fruit an inch from his nose. With an anguished little cry, Eddie jerked as though he'd been kicked, and his trembling hand worked its way up, out of his control…paused hovering an inch over the breast…molded itself agonizingly to the curvature…squeezed it twice. The girl turned around delightedly and slapped Eddie's hand with a scolding smile. Eddie squealed and fidgeted like a naughty little gnome, drew the hand spastically to his mouth.

Kevin turned away slowly, his breath shallow and rapid. His hands were shaking. Eddie was totally out of line here! If he, Kevin, had not been depleting his energy for the sake of Eddie's and Mike's welfare, it would have been a whole different story. He reasoned, unreasonably, that it was *he* who should have been tickled, and *he* the one to bring up a nervous hand for the quick double squeeze of that wonderful, teasing protuberance. Eddie had…*Eddie had no right!*

Sick, he shuffled off, his right hand softly, painfully cupping and fondling air, his left hand gripping the now creased and sweat-stained postcard. The incense smoke, competing for his air, agitated his distress, so he stopped and leaned against a sales counter. He looked up, directly into the lens of a closed-circuit camera fixed on his trembling face. He could almost see the pudgy little owner's neurotic eye glaring out at him.

"You," came a young woman's voice. "Hep?"

Kevin thought, *You bet your dumb whoring ass I am!* and tearfully swung to meet the sound.

The sales girl slouching behind the counter was a gaping, homely salute to estrogen gone wild. Only a supremely bored God could have produced such an outlandish exaggeration of the female form; a butt like two watermelons supporting an almost skeletal torso. What the sales girl carried upstairs Kevin could only guess, for she wore a tie-dyed peasant's blouse billowing like a parachute. The girl had no waist to speak of. Her outsize combat trousers were tucked into polished black jackboots, and secured by a tiny belt of entwined asps of anodized steel. Heart-shaped sunglasses with pink lenses took up half her face, exposing only a heavy jaw, lips painted the color of mercurochrome, and a forehead tattooed with the message MOO! written backward for rear-view mirror appraisal. Her hair, long and straight like her brother's, had been variously sectioned—clipped, banded, pinned, braided—ironed here, frizzed there, bleached in certain spots, dyed in others; loosely ornamented like a Christmas tree with dangling beads, feathers, gewgaws and the like. The whole rowdy mess was crowned by a tiny plastic silver-and-black birthday hat, its wide dayglo orange strap snapped tight under the girl's Peking Man jaw. The hat's shiny surface featured holographic grinning cartoon images of a wildly popular teeny-bopper band known as the *Monkees*.

Now Kevin, dazzled by the holograph, blinked and dropped the crumpled postcard on the counter.

"Hat? Buy hat too?"

He fingered the limp brim dully and grunted.

Leaning back, the girl looked him up and down while slowly shaking her trinket-barnacled head. The boy's eyes shifted side to side in response to the small movements of reflected light. After a minute of this she took him by his shirt's lapel and dragged him over to the leathers section. She bent down to root through a cluster of opened cardboard boxes.

Kevin almost fainted.

The contents of the girl's billowy blouse were now revealed in all their pendulous, braless glory. He clenched his fists, forced a quick look around. Surely everybody in the place was staring at him, absolutely crimson with outrage.

No one seemed remotely interested.

Then the camera…no, no, his back was to the camera.

Suddenly clammy in his armpits and crotch, Kevin felt his burning gaze drawn irresistibly to that spectacular dangling duo. The sales girl was wrestling with something heavy in one of the boxes, grunting and panting as she jerked up and down, up and down, up and down. And *up* and *down* and *side* to *side* and…*Up*…and…*Down*. Her long hanging hair formed two sides of a window for Kevin's bursting eyes alone, and within that window heaven just danced on and on; a performance way superior to the static displays in his girlie magazines, more vital by far than his steamiest fantasies. Kevin caught his breath as she straightened with a gasp, triumphantly holding a mass of fresh-smelling brown suede. Her eyes crossed.

*"You!"*

Kevin unclenched his fists and released his long-held breath. He was *busted*, Caught Ogling! "M-me?" he managed, the sudden center of attention for dozens of umbrageous shoppers, blushing clergymen, gaping schoolchildren, and grim plain-clothes detectives. The apparitions vanished. He tried to refocus.

The sales girl pushed the folded vest at him. "You," she said, frowning now. *"You."*

Kevin took the vest by its neck, let it fall open. The thing was bulky, with long leather fringing at the hem.

"You!" the girl said, exasperated. She mimed pulling on an upper body garment for Kevin's benefit. *"You!"*

Kevin shrugged the vest on. It fit tightly, smelled earthy and masculine. That tightness very agreeably made his chest and shoulders feel powerful and prominent. The vest's hem reached his waist. Those long strips of leather fringe hung limply almost to his knees. Little colored ceramic beads and roach clips were strung around the pockets. He slowly pivoted and noticed for the first time that a *Zig-Zag* (®) logo the size of a dinner plate was stitched onto the back. The rugged earthiness of this vest, he felt, gave him a likeness approximating that of a dignified dime store wooden Indian, and since the Movement ravenously sympathized with every Native American cause

Hollywood could dream up, Kevin saw the vest as a badge strongly identifying him with people like Guy and with all the Aquarian generation stood for.

Again holding him by the lapels, the girl dragged Kevin over to a full-length mirror standing against the wall. She then used her hands to patiently explain the advent of a mysterious third party, tapping a forefinger on his chest while the other hand indicated his reflection.

"*You.*"

"How much?" he panted.

The sales girl puckered. She spread her arms slowly, then rushed her hands together, halting when the palms were a few inches apart. Kevin, expecting an impact, felt his head jerk back. For a second all was blackness. The shop rematerialized, began to swim about him. The Cheshire Cat, leering from the far wall, morphed into a wolf, bayed in Kevin's slack mooning face. The girl's eyes rolled back in her skull.

"*Dirty night, nitey-nite,*" she chanted.

But Kevin wasn't so befuddled he'd buy into witchcraft or gothic verse. Physical art, poetic expression…these things were way too cryptic for like a totally plainspoken dude. *Besides*, that kind of stuff was only for nerds and losers. Kevin's testosterone level plummeted. She'd blown it. Babes, he acknowledged for the gazillionth time, just don't get it. Only minutes ago she'd been a funky, titillating goddess, and now she was nothing more than a gawky, pantomiming fool. Kevin exhaled quietly. He tried again. "How *much?*"

The girl snapped. She reached behind him, grabbed the vest's neck and yanked the garment around so hard she almost broke the boy's arm. She shoved the handful of vest in his face.

The label read: *Genuine Suede. Made in Mexico. XXL.* Below this had been scrawled in black ink: $39.99.

She smacked him across the forehead and stuck the scrawled price almost in his eye. "Dirty night, nitey-nite!"

Releasing the vest, she grabbed his shirt's lapel for the third time and hauled him back to the counter.

Kevin timidly pulled out his wallet.

The girl extracted three twenties and laid them out as a fan.

"Hat," she said, pointing at a twenty. She yanked twice on the vest while indicating the two remaining twenties. "Vet." She then extracted a ten dollar bill, slapped the wallet shut, and pulled from behind the counter a gorgeous snakeskin belt with a huge brass buckle. On the buckle's face were the words *DO YOUR OWN THING* in raised letters. It was a steal.

"Bet." She released Kevin's lapel. The boy gingerly picked up his belt and wallet and made his way out. He paused to slip on the belt and check his reflection in the display window's broad pane. A grin cut his face in half. Who *was* that together cat?

Mike and Eddie were holding their bikes at the curb. The setting sun was tinging a few streaks of cirri with flaming gold.

Mike guffawed wickedly when he saw Kevin's new outfit, then, apparently making an effort to stay on good terms, muttered, "Hey, that looks totally cool, Kevin. Really far out."

Kevin beamed. As they all rode away he sought Eddie's opinion.

Eddie looked at him feverishly. "I squeezed it, Kevin! I squeezed her tittie, I tell you! I squeezed her tittie!"

Kevin's grin collapsed.

"Big deal!" Mike barked, with a snappiness indicating this exchange had been going on for a while. "I pinched her ass."

Kevin looked one to the other, snarling. "So what? You guys act like it's your first feel!"

"What do you mean," Eddie shot back, "my 'first?' I've squeezed millions of titties! But it was so round and soft! And she liked it, I'm telling you, she *liked* it!"

Kevin sneered and looked to Mike knowingly, saying, "Oh, *bull!* Anybody knows they don't like it. Only guys like it."

But Mike, leaning inside as they coasted along, kept one eye on the road and rejoined in a sly undertone, "Yeah? Well, I didn't wanna tell you guys, but I not only pinched her ass, I *rubbed* it man. I could even feel her crack! And she liked that, too."

Eddie whipped his head to the side. He stared at Mike fiercely. "You didn't!"

*"So what?"* Kevin spat. "I don't give a shit. Why tell me?"

"I sure did," strutted Mike. "Not only that, I slipped my hand inside her bikini and felt 'down there.' Boy, did she ever like that!"

Eddie blew it. He pedaled so hard Kevin had to strain to catch him. Mike, gloating behind, called out, "Hey, *Eddie!* You wanna smell my finger?" and burst into vicious laughter.

"I'm telling you," Eddie panted, "Mike never touched her. Never! She didn't like *him*, she liked *me! She let me squeeze her tittie*, Kevin. Twice, I squeezed it twice. No! Four times."

"Well, what do you want me to do about it?" Kevin demanded. "Throw a parade? Break out the champagne?" He took a deep breath. "By the way, Eddie, I scored us a lid."

"It was nice and firm. Firm but soft."

"Eddie—"

"She let me squeeze it, Kevin. I could've squeezed 'em both if I wanted, if Mike didn't have to go and pinch her. No, he never touched her, never. She liked *me*, not him. I *know. She let me* squeeze her tittie."

"And I said I don't give a darn! Listen, Eddie, I hate to say this, but it really sounds like you never did it before. Otherwise you wouldn't be making such a big thing out of it."

"And *I*," Eddie shrieked, "said it *wasn't* my first time!" He looked away and refused to say another word. As Kevin rode alongside, mute, his frustration did not abate with the miles. He revisited the episode by the postcard rack; only it was he doing the squeezing, and it was the raven-haired girl, her wonders concealed only by a strained silky black bikini top, who was the object of his sensitive palm and pudgy questing fingers. In this fantasy, to upstage Eddie, he went farther than ever, brusquely pulling off the bikini top and ravenously suckling a nipple he pictured as a plump, firm strawberry. He swallowed hard and tightened his grip on the handlebars. The twilight deepened. A strand of fringe, flapping into the spokes of his rear wheel, was torn from his vest with a jolt.

A few miles north of Gaviota the highway twists inland, and for fifty miles remains inland, at last snaking back to the coast at Pismo Beach. This inland section passes through wild, dry country in hairpin curves.

The boys were making for the town of Lompoc, halfway between Gaviota and Pismo Beach. But after two hours of negotiating the endless curves they decided to sleep among the twisted trees just off the road. The area was thickly wooded and full of ankle-turning potholes.

"I heard a story about this stretch of road up here," Mike said offhandedly as he unrolled his sleeping bag. He kicked away a few pebbles poking up in his intended spread. "There's supposed to be a guy living up in these hills who comes down here at night to terrorize people who stop in cars—you know, guys necking with their chicks and people cooking at campfires. Anyhow, this guy's got only one hand, dig? He lost the other one in The War, and now he's got one of them hooks on the stump. He keeps it sharp as a razor blade, and every night he comes tiptoeing so nobody can hear him, and when he finds somebody he watches him for a long time, then sneaks up from behind and brings that hook down on the back of the guy's neck as hard as he can."

"Oh, great!" Kevin said sarcastically. "That's just what I wanted to hear!" Actually, he just loved a good bedtime story meant to frighten the pants off him, and although he was certain he'd heard this yarn, or one similar, before, he had to appreciate the storyteller's ability to entertain. So for the time being Mike was okay in Kevin's book. He lit one of two joints he'd rolled earlier. When he was snug in his sleeping bag he handed it to Mike.

"Yeah," Mike said, taking a deep draw and passing the reefer to Eddie. "He carries this satchel down with him, right? And in this satchel he's got all kinds of attachments he can screw onto his stump in place of the hook, and each of these attachments is for a special occasion. Like, if he sees a couple balling he'll knock 'em both out with this chrome-plated bludgeon attachment, and tie 'em up with this screw-on pulley gadget. Then he'll take this thing like a telescoping eggbeater, with a handle that turns the blades and everything." Mike demonstrated, turning an imaginary reel on his fist. "He's got this gizmo filed real sharp like his hook. So he rams it straight up her pussy and starts turning the handle. The blades whirl around and slowly go deeper and deeper until she croaks."

"Gawd!" Kevin said. "Where'd you hear about this guy? It sounds like you're making it all up." He hugged himself with delicious anticipation, imagining the stealthy crunch of footsteps just beyond the field of his vision.

"Cross my heart and hope to die if it's a lie," Mike swore solemnly. "I read this *in the paper,* man! They've seen the guy, 'cause a few people escaped. Only a few. But they've never caught him. He's known as The Hook. Just a couple weeks ago he snuffed some Marine, right about where we are now. He killed the guy by taking this long thingamajig like a knitting needle with a spiral ridge on it, see, and using this stump attachment built like an old hand drill to screw it into the Marine's eardrum real slow, all the way through his brain and out the other side. Then he chopped the guy's hand off with his hatchet screw-on and took it with him for his collection. He always cuts off one hand after he does in his victim. His way of getting even with everybody with two hands, I guess.

"Anyway, when he catches a couple balling, after the chick cools like I explained, well, then he takes this other attachment out of his bag and, chuckling and talking quietly to the terrified guy tied down butt-ass naked in front of him, he screws it on his stump. This little number he calls his Nutcracker. What it is is a vise which he sticks the guy's balls in. As he turns the handle the two sides of the Nutcracker slowly get closer, squeezing the poor thrashing guy's balls, and as he's screaming The Hook's still talking to him, and chuckling all the while. And when the guy's balls are purple and he's so far gone he's almost beyond pain, The Hook pushes this button on the Nutcracker. A spring that was tightening all the time is tripped like on a mousetrap, and the two halves smash together and crush the guy's balls into gonad puree."

Kevin moaned and instinctively curled up his knees. Eddie began to whistle shrilly, and they both quickly looked around at the black, ominously shivering bushes. They laughed nervously, in unison.

Mike yawned and stretched his arms. "Well, there's three of us, so we don't gotta worry."

Kevin blinked owlishly. "Whatta you mean? If we're all asleep we'll be sitting ducks. Maybe we should take turns watching."

"Nah. You'll wake up quick enough if The Hook comes around. I read he's got something wrong with his throat or his lungs. He breathes real fast and loud. So you'll know when he's coming." He yawned even wider and turned over in his sleeping bag, away from them.

Kevin blinked again. "But then why didn't the Marine hear…"

Mike raspberried him and yawned warningly.

Kevin and Eddie were quiet for a while. A small animal rustled the brush, momentarily hushing the crickets.

"You sca-a-a-red, Eddie?" Kevin whispered.

"Not rea-a-a-ally," Eddie whispered back. "I've got… I've got something else on my mind right now."

"What…what you got on your mind right now?"

Eddie looked at him directly, eyes ablaze. "I was just thinking about that girl's tittie I squeezed, about how big and soft it was."

Kevin groaned. "Eddie—"

"I squeezed it six times, Kevin, over and over and over. It was terrific. I wanted to squeeze 'em both, together, but Mike had to go and pinch her. No…no…*no he didn't!* I don't care what he says."

"Eddie—"

"They were firm and creamy, Kevin, just like big yummy marshmallows. All soft and squeezy."

"Okay already, Eddie! Jesus, now you sound like you wanted to eat 'em, for Pete's sake!"

There was a silence. At last Eddie said, guiltily, "You know what I wanted to do? I…I wanted to suck on them."

"Oh, Christ!" Kevin shot. "That's *wild*, Eddie; I mean like really, *really* wild! You know what that is? That's just plain *sick*, man. Sick! I mean, what are you, some kind of mama's boy?"

"Heck no! You're just saying that because you didn't get to squeeze it like I did. That's because she liked *me*. She didn't like you and she didn't like Mike. *She liked me!* She let *me* squeeze her tittie!"

"Okay! Big freaking deal, mama's-boy retard. I've heard all about it, you little sicko. Now why don't you just shut up and go to sleep."

To Kevin's surprise Eddie clammed immediately, and was soon snoring softly and rhythmically. This snoring had a lullaby effect on Kevin. His own respiration gradually slowed until his breathing was keeping perfect time with Eddie's. The monotonous chirring of crickets had the same quieting effect, and he was just about to sink completely under their spell into solid slumber when he was roused by a subtle change in Eddie's breathing. The soft snoring was gone, replaced by a quickening tempo in the boy's now-gritty respiration. Kevin unhappily let his eyelids come unglued and turned his head, seeing—poorly because of the darkness, and because his glasses were off—that Eddie was struggling with something in his sleeping bag.

"What's wrong, Eddie?" he mumbled thickly.

Eddie froze. "*Wrong*?" he asked tightly, after a moment of uncertainty. "Nothing...nothing's *wrong*. I—I have to take a leak, that's all. Be right back." He got out of his bag and stole into the bushes. Kevin yawned and prepared to drift off, but a sharp rock directly under his head had to be removed first. He flicked it away, massaged the sore spot on his head with a thumb, shifted in his bag...and found that now he couldn't sleep. He fingered the new leather of his vest approvingly for a while, wondered what was taking Eddie so long. He yawned again, cracked his knuckles. Grew worried. Wide awake, he listened intently, but there wasn't a sound. Even the crickets had ceased. He lay on his back with breath held, seeing indistinctly the immense field of uncountable still white stars, listening. The night was a warm, heavy shroud, and it made Kevin feel the world was holding its breath right along with him. Then Mike snorted loudly in his sleep, smacked his lips. Kevin, stepping silently from his bag, realized they had neglected to bring flashlights. Not bothering to don his glasses, he snatched a box of strike-anywhere matches and slipped between the bushes he'd peripherally witnessed Eddie passing. It was likely that Eddie had up and got himself lost, though Kevin couldn't imagine why his friend should wander so far from camp to urinate. He struck one of the long stick matches on his Levis and held it sputtering beside his head, hoping Eddie would see it. The light, so near his eyes, blinded him momentarily, so he raised his arm. The flame burned his fingertips. Kevin dropped the match with a whispered curse and crammed the fingers in his mouth. He listened. Total, utter, all-encompassing silence. Then a car passed on the road, its headlight beams swinging through the trees as the car rounded a curve. The brief glimpse chilled him:  the area was cemetery-still. But he'd seen a clearing, perhaps a hundred yards away at the top of a rise. He could get his bearings. Kevin struck another match and made for the spot, but, after five more matches, realized that somebody had managed to spirit away the clearing even as he was in the act of hiking to it. That was enough to stop him dead. Kevin struck no more matches. An owl flapped by like a huge clumsy bat, making him jump. He followed with his eyes, turning on his toes, and when he looked back down realized he was hopelessly lost. Immediately he began striking matches in quick succession, turning his head in every direction. He was just opening his mouth to call for help when he heard something that caused his nuts to race right back up their inguinal canals...*from fifteen yards behind came the sound of loud, excited breathing, hoarse and shallow*. Intense. Mike's words drifted whispering into Kevin's mind, as if the words, too, were desperately afraid of being discovered:  *He breathes real fast and loud, so you'll know when he's coming.* Kevin spun around. *You'll know when he's coming.* The Hook! And *there*, dressed to appear as an innocent shrub, crouched a wicked, scheming old pervert with one cunning eye and one trembling hand, his face and shoulders cleverly made up to simulate the black, star-speckled sky. His telltale respiration grew more rapid while Kevin gaped, transfixed. The leaves shook all around him, faster and faster, as he gathered himself to spring, and Kevin could now see that The Hook was carrying his notorious satchel, which, from where the boy was standing, presented the illusion of being merely a large rock. Kevin's left wrist throbbed with an imagined taste of the phantom pain to come. And just as The Hook's fiendish breathing reached a frenzied peak, Kevin gave vent to a mighty bellow of raw terror. He whirled round to flee and heard, after a second's pause, an answering shriek and tumultous clamor as The Hook set after him. Kevin ran blindly, snarling, screaming and waving his arms in front of his face, straight into a thick growth of brambles. The barbs gouged him, tore his arms and face, ripped long rents down his new vest. As he scrambled free he heard The Hook's demonic, gasping breath closing in. The fiend came crashing through the brush. Even in his panic Kevin could picture the old man dementedly swinging his long, wickedly curved hook like a sickle, cackling, muttering to himself, his one malevolent old eye fixed purposefully on the flushed nape of Kevin's naked neck. The scrambling boy tripped on a root and pitched face-first into the dirt, rolled onto his back with his arms protecting his face, expecting to feel the gleaming tip of the chromed hook come ripping into his throat. But there was nothing, only a heaving silence. He got to his knees, licked his lips. Not far off he could now hear hoarse, rapid breathing. Kevin sobbed, and the breathing stopped. Paralyzed with dread of this new silence, he *felt* The Hook's roving old eye, bulging with bloodlust, impatiently scan every leaf, every stone. The stillness was all-suffocating, as that old eyeball sent out an invisible beam of pure malice, passing over Kevin, moving on, and then, with dazzling speed, whipping back to impale him. Kevin croaked out one terrified vowel-thick syllable. Immediately the ghastly respiration sounds began, sobbing with monstrous lust and gore-anticipation. With a soundless shriek Kevin bolted, only to stumble in circles for what seemed hours, getting scratched and scraped to pieces, growing delirious, expecting one of The Hook's bizarre cleaving devices at any moment. At last he stopped and looked all around. Every shadow appeared to lurk, preparing to pounce. Rasping, exhausted breathing was in his ears. Wheezing painfully, he sank halfway to his knees, supporting himself by leaning on a blackened, scaly tree stump. And *there*, lifeless on the ground before his raving eyes, lay a limp, blood-smeared hand, palm up, the broken and hapless fingers splayed in dreadful self-commiseration. Kevin tasted vomit, his heart lurched as he tried to rise. With a final gasp he fell into the dismembered arms of the dry, dry shrubbery in a dead, dead faint.

# Chapter 7

## Planet Of The Humans

When Kevin opened his eyes the sun was already high in the sky, the air sizzling. His breath seared the walls of his nostrils, his mouth tasted of dirt and blood. He sat up slowly, totally disoriented, and gingerly picked his vest free of a thorny shrub.

On the ground by his knee was a withered gray workman's glove, its torn palm and fingers stained with axle grease. Kevin groaned and picked it up, but dropped it immediately as a small green lizard leaped out and vanished in the undergrowth. The boy looked around groggily, his neck taut and sore. Nothing for miles but dry, colorless shrubbery.

He stood and squirmed free of the vest, draped it over his shoulder, and began shambling about like a hopeless castaway. There was no real shade to speak of; trees were stunted, branches peppered with blanched, furling, and brittle leaves. He recalled tales of folks trapped in similar hells, wandering in circles, sucking on rocks, staggering aimlessly until the cruel sun pounded them into twisted heaps of scaly red garbage for the carrion birds.

A distant voice was calling his name. He called back, his own voice a painful croak. Mike and Eddie began shouting his name in unison, like a chant, until Kevin stumbled up, miserable and exhausted. He sucked Mike's canteen dry when they reached camp.

"Got chased by The Hook," he gasped. "Right behi...he

was right behi…he was right behind me."

Eddie's eyes ballooned in their sockets. "You too? He chased me for miles last night."

They blinked back and forth; each boy a mirror image of scrapes and scratches, of dirt and dust, of tangled hair clotted with burrs and twigs and bits of leaves.

And Mike was roaring with laughter.

Kevin looked his body up and down. His Levis were torn in a dozen new places, his feet leprous with scabs. Puffs of dust accompanied his every movement. He limped over to his sleeping bag and flopped down, rolled a joint, gently stepped into his boots. He lit the joint, slurped smoke up his silly face, and said, simply:

"Let's go."


joon 30 1967
jime
thu milz pas lik majik onle 30 mor 2 go an wel b in santu mureu an thn its onle 50 2 san loois obispo wich iz wut we figyr 2 b thu hafwa poent
nawt bad 4 3 daz ridn
akchoole frum san loois obispo awn its u lawt mor fr an u hek uv u lawt mor rugud but at thu r8 wr goen wel hav u kupl uv daz 2 chek owt thu h8 sen b4 we dig thu big gig
as uzooul nuthen but good vibz
iv bin metn u lawt uv groov ppl awn thu rod an tripn with thu chix hoo r awl bilt 2 thu hilt an hawt 2 trawt
mi bix bin holdn up lik u rel champ jime lik it kood mak it kler ukraws thu kuntre
edz iz dooen ok 2 but this mornen aftr we gawt in2 lawmpawk mix bik rele hasld him
yoo no that bolt wut keps thu handulbrz std awn u 10spd
wl thu nut kam loos awn mix bik wn he wuz ridn an he flipd hdfrst ovr thu frunt wel an praktikle skrapd hiz fac awf but hez ok jus soopr growche
wl thats awl 4 now jime hop yr lagz btr an awl that
tl awl mi budz i sd hi
rit yoo soon

kevin

"I can't *wait* to get back to the coast," Eddie shivered. "These flyboys are giving me the total creeps."

Another jeep full of enlisted men from Vandenberg Air Force base was slowing down. One of those young men blew Kevin a very wet kiss, another showed the boys a limp wrist and pouting lips.

"Hey...*sweet*-heart!" the driver called to Eddie. "Why don't you introduce me to your girlfriend (meaning Kevin) there? Does she like it from the front or the rear?" The others roared with laughter.

"Just you try it," Kevin mumbled, "and I'm gonna kick your asses all over your faces."

"What's *that*, honey?" a voice shot. "*What*'d you say, hot lips?"

The jeep stopped at the curb. The driver snarled, "Want some Free Love, butterball? Huh? How about eight inches of hot O'Henry? Think you can handle it all?"

And from the rear seat, another voice: "Don't you trolls ever take a bath?"

"Mind your own fucking business," Mike said, too grumpy to keep his mouth shut for long. His face was scarlet with Mercurochrome in a dozen places. An extra large bandage covered the scrape on his nose.

*"What was that?"* cried one of the men. He made to step out.

The boys cowered, but just then another jeep, this one containing a major general driven by his orderly, pulled alongside the first.

"You men move along there," the officer said tersely.

The men in the jeep immediately pulled away. The major general, a stocky white-haired man with heavy jowls, looked at the boys curiously through the thick lenses of his severe spectacles. His stare went on and on, growing darker by the moment. At last he said, "Harumph," looking as though he'd just swallowed something bitter and indigestible. He spoke sotto voce to his orderly, and together they laughed uproariously. Both stared back at Kevin, who was limply gaping at the twin flash of the general's stars. The orderly put the jeep in gear and drove away, his passenger craning his head over his shoulder to study the boys as if they were extraterrestrials.

"I mean it!" Eddie said. "I want out of here!"

They were in the town of Orcutt. It was three in the afternoon. The boys followed the highway grimly, keeping as far into the road's shoulder as possible. Convoys of jeeps and flatbed trucks from the nearby base were thick on the road, and from nearly all came derisive shouts. By five o'clock they had only covered fifteen miles, as they had to constantly pull over to avoid clouds of dust and flying gravel. Several jeeps deliberately swerved close. Not until seven o'clock did the hellish flow abate somewhat, and by then they were dusty, dehydrated, and dog-tired.

Much of the area was given over to depleted farmland, now mostly fields of withered weeds. Several dirt roads led off the highway, winding between ancient sycamores and dry rock gullies. Few of the decrepit houses appeared to be occupied, and, as twilight advanced, the dwellings grew dark and haunted-looking, the windows black and forbidding. The boys took a few of these unfrequented old roads out of curiosity, shattered windows in the deserted, looming houses, battled one another with clods of dirt. It was as they were firing rocks at rusty cans alongside one of these dirt roads that they became aware of a vehicle slowly bouncing their way, its headlights cutting uneven swaths in the crepuscular distance. Eddie, Mike, and Kevin stood stock-still, human scarecrows; one tiny, one scrawny, one fat—something in the low rattle of the engine striking them as ominous and probing. When the vehicle neared they saw it was an Air Force jeep.

"Down!" Mike said, too late. The jeep bumped to a stop, not twenty feet opposite where they lay.

"Well, well," drawled a familiar voice, "yes indeedy deedy-do. If it ain't them same three ripe sweethearts, and just when I'm feeling all hot and horny." Somebody belched. A beer can dropped from the jeep and rolled away clattering.

The boys rose slowly. Eddie was trembling. "Please, sir," he whimpered, "*please* don't hurt us. We don't want any trouble."

"Shit," Mike said, looking disgustedly at Eddie's cowering form. He addressed the six young men in the jeep straightforwardly. "Why don't you pricks just beat it. Scram."

There was laughter in the jeep. It was fully dark now, and the young men were huge and featureless. The hot engine ticked impatiently.

"Why, that's no way for a presentable young thing to talk," said a blur on the back seat. "Especially when she's just about to get her sweet little hippie ass kicked."

Another shape growled, "Why don't you kids ever get a haircut?" Although the delivery was full of rancor, this was a legitimate question.

"Oh, yes sir," Kevin said quickly. "We'll get haircuts, all of us. Right away."

"My ass," Mike spat. He stooped, grabbed a fist-sized rock from their arsenal, and hurled it just as hard as he could at the jeep. In amazing slow motion the windshield cracked, spiderwebbed, and disintegrated. Before the men could recover, the boys had hopped on their bikes and were tearing across the field toward a row of abandoned houses. The jeep's transmission bit into high gear. A correction in the shifting, and the jeep was in hot pursuit. Kevin felt its headlight beams scorching his back as he desperately drove himself on. On one side Eddie was crying and whining, on the other Mike was shouting instructions they were way too terrified to heed. Just as the jeep was upon them its rear wheels caught in a ditch. A whining roar, and the chase was resumed.

"*Over here!*" Mike screamed. They followed him to a gully's edge, over the lip and down. The gully was deeper than it looked; all three lost control of their bicycles and plummeted to the bed.

"My elbow!" Eddie cried, staggering to his feet and holding his hurt arm to his side.

"My neck!" Mike swore, dragging his bike up the opposite side.

"My God!" Kevin gasped: the jeep had come to a halt above them, and at least three of the young men were scrambling down with cries of rage and bloodlust. Kevin pushed his bicycle up the other side after his friends, nearly bowling over bawling Eddie in his haste.

It was a close scrape. The young servicemen ran hard, one on each frantically pedaling boy. Eddie's pursuer turned his ankle. Another stopped to assist, but the one chasing Kevin, as usual in the rear, kept after him, puffing and cursing, managing one solid punch to the right kidney.

The boys didn't even look back for five minutes, straining themselves to the very limit of their endurance, finally pulling their dusty bikes onto the porch of a sprawling, dilapidated two-story in the midst of a dozen drooping willows.

"Why," Kevin moaned, collapsing on the creaking old porch, "why'd you have to guide us down that stupid ditch, anyway?"

"Well, it was better than getting caught, wasn't it?" Mike panted. "Those guys are crazy or drunk or both. Besides, I didn't hear any better ideas." He turned on Eddie, still blubbering. *"Oh, for Christ's sake shut up, will you?"* He groaned and rubbed the back of his neck. "They woulda...they woulda killed us if they woulda caught us."

"I'm not crying," Eddie sobbed, wiping his eyes. He buried his face in his hands and wept convulsively. "I'm *not!*"

Kevin got to his feet and eyed the old house with a shudder. "Maybe we should get inside under cover."

This was no problem for Mike. The boy kicked on the door until the rusted old nails gave an inch, then tore a thick slat from the rotted porch railing and used this, with Kevin's assistance, to pry the door open a few more inches. One good solid kick from Kevin's sturdy boot opened the door another foot. They pushed to make enough space for their bikes.

Eddie hesitated, sniffling. "I don't like the looks of this place, you guys."

"Oh, c'mon, Eddie," Mike said soothingly. "We can be the Hardy Boys again. Just like we used to play, remember?"

But Eddie still lingered. "I'm too old to play Hardy Boys."

Mike sneered. "But you're not too old to play Flower Child, is that it? Shit. What a pantywaist." He edged in carefully.

Kevin shrugged sympathetically. He dug out another box of matches, pushed Mike's bicycle in, then his own, and finally Eddie's. "Hurry up!" Mike hissed, as though afraid of disturbing an unseen occupant.

"This—this is Trespassing," Eddie whispered, holding onto Kevin's vest as he squeezed in behind.

"Worse than that," Kevin muttered. "It's Breaking And Entering."

Mike scowled. "Sure beats Staying Outside And Getting The Shit Kicked Out Of You." He laughed harshly, testing his own courage. The laugh rang through the large front room and echoed faintly off the adjacent dining room walls.

Kevin struck a match, revealing blank walls and dusty floorboards. The sputtering light threw long black jittery shadows off the few sticks of furniture. "Spooky," he whispered. "I'll bet it's haunted."

Mike whirled on them, shouted "*Boo!*" and roared with laughter when they jumped. Eddie peeked from behind Kevin's elbow, still tightly gripping the vest. His teeth were chattering, his knees knocking. "Th-that's not funny, M-Mike," he whined, eyes wide and fearful. "D-don't do that again, okay? I'm not scared, j-just a little j-jumpy from that ch-chase."

"Okay, Eddie," Mike said, his voice rumbling. "I was only goofing around. C'mon." He led the way into the dining room. The remains of a crystal chandelier caught and scattered the light of another of Kevin's matches. The windows in this room, as in the front room, were boarded over. "I'll bet this place *is* haunted," Mike said. "It smells like somebody died in here and…*BOO!*"

This time Eddie gave a little shriek when he jumped. Now Kevin's teeth were chattering too. "Really, Mike," he said. "Don't be such an asshole."

"Aww…you guys are just pussies, that's all." Mike threw back his head and guffawed. He kicked a wine bottle across the floor to illustrate his disgust and disappointment. The bottle rolled, clattering loudly, up against a pile of fetid garbage next to an oblong closet. Kevin lit a match in time to reveal a couple of large brown rats scurrying from the pile with agitated squeals. The rats cornered themselves for a moment against the cabinets below the pantry, vanished into the woodwork.

Eddie shuddered. "Mice," he said in an oddly stifled voice. "Big mice."

Following the wall farthest from the pantry, they edged from the dining room into the spacious kitchen. Here it was much lighter, as the boards over a window had been knocked out by a previous explorer. Moonlight shone in sepulchrally, illuminating piles of trash and splintered wood. Kevin, instinctively moving to the window, peered out at the stars for comfort.

"Let's crash here!" Mike suggested, with the air of a decision already made. "It's warm and cozy and safe."

"Brrr," said Eddie. "And full of big hungry mice."

"Aw, what are you so darn—"

"Shush!" Kevin said. He crouched with his fingertips on the shattered sill, peeking out intently.

"What—what's the matter?" Eddie whispered, all ready to break into tears.

"Bats in his belfry," Mike diagnosed. When Kevin didn't respond, Mike sobered and cautiously crept up behind him, knelt to look over his shoulder. After a minute Eddie tiptoed over anxiously.

"What *is* it?" Mike hissed.

"I dunno," Kevin's reply was almost inaudible. "Something…" He strained his eyes until they burned with the effort. What was out there? A mountain lion? A stealthily padding ghost? In the coiling silence they all heard it: a throaty rumbling…the sound of something heavy rolling slowly…the crunching of small pebbles…excited whispering.

"It's those flyboys!" Mike sputtered under his breath, solving the mystery with uncanny rapidity. "That's their jeep rolling up in low gear. They're driving with the lights off."

"I wanna go home!" Eddie gurgled, the pitch of his voice rising alarmingly.

Mike turned quickly and placed a forefinger to his lips.

"Me too," Kevin said. He couldn't bear to look. "What are they doing now, Mike? Are they gonna pass us by?"

Mike had excellent night vision. "Couple of 'em are out on the ground," he reported. "It looks like they're following our tire tracks. Now one of 'em's got a flashlight. He's shining it on the ground. The light's swinging…toward the porch. Oh my God! Did anybody shut the front door?"

"I wanna go home!" Eddie whispered. Tears were rolling down his cheeks.

"Now he's shining the flashlight all around the house. He's pointing it at the—GET *DOWN!*" They crouched in a huddle as a beam of light lanced over their heads for an instant, played on the kitchen wall, vanished. There came a sibilant undercurrent…voices were whispering excitedly. The beam swung back to the kitchen window and remained there. The gentle thrumming of the jeep's engine was abruptly cut off.

Mike whispered, "We're cooked!" They got on their bellies and scurried to a doorway leading to the rear of the house, where they were presented with a choice of three rooms. With wordless consent they split up; Mike wiggling into a bedroom, Eddie choosing the playroom, Kevin making quietly for a jumble of rubbish in the laundry room. A door led outside, and Kevin was thinking of trying the knob when an instinct made him freeze. Listening intently, he made out footsteps crunching outside, quietly rounding the side of the house and proceeding toward the door. Kevin froze on all fours, head cocked, not breathing. A gentle rustling in the playroom as Eddie burrowed beneath a heap of moldy wallpaper, then utter silence. Finally the doorknob rattled slightly and turned a few degrees. But that was all. The lock's mechanism was rigid with rust. After a moment the footsteps crunched back around the house. Now there were voices at the front door. Kevin crawled to the pile in the corner, wormed behind a leaning infant's mattress stinking of old urine stains. He quietly pulled more trash over his legs just as the house echoed with an agonizing groan of bending nails: the front door was being forced wider. There was another interval of silence, but the boys could feel someone stepping lightly into the front room.

"Yoo-hoo…" cooed a voice musically, with a suave and malicious delight. "Anybody home?"

More silence. A soft creaking of floorboards.

"Why, looky here," marveled a different voice. "Three ten-speeds, just sitting here. Real nice bikes they are, too. Now I wonder who they might belong to." The whirring of a gear sprocket. Kevin's right hand, searching the floor for some kind of weapon, came up with a rusty trowel, its nose bent upward. He tensed.

Someone was in the dining room. The first voice called out softly, as though to a child, "Come out, come out, whatever you are." A crunching of trash underfoot. Then a full minute of absolute silence. Without any warning Kevin's little mattress was yanked away, revealing a black, towering form. "Ah *ha!*"

Kevin sprang up with all his force, slashed wildly at the black figure's head, felt the trowel rip into flesh, heard a scream almost in his ear. He stumbled through the doorway into the kitchen. A different man made to grab him. The boy side-stepped and slashed off-balance, missed and leaped out the window straight into the arms of two others. They threw him down and held him down. As he struggled to his knees he was kicked solidly in the ribs. Kevin doubled over. His glasses were torn from his face. One of the young men yanked back his hat and grabbed a handful of hair while the other twisted an arm behind his back. They dragged, kicked, and wrestled him to one of the willows. Each took an arm and pinned him against the tree, surprised at his strength.

A scraping sound at the kitchen window was followed by a dark form dropping to the ground, its left cheek sliced open and dripping blood. The shadow removed an Air Force shirt and held a lapel to the cheek. The lapel was instantly sopping. As the wincing form turned, it became recognizable as the jeep's driver. This man pulled the shirt away, studied the stains, held a sleeve to the wound. After glaring at Kevin he walked over calmly and slapped him across the face as hard as he could.

Kevin gasped as he struggled. A hard backhand caught him across the other cheek. The assailant grabbed his hair, yanked his head up viciously, and pressed his face up close. The voice was frighteningly calm, almost understanding.

"Pretty quick with the blade, aren't you, fat boy? Well I can be too!" He turned his head. "Johnny! Where's those shears?"

Johnny, a tall, gaunt, crew-cut blond, came padding up like a called dog. "Right here, Danny boy. You gonna clip this poodle?"

"That's right."

"Hot damn!"

At this Kevin began struggling fiercely, but a hard fist from Johnny caught him in the solar plexus. Kevin hawked and doubled over again, the fight out of him.

Johnny was grinning wildly, nursing his fist with his left hand. Danny, still holding Kevin by the hair, yanked his head back up with even greater force. He jerked Kevin's head left and right, snipping off large clumps on either side of his fist.

"Cut off his balls," suggested one of the men holding Kevin's arms. "If he's got any." He giggled insanely.

"You know something, Hank?" Danny commented in that same mellifluous tone, "sometimes that *ugh*ly thinker of yours comes up with some right dandy ideas." Danny grabbed Kevin's Levis at the waist and tore them open. Kevin screamed.

That scream was immediately followed by a delighted shout from the window. Another serviceman came forward, dragging Mike and Eddie by the scruff of their necks, one in either hand. Eddie, wailing hysterically, put up no resistance, the toes of his shoes plowing grooves in the dirt as he was hauled along, limp as a bit of washing. But Mike was flailing his arms and spitting like a cat. "Found these two girlies trying to hide," puffed the newcomer. "What you want me to do with 'em, Danny boy?"

Danny looked regretfully at Kevin and dropped the shears. He casually walked over to check out the latest development.

"My, my," he said. "Well, well." Mike spat in his face. Danny stepped back and all the young men laughed a nervous laugh. "Feisty son of a bitch, aren't you? You shouldn't have done that, little man. No sir, that was not wise at all." He wiped the saliva from his face, snapped his fingers, and barked, "Johnny! C'*m'ere!*" His eyes never left Mike, who seemed determined to stare him down. "But since you done it, little wise ass, I'm gonna hand you over to Johnny here. Now, Johnny's a real weirdo, you dig?" He twirled a finger by his temple. "Something missing upstairs. Don't know why the Air Force even accepted the guy; guess they're as crazy as he is. That right, Johnny?"

Johnny laughed harshly. "Guess that's right, Danny boy. Guess so." He grinned and cracked his knuckles.

Mike spat in Danny's face again. This time Danny didn't wipe. He said, quietly, "He's all yours, Johnny."

But as Mike was being transferred he kicked out hard, connected with Johnny's groin, and broke away. He bounded off like a jackrabbit. The kick only phased the big blond for a moment. "Johnny!" Danny shot. "Get him!" Johnny snarled and began jogging with long, measured strides.

Danny watched until Johnny was swallowed by darkness, then turned to face little Eddie, who quailed and sobbed traumatically. "Now, now," Danny said soothingly, "what's all the tears for, sweetheart?" Eddie withered beneath the big assailant's consoling tone, shaking violently from head to toe. Danny placed a gentle hand on top of Eddie's head, and the boy shrank further, his knees buckling. Eddie turned away, wincing through his tears.

"No need to cry, little one," Danny cooed. "There's no reason to be afraid. Not if you're a good boy. You are a good boy, aren't you? You won't make the mistake your friend made now, will you?"

"No sir," Eddie sobbed. "Oh no, only please—"

"Hush, hush, little one," Danny breathed. "Shh, shh. *Shhhhh.*" Eddie fought back his tears. "There, that's better; that's much better. We're going to be friends, aren't we, little one? Aren't we friends?"

"Yes sir," Eddie sniveled.

"Real good friends. Real close, *special* friends. Isn't that right?"

"Yes sir."

Danny caressed and patted Eddie's head lovingly, then gripped it tightly in his big palm, pulled it toward his crotch.

Eddie squirmed with revulsion. Danny laughed explosively and grabbed a fistful of hair. He held Eddie's head in that same demeaning position, made a motion to the man restraining Eddie, and snapped his fingers. That man now put an arm around the boy's bent waist. His other hand fumbled with the front of Eddie's Levis, found the snap and popped it open, roughly yanked the Levis down to Eddie's feet. Eddie, whimpering hysterically, tried to pull free, but there was no escaping the hold. His underpants were pulled down, exposing his trembling white buttocks to the night.

"Oh hush now, *hush!*" Danny said sternly. "Didn't you say we were friends? I thought you said we were friends." He savagely twisted up Eddie's head. Eddie froze in mortification, gritting his teeth against the pain of what he knew was to come. There was a grunt behind him. "Now, little one, we're going to show you just how friendly we can be."

But then the distant sound of a racing engine conveniently turned the worm. All the men stopped and looked in the sound's direction. Almost at the same time Johnny came stumbling around the side of the house, his eyes wild. "That little fucker got away from me," he puffed. "I couldn't catch him. There was a cop—"

The men sprinted for their jeep. Headlights blazed up the road. Just as the jeep roared to life a police car whipped through the willows in a cloud of dust. The dust washed in like fog, dimming the scene. A spotlight played over the area, found Kevin on his hands and knees. The jeep made a skillful turn around the police car and tore off across the field with its lights off. The solitary policeman jumped out, and Mike, Boy Wonder, scampered out the passenger side. The officer looked from the boys to the fleeing airmen with indecision. He pulled out his microphone, but before he made a call shouted, "Are you all right?"

Kevin nodded weakly. The officer made his decision, a very poor one. "Wait here," he said. "I'll call for help." He jumped back in his car and, absurdly, flicked on his flashing lights and siren and took off in hot pursuit. The boys watched the car slowly bucking and crashing across the field, headlamp beams slashing the night in all directions as the car lurched and bounced on tortured springs.

"Let's get out of here!" Eddie cried, zipping up his Levis. "They may come back!"

Kevin found his feet and rubbed his sore stomach. After pawing around in the dirt for a while he chanced upon his glasses, wiped the lenses with his shirt and peered through. Both lenses were intact, but his left eye was now peering through glass that was scratched and chipped. That didn't matter. He could see again.

Eddie came flipping head over heels across the porch like a tumbleweed in a gale. He picked himself out of the dirt hastily. "Let's go, Kevin," he panted, wringing his hands. "Let's hurry!" He darted back to the porch, caught his toe and skidded face-first over the wood.

Half a minute later Mike thumped off the foot-high porch on his bike, commanding, "Let's go, Kevin!" He cocked his head, said, "Hey, you're okay, aren't you?" Kevin, holding his arms in front of his face, was surveying the damage to his hair with rigid fingers. He pulled the hat's brim low on his forehead and ears.

"Yeah, yeah, I guess I'm okay." He couldn't mask the misery in his voice.

They heard Eddie before they saw him, calling, "Let's go, Kevin!" He flew off the porch on his bike, landing poorly. He and the bike bounced off in different directions. Eddie picked himself up slowly this time, his face almost obscured by dust. "Let's *go!*"

The police car was now about halfway across the field, still swaying and heaving. The jeep was long gone. The car's siren was off, so they could hear its frame rattling and crashing as it lurched along.

Kevin trotted into the house and walked his bike out, breathing a sigh of relief when he found his sleeping roll intact. He wasn't worried about the Air Force men returning; they couldn't possibly be that foolish. But he didn't like the idea of the police arriving and poking their snorting noses into the affair. Although quite unlikely, it was still possible they would go through his property and discover his contraband. That would bring this particularly unhappy adventure to a very nasty end.

The boys rode away hastily, diving into a ditch when a vehicle with whipping lights on its cab came roaring their way. But it was only a tow truck on its way to free the police car, stranded in the field with a busted motor mount and twisted tie rod.

"Man, that was neat riding in that cop car!" Mike

exulted as they rode on. "Who woulda thunk it! A cop smoking dope in the middle of nowhere! We musta been doing a thousand miles an hour! Guess you guys oughta be pretty thankful old Mike came to the rescue, huh?"

"Yeah, thanks Mike," Eddie said with all his heart. Then he was sobbing again. "They…they were gonna *punk* me, you guys! I just can't believe it. Why—why were they like that? Why?"

"I'm not surprised," Kevin said. "Brainwashed by the military. But I got that Danny dude a good one with that garden spoon. And I know it was rusty. I hope he dies."

"Yes sir," Mike sighed. "Good old Mike saved everybody's ass. That guy thought he was fast, but let me tell you, you gotta get up pretty dang early to beat *me* in a fair race."

"Why?" Eddie wanted to know. "Why'd they do that to me? It was sick."

"You got off lucky," Kevin said bitterly. "I got scalped." He lifted his hat.

Mike laughed so hard he almost lost control of his bike.

*"Why?"*

You'd expect even a prick to at least feign sympathy, but Mike was impossible. And the nasty, triumphant grin on Mike's face was the very last thing Kevin saw that night.

The next thing he knew, the morning sun was shining blindingly in his face.

# Chapter 8

## *Sacrilege!*

Kevin's equilibrium was so unstable he almost passed out in the act of sitting up. He spat dirt from his mouth.

Mike, who had turned to glower at the sound, looked away when he was sure Kevin had caught the look of contempt on his face. He waited. When he heard Kevin call his name he walked away pointedly, halting beside their standing bikes.

"Mike," Kevin repeated. He shook his groggy head, rested it in his sweaty, filthy hands.

There was a crash. Kevin looked up. Mike was poised with his fists at his sides, an expression of unbearable rage on his face. Kevin's ten-speed lay on its side. *"I'm sick of this crap!"* Mike screamed. He pointed a trembling, accusing finger at Kevin, kicked the fallen bike's front wheel and sent it spinning. "Every time we try to get going you pull this stunt and I'm sick of it!"

"What stunt?"

"You know what I'm talking about and don't pretend you don't!" He did a rude pantomime of an epileptic seizure, kicked Kevin's bike again. "Well, I'm sick of it, fatso! Y'hear me? Sick of it!" He kicked the dirt to help emphasize his words. "I'm *fed* up with your fucking *games*, man, and I'm *sick* of your ugly *face!*" He grew so distraught he began to weep, still kicking, alternating between the dirt and Kevin's bucking bicycle. "And after I saved your crummy life, too! You and your buddy-buddy friend," he charged, "have been planning this from the

144

beginning. You're ruining this whole trip and *I'm fucking sick of it!"* He gave one last hard kick at Kevin's bicycle, hurt his ankle and hopped away, heaving with sobs. Mike disappeared down the bank of a gully lined with wilted-looking willows.

Kevin shook his head languidly. Flies droned round his shoulders monotonously, lit on his throat and face. He let them be.

Eddie came scrambling up the gully's bank to Kevin's left, around the bend from where Mike was fuming. He trotted up to Kevin, showed him a scrabbling inch-long crawfish on either palm.

"Look, Kevin. Crawdaddies! There's a culvert around the bend. I found 'em half-in the run-off."

Kevin murmured dull approval. "What happened to me, Eddie?"

Eddie sat cross-legged in front of him and played with his crawfish for a minute. He said, quietly, "You pulled another one of those freaky numbers, Kevin. Like a couple days ago, remember? Only worse. I tried to do the bit with your glasses again, but you were shaking your head so hard I couldn't do it. And you bit my thumb." He showed Kevin his right thumb, still red and swollen. "But it's cool. It wasn't your fault. Anyways, after bouncing around for a few minutes you just froze up like you were dead. I'll be honest; I was scared. Then you flipped over on your stomach and started crawling away, making these spooky gargling noises. You kept crawling, right out into this field, but after a while you weren't going anywhere, just making the motions. Then you passed out, and we couldn't wake you up no way. So we had to crash here." He was quiet for a moment, moving the crawfish back and forth like cars on a highway. "Maybe you ought to see a doctor, Kevin," he said finally, helpfully.

Kevin hung his head. "D'you remember that first night we met, Eddie? When my old man busted us getting high?"

Eddie shuddered. "I try to not think about it."

"Well, I get the feeling that's when it all started. But it seems funny it should take so long before it started turning hairy like this."

"You never had these fits before...before *that* night?"

Eddie asked, still avoiding Kevin's eyes. He scooped out a clamber-trough for his crawfish, pushing dirt back into the trough when the little crustaceans reached the top, causing them to topple down and start back up.

"Not before we left. At least I don't *think* so. It's strange, though. I get the feeling I've been having these creepy blackouts for a while. You know, suddenly you find yourself thinking: 'Wow, man, did I just flash off, or am I imagining things?' You know what I mean."

Eddie shook his head. "Nope. Never happened to me. Um…you been taking downers, Kevin?" 'Downers' is a slang term for barbiturates, which are notorious for causing, among other things, loss of motor control and lapses in memory.

It was Kevin's turn to shake his head. "Uh-uh. You remember we agreed that downers aren't good for a true revolutionary's head? Only lowriders and rowdies fool around with that hard stuff."

Eddie was silent. He was thinking of that cold wet night last November, when he had smoked a fat initiatory joint with Kevin, and the two had grown painfully embarrassed while sitting cramped in the little wooden cubicle of the garage's loft. The atmosphere had grown electric, the silence echoing around them and making the walls seem even closer. There had been a thousand things to talk about, a whole burgeoning philosophy to discuss, and Eddie had been, already, toying with the idea of asking Kevin to accompany him up the coast during the summer. Still, that awful silence had grown and grown. The marijuana had made clumsy, unwieldy things of their tongues, made wounds of their minds. And that silence became heavy as water, clogging their mouths and ears, seeming to dim the single yellow bulb hanging like a hot scrotum between them from the loft's ceiling, which was so low Kevin had to slump forward as he sat. This thrust-forward posture made him appear about to deliver a sapient observation, when actually his head was as dense with that paralyzing silence as a filled goldfish bowl. And, like a goldfish circumnavigating its prison, Kevin's attention swam round and round, looking hopelessly for an object to focus on so he wouldn't have to meet Eddie's eyes. Belatedly, he remembered he'd planned on bringing a radio into the loft. At least, with a radio present, he could go through the spasmodic motions of pretending to be absorbed in some raucous rock and roll. And he knew Eddie was going through the same struggle, looking furtively about to avoid Kevin's eyes. Yet their eyes seemed almost to have a magnetic attraction, and, in their effort to break this influence, each boy had swiveled his neck, Eddie to the right and Kevin to the left, so that both were facing the thin rectangular doors of the loft. The symmetry, a door for each boy, had actually enhanced the trip rather than refocus it, and then, to make matters worse, rainwater had begun to tap and ping monotonously on the aluminum downspout. The embarrassment had wound up maddeningly, intensifying until it bore the imminence of a volcano on the brink of eruption. And suddenly both doors had been wrenched open to reveal giant Joe Mikolajczyk, his perspiration-soaked face insane with rage, his expression more like that of a voracious, prehuman predator than a contemporary man. The damning aroma of the marijuana smoke had burst out, and for several seconds no one had moved or breathed. Then, with a primeval roar, Big Joe had reached in, grabbed Kevin by the hair, and torn him bodily from the loft. Following through on the motion, he hurled the boy clear across the garage, doorless since Kevin's mother's one and only experiment with driving. Kevin's head had cracked hard on the cement floor. Now, this had been a very violent move, and had certainly done serious physical harm to Kevin, but the immediate psychological damage to Eddie had been greater. Eddie had gone colorless with shock, certain he was next to be attacked by this enormous, bellowing madman. He had screamed and screamed and screamed, and Joe had turned blind bulging eyes on him. But, even as Eddie's short life was passing before him, Big Joe had turned like some berserk, jumbo automaton, gasping and sputtering, and his eyes had centered on the whimpering target of his son as the boy weakly crawled away. With his fingers splayed, Joe's hands had become great mauling machines. Completely out of his mind, he'd crosshaired the laboring target and advanced thunderously.

"Maybe I *should* see a doctor," Kevin said hollowly, snipping the ribbon of Eddie's recollection.

Eddie nodded.

"Ummm...Eddie," Kevin appended, "I've got to get something together in my head...or I think I'm gonna lose it. Like, I know you do a whole lot of thinking, Eddie—no offense—so I figure you might be able to clue me in on something that's really bugging me way down deep. I guess it's maybe the biggest question there is."

"Sure, Kevin," Eddie said quietly. He smiled. "And no offense taken. You know I'll always help you out any way I can. We're brothers."

"Tight as they come," Kevin declared. "Eddie...I...I really don't understand what's going on in life; like why some people are so uncool when they don't have to be. Or why I've got to be having these stupid blackouts in the first place. I mean, what did I do so wrong that I should have to be punished? It would make more sense if it happened to, like, Mike for instance. Eddie, nothing, I mean *nothing* in life is right, or I've got it all upside-down. You're the only guy I ever met who even cared about whether things are right or not. The rest of just pretend we've got it together. So Eddie, I mean, like man-to-man now...in all this crazy crying out loud shit and more shit, I mean, Eddie, like, is there *really* a God?"

Eddie gave a short whistle in imitation of a falling bomb. "Just like that?" he asked. "All you want's a simple yes or no?"

"Actually," Kevin said, looking away, "I don't think yes or no would answer anything. I need to know what's going on, Eddie. Do I listen to that Jesus freak we ran into on the beach? Look what God made out of him. I don't wanna be some holy motormouth. And if you say there isn't a God that's okay too; it's not gonna do me in or anything. At least things might make some sense if I can look at it as all being out of control. But I can't go through life in the dark like this. Not any more. So...um...*is* there a God, Eddie?"

Eddie exhaled noisily. He looked down at the mindless labor of the crawfish as they struggled to overcome the lip of their trough, then at the way the fingers of his own hands were able to smoothly perform motions independently or in concert. He took a deep breath.

"Yes and no, Kevin. There is and there isn't. It's pretty complex, and it really hangs on how able you are to be objective, because all the answers to the universe—subjectively speaking—are negative ones. You ask the question: *Is there a God?* But that's subjective. Built into the question is a kind of spiritual plea. Honestly translated it would come out more like: *Is there a bigger reality than all this; a reality that'll make me feel better, so that if I sense my life is going nowhere maybe I can still hope it's really just going somewhere I can't see?* What it comes down to is that you're vocalizing a feeling, not a thought. I guess a good comparison, Kevin, would be love. Now, you take some guy or some chick who's in love. That feeling's as real as all get-out, right? And there isn't a whole bunch you can say that'll convince that guy or that chick that what's being experienced isn't rational. As a matter of fact, you're gonna find that that somebody *knows* the object of his or her affection is light years more attractive, in both subtle and obvious ways, than any of the other suddenly half-assed specimens he or she used to dig—even though this new loved one may have never rated a second glance before. And it'll be a waste of time trying to be objective with either lover. The lover 'knows,' and feels he or she can see qualities which you, in your objective ignorance, are blind to. You see where I'm coming from? Love isn't reasonable, it isn't objective, and it isn't honest. It's a process, a response, a reaction. The brain has been saturated with hormones, and the lover is operating according to a program that'll make the guy or chick *feel good* when behavior is conducive to procreation, and *feel bad* when the behavior frustrates the process. Faith is also a part of this process; only it's self-preservation instead of procreation that's running the program. The big difference here is that the brain has developed to the point where we're conscious of our mortality and our insignificance, and so we've got this, like, new and unique horror of our impending demise—something separate from the brain's basic job, which is to get us to survive the physical environment. It's *abstract consciousness*—the newly acquired ability to be aware of non-concrete things like justice, order and impermanence—that gave birth to ideas like a deity and a devil, and to concepts like good and evil. So faith is a reaction to a threatening situation; only the threat is abstract, not concrete. God only exists when necessary. Put his focus back on the real world, and the most religious of men has a brain working like anyone else's. So you see, faith isn't objective at all. It's a response to hormones, just like love is, and it's just as important, and just as foolish, as love is." Eddie spread his hands. "I hope you won't want to shoot the messenger, Kevin, but...God just doesn't exist. The super-natural is a product of imagination." Then he went on eagerly: "Nothing *really* exists, Kevin, even though we use words, like *nothing*, for instance, implying the existence of a *thing*. But there isn't. I don't exist and you don't exist, despite the impressions. Every 'thing' is a process, or actually an aspect of countless processes, all taking place far too rapidly for anyone to discern. The bottom line is that you have to deal with reality in verbs instead of nouns, and that's flat-out impossible, given the fact that organisms react with the environment at the sensory level. Abstract consciousness is something relatively new in nature, Kevin, and people will learn to deal with it in good time. I mean, try to imagine a spider with a conscience. Or a lizard. Or a barracuda. They don't murder or rape; they just kill and screw. And they sure as heck don't dwell on penetrating questions concerning morality, ethics, or some kind of Great Lizard in the sky. So you're not gonna find any crazy or despondent spiders. But to answer the question truthfully: 'God' is a concept. Yet it's a concept that's as viable as the neediness of the question."

"But Eddie, how can you say nothing exists, when a blind man can see all the things that *do* exist? Or at least he can feel them. I'm not saying you should be able to see or feel God, but I know I'm sitting on something solid; and that that's my boot there, and that inside my boot is my foot, and so on. And I can see you, right in front of me. Or are you trying to tell me you're a ghost?"

"Pretty much," Eddie said eerily. "An instantaneous ghost, or a series of instantaneous ghosts, that is, each a microsecond removed from the last. But are you really so sure our ghosts are 'sitting on something solid,' as you said? Let's take it logically, Kevin. A rock, for instance. You see a 'thing,' right? But you break it down and you've got a whole bunch of pebbles. More 'things.' Let's keep going. Take one of those pebbles, and you break it down to a whole bunch of grains. Break a grain down and you get dust. Break down a speck of dust in your head, Kevin. Keep going. You'll get down to the molecular level. Then what? What's a molecule, Kevin? It's a process, a bonding of atoms. And an atom isn't a 'thing' at all; it's also a process, a force. So all you really have is an accretion of processes and subprocesses masquerading as matter."

"But if I can't see or feel an atom, how come I can see and feel 'em when a whole bunch are stuck together?"

"You can't, Kevin. You keep forgetting an atom isn't a thing. Any more than a billion atoms equals a thing. Try to see an atom as a verb. What's happening is this: the attraction between atoms is resistant to any force less energetic than the bond. *It's this resistance that seems to be substance.* Matter is really energy. But you've got to go a long way to get to a speck of dust."

"I'm not trying to argue with you, Eddie," Kevin said bravely. "But none of that proves anything. Why can't we just say, y'know, that God decided to put everything together with atoms?"

Eddie's eyes twinkled. "Kind of a cosmic erector set? Neat! But a whole lot easier to just breathe life into nostrils and refabricate a rib. We all do love a good magic show every now and then."

"Then who *did* start it, Eddie, and when?"

"Nobody started it. Because it didn't start. And it doesn't end. That's, in a nutshell, the whole trip where this business of trying to figure out how everything got this way gets freaked out. People instinctively start out with a model of a void, you dig? And then they in effect say, 'Okay, now how does everything come from nothing?' So they've gotta throw in this deity, y'see, and—never mind the fact that the same problem about the deity's origin remains—and let the deity do all the work, then say it's beyond our ability to comprehend further and just rely on faith. Oh yeah, groovy man, and hallelujah. Problem solved. The brain is so dependent on sensory input that it barfs up any idea it can't put in a box. What people can't deal with, and don't *want* to deal with, is that the whole analytical process is off to a false start *when* it starts. 'Quit picking your nose, dear reader, and check this out: *inactivity is a physical impossibility.* Peace, 'nothingness,' void, 'absolute zero' *cannot occur!*' That's what I'd say if I was, like, writing a book and there was a cheese-eater out there who really wanted to know what's going on instead of picking one of the tunnels in this ant farm we call enlightenment. Biology, chemistry, physics…they're all the same subject.

"And this junk about finding a start point. Sure, maybe there was a 'Big Bang.' But that's not a start. It's a hiccough. So we're prey to this premise that the cosmos somehow had to 'start' at a certain 'time,' and I guess infer it has to 'end' at a certain 'time.' And that this 'start' took effect at a specific 'place.' And now a drum roll…a-a-a-and…*trip*: 'when' is just another convention, like 'where,' which we've come up with to orient ourselves! *Time*, Kevin, is also a *concept*; but it's just as useful as, say, drawing a line on a map to create a border, or saying the sun rises when it's really the world that's turning, or claiming what's above us is up, when the Australians would swear it's down. But…there was no 'Prime Mover,' Kevin. That's part of the problem. People are mortals, and mortals just can't imagine things without a birth and a death, a beginning and an end, a cause and an effect. Like I said, the brain's job is to deal with the plain environment. It freaks out when it comes down to paradoxes."

"Too trippy;" Kevin said, slowly shaking his head, "much too trippy. I mean, like, how can you say there's no time? There was a yesterday, wasn't there?"

"And what came before yesterday?"

"The day before yesterday."

"And the day before that? And the day before *that*? And so where does it all 'begin?' On a first day? Well, what came 'before' this first day? Yesterfirstday? And do you think atoms respect our calendars? Or how about space? Pick an end or a beginning and you're stuck with the same problem. What's *beyond* these hypothetical points? Obviously 'end' and 'begin' are concepts, just like in and out and up and down and over and under and on and on and on. Everything's relative to the subjective observer."

"Um…" Kevin said. "So then, Eddie, I mean what are we *here* for? What's it all about? There's gotta be, like, some kinda purpose for everything. There's just gotta be, Eddie. Eddie…Eddie, what's the meaning of life?"

"Same deal," Eddie said. "Concepts again. Why, Kevin, *why* does there *gotta* be a meaning, and a purpose, and all that? Some kind of security blanket for your self-preservation instinct? Like I said, the brain will have to adjust to abstract consciousness eventually. All that rap about predestination and chosen people and good and evil is just a bunch of garbanzo beans. You're here because your mom and dad got horny, just like all the moms and dads before them, and all the moms and dads to come. But just because there's no high-falutin' purpose and grand design or whatever, it doesn't mean we can't organize our lives around inspired ideas of our own.

"The great challenge of existence, Kevin, is for all of us to be quality human beings who embrace deep, positive values. In other words, to live exactly as if there really *is* a God. We can still make a commitment to behave decently, without having to bow and scrape and genuflect and supplicate. We don't have to trash our brains; we don't have to turn into a bunch of hands-wriggling dildos shouting hosanna, as if the universe had ears or something. We've got a real obligation to be humane and wise and self-restraining, *simply because it's beneath our dignity*, collectively and individually, to let our appetites lead us around on a leash. And *not* because we think it's gonna get us a ticket into some happy hereafter. That attitude makes religion into a sort of holy bribery.

"What's rough is that honoring principle means saying *no!* to some very strong and very basic drives, throughout your lifetime. Do you resist the instinct to exploit because it's profitable to? Of course not. The thief gains, the liar outmaneuvers, the weasel scores. The man of principle gets zilch. So why not be smart like the thief? Why not grab whatever you can get your hands on? Well, when the opportunity's there it *can* be tough to stand tall, but the trip is you've got to say: 'because I'm *not* a thief, because I'm *not* a liar, and because I'm sure as hell no motherfucking weasel! I'm *better* than that.' But wait! I know there's no God. There's nothing to punish me for living contrary to the Bible's teaching: Far out! I can get away with all *kinds* of shit! But no…oh no…I can't be a common pig and live with myself. I've got to be my own god and guardian; respect myself, respect my mind, and believe that all the brutal instincts urging me on are not in mandatory control. *My mind must drive my body, not the other way around.* Y'see, Kevin, everybody *knows* what's right and what's wrong. They *know!* It doesn't take a genius or some fuzzy sage to define morality, or correct ethical behavior, or proper comportment in any sense. It takes guts, and it takes honesty, and it takes sacrifice. It means admitting the truth, but it doesn't mean the truth is something you're supposed to *feel good* about. Is that digable? It means, like, you know, 'I *want* this.' Okay? But that's not my mind, that's my hormones. Just because I feel that want, that doesn't mean I have to be, like, mesmerized. I *appreciate* that want. Or that want might be an urge against somebody else. It's just as selfish. And so I might feel, 'I *hate* him,' or 'I'm *wounded* by her,' or '*they* are inferior.' These are instincts, and the instincts are there because, way down at the genetic level, nature is leading me to respond aggressively or passionately to preserve my tribe, or to perpetuate certain sexual qualities, or to claim my stake. And I don't gotta give up that claim, or spurn that cute little chick who turns me on, or, for that matter, love and respect that creep who gets on my nerves, *just because* I happen to know that what I suppose is a thought is really a feeling. I've gotta ride that beast, and tame it so I'll never end up regretting being carried along by some momentary impulse. I don't want anybody to be hurt by my actions, even if he's got it coming. And I don't want to be in possession of anything I don't deserve, no matter how much it may appeal to me. So, like it or not, for the most part I'm gonna have to go without. And that makes me a loser. Take my word for it, Kevin, it's no fun being a determined, self-made have-not in a world of greedy grubbing gophers.

"And I'm not just talking about not being a criminal, or about not being immoral. There has to be something higher in your outlook than the real world. Check out Mr. Suit-and-tie, for instance, in all his little cocktail party gobbledygook bullshit, with his neat and clean façade and his pretty car, his home and his credit cards; all the plastic crap he wraps himself up in to let his boot-licking competitors know how smarmy-ass successful he is. But who *is* he? Nobody knows. *He* doesn't even know! All his adult life he's been busting his ass to turn himself into a grinning mannequin out of some J.C. Penney catalogue. He's done a good job of it, too; at least as good as his buddies. Not a hair's out of place, and his car's so clean you won't find a bird turd on it. And he smiles at just the right time, and goes *'Har har har'* when he's supposed to. Good little mannequin. And then this prissy puppet will see some *real* person, who's got his head into something deeper than appearances, and go, 'Jesus! What a jerk! Lock the doors, honey, he might be after our best china.' What would Mr. Suit-and-tie think of Socrates, or Ghandi, or Jesus of Nazareth for that matter? Buncha bums, that's what. And can't that Jesus guy afford a haircut? *Sheesh!* Creeps and losers; not like him—not like Mr. Suit-and-tie on his way to drop off Johnny and Marge at the P.T.A. meeting before he grovels up to J.B. for the big Moneysucker contract. Life by the book. I tell you, Kevin, I'd rather die than put on a suit and a tie! Serious as all shit. And that's not only the Movement's philosophy, it's my personal vow. And…when I die, if some mortician even tries to suit me up…I swear to your God I'll reach outta my coffin and stuff the phony fucker in there in my place!"

"Ah-ah-ah," Kevin said, wagging a finger. "What happened to all our groovy dignity, Eddie?"

Eddie blushed and looked down at his tightly locked hands. "You're right, Kevin. I shouldn't let it get to me. It's just, y'know, when I see all these Mr. Suit-and-tie clones coming off the conveyor belt, with their little briefcases and wristwatches, it makes me want to puke. It's like they're all giving the finger to human potential."

Kevin nodded sagely. "I'm hip. Sometimes when I see 'em filing in and out of the bank building I think I'm having a flashback; like I'm seeing trails. They've all got newspapers under their arms and sticks up their assholes. But then I think, 'at least they're going into the bank. They must be doing something right'."

155

"They sure are, Kevin. They're doing everything *exactly* right. They've got phoniness down to a science and butt-kissing down to a fine art form. I mean, it's their fucking *careers* for Pete's sake! They know, from checking out their peers, that if they march in time it'll pay off."

"Sorta like your dog story, huh, Eddie? The one about it's the dogs who do the tricks who get the goodies."

"Same animal," Eddie nodded. "But we got off track somewhere. What were we talking about before Mr. Suit-and-tie?"

"You were saying, like, there really isn't a God, but that's no reason to behave bad."

"Right," Eddie said. "Right. But it goes deeper than that. I mean, it's *accepted* that there's a God, see, and that's the *reason* we shouldn't behave like pigs…because we'll be punished later on. There's no proposition implying we should behave with dignity simply because it's unconscionable not to. There's gotta be a threat or a promise thrown into the equation to make it work. And, since the whole idea behind religion is to better people against their basic drives, I always get bent out of shape denying the physical side of the issue while defending the ethical side of it. If it wasn't for the simple fact that I don't believe in God I'd have to say I'm a heck of a lot more religious than most of these Bible Thumpers I've run across. Anyways, when I'm trying to separate these aspects—the physical and the ethical—it's *so* difficult," Eddie said uncomfortably, "to put it in words that won't be taken offensively, or to get the point across in context. Look…The issue really isn't: 'Is there a God?', or: 'Is faith good or bad?', or: 'Well, then just how the heck *did* we get here?', or anything about who's right and who's wrong and why. As simply as I can put it, the real question is this: *Why* do people automatically accept the notion of a supreme being? Or even waver between faith and doubt? Why isn't the idea of a conscious universe laughed at outright? You'd expect a retarded six-year-old to wonder if you were nuts or just putting him on with rap like that, yet the concept is universally accepted. Why? It's absolutely silly, but that doesn't seem to make the slightest difference."

"Okay," Kevin said. "Then why?"

"I really have to guess at it," Eddie returned, almost apologetically. "I've never read anything about it from that end. It's like there's some built-in taboo, like you strike a really deep nerve. It's like…uh…y'know how it is when you question the virtue of somebody's girlfriend, or his mother, or his country? Or, if the bond's strong enough, it could even be his school, or the crowd he hangs with. Maybe just a friend of his, or his pet goldfish, or sometimes it can be anything at all that he *feels* strongly about. And I don't mean insulting whatever he loves, I mean asking an honest, legitimate question, or just pointing out some little flaw. It's like…BAM: 'that's my mama you're talking about!' or, 'hey buddy, if you don't dig this country then why don't you just get the hell out!' You know what I mean? You hit that nerve. And God's a big part of that nerve."

"Well?" Kevin said. "What do you expect? You want somebody saying things about your mother?"

"Of course I don't, Kevin. But if what he's telling me's logical I'm gonna wanna know the facts. And the way you put it: 'saying things,' is just what I'm trying to get at here."

"Like what?"

"Like hitting that nerve, like crossing that line. It's all: 'I love my mother and my family and my country and I stick up for my friends and I have faith in my God and I fucking refuse to hear anything about them that doesn't jibe with my feelings.' It's *taboo* to objectively analyze your bonds. And…" Eddie sighed, "why not? Will the truth make your love stronger, or make you more patriotic?"

"Truth," Kevin interjected, "is what everybody agrees on. And people have all agreed there's a God for…for…*forever*. And people have always stuck up for their friends and fought for their country. Eddie, you can't say everybody's always been wrong about everything until you came along. The whole trip wouldn't have been around as long as it has if it was half as dumb as you say it is. It's gotta be based on something real."

"That's the bummer," Eddie said. "*What's* it based on? It's practically a law of life that if you, like, *accept* a given premise as fact, then anything that follows in support of that premise must be fact, too. *The premise is everything*, Kevin. If something's established by society as truth, or as being good, and it just keeps getting hammered home, eventually it'll be taken for granted. Let me throw another analogy at you. Let's suppose, for example, that it was just a *given* that human beings were put on this planet by some Martian super-race, millions of years ago. Okay? As silly as that sounds, just so's I can make my point, we'll pretend that you and I and everybody else grew up in a world where our money says, 'In Martians We Trust' on it, where principle is a matter of 'Martians, mother, and country,' and where *things Martian* creep into our everyday language, such as, 'For the love of Mars!' or 'Good Martian, man, what's got into you?' and so forth. We can even throw in some Son of Mars sent to Earth to die for our sins, and maybe make Pluto into Hell. Whatever. The point is, if this premise is simply taken for granted as the truth by everybody, without serious inquiry, then for all practical purposes, *it becomes the truth*. And if you or I or anybody else say, 'But wait a minute! What Martians? I don't see any Martians,' well, then you and I and everybody else who demanded some evidential account-ability are either crazy, evil, or blind. 'But you must *believe*,' the Martiavangelists will tell us. 'You must have faith!' And so here we are, gone astray, faithless and damned, sick sinners who'll never go to Mars after we die. And it just freaks people out. What's *wrong* with us? Why do we fight the 'truth?' Do we *want* to go to Pluto when we die, or something? 'But look,' we answer, 'Mars is a dead planet. There are no Martians. What gives you the right to pronounce all this specious crap our natural history when it runs contrary to scientific evidence and to plain sense?' And what can a Martianist do but smile sadly and sigh and try to get it through our thick skulls...'Look,' he'll say, '*of course* you can't *see* any Martians, you silly fool. Martians are invisible! They're not like you and me, for Deimos-sake—they're Martians! And they're not just on Mars. They're *everywhere*, at all times, and they know what we're thinking; so you'd better get all those nasty unMartian thoughts out of your head right away, boy, or you're gonna end up a popsicle on Pluto for sure.' Eventually you become cynical to the max, and you realize an argument for sanity in Bellevue is just treading water, and that there's nothing you can say that'll effectively counter what society's been blathering for centuries.

What I'm trying to say here, Kevin, is that society has done a great job of programming. And it's positive programming. I guess if a white lie brings favorable results then all lying ain't necessarily a bad thing. But the lie itself, like laws and rules, shouldn't be exalted. Honest men and women are above all that. In other words, my friend, people who 'believe' in God are weenies: they're good pets. Here's your choice, Fido: There is a God, or there isn't a God. 'Believing' there's a God is just bursting with bennies. Immortality, redemption for all your sick behavior, being on the 'right' side, et cetera. But not having a God means a negation of all the above. Fido likes the taste of the former, therefore there 'is' a God. Munch munch. Only a really dumb pet would turn down a goodie like that. So people who 'believe' in God are smart and good, and people who don't are stupid and evil. What could be more obvious? But *don't you dare* ask the good dog to analyze the goodie! Don't you *ever* ask one of these white knights to describe their God, or define Him in any sensible way. They 'know,' and that's all there is to it. They'll stick their fingers in their ears and just start parroting the Gospel if you *dare* ask them to even *consider* the preposterousness of what they're jabbering. A universe that thinks? Man oh man, that's so asinine it's downright scary! *Thinking*, Kevin, is a process; a process that originates in a specific organ, the brain. Like the heart's an organ for pumping blood, and the lung is an organ for respiration. The cosmos can no more think than pump blood or breathe. 'God' is a product of the brain, not the other way around."

"But, Eddie," Kevin said, "I mean, how do you *know*? Maybe, just maybe, like…what if the universe *can* think, after all? What if there's another way of thinking you don't know about? Who can say how God's Head works, or what His whole trip is? Maybe He's invisible and put together in all kinds of different ways so that He doesn't *need* a brain to think. Maybe He doesn't breathe or have blood or *anything* like us. I mean, you don't *know*, Eddie. No offense, but can't you see how stupid it is to judge God when you don't know the first thing about Him?"

Eddie shook his head slowly. "You're right, Kevin. I'm stupid; and again, no offense taken. But all the maybes, what ifs, and just supposes you can dream up are just evasions. They're not answers. But I'll bite anyway. Fancy away."

"Huh?"

"I told you what I know, and you deserve your turn. So tell me, Kevin; tell me the first thing about God."

"What do you mean?"

"Well…what He looks like, for instance."

"He looks like God, Eddie. He's real big; I mean really, *really* big. And He's all white, with a big white beard, and muscles like Hercules."

"Pretty impressive Guy," Eddie said. "So where does He live, Kevin? What's His address?"

"God doesn't have an address, Eddie! Now you're being just plain dumb. God's *everywhere*." He looked up, furtively. "Up there."

But Eddie's eyes remained firm. "If He's everywhere, Kevin, why do you say He's 'up there?' Doesn't everywhere include 'down here'?"

"Uh-uh," Kevin said. "The Devil lives down here, underneath us, in Hell."

"The Bad Place."

"Real bad. I mean really, *really* bad."

"So God's everywhere but here. God takes up the whole universe, which is infinite, except for this flyspeck in the middle of nowhere. Why can't God get in here, Kevin?"

"Because the Devil won't let Him in, Eddie. The Devil's *evil*. He hates everybody and everything. But most of all he just hates God to pieces, because God wouldn't let him wear wings. So when he fell out of Heaven he couldn't fly and ended up falling and falling and falling until he landed here, where he turned into a snake who lived in an apple tree. Then, after God made Adam and Eve, well, the Devil talked Eve into eating an apple, which sort of made Adam go from holy to horny. And that got God super-pissed. But He was mad at the Devil, Eddie, not at Adam and Eve. That's 'cause God loves His children, no matter how many apples they eat. So to let Adam and Eve know He still loved them He decided to show 'em it wasn't cool to be all naked in the garden like that, and told Adam to put on a fig leaf. And ever since then the Devil's been causing trouble, on account of God outfoxed him with the fig leaf trick. Now the Devil lives down in Hell, and he spends all his time barbecuing people who couldn't get into Heaven, and trying to figure out trickier ways to get back at God."

"And you *believe* that?"

"Well...you gotta admit it makes a whole lot more sense than what you were talking about; what with a whole bunch of little atoms being stuck together and all that. Besides," Kevin said defensively, "I'm not saying it's like I believe it all the way. It's what my Sunday School teacher told me, and I don't thing they'd hire her just to lie to everybody."

"I wouldn't lie to you either, Kevin."

"Oh heck, I know you wouldn't, Eddie."

"So you don't have to worry about me handing you a line here. I only want you to accept my input because you're my friend—and because you asked me the question in the first place. You can believe me. I'm giving you the unadulterated upshot."

"Yeah, but...but there you go again, Eddie! It's that same attitude that gets people all pissed off in the first place. You can't say your opinion is right and everybody else's is wrong...and expect anyone's gonna respect your opinion. 'Cause all you're saying is you're so smart and we're so stupid. It's like, y'see, you don't *know* what it's all about after you die, Eddie, on accounta you ain't died yet! Can't you dig that? So when you say we don't go to Heaven, or that there's no ghosts or reincarburetion or any of that stuff, well, it's like that's your trip. That's your thing, and it's your opinion, and I don't wanna take it away from you. But you got no better idea than anybody else."

"You'll notice," Eddie said wryly, "that I'm not letting frustration get the better of me. Maybe this is just too simple for clarity, Kevin. Look, *I'm not giving you my opinion*, okay? Anybody can form any opinion he wants about art, or politics, or food—but not about the physical universe. Consciousness exists *because* we're alive; it's not some mystical entity your body plays host to, that just happily flits away after your body dies. It's part of your metabolism. What's after life? What's death like? Ask yourself: 'what was it like before I was born?'

and you'll have your answer. You weren't alive before you were born, and you won't be alive after you're dead. Therefore you won't be conscious after you're dead. It's like this 'out-of-body experience' stuff. You know what I'm rapping about here? You get all these traumatized geeks saying they were at death's door, see, and then suddenly they're looking down at their bodies and feeling all toasty-warm and being aware of this white light. This phenomenon is 'proof' of a soul or whatever. What seems to elude everybody is the fact that they're talking about it. They never died! What they went through is a subconscious experience; very much an 'in-body' thing. It's not my 'opinion' there's no God; it's your opinion there is. What's really happening is the nitty-gritty of nature: all the processes taking place whether consciousness is introduced into the picture or not. The rest is mysticism, animism, wishful thinking. Personification of the elements. It's all, like, a really profound and touching attempt to take the bare bones of reality and slap on some spiritual meat. But it's not honest. It's self-defensive, and *deliberately illogical*. Science, Kevin, isn't around to try to make anybody believe anything. Everything has to be proven one hundred per cent, over and over again. Science is fact. Religion is fancy. But science is spiritually unpalatable. Swallowing religion is easy, 'cause it *feels good* to believe things *are good*. Yet it's all a bunch of primitive, superstitious bullshit. We've got to develop spines if we're ever to get the spiritual side of our thought processes out of the Dark Ages, or some airhead's gonna start World War Three because his silly 'god' told him to. Kevin, I'm convinced that mankind's true evolution will commence when this whole aboriginal God trip is junked! It took *guts* to accept the fact that Earth isn't the center of the universe, *and it took guts* to reason our way through ghosts and black magic and all the other nonsense which used to be the only was we could explain things. People are gonna have to take the humongous step of their own accountability...they're gonna have to stop thanking gods and blaming devils for their ups and downs, and accept life as the brief phenomenon it really is. Then they've gotta see life as all the more precious for its brevity, and build on their assets and overcome their flaws. *As long as we've got beliefs and prejudices and good guys and bad guys we're savages!"*

Eddie found he was breathing hard: anyone attempting to reason graphically soon finds just how taxing it can be when the second party, while perhaps earnest enough, is still essentially interested in something that SOUNDS GOOD to him, something that portends favorably. It can be as stressful as gridlock. (Expressed with great, with difficult, with heartfelt poignancy: I wonder if our poor dead, oh-so-very human Jesus was just, oh-so-very humanly, indulging, to the point of addiction, in audience manipulation.) *Here's a simple trick you can try at home:* First, take a handful of twenty-dollar bills, crush 'em into a ball and wrap the ball in a funky old piece of newspaper. Then take a piece of shit and cover it with the prettiest, fanciest gift wrapping you can find. Now go up to your oh-so-very earnest friend, with specimen one in your left hand and specimen two in your right, and say, *"Pick."*

"So," Eddie continued, after sufficient time had elapsed to make it plain the author had just called the reader an asshole, "it *always* comes down to the bottom line. And the bottom line here is…*interest.* Meaning: what's *in it* for you? It's like the guy who goes 'searching for the truth.' He's not concerned with the truth; he wants to satisfy his conscience and his spiritual needs. He wants what he wants. Truth is seven minus four equals three. Truth is a given amount of water will boil at a specific temperature. Truth is photosynthesis. Nobody'll argue with any of that, but there're darned few people who'll be satisfied, because it doesn't make you *feel* anything. So why should I be an 'atheist,' Kevin? What's in it for me? *Why in the world would anybody* pick *'atheism,'* or want to get old, die, and have that be that? What's my interest? And the answer is: *there isn't any!* I don't accept what I accept because I *like* what I accept. I accept what I accept because it just so happens those are the facts, whether I like 'em or not. And I *don't* like the facts. *I wish there was a God*, dammit, and I wish I could go to a Paradise after I die. But there *isn't*, and I *can't*, and that's just tough fucking tamales for me. So somebody can swear seven minus four equals five if he wants. That's his right. But it won't make him right, and it won't make seven minus four equals three just an opinion.

"And then all these noble weenies will glorify their illogic by saying, 'my belief *requires a leap of faith.*' What a load of sanctimonious bullshit! The only 'requirement' is that you be a pussy; that you don't have the balls to be honest with yourself. This so-called 'leap of faith' is really just an intellectual belly flop. And it's the biggest cop-out there is. Because all they're saying is they *know* what they're saying is crap. They *know* it, Kevin! Every 'believer,' from the lowliest pew warmer to the Pope, *knows* there isn't a God. The fucking village idiot knows there isn't a God! I don't want to get upset with people, or interfere with their right to be jackasses, but when I hear somebody braying he believes there *really is* a God, I mean, as if he's making an intellectual statement or something, I...I feel like spitting in his filthy fibbing face. And when you get it from all sides; from school, from the press, from your family...all you're left with is contempt for your species. You know they'll lie about anything, and they'll do anything, to serve their self-interest. So don't be surprised when you get burned by the friendliest of strangers, Kevin, and don't exalt popularity too greatly; all truly honest people are, by definition, misanthropes. But...gotta be cool, Eddie. Gotta hang tough. If I lower myself to the level of a 'believer' in God—by 'believing' my feelings are objective—then I've lost my war against my own subjectivity. Truth can be anything I want it to be.

"And so, Kevin, and so I'm going to San Francisco, and I'm going to mingle with people who care more about love and peace and harmony than about self-serving hypocrisy. And if I run into people who spout God crap I'll know they're doing it because their motivation is love and peace and harmony, and that their rap's a device for bringing people together, a stratagem. And I'll offer those people a toke off my joint. And they'll wink and smile and we'll flash each other the peace sign and be on our separate ways together.

"Because I understand, Kevin. Because I understand that ethical values originate with abstract consciousness. The so-called 'meaning of life' begins with man's capacity to overpower his animal drives. It doesn't start somewhere out in space in some deity, and it doesn't start in animal nature, and it ain't got nothin' to do with reward and punishment. It's where the baby stands up and walks on his own. And it's just busting loose now, Kevin, and we're on our way to meet it!'"

Eddie paused, once again breathing hard. The boys stared at one another. Eddie coughed.

Kevin stirred the dirt with a forefinger, feeling the subject wasn't closed. Like all nonthinking persons, he was totally thrown out of whack by the notion of an unconscious universe, was just self-centered enough to instinctively dread a system that could proceed without a specific and meaningful role for him. A mammal saddled with a conscience, he'd been bitten by the *me bug*, found it incomprehensible that the stream of consciousness that was his could just be diddling along without some transcendent "purpose." Such persons, however, eventually "mature" when they are bitten by the *us* (vs. Them) *bug*; that is, once they can no longer feign significance on a personal level.

*Snap out of it, people!*

You and I are merely energy packets; like all "things" simply dissolving components of the elemental carousel, steadily and unconsciously disseminating the sliver of sunlight this pretty little rock captures, redistributing it as some other organism's breakfast. Beat the system; opt for cremation. No, *no*, No, *No*, NO! *This is all a breaking down, not a building up!*

Kevin, having ceased stirring the dirt, saw that the resultant spiral was reminiscent of a nebular swirl he'd seen in a science class photograph. Defiantly, he jabbed in two eyes and drew a smile on the swirl. He looked back up. "And that's *it?*" he countered. "You want everybody to just look at everything like it's some kind of a dumb machine, with no feelings or love or hope?" He spread his arms just as wide as he could, trying to adequately convey the sterility of Eddie's outlook. "Go ahead and trip around you some time, Eddie. Haven't you ever seen a rainbow, or tasted good food, or played with a puppy? That's where you and all the scientist guys are out to lunch. Machines don't make nice things that make you happy. The world can't be so beautiful out of dumb luck."

Eddie clasped his knees in his hands and gently rocked back and forth, staring at nothing. "Right," he muttered sourly. "The Great Thinkers' argument: 'Only intelligence could devise something so marvelous.' Aw, get fucking real! *Only intelligence could perceive something as marvelous!* Or, of course, 'Gaze ye upon yon automobile. Intelligence constructed this contraption, ergo it stands to reason that intelligence constructed the animal and vegetable kingdoms, and everything else that functions.' O priceless sillygisms!" He looked back at his friend. "Y'know, Kevin, one thing that really gores me is the way people always say, 'how can all this just be?' Well, why the heck *shouldn't* things be the way they are? How else *could* it be? Fish should have feet, maybe? We should all eat with our rear ends? Then they'll all go: 'Oooh, look at the pretty sunset! How can you look at that and say there isn't a God?' And I'll go, 'Nothin' to it!' and I'll look at the sunset and say, 'There isn't a God.' And believe it or not, Kevin, I haven't been struck by lightning yet, not once. And why *shouldn't* a sunset be stirring? It's a very sensory experience, not an intellectual one. I mean, it's like your retinae are being bombarded, for Pete's sake. But people always let their senses do their thinking for them, and then associate their feelings with some kind of rationale. And, to be honest, scientists don't help matters either, when they explain something as physically determinate as the processes in nature with words like 'accident' and 'chance.' Fido gets stuck with a choice: like, is all this a miracle, or just an accident? Gee, I wonder which one he's gonna find more appealing? And then I guess it's all only chance that life *just happened* to appear here, under ideal circumstances, instead of on some hellhole like Mercury. Just good luck on our part. They gotta replace all these misleading words with something like *inevitable*. Anywhere like *can* appear, it will, eventually. Just look at this planet: it's filthy with life, in every nook and cranny it can possibly cram itself into, until it reaches a place where it's too cold or too dry for life to be supported. That's why you can bet your bottom there's life on other planets, and all over the universe where conditions aren't too extreme. It won't be exactly like it is here, 'cause there are no carbon copies in nature, but you can be sure that, whatever it's like, it'll fit whatever the planet it's on is like. And even though their sunsets will be just as pretty as ours, we'll be ready to fight to the death any smart-ass who isn't democratic enough to admit our sunset is the prettiest in the whole damned, ever-lovin' universe."

"Um," Kevin said. He looked up, at the dumb parade of puffy cloud masses seemingly inching across the no-less-lovely field of bottomless blue. There was one clump that looked a whole lot like an angel's head, sadly staring down on these oh-so mortal proceedings. But the angel began distorting, taffy-like, even as he watched her. "So there's no God, no meaning, no beginning…no such thing as time or space. I don't really even exist; just a lot of ghosts what seem to be me. I'm gonna get old and die, and a bunch of worms are gonna chow down on my corpse. But it's no big thing, 'cause the worms don't really exist either. And there's no good or evil or right or wrong or up or down or in or out. It all comes from some whoremoans; from some relative of some observer, who only thinks he thinks; but even that's cool, on accounta thought don't exist neither." He looked back down. "Thanks for cheering me up, Eddie."

"No problem," Eddie said softly. "But you said you wanted to know what's going on, Kevin; not cheering up. If you want something positive you can still go back to the Bible. That's what it's there for. Then you can have your Heaven and your immortality, your heroes and villains, your reward and punishment. The good guys will be vindicated and the heavies will get theirs. Y'see, even though it's full of agony and passion, the Bible offers a light at the end of the tunnel, and a proposition for good behavior coming out ahead in the long run. People who follow the ethical guidelines will behave better, even if—especially if—they're of a rotten disposition to begin with. Personally, though, for my daily dose of Western ethical input, I prefer the Adventures of Superboy; although the Lone Ranger can really get my adrenaline going."

"Are you trying to say the Bible's a *lie*, Eddie?"

"Oh no, Kevin," Eddie said hurriedly, "I'm not saying it's a lie. It's a history. And it's the finest, wisest book I've ever come across. Pure poetry. The Lone Ranger isn't a *lie* either, but you see, you have to use metaphors and heroization to get people to *feel* that good behavior is correct. Thanks to the apostles the suffering of common people doesn't have to be in vain, and thanks to Jay Silverheels we can stop being convinced that Indians are a bunch of bloodthirsty savages. All of this is positive propaganda, Kevin. Like our own American history. How much patriotism's gonna be mustered by relating a history of some treasonous foreigners coming over here and ripping off land, using other people as beasts of burden, and aggrandizing it all with a lot of pompous rhetoric about it being the will of your God? So you've got to paint a pretty picture full of righteous reasons for your actions, and make people believe they've got cause to be proud. Otherwise they'll just go on their angry, horny, frightened little ways and we'll have anarchy all over again. That's why we've got laws and taboos; not to intimidate decent people, but to stop the natural predators from overextending themselves. And God's really a kind of big invisible policeman; He's walking a beat along the avenue of your darkest thoughts. Instead of jail, though, you may be looking at Hell without possibility of parole. No...you can't give somebody a single good reason to not give in to his animal appetites, except that if he gets caught there's a more powerful authority that'll punish him.

"So there it is. You invent good and bad characters to dramatize your message, and hope you can influence folks positively without resorting to locking 'em up. Or else you try using entertainment as the vehicle for your message, knowing people have attention spans rivaling that of a baboon's unless they're focused on something that makes them *feel good*. It's like the guy who's writing this novel, for instance. What's he doing but playing God by using us to communicate something to an audience that couldn't care less? *He's* the one who's making you have these seizures, Kevin. But he's not doing it just to be mean. You're a hero, my friend, whether you like it or not, and all your suffering is just to soften you up for your redemption at the end of the story. So don't worry about the 'here' and 'now.' You'll never meet your maker, but salvation's waiting for you with open arms."

Kevin looked up sharply. "Huh?" He'd been on the verge of nodding off, hypnotized by the sun's warmth, the droning of flies, and Eddie's softly tapering monologue. "What's that you said about suffering scissors in the Salvation Army?"

Eddie grinned. "Caught you nappin', didn't I? Now you see why this kind of rap doesn't get much action. I was just joshin' you, Kevin. This really isn't a story, and old terra couldn't get much firma." He patted the ground between them. "And yes, of course there's a God and a Devil, and a darned good reason for us being here. So pick your opinion. Collect 'em all." He juxtaposed his crawfish, then scooted them along by brushing at the dirt behind them. "Now, this one's a Jaguar, and this one's a Maserati. Vroom, vroom."

Kevin looked away, just as Mike came shuffling back, hands deep in pockets, avoiding his friends' eyes. "I guess it's really none of my business," he said bitterly, "but do you think you two comrades might be willing to go now?"

Eddie was caught off guard. Mike's tone implied a real rift in their friendship; a friendship Eddie had always believed was unshakable. "What do you mean, Mike? Of course it's your business. We're ready to go whenever you are. I was wondering where you were." He scooped up his crawfish and displayed them with the same enthusiasm he'd shown Kevin. "Look, Mike! Crawdaddies! There's a culvert around the bend. I found 'em half—"

Mike swatted them off Eddie's palm with a vicious swipe.

"I don't care!" he cried, and stamped on the fleeing creatures. "Don't act all friendly with me, Eddie! I know just what you and your kiss-ass buddy are up to!"

Eddie's honest face went through a gamut of emotions, from gaping astonishment to an impotent rage. He looked down at the smashed crawfish, then back up at Mike with a crestfallen grimace.

Tears were coursing down Mike's face. "We used to be friends, Eddie! We had good times together, all the time. Everything was great until this fat faggot showed up." He looked at Kevin and his face shook with emotion.

"That's not true, Mike," Eddie said. "We're still friends. We'll always be friends. I don't know where you got this idea we're against you. You're wrong."

Mike ignored him. He showed Kevin a bony, threatening fist. "I swear to God, Polak," he said viciously, "sooner or later I'm gonna kill you. I *mean* it! Don't you ever turn your back on me or you're dead!" He kicked Kevin's felled bicycle, hurt his ankle again, and, after hopping around wailing on one foot, jumped on his own bike and jammed.

Eddie said quickly, "I don't think we'd better ride together anymore, Kevin." Without another word he mounted and took off after Mike.

Kevin rose wearily, picked up his bike. He rode well to the rear; feeling awful—filthy and smelly and hungry and tired—but content with the new single-file arrangement. Although he really needed to think things through, his thoughts were aimless and meandering. *Trying* to think constructively can be as futile as trying to sleep; the very effort causes the mind to revolt, to wander and to peck compulsively at nonsense. All the stimuli—traffic, the glare of sun, his companions, his own exertion—served only to distract his mind from the cogitative process. By far his most substantial mental inclination—the one thing he was really aware of—was his fear. Kevin was scared silly. And not of anything he could identify and grapple with, discern and resolve. He felt himself the helpless victim of some whimsical internal bogey, whose outbursts, in the form of blackouts followed by convulsions, were extremely potent and entirely unpredictable.

Not until the highway had returned to the beaches did the boys begin to ride together again, and approximate their Santa Monica chumminess. The mighty ocean dwarfed their puny differences. The impermanence of their arguments was made plain by time and freedom in plentiful supply. All was forgiven in the exhilaration of being young and full of energy in a familiar world of sand and suntan oil and splashing brown bodies.

Kevin, Mike, and Eddie stopped at the north end of Pismo Beach. Farther up the highway began the sprawling community of San Luis Obispo, thier designated halfway point.

The beach was swarming with tanned vacationers in all stages of undress, so packed there was hardly room to walk, much less recline. Footballs and Frisbees described their trajectories smoothly, while sea gulls screeched and fluttered between blankets, fighting for leftover goodies.

170

"Halfway!" Eddie cried exuberantly. "We're almost halfway in four days! We oughta make it with time to spare."

"Yeah," Mike said. "Now I feel really good, despite everything. We just gots to celebrate. How much grass you got left, Four-eyes?"

Caught up in the moment, Kevin produced his stash gleefully, only to hesitate, wary of the prying eyes of pedestrians. "Still over half a lid. You guys form a screen while I roll one up." Mike and Eddie stood nonchalantly on either side while he sat and rolled an exceptionally fat celebration doobie. The boys burned it true.

"That *was* good!" Mike exclaimed. "So good I feel like I could smoke a dozen more."

"I sure do have the munchies all of a sudden," Eddie moaned.

Kevin echoed the moan. "I *wish* you wouldn't have said that, Eddie. I'm so hungry I could eat a fatcat." The aroma of barbecuing hamburgers came to him. His stomach growled. A little way down the beach he made out a small bunker-style snack bar. "Over there!"

His friends' eyes followed his finger. They walked their bikes along the strand until they stood just opposite the little building.

Mike blurted, "Wait a minute!" just as Kevin and Eddie were picking up their bikes. "I wanna smoke another joint first."

Eddie stared. "You actually have *zero* self-control?"

"Let me just get a little higher first."

Kevin's stomach voiced its demands again. He handed the baggie of marijuana and a book of cherry rolling papers to Mike. "Okay then. Go ahead and roll up a couple small ones and watch our bikes for us. What do you want to eat?"

Mike appeared simultaneously confused and affronted; an odd kid. His eyes flashed back at Kevin. "Uh, just get me a fat dog and a choke. I'll pain you when you fat back."

Kevin and Eddie raced through the crowd, laughing and kicking sand. The lines at the snack bar were way-long. Kevin's appetite rose incrementally with each slow-ass motherfucking customer who didn't have the common courtesy to just pay and get the hell out of the way. For Mike, he ordered a hot dog and a large cola, and for himself a bacon chili cheese dog, French fries with tartar and cream, two slices of double-anchovies pepperoni pizza, cinnamon sand dabs, a lemon-lime turnover, and a large root beer float with neopolitan. Eddie purchased a double cheeseburger and a pint of milk. With their arms and nostrils thus laden they made their way back. Once they'd devoured their lunches on a strand bench, the boys broke into a delightful belching contest which Kevin won by virtue of his bovine powers of projection. Enormously pleased, he leaned back with his hands on his belly.

"This victory, comrades," he groaned happily, "calls for another joint of my most excellent herb, don't you agree?"

"Indubitably," Eddie giggled.

Acting the part of an awards master of ceremonies, Kevin casually flipped out his palm. "Michael. The reefer please."

Mike was slow on the uptake for his part. "Er...yeah," he said. "Here you go, man," and handed Kevin a rather thin, poorly rolled cigarette.

Kevin fired up the joint, held in the smoke for a long moment, let it out with an exaggerated "*Ah-h-h-h...*" He smiled angelically, passed the joint to Eddie, closed his eyes and again held out his hand. "Now," he said, continuing his performance, "the envelope, please." Mike handed over the baggie wordlessly, just as Eddie was handing back the glowing joint; so for a space Kevin's mind was distracted. He was taking another deep hit when something compelled him to survey the baggie in his hand. It felt unaccountably lighter.

"Hey!" he said, astounded. "What happened to all my pot?" There was surely more than the equivalence of two joints missing. More like eight or nine.

"What do you mean?" Mike shot back quickly; too quickly. "What are you talking about, man?"

Kevin turned his head to darkly examine Mike's burning face. "I mean, *where's all my pot?*" he spat. "I only see one joint."

Mike stood. On his palm was another thin and poorly rolled cigarette. "Right here! You said to roll two, and I did!"

Now Kevin stood also, his gray suspicion gelling to

black certainty. "Two skinny joints," he said slowly, "wouldn't make my stash so much lighter."

"I—I spilled some," Mike sputtered. He looked up sharply. "Hey, man," he growled, staring into Kevin's eyes aggressively, "are you trying to say I ripped you off, man? 'Cause you better not be, man. You know I don't dig that kind of rap, man."

Eddie broke in quickly. "Come on, you guys. Let's figure this out cool. Don't jump to conclusions."

Both boys ignored him completely. "*Yeah?*" Kevin said. He tore off his glasses and handed them to Eddie. "Well I don't dig rip-offs, *man*. Especially when they're supposed to be my friends, *man*. So I'm telling you right now, *man*, you better hand over my fucking dope before I lose my fucking temper!"

Kevin didn't really believe Mike would ever seriously attempt engaging in fisticuffs a boy as huge as he. The bloody consequences made even entertaining the idea absurd. So he was totally unprepared when Mike reared back and socked him in the eye just as hard as he could. Kevin was so startled that he didn't at first retaliate, but went down with little Mike on top of him; Mike's hands alternately kidney-punching and tearing out his hair. With an ursine roar, Kevin threw his massive arms around his opponent in a death-dealing bear hug. But Mike's wiry body slipped out of the embrace. Mike managed to get behind him, where his tight little bony fists could rain down on Kevin's ears and cheeks. Blindly reaching back, Kevin was able to grasp Mike's shirt, and then, in a burst of blind rage, to pull him over his shoulder and onto the ground. Kevin got in two good solid punches to Mike's ugly little face, and then the smaller boy was scrabbling at Kevin's eyes with his fingernails. Kevin backed off, still surprised at Mike's ferocity. He punched him once more in the face, and then Mike was all over him, kicking and biting and spitting, which was downright dirty fighting. Kevin saw his opening and lunged, got his hands on Mike's scrawny throat and wrung it like a wet towel. He heard Mike gasping, felt his hot cursing breath in his face. Somehow Mike found the wind for a final lunge, and with all his strength delivered a thrust of the knee squarely into Kevin's groin. Kevin hissed and drew back, releasing his stranglehold. As he wove to his feet he was seized at each bicep by an intervening bystander. He flung them aside as if they were children and took a step toward Mike, who was just making his feet. The one step was all he could manage before that excruciating pain only males can experience dropped him to his knees. He groaned, toppled over, curled up his legs. With his hands tucked between his thighs he lay on the verge of vomiting, deaf to the commotion around him. When at last he could get to his hands and knees the crowd had dispersed. Mike offered a hand up, but Kevin refused it with a warning growl.

He slumped on the bench, getting his wind back. One of his eyes was swelling shut, but with his good eye he could see that he'd scored with a number of punches. The bottom half of Mike's face was red with drying blood, especially around the nostrils, and one of his premolars was missing. Kevin felt drained of heat. As the boys stared steadfastly at one another, panting, that peculiar post-combat truce passed between them. Kevin stuck out his bloodguilty paw. Mike grinned wryly and shook hands.

"Black eye, some bruises, sore balls," Kevin wheezed. "You?"

"Two teeth, at least," Mike said. "Almost broke my frigging nose."

Eddie heaved a sigh. "That's better! What came over you guys?"

"Beats me," Mike said. "I just don't like being called a rip-off, that's all. But everything's cool."

"Well," Kevin said, "*something* happened to my pot. I mean, I trusted you with it."

"And *I* said I *didn't* rip you *off!*"

Kevin found he was back on his feet, fists all ready to go. He blinked and realized that, revolution or no revolution, Mike was an enemy to the bitter end. And Mike *had* ripped his off; it was written on his face.

Eddie was back up between them. "Come *on*, you guys! I thought you made up. Just drop it, will you?"

Kevin glared at Mike before quietly turning away to find a restroom. Something told him his lunch was about to make a detour.

He was wrong. In the little brick restroom, assailed by standing urine and the ghosts of a thousand bare feet, all he lost was another load of soul. The truth was all over this trip; it was every man for himself. But his heart told him he could still trust little Eddie, who had clearly demonstrated his honesty that dreadful night of the beach party, when a lesser individual would certainly have taken advantage of Kevin's intoxication by glomming his weed.

His mind made up, Kevin lumbered back to the strand and drew Eddie aside.

"Eddie, I'll tell you the truth, I don't trust Mike any farther than I can throw him. I've been thinking he might swipe my lid when I'm not looking, or when I'm asleep. We've been partners, Eddie, you and me, forever. I know I can trust you. So maybe you can do me a favor and hold onto my pot for me. Okay? Mike won't ever think you've got it, and if he *does* try to rip me off again he'll just think I'm all out."

Eddie looked up nervously. It was a responsibility he didn't want to bear, and besides, it made him feel like a collaborator. But if it would help keep the peace he would do it. He nodded assent.

"Thanks, Eddie," Kevin said glowingly.

Eddie nodded again, and no more was said on the matter. When Mike was looking elsewhere, Eddie obediently tucked the contraband into the rolled sleeping bag strapped to his bike's rack. Eddie's mood was grave. He was pretty sure the fight had destroyed all chances of his friends reconciling, and was wary of speaking with either boy separately.

They set off in gloomy silence. At the outskirts of San Luis Obispo, the highway describes a gentle crescent away from the coast. Presented with an option to more beach, they elected to follow the highway into the heart of town. This was due to a mutual, instinctive feeling of discontent with the sea. Wide open spaces were beginning to make them feel uneasy. They were just boys. What they needed was the funhouse of hell-raising only an unwary city could provide; a fairgrounds of refuse cans to kick over, pedestrians to insult, fire alarms to trigger. This course they followed jubilantly, and less than a mile into the city they were bosom buddies again, and in their wake lay a trail of garbage and outraged citizenry. On Washington Avenue Mike made the mistake of swerving in front of a battered old pickup truck, forcing it to a squealing stop. There were three Spanish-American men in the cab; an old man and his adult sons. The old man shook his fist out the cab window dramatically. "¡Degenerados!" he cried. "You kids should drive more careful!"

"Aw, we're just kidding around," Mike said. "So don't go getting your mariachis all rattled."

"Es no comico..." the old man responded, struggling. "Is not a funny! ¡Es malo chiste! Es...is...is bad jest!"

"Bad jest?" Eddie said delightedly. "*Bad jest?*" He screwed up his face into a countenance of burning outrage. "We don't need no stinking bad jest!"

But Mike came right to the point. "Up your burrito, you old bean fucker!" He spat at the truck, just catching the grille.

The old man threw the truck in reverse. As they took off he backed into a driveway, straightened out, and screeched in hot pursuit. There were two things the boys hadn't reckoned on. One was that the old man knew this part of town like the back of his hand. The other was that he was a mechanic who took loving care of his old truck, which, despite its battered appearance, tore after them like a lusty rhinoceros. Whether they fled down little alleys or seldom-used side streets, the driver seemed to anticipate their moves, and the truck's mighty shifting roar was always just at their backs. The boys ran their bikes over a dirt lot pocked with holes two feet deep, up a steep incline, and over railroad tracks. They thought this obstacle course would stop the truck, but it didn't even slow it. They rode hollering and yelping down the opposite side, over another dirt lot, and into a supermarket's parking lot.

Kevin, dragging the rear, was terrified. He was too naïve to know the men in the truck were merely enjoying a game of cat and mouse, and too disoriented to realize they'd been chased halfway across town. He only knew that his heart was hammering between his ears, and that his second wind was history. He zigzagged recklessly between parked cars as he followed his shouting friends, bruising his shins and elbows on bumpers and side-view mirrors. The truck rapidly lost ground while the boys row-hopped. Kevin saw Eddie frantically sideswipe a shopper attempting to unlock his car while balancing four full shopping bags. Jerking his handlebars to avoid the man, Kevin found himself careening off the pavement. He was only able to maintain control by running staggeringly while straddling the eunuch-maker, bouncing painfully against the cleverly-situated bar until he pitched headfirst into a narrow ditch. Mike and Eddie, who were already cowering in the ditch, hissed at him to be quiet. Kevin swallowed his pain, immensely relieved to find his panting friends so near.

It was well he kept quiet, for very soon they heard the pickup slowly cruising by. It stopped directly opposite the narrow ditch. Kevin held his breath until his chest felt about to burst, not realizing the lazily revolving front wheel of his bike was sticking up in plain sight. The boys heard laughter and rapid, incomprehensible Spanish, the sound of tabs popping on beer cans. More laughter. The truck's rear wheels spun for a few seconds. It roared off with a squeal and lurch. Mike and Eddie poked up their heads in a choking cloud of dust and drizzling gravel. Kevin pulled himself from the ditch looking like a beached whale.

Eddie was an emotional mess. "Let's split, you guys!" he cried. "Fast, man, *fast!* Before they come back!"

"Yeah. Let's *go*, Kevin!"

But Kevin was out of it. His mind took him on a delirious rerun of all the Combat shows he'd watched religiously at home. "You guys go on without me," he croaked, pawing the dirt.

"God *damn* you!" he heard Mike shout. "You got us *into* this"—which wasn't true—"now you get us *out* of it!"

"Let's drag him, Mike!"

"*You* drag him. That fat fucker weighs a ton."

This cruel exaggeration of his girth drove Kevin to his feet. He was going to kill Mike, right here and now, literally. Exterminate him, erase him, delete him. Pop him like a zit. But, even as he rose, Mike and Eddie mounted and took off. The fight drained right out of Kevin. It was all he could do to keep up.

"Wait!" he cried. "Aw, for the luvva Christ, *wait up!*"

"Wait, *hell!*" Mike shot back.

And soon they had reached the far, residential side of town. Their common peril breached the feud. They all kept their eyes peeled for the pickup truck.

"Don't look now," Mike hissed suddenly, "but the pigs are following us."

Eddie jerked his head around, eyes wide. Kevin quickly looked back.

"Jesus!" Mike snapped. "I *said* don't *look!* You want 'em to think you got something to hide?"

"I'll look if I want to," Eddie whimpered.

"How do you know they're following us?" Kevin asked. In his mind he could still see the car, still see the lights on the roof, still see the siren. They were so close he could have seen their faces, had he the courage.

"I *don't* know," Mike said testily. "Turn the corner."

They turned off the main road onto a tree-lined avenue. The police car nosed around the corner like a curious shark. An amplified voice said: "PULL OVER TO THE SIDE OF THE ROAD."

"This is it!" Mike cried. The car pulled beside them. Kevin and Eddie stopped and clumsily dismounted, but Mike zoomed to the middle of the road and pedaled frantically to the street's other side.

Both of the car's front doors flew open and the driver sprang out yelling, "Hey! *Hold* it!" But Mike was dodging back and forth on his bike, as though he expected the officer to take a shot at him. He disappeared behind a gas station on the corner, reappeared hurtling across the main road, vanished again behind a restaurant.

The passenger cop whipped out his nightstick and cornered the boys. "Don't nobody move," he said. They cringed in terror.

The driver reached for his radio microphone, thought better of it, and walked around the front of the car to join his partner.

"Hey now," he said smoothly, "what's the hurry?" He smiled slyly at his partner. "Wouldn't be surprised if a couple weirdos like these had warrants out for 'em."

Kevin and Eddie were mortified. The policemen were giant, evil Batmen in their black uniforms, badges catching the sun. The car's radio crackled.

"Okay," said the passenger cop, "let's see some I.D."

Kevin shakily reached into his hip pocket. All he had in the wallet was his library card and the Free Press clipping…and he still had plenty of cash. A terrible thought struck him: the cops might steal it! Then came an even worse thought: for sure they'd think *he* stole it.

"C'mon, fat boy," said the passenger cop. "Give."

The driver watched the proceedings with a detached amusement. He was older than his partner, more used to this kind of little comedy. "My, my," he said breezily. "The carnival's in town."

But the other cop was tougher. He snatched Kevin's wallet and indicated with his nightstick that the boy should move up against the car. "Okay, frogface;" he said when Kevin was beside him, "hands apart on the hood, legs spread wide…I said *spread* 'em!" He looked at Eddie, who was bent in fear, eyes wide and liquid. "All right, now you, gimme your I.D., nice and easylike, and get over next to four-eyes here."

"It's…it's in my sleeping bag," Eddie said. A look of horror crossed his face: *that's where he'd stashed Kevin's grass!*

The older cop grasped the seat of Eddie's bike. "Keep 'em covered," he said to his friend. He unfastened Eddie's sleeping bag from the rack.

"No!" Eddie cried. "You can't do that! You don't have the right!" His eyes appealed wildly to the other officer.

"You keep your mouth shut, punk."

Kevin, spread out painfully against the hood like an obese starfish, all at once realized why Eddie was so terrified. He very carefully turned his head and watched the senior cop unroll Eddie's sleeping bag on the sidewalk. Eddie's shirts and private effects rolled nicely on top of the bag. The only article that fell out onto the sidewalk was a half-sealed sandwich bag. The officer picked it up. His eyes gleamed.

"Well, well. And what have we here?"

Eddie croaked out something unintelligible.

"You been asked a question," said the younger cop, threateningly.

Eddie shuddered violently. "It's *his!*" he cried, pointing at Kevin. "It's not mine!"

Both officers looked at Kevin's gaping face. The driver looked back at Eddie.

"Hmmmn..." he said judicially. "You were riding this bike and assume a responsibility for what you were carrying. I'm sorry, son, but—

*we're going to have to have you booked for possession of marijuana.*"

Eddie reeled, gasping for air.

"Move it, kid!" snapped the other cop. "Up against the car next to your girlfriend." Eddie moved over next to Kevin unsteadily, copied his position. Quick tears came to his eyes. "This is all your fault," he whispered.

Now the young cop patted them down, neatly and completely. "They're clean," he said. "Okay, move back—*away from the car!* No funny business."

Kevin tottered as he stood upright. His shoulders and legs ached from the strain. The senior officer began speaking some code words into the radio's microphone, words which, Eddie knew, amounted to his death warrant. The cop replaced the microphone and stepped to the back of the car, unlocked the trunk and opened it high. Eddie hung his head as the other officer put the boy's hands behind his back and cuffed them together. "You and us..." said the cop in a vicious saccharine undertone, "...we're taking us a little *ri-i-i-i-de.*"

Kevin stared incredulously as the older policeman stuffed Eddie's bicycle into the car's gaping trunk. He was beginning to realize he was still free, that he was not going to the big house after all.

Eddie was made to sit on the rear seat with his hands locked painfully behind him. Kevin saw Eddie turn and look back miserably; then the officer had returned Kevin's wallet, shut the rear door, and climbed in front.

The driver looked over the roof at Kevin and frowned

avuncularly.

"Some advice," he said. "When you find your buddy, you guys stick to the coast route. Kids who look like you are always getting in trouble in the city."

Then the head was gone and the car, amazingly, was being driven away. Barely visible, the back of Eddie's neck seemed to await a guillotine blade. Kevin shuddered. He was free.

Free!

He looked around, aware for the first time that people, free people, were everywhere; staring out windows, pointing from porches and driveways. An adolescent brother and sister stuck out their tongues and wiggled their fingers behind their ears.

Kevin mounted and rode to the corner, looking for Mike. With a start he realized the cops had never even searched his sleeping bag, and that made him laugh nervously. But when he thought of poor, doomed Eddie a wave of shame swept over him. And how long had it been since he had guaran-*teed* Eddie's eventual arrival in San Francisco? Was it really only the day before yesterday? And he, Kevin, had been the useless instrument of honest Eddie's crushing demise. Kevin pounded his fist on the stem of his handlebars until it was raw and bleeding.

He waited for the light to change, then gingerly walked his bike to the back of the restaurant—paranoid, absolutely certain an old lady in one of the phone booths was reporting his every move to a squad of detectives intently positioning push-pins on a grid of the area.

"*Mike!*" he whispered.

No answer.

So he rode around the restaurant and began calling. Still not finding his companion, he pedaled down the main street, trying to figure which way he would have gone if he were Mike. His search took him down side streets and alleys, and at long last, when the sun was beginning to set, the road he'd been following came to an abrupt end. An infinite highway stretched north and south, and just beyond a cliff dropped off into oblivion. Kevin heard the pounding of surf. A single sign poked up next to him and the boy looked at it stupidly.

*State Highway 1* said the sign.

All at once Kevin understood he'd been searching in vain, and that the community of San Luis Obispo lay behind him, unfriendly and darkling. He knew in his gut that he had lost Mike, been separated from Eddie, and was, most likely, finally and irrecoverably alone.

He looked north up the lonely stretch of highway. Somewhere, far away at the end of this road, lay the magical, utopian city of his dreams. Colorful people adorned the happy streets in that enchanted city, flowers in their hair. Dope was free there, the people were free, love was free. Soft young girls walked about in sheer white robes, begging you to do them the favor of accepting their free love.

The boy looked south toward his home. Big Joe notwithstanding, he'd be safe there. A nice warm bed and his record player were in that direction. And no more toil, he reasoned. Shit, the way it looked he could probably coast all the way home. Then, to sweeten the pot, the tender, supplicating vision of the raven-haired girl returned. Kevin licked his dry lips.

An old bus appeared lumbering toward him, the only traffic on the road. Sounds of rock music and laughter, of singing voices. Since it was a warm summer evening, most of the remaining panes were down, and Kevin could see that the bus was crammed full of joyous people with long, unruly hair. As the bus approached, he noticed words sloppily and exuberantly splashed on the side with fluorescent paint. He strained to make out their message:  SAN FRANCISCO OR BUST(ed).

Now the bus passed him and a freaky-looking character leaned out a window, flashed Kevin the peace sign with his left hand, waved a joint in his right. The bus continued lumbering up the road, seemingly dwindling in size. The laughter and singing grew fainter. The bus rounded a bend and vanished.

The boy looked down the highway. It was deserted. He looked north, saw the bus appear as a tiny moving toy before vanishing again. He looked behind him, and the road to town was being swallowed by a malevolent shadow. Night was coming fast.

Kevin changed gears and, wearily at first, began pedaling north in the wake of the bus.

# PART TWO

## WEASELS AND PEACOCKS AND WHORES, OH MY!

# Chapter 9

## Save The Cockroaches

Kevin's loneliness was brief. He didn't have far to ride before he came upon merry lights in the gloaming. He had a pastry, a candy bar, and a candied apple for dinner, and spent the night with a troll under a pier. Here's how it came about.

The pier was a quaint place of gift shops, of pinball machines, of stolid fishermen rolling mirthlessly with the sea. Kevin approached it almost unknowing, still mourning the loss of his friends. There was nothing he could do about Eddie, who would get one phone call home and catch hell from his parents. It was Kevin's contraband, and Eddie would certainly tell his own parents this, and they would of course inform the Mikolaj- czyks. But in a way, Kevin thought, Eddie might actually come out ahead in the long run. After all, being busted for possession *was* an honor—it meant gaining the reputation of a rebel and dreamer, sharing your views with other heads and heavies, and becoming a veteran of prison life. Kevin would spend the rest of his days eluding Joe, who would refuse to die before he had caught his son and tromped the life from him, while Eddie, with a few breaks and a lift from a liberal probation system, might end up a hero next semester. Kevin winced and quit this line of thinking immediately. When he owned up to it—that he was directly responsible for the destruction of Eddie's dream—he almost wished Big Joe would find him and give him the thrash- ing he deserved.

As far as Mike was concerned, Kevin was at a loss.

Even the scrawny boy's pugnacious company was better than being lost and lonely. He was sure Mike was still in town, a fugitive; stealthily haunting the sewer system or doing the roof-top route. Kevin, with a sense of fatality brought on by soul-fatigue and remorse, was also certain this severance was permanent—that if he went back into town looking for Mike, Mike would simultaneously leave town by a different road to search the coast. So Kevin was very miserable indeed when he parked outside the coffee shop-restaurant-fish market on the little pier, and somehow the passing of strolling window-shoppers and skateboarding pinballers was just what he needed.

The restaurant was constructed as a truncated hemi-sphere; the upper portion all glass panes cut hexagonally, the lower section paneled laterally with salt-pitted redwood slats. The dome's flat top was capped by the plaster figure of a smiling sea bass wolfing down a steaming cup of java. All this glass bared the shop's innards to passersby, making it difficult to miss tier upon tier of hot fresh pastries displayed within. Kevin chose a little table by the entrance, where he could keep a close eye on his bike. There he sat and pouted over his hot coffee and sweet cinnamon roll. He was dining alone…

…when…

…without a sound the table's other chair had been occu-pied by a repulsive creature wearing a hideous hat of mangled felt, almost identical to Kevin's own. Kevin became aware of a particularly offensive odor, an absolutely vulgar stench that trig-gered feelings of anxiety and loathing. His reaction wasn't just a healthy individual's natural aversion to a foul-smelling pres-ence; it was something deeper. He was being bombarded by pheromones. The intruder's age was impossible to gauge, as his face was streaked with grease and grime and other, unrecogniz-able patches of filth. Under the tiny yellow eyes projected a long crooked nose, a thin slice of mouth, a transparent shock of goatee. He was wearing a torn old coat stained so badly its original color was anybody's guess, and a pair of obscenely eroded cutoff trousers which must have originally belonged to a child. Kevin saw with pity and with revulsion that the stranger's skeletal legs were peppered with scabs, and pocked with what looked like the craters of old boil scars. He wore tennis shoes coated with a rank, bile-colored slime, and corroded, collapsed socks of the same nauseating extract. He laid a wormy upturned hand on the table, saying, "You got some change, friend? It's an emergency. It's like my car ran out of gas and I lost my wallet in the cab. I can't apply for a new credit card until the bank opens in the morning...all my bags, man...all of 'em, lost, lost forever...airport snafu, terrible thing." His fingernails dug into the tabletop. "Terrorists, man. But what you gonna do...free country." He inhaled until it looked like his head would pop. "Hotels, man, socked in for the holidays...muggers... appointments...cops with attitudes...missing ID." Scale by scale, the tiny eyes sank back into his skull. "Man, I gotta call my wife, I just gotta let her know the kids are all okay. Suzie...Mitch... Cupcake...Corndog." His stomach growled through a bottomless decrescendo, finally petering out in a wrenching gastric death rattle. "Long distance," he gasped.

Kevin nodded with compassion. This guy's situation made his own troubles seem a lark. Also he needed company, anybody's company, badly.

"Sure, man;" he said, "let me get you something to eat." Kevin rose and studied the menu. Feeling strangely pleased with himself, he ordered steak and lobster, corn on the cob, and a glass of milk. When the meal arrived his beneficiary devoured it without a word of thanks. The tab had come to, surprisingly, over twenty-one dollars.

Once the meal had been consumed with an atrocious lack of manners, Kevin asked, "Feel better?"

"You got a cigarette?"

"Sorry. I don't smoke."

"Christ. Now I gotta have a smoke." The wretch rose on wobbly legs, standing barely five feet tall while stooped at a curious angle. He seized the arm of a customer waiting at the cash register. "Hey man, you got a smoke? It's like I left all my shit in the van, man, and I just know this chick ran off with it. Women, man. But what you gonna do?" The customer looked at the filthy claw on his arm, peeled it off with disgust. He was tempted to take the little troublemaker outside and whip the pants off him for being so rude, but it was clear nature had already worked him over.

"Beat it," he said mildly.

The little guy threw his arms in the air. "Christ!" he said, turning and limping back to the table. "Some people just blow me away! I mean! Here I been working this joint for five years, and he tells *me* to beat it. Christ!"

"Come on," Kevin said. "I'll buy you a pack."

He stepped up next to the customer and said under his breath, "Sorry about…him." The man stared sourly, jangling the change in his pocket, and thought, *Jesus. Another one.*

After paying, Kevin walked outside to join his new companion, who was mouthing obscenities at the passersby. He walked his bike slowly, trying to not wind his limping partner. They came to a little stand which sold newspapers, candied apples, and tepid beer. A very comely teenage girl sat behind the makeshift counter, polishing her nails.

"Gimme packa smokes."

"Which brand do you want?" she asked, not smiling.

"Christ…Gimme Pall Malls."

She handed him a pack and a book of matches. Kevin paid as the little viper hobbled to a rail overlooking the ocean.

"Friend of yours?" the girl asked, her wholesome face twisting with distaste.

"Just a stray cat," Kevin said absently. It was a fresh scene for him. For a crazy moment he thought that, contrasted with *that* guy, he might actually look *good*. He squared his shoulders and half-turned to display the famous logo on the vest's rear. "But he's a heavy dude. We're like talking about maybe starting a band."

"Ugh. He gives me the creeps. He's out here panhandling every day, swearing at people, scaring off business. I wish he'd just fall in the water and never come up."

Kevin's shoulders sagged. He bought a candy bar and a candied apple for his own dinner before walking over to rejoin his sorry new sidekick. He would really have to start watching his money.

"You live around here?" he asked.

"Yeah. I sleep under the pier at night and hustle up here during the day. It's not great, but I do okay. Sometimes, if you're fast, you can skip into one of the restaurants and swipe the tips off the tables before the waitress can get to 'em. Just last week I rolled some old man for six bucks, and people are always dropping change. Hang on a second."

He leaned farther over the rail and casually vomited the entire dinner. Kevin's stomach wrenched at the diarrheic sound of undigested steak and lobster spattering the waves. Twenty-one bucks down the drain.

"Yeah, I do okay," he continued, snuffling residue up his nose. He lit another cigarette.

Kevin turned away. He was weary with the day, aching and depressed. "Where's a good place to crash around here?" he asked unwisely.

"Only one place, under the pier. Sleep on the beach in the open and the cops'll bust you, or the drifters'll mug you. You can sleep downstairs if you want, I don't give a fuck; God knows there's room enough."

"Thanks," Kevin said prematurely.

The wretch shrugged.

"My name's Kevin; what's yours?"

The little cripple shrugged again, and from then on Kevin thought of him only as the troll. Although trolls tradition-ally inhabit caves and foothills and the like, Kevin saw no rea-son one couldn't master the underbelly of a pier.

After a few minutes of ignored small talk on Kevin's part and foul muttering by the troll, they walked back off the pier and onto the beach. Kevin had a spooky feeling as he carried his bike over the sand, and this feeling intensified as they ducked under the pier's sodden timber framework. Under-neath it was inky dark, but the surf reflected colored light from above, and this light, playing games with the eyes, seemed to dance around the pillars, sculpting otherworldly Things out of shadow. The only sound was the distinct crash and suck of breaking waves.

"Over here's a dry place," the troll whispered. Why did he whisper? The troll lit another cigarette, and in the brief sputtering glare of the match Kevin saw salt-softened beams gently rocking and groaning with the ocean. Trash and foul-smelling seaweed lay heaped on the sand, along with small, indefinably gruesome blotches. Kevin shivered. The troll stopped and perched on a beam, so Kevin carefully wedged his bicycle in a crotch of timbers. He took his sleeping bag off the bike's rack and used it for a cushion.

"You sure the tide won't come this high?" he asked in a voice which seemed unnecessarily loud.

"Would I of said it's a good place if the fucking tide came this high? Christ, I slept here I don't know how long, haven't got wet yet."

"You—you actually *live* down here?"

"What of it?"

"Nothing...I just, well—how long?"

The troll looked away. By now Kevin's eyes had adjusted to the dark, and he could see that the troll's expression was bitter.

"Seems long as I can remember. Maybe six, seven years. I use to bum in the parks and railroad stations, but there was too much competition. Before I come down the coast I use to hang out at Golden Gate Park, and then at Big Sur. Too much fucking competition."

Kevin started. "Did you say Golden Gate? That's where I'm going." He asked eagerly, "What's it like up there?"

The troll doubled over with a humongous fit of coughing. Kevin waited impatiently. Recovering, the troll flicked away what was left of his cigarette and lit another. "Too much fucking competition," he said at last.

"No, I mean what are the vibes like? How are the people?" He was still eager to compare the descriptions of others, to build an accurate visual. If only Eddie were here now.

"People are fucked," said the troll. "Too fucking poor to bum any money off, always spouting crap about love and religion. Christ, I couldn't live around freaks like that." He began to idly pick his nose, lazily eyeing the results rolled between forefinger and thumb. Kevin had a disturbing feeling the troll could see well in the dark, having survived so long in this chilly shadow-world. He grunted, figured the subject was a touchy one, and better left closed.

"Well, I'm tired. I'm gonna crash."

The troll turned and looked at him with frightening speed. His eyes glinted. "You wanna let me use your bag, man?

Christ, I been sick lately, real sick. You seen."

"What about me?" Kevin demanded.

"Oh, it's not cold here, you'll see. You don't need the bag, and the sand's soft. But man, I been so fucking *sick*, you dig? Hey, I'm letting you use my place to crash; you can be cool too." Again the glint of eyes.

Kevin composed himself. At last he said quietly, "Go ahead then."

"Hey, that's groovy, man. This'll all come back to you someday. It all evens out." The troll snatched and unrolled the sleeping bag. Without even removing his shoes he climbed in and zipped it up.

Kevin watched silently before moving back a few yards to sit against a barnacled pillar. He shivered and half-closed his eyes. Somewhere out of his line of vision a buoy clanged its doomsday bell, and a small boat tooted its horn twice. The piles stood about him like the ribcage of a long-disintegrated dragon, calcifying while tiny things scurried and sucked, picking its bones clean. The faintly phosphorescent waves broke stinking, monotonously and mournfully, and ghostly shadow people darted about in the darkness, playing a deadly hide-and-seek, waiting for him to close his eyes completely. He continued to monitor his surroundings, determined to remain alert. The night wore on.

It was head-to-toe discomfort which at last tugged him from the depths of a peculiarly heavy sleep. He felt drugged and stiff and sore. His back and shoulders ached arthritically.

He had dreamt of grisly many-pincered crustaceans clambering over his legs, and of a horrible thing like a tentacled lamprey with a firm suckerhold on his heart. A subconscious fear of waking to find these horrors a reality had kept him under during the long night. Now it was another hot beautiful morning, but under the pier it was still dreary and foul.

Kevin froze.

Something was crawling on his backside, tugging very gently. Perspiration broke out on the boy's forehead...he hadn't been dreaming after all! The instinct to survive caused him to hold his breath while he tried to imagine just what disgusting, smelly, obscene creature was assailing him. Was it a primitive, spiny, fierce-eyed crab? Or maybe a blind, hideously deformed, radioactive rat; one of the hapless few washed up along the coast after escaping the Government's sadistic experiments in hippie behavior control. Or maybe it was—

"*Hey!*" Kevin cried. He turned just as the troll was leaning over him. The troll jumped back, trembling.

"You!" Kevin gasped. He shoved his wallet all the way back in. "You were trying to pick my pocket! You—"

"Hey, man," the troll spluttered, "what're you talking about, man?" His mouth worked convulsively. Kevin got to his feet. The troll looked around wildly. Kevin was standing between him and a cul-de-sac of crisscrossing timbers. The troll dropped to his knees.

"Would I do that?" he whined. "I mean, *would* I? After you bought me dinner and everything? Christ, man, gimme a break, willya? I got a family to look after, man; a wife and kids…Seka and Oprah…Rover and Babs. Look, I'm still on probation, man! Christ! *How in the fuck does doing time make a better man of anybody?* You tell me, pal—yeah, *you* tell *me*; it's not like anyone gives a good long crap about what I have to say anyway. Public defenders, man. But what you gonna do? They gotcha coming and going."

"Well, how do you explain it then?" Kevin demanded.

"It was…it was falling out of your pocket," the troll said. "Yeah, that's it, man; swear to God. I was afraid you might lose it, so I was trying to push it back in before it slid all the way out. You shouldn't be pissed at me, man. You should be thanking me."

As Kevin's mind, still sleep-bedraggled, tried to deal with the troll's lame explanation, he became increasingly disoriented. Either he'd blinked or the sun had just been swallowed by a black hole and just as suddenly regurgitated. Kevin tensed. Air. He needed air. "Thanks," he mumbled, and stumbled toward the pulsing squares of daylight. He lurched into sunshine. Kevin sat on the clean sand for five minutes, recovering. At last he looked back at the pier. He missed his bicycle. Underneath was all vile, impenetrable darkness. The idea made him shudder, but he had to retrieve his bike and sleeping bag. Then he was clearing out, no doubt about it. He rose, shook himself, and grimly made his way back in.

The troll was asleep in Kevin's bag. The boy angrily unzipped it and rolled him out. The troll didn't waken, but coughed feebly and curled into a fetal ball. Kevin rolled and tied the bag, strapped it to his bike's rack. He was about to leave when his heart took a turn. Nodding, he pulled a five dollar bill from his wallet and stuffed it in the troll's front pocket. He carried his bike out quietly, shaking his head and aching all over. He would have to make a note to scout out his sleeping spots before dark in the future, and from now on he'd have to think ahead before getting involved with strangers. And he really had to start watching his money.

# Chapter 10

## Homo Erectus

jooli 2 1967
jime
thengz hav gawtn awl scrood up fas
mik haz gawn undrgrown an edz bhin brz
thu man bustd us ystrda in san loois obispo an took ed an mi
pawt but it wuzn mi fawlt ed wuz holden it 4 me az u favr an
thu pigz kawt him with it
i don no wut hapund 2 mik he split az soon az thu pigz pold us
ovr an iv bin siten her awl da awn thu hiwa in kas he kumz bi
but if he duznt iv dsidud 2 kep goen newa bcuz im nawt thu kin
uv dood 2 kawp owt wn thu shit gts thik
ukordn 2 mi map its ruf stuf frum her awn no mor big sitz until
mawntra
frs theng iv gawt 2 doo iz gt u hold uv sum mor pawt but thu wa
it loox thaer won b much chans uv skoren 4 u yl so il hav 2 w8
an c wut wrx owt
kevin


   And now Kevin, in the shade of a rare palm, slipped the
letter into his last envelope and dropped it in the mailbox. All
morning and much of the afternoon he'd loitered here in Morro
Bay, watching the highway on the off chance Mike should come
pedaling his way. Kevin wasn't holding his breath. Odds were
Mike was on his way back to Santa Monica. And even if the

little punk were to continue north, he'd surely be too paranoid to travel in plain sight. No, whichever direction Mike chose, he'd move by night, and by the most circuitous route available.

Morro Bay is one of the loveliest stops the coast highway has to offer, but Kevin wasn't moved. The hauntingly picturesque windmills and sun-buttered marinas seemed incredibly alien, and the enormous hump of rock rising majestically from the bay only brought to mind Big Joe, who loomed in his thoughts at every turn.

Kevin found a small, clean, family-run café. He wasn't all that hungry, but the café's windows offered a superb highway view and, beyond, the gentle crescent of the sailboat-dotted bay. The café's outer wall was painted in washed blue and marine green, with infantile illustrations of sea life; seahorses, lobsters, crabs, a many-tentacled blemish meant to represent an octopus. Kevin parked his bike and stepped inside, took a chair at the table nearest the door. The dining area was deserted, but there were active voices in the kitchen, arguing in rapid Greek. The menu contained a lot of unfamiliar and unpronounceable dishes. When at last a squat, swarthy man in janitorial white came to take his order, his dark eyes beaming with false hospitality, Kevin tentatively ordered *falafel*, which turned out to be some mildly spiced deep-fried vegetable mush, and a large Pepsi.

While eating he heard a vehicle pull into the lot. A classic powder-blue Ferrari 250 GT parked in front of the café, and a youthful man of thirty-five, after spending a few minutes fussing with his wavy blond hair in the rear view-mirror, stepped out with a neat sashay and proceeded cheerfully up the walk. At the door he stopped to study his overall reflection in the glass, whipped out a fancy comb and spent at least another minute on details around his mane's part. Kevin saw that this man's complexion was very smooth and fair. An exaggerated grace imparted an unpleasant suggestion of effeminacy. There was something of this, too, in the eyes, which were slightly strabismic and of a twinkling and distant blue, like aquamarine rhinestones. He was dressed as a pseudo-hippie. Kevin imagined he'd told his tailor, "Dress me for the New Generation. You know, like all these young rebels go about nowadays." But the attempt to mix was simply too obvious. The brightly colored Nehru shirt and alabaster peace medallion were excessively "mod." The suspiciously soft Levis, though bleached and patched, in no way exemplified the proud, hardy dropped-out set. And the rope-soled sandals were so unworn they appeared virtually brand new. There was a familiar look to his hair...*that* look of being long enough to be non-conservative, yet too well-tended.

Kevin, gloomily munching his vegetable mush, couldn't help taking all this in. A window should never be used as a mirror. It really didn't make any sense, unless the man was some kind of a...Kevin guilty looked into his drink. There was a puff of hot air. The blond man waltzed in and stationed himself by the cash register while studying Kevin with an unwavering merry stare. After a bit the boy grew uncomfortable; he turned his head in the man's direction and nodded curtly. The stranger continued to eye him twinklingly.

The squat proprietor came back out and made much of this newcomer, apparently a regular and favored customer. The proprietor wrung his hands with grotesque servility and lavishly flattered the Ferrari. But the blond man's eyes never left Kevin. He shooed away the proprietor and, without preamble, joined Kevin at his table. Kevin looked away.

After an interminable span the stranger said in a wheedling voice, "You're certainly an intent road-watcher. Waiting for somebody? Hmm?"

Kevin shrugged a shoulder—the shoulder farthest from his unbidden guest. "Sort of. I got separated from a friend of mine back in San Luis Obispo. I'm hoping he'll come riding by. Sort of."

The stranger folded his arms on the tabletop, still smiling. "So you're *new* in town, is that it? You live in San Luis Obispo, do you? What brings you up to our sunny little resort?"

Kevin grinned lopsidedly. His resolution concerning strangers was easy prey to lonesomeness. "No, I live down near Los Angeles. A city called Santa Monica; maybe you've heard of it. Me and a couple partners were riding our bikes up to the Haight to catch the Big Jam at the Park."

The blond man was delighted. "That's *mar*velous! Riding your bicycles up you say? That's thrilling. How very, very camp. Are you carrying the banner of the Movement? Flying your freak flag? Participants in the Summer of Love?"

Kevin looked at him narrowly, wondering if he was being put on. But the answering twinkle was candid. After a moment he felt satisfied the stranger's enthusiasm was genuine.

"More or less," he admitted proudly. "A guy would have to be a fool to miss this big a happening." He looked up, trying to jog his memory. "—'The world has too long saved itself from becoming meaningfully involved'," he mumbled, "—'and now to become meaningfully involved is to save the world from itself'."

"What lovely thoughts you have in your head."

"Not really," Kevin said quietly. He looked back into his glass and let the ghosts coalesce. "A good friend once told me that. My...best friend."

"Still, it's the conviction that really matters, especially in these turbulent times. But what about your little friends? I'm quite sure you said you were traveling *en masse*. Where are they?"

Kevin shook his head. "That's the real bummer. Yesterday the man stopped us and busted Eddie with my pot—" He raised a hand halfway to his mouth.

The blond man placed a thin hand lightly on Kevin's arm and squeezed. "You don't have to worry about being discreet with *me*. You can rest assured *I'm* no pro-establishment straight. Believe me, I turn on with the best of them."

There was something really ugly and leading about the way the phrase "turn on" was used here. Kevin squinted. The moment was gone.

"Really?" he asked, curious and skeptical. "You get high?"

"Oh, assuredly. Pot, hash, acid, some of the best pharmaceuticals money can buy. And let me tell you, none of the lovelies passing through my system are cut, mixed, or tampered with in any way. There is no high like a clean high."

Kevin used the straw to stir the ice in his glass. At last he said, trying to not appear *too* eager, "You think you can maybe score me a lid? Like I said, I'm all out of pot."

The little stars dancing in the irises of the stranger's light blue eyes now blazed with some inner secret transcending merriment. "Can I score you a lid?" he asked with mock indignation. "Why, do you realize (and you'll keep this to yourself, please) that you are speaking to *the* individual solely responsible for stoking the heads of ninety percent of this quaint resort? That is, of the gross *turned-on* populace. I don't think more than sixty percent, all totaled, of the men, women, and children of Morro Bay *turn on*. But, believe me, the time will come, and it won't be long, when there won't be a living soul on the face of the globe who doesn't use pot, acid, and pharmaceuticals. Why, did you know that the Chief of Police in this town has been known to *turn on* before coming to work? The *Chief of Police*! Of *course* you didn't know. How *could* you? How could you even *guess*? But—and I'm not fabricating a word of this, mind you—you wouldn't believe the number of prominent and ascending socialites who *turn on* in this cheery little community. It's the *in* thing to do. But I don't have to tell you all this; I can see by that clever look in your eyes that you *turn on* too, hmmm?"

But Kevin, strange to say, was just too dumb to be subliminally influenced. "Well," he said, "of course I couldn't have know those numbers. Things are a lot tighter where I come from. But really," he said, trying to look the smiling blond man in the eye, "I had you figured for a head as soon as I first saw you. I was just fooling, you know, so you wouldn't be worried about me being a nark or anything. I mean, really, I *believe* what you say."

There was a weighty silence. Again Kevin looked away, totally disgusted by this flashy sweet peacock. For, dumb as Kevin was, he wasn't so dumb he couldn't recognize a lousy sticky-lipped, bottom-feeding, heinie-humping rectum reamer when he saw one. Yet the stout boy wasn't afraid of any physical advances. He'd heard that homosexuals were easily put off, and he knew that, if the situation should arise, it would be no problem to overpower this frail little man. Besides, Kevin held his own appeal in such low esteem that it seemed ludicrous to imagine a member of either sex seriously propositioning him. So he could pursue the matter.

"Well, do you have the pot on you? I mean, is it here, or do you have to go get it?"

"Oh no," the stranger said dreamily. "I never carry quantities with me. We can just skip over to my place and pick it up."

"But my bike," Kevin objected. "I can't leave it here. It might get ripped off. Can't you just go get the stash and meet me back here?"

The stranger waved a limp hand, stood and picked up Kevin's tab. "Nonsense, nonsense. I've got a way around that. You just leave it to me." When they had exited he showed Kevin a gleaming chromed bicycle rack on the Ferrari's trunk. He laughed. "What did I tell you—no problem!" He gracefully lifted Kevin's bike onto the rack, saying, "Upsy-daisy now!"

Kevin awkwardly climbed into the sleek little car. As the blond man put the Ferrari in gear and started away, a cassette tape featuring Rod McKuen began immediately. The driver pulled a neatly rolled joint—rolled in paper the same powder-blue as the car—from above the sun visor and lit it with a delicately embossed gold-plate lighter. He handed the joint to Kevin, who knew immediately from the smell and taste that this was foreign grass of high potency. He took two draws and began coughing. When the fit was over his mind was bobbing.

"Wow!" he fumbled. "This is—this is really dynamite. I mean...*wow!*"

The blond man looked at him with his widest smile yet, extremely pleased. "What did I tell you? Nothing but the best."

Kevin hit it again. Wow. There was a gustatory undercurrent, whatever that meant, giving the weed a slightly off taste, as though it had been cut with a Plutonian synthetic, perhaps, or maybe even an opiate-based multiabracathumbafarcture. Kevin's balls scrunched up his butt. Meth? He turned to face his benefactor.

Lance's smile was an enamel cartoon. "Goo-oo-oood?" He cupped Kevin's knee playfully. "So glad to have *turned* you *on*."

They motored along. Kevin shook his hard and grinned. As they were humped at an intersection he offered his hind in appreciation. "My name's Kevin."

The blond man took his hand without the slightest pressure. Kevin had a fleeting impression of an indecipherable change in the man's smile, but he put it down as a strange effect of this powerful marijuana.

"And I'm Lance." This statement was made in a velvety undertone. He removed his hand as though Kevin's body were a thing diseased and unclean. They drove on.

Kevin looked at the beautiful car dazedly. "Wow," he said, "I just can't get over this. What…what do you do for a living, Lance?" He blinked, adding quickly, "If I'm not being too purseonal, that is."

Lance laughed. "Me? Oh, I bugger the mayor for a living, and any of his friends who're feeling generous. I'll bet you didn't know the mayor was gay, did you?" He laughed again, and gave Kevin's thigh a generous squeeze with his free hand. "I'm kidding, of course. Now this Ferrari is a real jewel. Mint condition. Original paint, would you believe it? Not a ding or a dent when I picked him up; never had a bit of trouble with the motor, runs like a dream. And *feel* these seats. Original interior; not a rip, not a stain." He caressed and stroked the leather of the seat, reached up to lovingly pat the dashboard. "Oh, he's a real beauty, all right."

Lance pulled to a stop before a rather ordinary-looking apartment complex with an outstanding view of the bay. He carefully removed Kevin's bicycle from the rack and told him to lock it to a cast iron ornamental lattice bordering the ground floor apartment's front door. Kevin was by now too stoned to do anything but wordlessly comply, but as he passed the lock's chain between the rear wheel's spokes he grew increasingly apprehensive. He left the lock disengaged, just in case, for any reason, he might have to make a quick getaway. Then he followed his strange host into the apartment's living room.

The décor was expensive and tasteful, but definitely effeminate. Scattered about the room were huge silky pouffes in variant tones of pink, from flesh to shocking; the lamp shades, as diaphanous as babydolls, conformed to this tone scheme with subtle seductiveness. Conspicuously lacking were the materials a man generally uses to mood his lair: leather, chrome, rich woods were nowhere to be seen. With a start Kevin realized that all the framed nudes were males. Hiding his revulsion, he tried to focus on what his host was saying.

"Oh, I *know* it's not much," Lance gushed, slouching against a delicate rice paper partition and growing prissier by the second, "but I make do."

Knowing it was expected of him, Kevin murmured, "Oh, it's really...really swell, Lance." He quickly brought the small talk back to basics. "Look, I don't mean to rush you, but could I just get that lid?"

Lance pooh-poohed the interruption. "No bother; I'm in no hurry. Gracious! What kind of host *am* I, anyway? Do sit down. Make yourself comfy. What's your drink?"

Kevin remained standing, unconsciously balling his hands into fists. After a moment he said, very quietly, "I don't drink." Then, with barely concealed anxiety, "Listen, Lance, I didn't tell you before, but I'm really in a hurry. No offense or anything, man, but just let me cop a lid and split, okay? Don't get me wrong, I sure do appreciate the hassle you're going to and all, but I've really got to be on my way. I don't want to go into details, but I've got a heavy date, right away. With a *girl*," he added quickly. "My girlfriend'll be waiting and I hate to make her wait." He managed a sickly grin. "You know how women are...I—what I mean to say is, like, let's just forget about the lid, 'cause I'm in a like super-hurry so I guess I'd better just split. Nice to meet you and thanks for the ride. I really dug the ride, that's a really nice car you've got there, really. Well, I guess I'd better be going, so take it easy." He ended lamely, "Thanks again." He had to look down.

And the room frosted over. Lance's aquamarine eyes weren't twinkling anymore. He said softly, "You're nervous. I'm making you nervous."

Kevin nearly blacked out. Something absolutely primitive in his subconscious caught his courage before it could hit the floor, and his mouth, on its own, replied: "Just who the fuck are you to tell me whether I'm nervous or not, huh, man? I mean, where the fuck do you get off thinking you can read my mind, huh, prick?"

"You're getting rowdy," Lance responded. "I'm making you rowdy."

"I'm not getting rowdy," Kevin gasped. "It's just that you keep coming on like...like . . ."

"Go ahead and say it," Lance hissed. "Like a queer, is that what you mean? Like a fairy? A faggot?"

"I...I . . ."

"Well, that's just an assumption. That's not only unfair and premature, it's characteristic of a bigot, and if I'd known you were a bigot I wouldn't have gone out of my way to help you score like this."

"You...you said it wasn't any hassle."

"It's going out of my way to entertain a bigot."

"But," Kevin groped, "I'm really not all *that* big. I just come from a...large family."

And Lance was smiling again. "You know what, cream puff? I believe you. There's nothing more disarming than innocence. And," he divulged, "just to put your mind at ease, I want you to know you're not the first person to jump to that conclusion."

There then ensued another of those excruciating silences, punctuated only by a slender crystal grandfather clock ticking patiently in the corner. Something about the steady tapping made Kevin's mind hark back to that crucial November night in the garage loft, when Eddie'd got his head just as stoked on pot, and a similar tapping had portended an explosion that would profoundly affect his future.

"I just don't know what it is," Lance sighed, alternately sagging and recovering, "that would cause some people to get that impression." His gaze oozed across the framed male nudes. After a reflective pause he began to discourse:

"Y'know, jelly bean, we've all heard this label-linking about 'lifestyles,' and 'sexual preferences,' and all the speculation about whether it's a genetic thing or something an individual, presumably heterosexual by nature, gets sucked into through exposure to sickies and horniness—as if straight young men are caught in a helpless spiral; from pornography to prostitutes to queer dives. *As if* to say there's a lurid substratum of compulsively masturbating thrill addicts needing a harder fix each time; and so moving up the sin ladder. That's like assuming a pot smoker 'does it' for a voluptuous thrill until it just isn't 'good enough' anymore, and so goes on to sniffing glue or dropping downers, finally ending up in a rat-infested tenement sharing needles with another little engine that couldn't. So you see, passion fruit, the assumptive personality, adamantly indifferent to the facts and completely ignorant of the experience, is the party with the least valid voice in the matter. But everybody knows that. It's just that honesty takes all the fun out of a witch hunt.

"*Anyways*," Lance elaborated, "there's a mutual insensitivity that guarantees both sides'll remain polarized. You take queer factions, for instance. Now, *what outspoken homosexual groups are unable to understand*, pudding buns, when they publicly attempt to assuage the straight community with all their rationale about 'preferences' and 'lifestyles,' is...is...the absolute, soul-deep *revulsion* the heterosexual majority is going to experience. As an example I could say...oh...like I'm a member of the pro-cannibalism movement, okay? Just an analogy."

"I know," Kevin said remorsefully, "all about analogies."

"Groovy. So we'll suppose that cannibalism is my 'preference,' or my 'religion,' or my 'philosophy.' Right? So...why in the world, my camp wonders, do you goobers react so violently, so *canniphobically*, to our druthers? I mean, we don't castigate you for being strict vegetarians, or for being steak and potato guys, or even for being Sara Lee junkies. So why should it bother you that we eat our relatives? You've got your thing, and we've got ours. All we ask is that we cannibals are treated the same as so-called 'normal' people. You see what I mean? And I can stretch this kind of inductive nonsense as far as necessary. I can say, for example, that the morgue is an *eco-friendly* source of protein, and I can say additionally that people have been ceremoniously eating other people since people began, and that it's only some weird right-wing taboo which prevents we finger-lickin' liberals from enjoying, let's say, the pleasures of the flesh."

"That's disgusting," Kevin said.

"Exactly. But to our hypothetical cannibals' society it's absolutely reasonable, and your aversion is just a popular prejudice. And that's why queers miss the mark so badly. Apparently they don't understand that homosexuality is nauseating, infuriating, and absolutely *ugly*; ugly in a way that deflects sympathy and snuffs any desire to reach a compromise. When a faggot announces his fairyness to someone in the straight community, he's not communicating to that straight someone: 'I am simply a person like any other, who just so happens to be oriented toward members of his own gender rather than the opposite gender.' What he's communicating is: 'I am a male who loves to suck on another male's penis while my punk lover rams his penis in and out of my anus. I crave the sickest, most obscene behavior imaginable'."

There was a lull while Lance collected himself.

"The premise," Kevin said brightly, "is everything."

Lance blinked at him. "What premise?" Then he said, "Oh, oh, oh! I see what you mean. Queers, cannibals, and democrats aren't aware of their transgressions because they're morally ignorant. They take the Constitution literally. In other words, liberty, perversion, and cannibalism are synonymous: we're freemen."

Kevin looked away, seeking words to encapsulate and close this increasingly uncomfortable subject.

"I really don't care what people do in privacy," he said. "But if it's a bad thing it shouldn't be in everybody's face. I mean…I don't think I should even have to *know* about it, except maybe from some book. Instead, there's these parades and all this public stuff. They even say they're proud of it. I don't understand that."

"Gay Pride," Lance replied, nodding and slouching, "is definitely an oxymoron. But I guess closets can become suffocating after a couple thousand years or so. Yet," he said, holding up a hand to obviate any possible interruption, "after all the dirt has been swept aside, there remains one critical, totally unprejudiced question: *why* is homosexuality?

"Now, it's a simple, undeniable fact that nothing occurs in nature, as a steady-state, without being a part of the Big Picture. Ergo, sweetmeat, homosexuality *has* a place in nature; it's not some temporary phenomenon or transient mutation. It's always been with us, even though it's been in the closet, retaining its natural hold on a percentage of the population. You can read about it in the Bible, or in the Wall Street Journal, for that matter. But *why* does it exist?"

Kevin shrugged. "The world doesn't need more babies."

"That *does* seem to be the only logical answer. A queer won't get his faggot sweetheart pregnant. But why would the population be regulated like that? Why not more miscarriages? Why not an asexual continuum? Or a naturally-regulated quota of infertile women, or impotent men?"

"Maybe because—"

"I'll tell you why," Lance interrupted. "I'll answer my own questions, deary, if you don't *mind!* I'm not making idle chatter here; I'm attempting to probe the deepest recesses, to get my hands on the naked truth. So…notwithstanding that homo sapiens is, to all effects and purposes, out of the food chain, and that our numbers don't have to be regulated according to how many of our offspring are likely to be scarfed up, and…*given* that there are more effective ways for nature to maintain population control, *and* disregarding any ecumenical tripe about good and evil, we're left with a sexual anomaly that resists logic and persists throughout history. And the answer is not to be found in mathematics, and it's not to be found in reason. It's even more abstruse than the queer community calling itself 'gay.' Now *there's* a dignified, ennobling title for you!

"Anyway, as I was attempting to impart here, the answer is far more basic. You see, peach, testosterone is an intensely powerful chemical influence. The sexual receptor is the libido, which is a blind area. Men will fuck women," he sang, "men will fuck men. Men will fuck boys, men will fuck sheep. Men will fuck anything that will accommodate them. A man will fuck himself if he can figure out a way to do it. And it really doesn't reflect on the individual, except where there's no restraint. No matter how intense the provocation, each man still has an obligation to govern his reaction. It's the *mind*—not the brain, the *mind*—which gives us the right to call all other species 'lower animals.' We can't spiritually go through life on all fours."

"Now you're starting to kinda remind me of my best friend."

*"Really!"* Lance gushed. "I'm flattered. Is he cute?"

"I...don't know," Kevin fumbled. "I never thought about it. What I mean is the kinda stuff you're talking about reminds me of him. I guess there's a lot I haven't given much thought to."

"Well, shame on you. You don't want to live in the dark, do you? That's what this whole revolution's about. People are opening their minds and their hearts, instead of just running around following orders and feeding the system. It's not only the gays. The entire human race is coming out of one closet or another."

"I just wish they'd do it without the parades," Kevin said, "and quit trying to make everybody feel guilty about 'em being in there in the first place."

"Hypocrisy," Lance prognosticated, "is one practice that'll never go out of fashion. So there might be a whole lot less of this homophobia if queers would just quit pretending there's nothing disgusting about *being* queer." Lance, placing his hands on his hips and pouting dreamily, now embellished, "Yet, you know, it's the same thing, heterosexually speaking, when you put the pump on the other foot.

"Take the way women come off making *statements* about how they're oppressed, and not seen as anything other than sex objects, whilst they demand *equal access* to the power thought-pool. Reverse the broadcast imagery, if you will. Now...just *picture* a man in a skirt, wearing special under-clothing designed to 'lift and separate' his private parts into your focus, wearing lipstick and mascara and eyeliner, his hair dyed and his nails polished, stamping his heels in pique because you won't take him seriously as a cool, deep, intellectual individual. Imagine it! Women are either as naïve, or as dishonest, as fags. Hell-o-o out there, women! You're *painting* yourselves, for goodness' sake! What are you, aborigines? *You're painting yourselves!* You're dangling baubles from your body parts. You're boldly walking around in public trying to be just as naked as you can legally be. Everything you do, everything you stand for...your entire 'statement' *is* sex—not gender, sex—yet you're brought up to believe anybody who reacts to what you're deliberately radiating is dirty-minded.

*You're* the ones who are dirty-minded! I mean," Lance shivered, "can't you just *see* some curvy guy in drag, expecting to be taken seriously! Why, that's so ludicrous it's…it's…*delicious!*"

But Kevin wasn't salivating. Now the grandfather clock was pounding in his head, and Lance had become something out of a nightmare. "I gotta go," he said. "Later."

"Nonsense! Just relax. Pull up one of those cushions and take off your shoes. I'll be back in a sec'." He sauntered into the kitchen.

After a moment Kevin sat on a lavender couch and gnawed his nails. If Lance would have stood in his way…it would have been different. But take off his shoes—hell! No way was he about to remove a single article of clothing. He told himself to be a man: a tough, resolute lumberjock with thighs of steel, a no-holes-barred hardon who wasn't about to shake any lip off of some pretty-ass blond weenie wagger. He'd come to screw a lid and, dammit, he'd sit here surrounded by posters of hot shiny naked guys all day long if he had to; it was no big deal, 'cause he didn't lean that way, wouldn't ponder leaning, wouldn't dream of leaning. Kevin actually thought it was fall-down funny that dudes would even pose for other dudes; that was lady stuff, and since only guys liked to look at pictures, only women should spread for 'em. That one guy there, Kevin marveled, must have exercised forever to get abs like that. Or maybe it was just fairy luck: a bi-product of nibbling tofu and sprouts and other leprechaun food instead of real macho grub like hot dogs with heavy mayo and tight sesame buns. A string of saliva joined Kevin's lips. Or maybe that guy didn't just diet and work the abs; he was absolutely ripped, from his taut glistening pecs all the way down to his rock-hard thighs. It was really kind of funny looking at another guy's penis like this. Not funny-haha, but funny…well, funny. It wasn't an actual photograph anyway, just some kind of special effects mock-up, where great equipment augments a hairless model's doink and doo-dads so whoever's staring hard at it simply can't look away. Kevin had heard of such stiff in orgio-video class; cameras and filters and lights and codpieces. Manimation. 3-D graphic sensories that feel the observer into believing a picture of some guy's ripe rolling riftwhomper is, you know, engorging or whatever the hell they call it, getting bigger and shinier and closer and thicker and oh for the love of God; Kevin closed his knees and covered his peaking lap with his forearms. Something totally *wrong* was going on here. And definitely not wrong-haha. He'd heard of such stiff in science class; bi-ochemistry it was called, where the bodies' organs could penetrate even the tightest wad until some poor son of a bitch dropped to his knees and embraced a great God in Heaven something really queer was going on here. Kevin bit his lower lip and stamped a foot. For some reason a vision of his mom doing a striptease came to mind, and that was that. But man oh man oh men, somebody must have slipped him something. That grass must have come off a Thighstick. He'd heard about such stiff in Jim class...

The muzak of a string queertet swished sweetly from speakers lurking in the balls. Lance pranced in, gaily jiggling a sticky woody tray. "Cumfy?" he queeried. On the shiny round tray were: a carafe containing a foggy liqueer, a tall glans of wine, and a bulging, ornately splayed hardwood box.

Lance laid the tray on the rump-end of a pronated coffee table. He opened the box, exposing its contents to Kevin's frankly curious gaze. The boy half-expected to see a ghastly rectal arsenal of gadgets and lubricants, but the box contained various articles of smoking paraphernalia, little trays of hashish and marijuana, a variety of capsules and tablets, and several vials of powders. Now here was something to focus on.

"Did I lie?" Lance prompted gleefully. "Nothing but the best!"

Kevin threw his whole attention into the box of goodies.

"What kind of pot is this?"

"Here, Panama Red. This here is from Viet Nam. And this is Acapulco Gold. *Real* Acapulco Gold, not the bunk you get on the street."

"Wow! And the hash?"

"From India, here. This is from Iraq, and this here's local."

"Man! What's in these little bottles?"

"Cocaine here, absolutely uncut. Pure PCP here. And this little vial contains *s-s-s-mack!* for those rare moments."

"No kidding! And all these pills!"

"That's right, spongecake. Uppers, downers, in-betwee-ners. Mescaline and Orange Sunshine. Pressed powder of peyote. And *this*...is for *you*." He handed the boy a neatly bagged ounce of pungent marijuana, and refused to accept a cent in payment.

Kevin looked up in awe and deep gratitude, a good deal of his natural repugnance replaced by envy and a sort of diluted idolatry. He stuffed the baggie in his left trousers pocket.

"Would you like a toot of that coke?" Lance offered delightedly. "I can guarantee you won't soon, if ever, sample its equal."

Kevin's mouth opened wider. "*Could* I?"

"Of *course*! That's what it's *here*, for, Silly. You didn't think I brought it out just to *tease* you, did you? Here's the vial, and here's the straw, mirror, and razor blade." He pointed out these articles and settled next to Kevin on the lavender couch, watching over the rim of his wine glass as the boy indulged. He laughed with a trace of the old merriment when Kevin got a nosebleed from snorting the drug.

"Wow-w-w—" Kevin said at last. He felt he was out to sea, without moorage, without memory.

"Goo-oo-oood?" Lance asked. His voice was distant, soft as cotton on the eardrums. Kevin watched entranced as Lance leaned forward to extract a tiny jade pipe from the box, a slender hand on Kevin's thigh for support. Lance filled the bowl with a large chunk of hashish and placed the pipe in Kevin's numb fingers.

Some part of Kevin heard a voice say, "*Here. Smoke this. It'll make the high flow easier. It'll soften you up. But first...as an everlasting symbol of our very, very* close *friend-ship.*" Lance removed his alabaster peace medallion and draped it around Kevin's neck. "Now!" The boy obediently puffed on the pipe's stem while Lance held a sputtering match to the bowl. After three hits he was hacking uncontrollably. He felt the chill of a glass in his hand, and was gratefully gulping down a cold foggy drink.

The combination of all these stimuli had Kevin com-pletely confused, but delightfully so. If he had previously been frightened and repulsed by his host, all was now forgotten in this wonderful cool weightlessness. He was bobbing and drifting, grinning lazily at the room. Lance's smiling countenance became just another prop highlighting the strange backdrop floating round and round, and Kevin's body had grown so numb that it was a full five minutes before he realized Lance's hand was resting on his knee. He gawked at the man, or tried to gawk. Kevin Freaking Mikolajczyk was made of stone. Lance must have seen something in his face though, for he removed the hand and busied himself with the contents of the joybox.

"Come in, come in," Lance was jabbering. "This is planet Lance to outpost station Kevin; do you read me? I say, you don't seem to be receiving me, Station Kevin. Come in, come in. Are you receiving me? Are we making contact? Come in, please." Lance passed a hand like a fluttering bat in front of Kevin's face. "Dear me, what's it like out there, Station Kevin? What do you see? Tell me. Tell me what you see."

Kevin grinned at the jackass and his stupid room. He certainly *did* feel out in space, and this certainly *was* good cocaine, and mighty choice hashish, but there had been something in that drink…he felt oddly open to suggestion. He didn't want to offend his generous, if comical, host, so he did everything in his power to pay attention, to focus his glassy eyes.

"Planet Lance to Station Kevin, Planet Lance to Station Kevin, we are sending up a shuttlecraft. Please open your receiving hatch. Repeat, we are sending up a shuttlecraft. Come on now, plum, open your mouth."

Station Kevin saw a capsule-shaped shuttlecraft growing in his viewscreen, and obediently opened his receiving hatch. There was a sudden obstruction in his throat—and he was choking, but his good friend and benefactor was helping him, holding his head while administering increasingly large doses of that same acidic drink. The offending lump slid down his throat.

"You know what *that* was, biscuit? Seven-hundred and fifty micrograms of Latvian LSD cut with estrogenic esters of Eastwood. Margarine, anybody? Soon you'll be orbiting out of all known planes, just a big juicy nebula lost in space, a happy creature of godlike luminosity. How does that strike you, sweets? Isn't it goo-oo-oood?"

And Kevin closed his eyes to hide from the hypnotic voice, becoming an astronaut in a huge clumsy spacesuit, floating in a starless void. Far, far away drifted the squat body of his truncated module, a dazzlingly lovely thing shimmering in its own light. Kevin, groping for it, became aware he was without lifeline. He took that news in stride, and began swimming for the module. But the module was moving away, at a velocity precisely mirroring the little forward lurches he managed. He threw out his arms in despair, only to find himself tumbling over and over like paper in a gentle breeze. Kevin resigned himself to this tumbling, which soon steadied to a smooth spiraling. Abruptly the great body of the module was before him, and he was closing with outstretched arms. Once he'd embraced it, the module began rocking violently, as though a captive beast raged within. And from out of nowhere a great slug monster clamped itself to his back, growing, growing; bigger than he, then bigger than the shaking module, then bigger than space itself. Kevin cried out in alarm and opened his eyes. And the wildly bucking module became the lavender couch, and the slug monster on his back became his frantically humping ex-friend Lance.

Shock prevented his reacting for a moment. But only for a moment. Kevin scrambled to his feet with a wail of horror and disgust.

There were some really strange visual events taking place all about the room...and Lance was facing him, his Levis and shorts down to his ankles, panting, flaccid.

"Are you out of your mind-your mind?" Kevin cried, his voice splintering in his ears. "What do you—what do you think you're *doing*?doing?do-ing-g?"

Lance was staring with vacant eyes, his mouth working soundlessly. At last he said, viciously, "I should paddle your fanny for that, you know that? You'd *like* that, wouldn't you?"

"No!" Kevin gasped, close to tears. "Get away! Leave me alone!"

Lance advanced threateningly, only managing small steps due to the Levis fettering his ankles. "Or do you want to paddle my fanny? You can do it if you want! Yes. Do it! *Do* it!" He turned and proffered his skinny pale buttocks.

*"No!"* Kevin screamed. The powerful dose of LSD was taking command quickly, and with attitude. Kevin, cringing on the edge of the couch, covered his face while a dozen trail-images of his arms dissolved into multicolored streamers. Green paisley patterns oozed down the walls.

When he looked again Lance was gone, but he could hear a soliloquy from the next room,

"Insolent puppy! Telling *me* to get away! In my own house!"

Kevin stood shakily. He made for the door in slow motion, forcing the lead stilts of his legs through a thick, sluggishly flowing medium while the ocean roared in his ears. He finally reached the door, hauled it open. Behind the door was only a closet containing dainty garments. He willed himself to close the door but his arm would not obey, so he stood frozen, staring into the rustling disembodied finery. From the adjacent bedroom came an odd snapping, and Lance's thin voice, "Rude. Naughty. Selfish." Each word was spat out and punctuated by a cracking report. The voice was nearing. In a panic Kevin freed his hand from the doorknob and swam toward the center of the room.

"So *there* you are!"

Turning, Kevin was horrified to see Lance attired in powder blue panties, red high heels, and a limp black brassiere. In his hand was a flexible thing like a rubber ping pong paddle with a phallus handle, its diaphragmatic surface covered with slender, villi-like nylon protuberances. He was slapping the device against his palm.

Kevin cried out and slowly dog-paddled away, assaulted from all directions by the most amazing and terrifying hallucinations. The room would yawn to swallow him, then tilt and revolve, drawing him deeper into its crazy reeling belly, and he'd be running along an unending, whirling hallway, puffing up a DOWN escalator, hacking his way through a vacuum, while colors and sounds strafed him from all sides. And everywhere he turned Lance's feverish voice was in one ear, the smacking of the paddle in the other. The whirling hallway came to an abrupt end. Kevin was cornered. He turned with a snarl just as Lance pounced, both hands scrabbling for the fly on his

Levis.

Kevin grabbed the first thing within reach, which happened to be the slender neck of a plaster lamp. With all his strength he brought the base of the lamp down on Lance's intent, sweating face. The lamp exploded in his hand and the grip on his pants was released. He opened his eyes to see Lance's grinning face next to his. There was blood all over that silly mug, and sharp chunks of plaster imbedded in the cheeks and forehead. The look on the man's face was ecstatic. Kevin, in pushing him away, undulated to his feet. Lance rolled on his back like a submissive bitch, grinning up at him.

Kevin whirled, flipped over the lurking lavender couch, and somehow made his way to the front door. As he threw it open the fading daylight burst on him like a tidal wave. In the space within the door's frame, the horizon was revolving kaleidoscopically about an angry, throbbing sun. Exotic shrieks filled his ears. He reeled into his bicycle and stumbled over it, rolled, picked himself and the bicycle up, mounted it backward, pitched headfirst off the porch. The lock's chain was fouled in the spokes. He tore out the chain and left it where it fell. A sound of stumbling from the front room. Kevin frantically threw himself on his bike as Lance came clopping out in his bra and panties, covered with blood and bawling, "Wait, Honeyhole! *Wait!*" Kevin kicked at him twice, missed twice, and wobbled onto the walk. Lance, doubled-over on the railing, shook his fist, cried, *"Cockteaser!"* and began hollering for the police.

Kevin insanely pedaled down the street, hallucinating parked cars rushing at him. The road pitched and yawed.

It was fortunate he found his way to Brokeback Beach, where someone in his condition posed little threat to himself or the community. He dragged his bike through the sand until the front wheel turned on him: bitch. With the pink light district in front and the lubricant sea behind, Kevin found himself going south in the petering light. Butt he'd really pulled a boner this time: Kevin had stumbled upon an all-male nude beach! He backed onto a peephole grate, only to have a hot blast of air blow his sheer frilly skirt billowing around his eyes; and that wasn't the worst of it—*Kevin wasn't wearing any underpants!* Blushing bright crimson, he flitted off squealing, his hands desperately cupping his front and rear, an old man on crotches in hot pursuit. There was nowhere to run, nowhere to hide; the Marvellettes were fingering him fully while searchlight beams danced gaily over the sand, exposing Kevin's quivering spunk-hole to landlubbers and semen alike. Queens to the left of him, jerkers to the right, and cuming up ahead—*no*, not sperm whales! This was nuts! Kevin screamed as Lance rose from the sand, violated an ankle, and tried to drag him down. The boy kicked and kicked until a snarling wedge of spokes bit into flesh. His bike's front wheel half-turned, but it was enough to throw him face-first into the sand. In one lunge the faggot was on him. Weeping with the pain, Kevin dug himself deeper, a bottom-up bitch in a gangbanger's glory hole, holding his own while the naked night punked him to sleep.

When he woke it was just getting light. The sand was damp and cold, the area stinking of beached seaweed. His body felt sticky and limp, elastic, as though it no longer belonged to him. He spat the sand from his mouth and sat up. His left foot was swollen and numb, still wedged between the spokes of his bicycle's rear wheel. With the utmost delicacy he extracted the foot and let it rest on the sand. Curiously, his first concern was damage to the spokes. When he saw there was no problem he let his Gumby body fall back on the sand.

And so the memories came rushing back. Kevin struggled to suppress them, to think of other things, but the drug's effects still had him. Chief among his remaining sensations was a nauseous weightlessness, very much like an alcohol hangover. Yet faint traces of colored light still wriggled in the air, and the cottages off the strand exuded a sickly radiance.

He limped across the sand to the mouth of a little waking avenue, where he caught his reflection in the window of a notary public's office. He hung his head. He looked and felt like hell. Kevin ran his hands over his matted hair, pulled his hat back in place, wiped his hands across his face and down his sides. He stopped when he felt the bulge in his pants pocket, fished out the squashed bag of marijuana. Only then did he recall the full horror of the assault. Kevin was filled with a rage so intense it left him limp and spent without having moved a muscle. He wanted to take Lance by the ears and smash his grinning face into a wall, a window, anything that would maim. But that, he realized, was exactly what the man craved. The world was just too sick and perverse to fathom. He continued shambling down the sidewalk.

He came to a tiny cafeteria and drank steaming black coffee. Now he could accept the looks of disgust and amusement he received from other customers; he'd become *empathic*. Not long ago, in another world and another life, he could sneer right back, Now he only felt guilty in public.

Shunning any solid breakfast, he dragged himself from the cafeteria and back to the beach, where he grudgingly rolled a joint. After two inhalations he began to hallucinate. He snuffed the joint and dropped it back in the bag.

Kevin, returning to the avenue, eventually found himself back on Highway 1. Resting there, watching the gorgeous morning stretch awake, he weighed the urge to chuck it all and just head on home. What prevented him he wasn't sure, but, as he realized for the first time that Lance's alabaster peace medallion still hung from his neck, a grim resolve shooed away his thoughts of submission. He raised the medallion to his eyes, prepared to tear it from its chain and hurl it into the nearest storm drain as a proclamation of his outrage. He hesitated. It was a beautifully carved piece. No, he would keep this medallion, along with all the other junk he'd acquired—he was a pack rat at heart. Kevin stared at the gently shimmering houses, at the radioactive gulls scudding over the broad sparkling bay, then, in his mind, at the miles and miles of highway yet to be conquered. Slowly a hard smile turned away the furrows of tension on his brow. The sun, small and round in the east, was glazing the rooftops with gold. Like it or not, it was going to be a beautiful day.

# Chapter 11

## Why I'm Single

Getting back into the highway groove was the quickest way out of his funk, and the best way to override the acid's lingering effects. Kevin pedaled with a will, concentrating only on that next downward pump of the leg. Yet for several hours and many miles the ghosts pursued him. The phenomenon of "flashing back" continued to nip, as if insanity, an eager demon, rode puffing just behind. He was afraid to turn and confront this demon, but in his mind he could visualize its face. It would be grinning and bathed in blood, with jagged chunks of plaster protruding from its forehead and cheeks. Kevin scrunched his neck and pumped his legs like pistons. He drove himself on.

At one o'clock he broke for lunch in the tiny seaside resort of Harmony.

The exertion had all but cured him. Kevin's demon, unless it lay ahead in patient grinning ambush, had at last been given the slip. He felt so much better, in fact, he could smoke a whole joint with only the slightest discomfort.

He scouted around, bought a new lock and chain for his bicycle.

Kevin coasted the strand, enviously watching the happy beachgoers. He found a vacant bench along the promenade, sat and rolled another joint, drew on it hard as he could. He began to doze, snapped out of it. A weird sense of alienation overcame him as he took in the casual parade of passersby. Everybody seemed absorbed in participation, as opposed to observation. He felt he could expire right there, in plain sight, and the parade would go on as ever.

And while he sat, intoxicated, Kevin was treated to a haunting insight.

First came three young women wiggling by in their most provocative summer sex costumes, rudely jiggling their tits and swaying their asses—exhibiting these unbelievably affecting parts, it seemed to Kevin, solely to provoke his rolling, burning eyeballs—while giggling nervously, their own eyes flashing as they pretended to not be inflamed by the four whooping and whistling young men who were hungrily pursuing, no less mesmerized than the lonely fat boy craning on the bench. The horniness was so intense it was almost palpable. Everyone involved was drunk with lust.

Behind this barely restrained aspect were two couples in their late twenties. The women were doing all the talking and gesticulating, at this age still giggling, clinging to their goofily blushing and occasionally mumbling men as if they were life itself, shrieking with brainless vivacity while slapping the men on their behinds. This phase of mating was somehow even uglier than the lust phase.

Next in line came middle age:  the Bermuda-shorted, wingtipped males shuffling along vacantly, hands in pockets, pot-bellied. Their females waddled beside them, hanging on as though they were the jealous guides of blind gods, their tits and asses now nauseating masses of funky flopping fat. Their infants they fondled obscenely, slipping readily into baby talk; their growing children they berated almost casually, snapping and scolding and threatening. These women would then effortlessly glide into yammering at their hubbies, whose minds were clearly elsewhere.

Finally came old age; senior citizens looking desperately alone, desperately deprived. Nobody was giggling or blushing anymore.

And subsequent to the seniors came…

Nothing.

Suddenly there were tears rolling down Kevin's cheeks, and he didn't know why. He kept waiting for somebody, for anybody, to follow the procession. But the promenade was deserted. For some reason Eddie's face came to mind, and now Kevin could clearly discern what before had been only a vagabond impression. Eddie had wanted something too badly. He heard Eddie's voice: *"You'll never meet your maker, but salvation's waiting for you with open arms."* Kevin mounted and rode on without looking back.

The highway became progressively desolate after Harmony, the road's regular tenor giving way to long murderous climbs and to brief, exhilarating descents. Kevin removed his vest and peeled off his reeking shirt, once again exposing his upper body to the brutal July sun.

It was always one more climb. From the top of the next grade he was certain to gaze over the panorama of a little green valley where children splashed in crystal fountains. But time and again he found himself commanding a lonesome view of an unending highway shimmering in waves of heat, often snaking well out of sight of the ocean, only to return, inevitably, to this backbreaking range. He broke his climb to study his crumpled map of California, certain that Gorda must be very near. But either exhaustion had addled his sense of distance or the map was a liar (Gorda, it turned out, was nothing more than an old house with a rusty gas pump. Maps don't lie so much as tease). He coasted down the opposing grade barely enjoying the cooler rush of air.

Just one more climb! When he reached the top he was going to stop and find shade, or make shade, and perhaps snooze until the sun had eased low enough to make this kind of exertion reasonable. Maybe, he thought, maybe he should henceforth travel only by night. He wasn't even sure he wanted to see San Francisco any longer, or catch the great concert. He was pretty sure, with almost four days left, that he'd arrive in time, but his mind no longer soared with grand images. The struggle was now automatic, his game plan confused. His basic motivation had become a soporific, singsong mantra on the benefits of rigorous exercise, which only seemed to be killing him, and on the ideals of Love and Peace, concepts which were only applicable in the half-world of his Shangri-la waiting just beyond the next climb. The whole trip made much less sense without his buddies. Guilt made him bitter and defiant. Kevin repeatedly visualized them at home, smugly expecting him to come whining into Santa Monica at any time.

Just *one* more *climb!*

But this grade seemed to rise forever.

Grunting, he closed his mind to it, labored up the highway mechanically, head bowed. The sun was vicious. Kevin once more donned his shirt against the rays. The rough fabric scraped maddeningly on his back with each forced pump of a leg. Sweat soaked his hair and collar. Traffic picked up. He thought of stopping halfway to the top, but to arrest his painfully slow progress would kill it. He'd never get going again.

The highway began to wind. And wind. The yellow caution signs became redundant. "Jesus," Kevin said. Dismounting, he almost lost his feet. Kevin pushed his bike along. The space between road surface and cliff tapered until he was almost in competition with automotive traffic, and suddenly there was no space. Ahead, he could see cyclists and hikers darting to the road's other side, which didn't look any better. Traffic intensified. "*Jesus!*" Kevin gasped. He stopped at a cliff depression, squeezed himself into the niche. Even the sea breeze was hot. Eventually traffic abated and Kevin made his break. He took three steps and stopped dead in his tracks. What was he doing? Who was he kidding? A close call from a passing flatbed got him moving again, inching along, until he reached a roadside emergency turnout. Kevin pushed himself to the far end of the turnout, where a slight overhang crowned by a few stunted shrubs provided a bit of relief from the sun. He wearily swabbed the lenses of his glasses with his shirt's tail, elevated his feet.

Came hiking round the bend one of the oddest people he'd ever seen.

This guy was dressed in a pair of tie-dyed corduroys eighteen sizes too large for his gaunt frame, held up by green-checked purple suspenders. Dangling from the suspenders were several shells, a starfish, various found oddities, and an unopened summer sausage. His left foot sported a scuffed brown wingtip, his right a filthy pink slipper. Painted on his bare chest was a serrated black swastika, superimposed on a stars-and-stripes field. Atop his long, wildly disheveled hair perched a tall dunce's cap featuring, as on a barber's pole, a bright red cork-screw spiral. Additional odds and ends were pinned haphazardly to this cap, and he'd topped it off with a slinky toy which bobbed and lunged as he moved. Perhaps most arresting of his paraphernalia, however, was the miniature purple plastic hula hoop suspended from a hole pierced in his nasal septum. Rattling about on this hoop were large mahogany letters spelling out P-E-A-C-E. He was pushing a bashed and battered shopping cart filled to the brim with a variety of found junk—rocks, shells, hubcaps, etc. The cart was candy-striped with red, pink, and white paint, and bore on its front a sloppily painted sign that read FREE NUTS; apparently less an advertisement for pecans at no cost than a timely plea for the wholesale liberation of lunatics.

Kevin watched this character schlepping along, fascinated. Now there, he thought, is one together dude.

When the guy reached the turnout he stopped pushing his cart to survey the winding grade ahead. He closed an eye and positioned a thumb in front of the other eye like a painter judging perspective, then slowly pivoted round in the manner of a toy drummer. He was now facing traffic with his thumb displayed for the purpose of hitching a ride.

Immediately three cars pulled over. The freak took his pick—a late model Mercedes Benz driven by a voluptuous redhead in a nude body stocking, who helped wrestle the shopping cart onto the back seat with squeals of delight—and was last seen being happily shunted along.

Kevin considered this transaction for a few minutes.

What the hell.

He stuck out his thumb.

The response was not so immediate in his case. He tried various poses, including lost and lonely, seasoned and aloof, personable and eager. Zip.

Finally his nymph arrived.

She was of indeterminate age—sixty to be generous, eighty tops—wearing a frayed black halter top, faded blue slacks, open white sandals. She had come for him in a 1960 Chevrolet Impala convertible, which produced the racket of Rommel's Egyptian campaign and enough black exhaust to obscure whatever lay behind it. Oddly, each toenail was painted a different shade of pink, and there were what appeared to be bite marks all over her feet and hands. Her face possessed the singular property of apparently having its contiguous parts in a state of flux. It took Kevin a minute to realize she wasn't melting after all, that this effect was produced by the woman's liberal and reckless application of makeup. Her scarlet lipstick, for instance, careened off the right side of her mouth and down her chin, while lumping up under the left nostril. Massive amounts of cobalt-blue eye shadow stained her upper lids and parts of her forehead, where a pair of black squiggles had been drawn to hide the fact she had no eyebrows to speak of, and some weird dark goop had been applied to her lashes so as to produce a few uneven spikes. Handfuls of pancake makeup made her face a bone-white mask, except for those areas where rouge had been carelessly smeared across her cheeks and into her black-dyed, alternately snaking and crimping hair. Eczema was evident in a few bald patches, on the right ear, and on her throat. She now placed a shaky hand on the seat for support, leaned toward the boy and smiled boozily. "Goin' my way?" she asked, in a voice that would nauseate a grackle.

"Umm..." Kevin said hesitantly, "this...this is my bike," half-hoping she'd change her mind after considering the extra cargo.

"Pleased ter meetcha," she replied, addressing Kevin's bicycle. There was a pause. Finally she said, "Well, do you expect me to load the damn thing in for you, too?"

Kevin lifted his derailleur and placed it in the back, brushed aside some of the trash on the front seat to make room for himself. The crone took off hurriedly, barely giving him time to shut the door.

"My name's Nefertiti," she said, once the car had settled in traffic.

"I'm Kevin."

Another pause.

"Pretty coastline," Nefertiti said.

"I'm hip."

The driver of a white sedan, apparently peeved at having to suck down the Impala's jetting black exhaust, sounded his car's horn sharply. Nefertiti flipped him off. The sedan then swerved into the opposing lane and passed the Chevy easily. Nefertiti came half out of her seat. "Fucking showoff asshole!" she shrieked, and hammered her fist repeatedly on her own car's horn plate until the sedan had rounded the next bend.

"Oughta be a law preventin' creeps like that from obtainin' a license in the first place," she declared. She hunched her shoulders and swiveled her neck to get out some of the road stress. "Anyways," she said. She hiccoughed. "So where you headin', sweetheart?"

"Oh..." Kevin answered nonchalantly, "just up the coast."

"Ah, c'mon now, don't give me that. You can't fool Nefertiti. I been doin' readings since I was half your age."

"Readings?" Kevin wondered.

Nefertiti swatted him with her free hand. "Now hush up!" She placed the hand on her forehead and looked grave. "So..." she intoned, "you're in your late teens and you're goin' solo up north and you don't wanna talk about it. You're all dressed up incognito to be some kinda freaked-out hillbilly cowboy or something. The jollied-up bike's just a part of the disguise. I'd say Uncle Sam's just declared you're 1-A and you're scootin' your ass right on up to Canada 'bout as fast as you can."

"Nah," Kevin said. "I'm no draft dodger, not yet anyway. I'm only sixteen. With any luck, by the time I'm eighteen there won't even be a draft."

"Okay, sugar. Don't tell me. It'll just be our little secret. 'Cause y'see, honey, ol' 'Titi's never wrong. Never. It's a gift. But you can forget all about this great big ornery horse takin' you clear to the border. I'm only goin' far as Big Sur."

"Big Sur would be right-on!" Kevin said excitedly.

"Oh? So you wanna party with the animals, too?"

"Damn straight!"

"Then sugar, you got yourself some like company. Gots me two nephews and a grandson camping up there right now. Visited 'em during the hollydays an they invited me back for the summer. Hardly recognized 'em, but boy, do they ever know how to party. I didn't realize how squaresville the world really was till I got out and decided to let my hair down. I gotta hand it to you kids nowadays. You can really get it on when you've a mind to."

Kevin nodded. "It's really evolving," he asserted, eyeing the audacious array of freaks they were passing. "The world is, I mean. Kinda like having Halloween every day of the year."

Nefertiti smiled. "Y'know, sugar," she said, "all this reminds me of a big ol' festival they have every year down in Rio de Janeiro. It's called Carnival. Sort of a giant contest to see who can make the most obnoxious asshole of hisself." She laughed shrilly.

"Yeah," Kevin replied. "I love America."

Nefertiti swatted him again. "No, silly! Rio's *way* down south, down in that other America. One year Hank—before he died, God rest his soul—I says one year Hank and I was down there on a business layover from that stupid computer company that couldn't make a dime if you programmed it to, and Hank, well, he just got all dolled up in the cutest little Tarzan costume you ever seen, with his little round belly hanging out there and everything, so don't you know I just had to go as Jane," she gushed. "I mean I just *had* to. I mean *me*, Nefertiti, queen of the freaking Nile, for god's sake! Isn't that a *scream*? So I got out this smelly old wombat pelt Hank had wrangled out of some curio shop owner for next to *nothing*, sweetheart, and I fastened it in place with a buncha safety pins, and you know what? Honey, it *worked*! Even though it did smell like the devil, but whoever said Jane was supposed to be some kinda scent queen in the first place, if you know what I mean. And Hank, well he just looks at me with this darling little sarcastic look of his and he says, 'Oh, you'll really create a stir, Pinky, that's for sure,' like he was supposed to be Mr. Fashion Plate or something and—Pinky's what he used to call me, God rest his soul—and so I just looks him right in the eye and I says, 'Stir?' I says, 'you want a *stir*?' and I just took the top part of that smelly old wombat pelt and pulled it right down, like, like, like...*this!*"

To Kevin's astonishment, she freed her hands from the steering wheel for an instant and yanked down the front of her funky black halter. Her naked, burned-out dugs flapped in the breeze.

"Jeez!" Kevin hissed. "Cover up, willya? You want the pigs to come down on us?" In spite of himself, he kept his eyes glued to the dashboard.

Nefertiti glared at him, offended. "Ah, lighten up, huh, sourpuss? I'm just exercisin' my right to expose myself, like it says in the—what's that damned thing—the Constitution. You aren't unAmerican, are you?"

"Of course not," Kevin gasped, hyperventilating. "But I'm on the lam. I just don't wanna end up in the slammer, that's all."

Nefertiti wagged a limp hand. "B'lieve me, sugar, y'gots nothin' to fret about. If any copper tries to harass us, why, you just leave 'im to me. By the time ol' Nefertiti's done with him, he'll have traded his six-shooter in for a pacifier. B'sides, wasn't five minutes ago you was rappin' 'bout how it's all bully-bully and hallelujah to the good times you kids got goin' for you these days. So what's it gonna be? You gonna hide the goods or let it all hang out? Shit, I seen eunuchs got more balls than you got." Then she whinnied mockingly, half to herself, "cover up, *willya*? Cover up, *willya*? That's just what that stupid son of a bitch Hank says to me, like I'm standing there in some stinking rat's fur for my own freaking amusement or something, and...and...*oh, Hank!*" she cried, and the waterworks came on. "You know I was only doing it for you, baby; you know li'l Pinky never meant no harm to come to nobody, smoochypoo, you know I never meant no...aaah—*men!*" she spat, and looked daggers at Kevin. "*The way you act!* Why don't you *listen* to yourselves sometime!"

Kevin stared at her, speechless. Nefertiti gunned the engine and began taking the curves hard, braking halfway into the turns. It was all so very, very unnecessary. After a while she relaxed a bit, pulled her halter back up and said, "Oh, Christ." Kevin sighed with relief. They drove on in silence for a few miles until Nefertiti said, "*And* I'm a poetess. How about that?" as if it were one fragment of an ongoing conversation.

"Huh?" Kevin grunted. He'd been thinking about maybe rolling a joint. "How about what?"

Nefertiti reached over and slapped her palm against the glove compartment's door, causing it to pop open. A half-full pint bottle of local rotgut in a brown paper bag fell out, but Nefertiti caught it before it could hit the floor. Instead of gripping the cap with her teeth while turning the bottle, she held the bottle steady while unscrewing the cap with her lips—not a pretty sight—and chugged the contents without blinking, all the time dead-eyeing the road. She then tossed the empty bottle over her shoulder onto the back seat, maintaining a grip on the bag with her forefinger and thumb. Now Kevin could see that a number of lines had been scrawled on the bag in pink ink. She smoothed it on the dash, slapped it once for good measure, and stuck it in the boy's face.

"Here. Digest this."

Kevin read:

> Ah, the tenable lie, the ready pique / the cool denial, the dire eye / Conscience be still and / quarry be damned; you can't help it, it's / "human nature."
>
> Cheat, compete, sweet the blade / in the back of the dog your friend / Your vile pride is justified: / it's not your fault, *it's not your fault*, it's / "human nature."
>
> O Irony, worm! Cerebrate; / in the ooze and ashes / of time's distemper fly / headlong into madness. Imposters! / How must it grate: *forced* to primp and posture / and all because of The Whip, / that loathed and unflagging fiend you call / "human nature."
>
> No rest, no peace, / no recompense—On: / you struggle on / for honesty, for honor, for equity / only to be foiled, alas, alack, / ever soiled by that accursed demon you deem / "human nature."
>
> What *pain* must you endure in the keeping of your / crimes! / How *insufferable* must be the consideration of your / profits, / the memory of your slanders, your hypocrisy, / your double-dealing endeavors / as you valiantly strive to overcome your lust, / your greed, your mendacity / only to be so predictable drubbed / by that crazy dragon you call / "human nature."
>
> Rust not, brave warrior now fallen. / Your rest is /

prosaic. / Your camp is / populations-deep and / generations-wide. / And upon your common, gilded headstone / thine epitaph shall read, / with veracity, with humility: / I'M ONLY HUMAN.

Kevin looked up.

"Whaddaya think?" Nefertiti wondered.

"What does 'drubbed' mean?"

"It means," she hissed, "it *means* you can get your big fat ass outta my car!" She whipped the Impala into a dirt turnout and slammed on the brakes, sending the car into a tailspin in a choking cloud of dust, jumped to her feet and began kicking at Kevin's head. The boy somehow got the door open, tumbled out. Nefertiti lifted his bike over her head and hurled it at him, threw the car in gear, and roared away in a storm of dust and black exhaust.

Kevin picked himself up slowly, uncertain whether to (A) shake fist and shout obscenity or (B) stand with hands on hips while wagging head and smiling wryly. As no one on foot or in passing cars seemed to be paying him the least mind, he simply (C) swatted dirt off clothes, picked up bike, walked away with dusty head held high. He wasn't about to do any more hitchhiking, that's all there was to it. Chalk it up to experience. It was time to roll a joint.

After he'd embroidered his gray matter he resumed the mechanical upward climb. It just seemed to get hotter and hotter. When the grade became workable he stopped pushing and remounted, determined to prove himself. He came to a section of highway that was relatively straight, but murderously consistent: up, up, up. So he put his head down, down, down, and threw himself into it, becoming woozy and colicky, but refusing to give in.

Finally he raised his gaudy gourd and searched through sweat-streaked lenses for the top of the grade. Perhaps a hundred yards ahead it *did* seem to level off somewhat. Kevin could see something like a red handkerchief about half that distance, motionless at the side of the road. As he slowly drew closer he could distinguish white polka dots on the material, and then that it was a scarf, and then that the scarf was connected to the head of a sitting form. The person was hunched forward, exhaustion embodied; face buried in the arms, elbows resting on raised knees. Nearing, Kevin made out a nest of fine chestnut hair escaping from the scarf and falling about the arms. Closing, he saw the firm brown shoulders and abdomen of a slender teen-aged girl. Stopping, he saw long, tanned legs connected to a sun-bleached pair of cutoff blue jeans.

The girl raised her head and looked up at Kevin out of astonished brown eyes, her forehead white from resting on her arms. She was sweetly pretty, maybe seventeen or eighteen.

"Oh, thank *goodness*! I thought I was the only living person on this road."

Kevin stared blankly at the mirage, marveling its precision, its realism. The girl stood quickly.

"Oh, you *will* help me, won't you?" she decreed excitedly. "My bike got a flat, and I'm so...so *helpless* with these things."

Kevin's stare dropped from her face to her chest, where he could see she wore a halter of the same color and pattern as the scarf over her small breasts. His gaze oozed along to her shoulder, followed her brown arm until it came to her bicycle leaning against the rough rocks of the hewn-away hillside. It was an old, clumsy, three-speed bike, sporting a plastic basket adorned with artificial roses above the front mudguard. A rickety affair like that should never have been used on these hills. Kevin gasped. He shouldn't have stopped. Every muscle ached. His legs screamed with pain.

He dismounted awkwardly and limped over to her bicycle.

"Oh, *thank* you," the mirage gushed. I just *knew* you'd help me." She moved up close, and as he sat he bumped into real flesh.

That opened his eyes. Kevin looked at her closely. She was anxiously wringing her pretty brown hands. He closed his eyes and let the crimson waves of near-nausea rock him, let his respiration slow. He could feel the sweat seeping from his hairline and crawling down his forehead. He ran a hand over his face, gently massaged his brow with pudgy fingers, slowly re-opened his eyes.

She was still there, hovering like a hummingbird eager to get at those slow drops of sweat.

"Are you *okay*?" she asked in a faraway voice. "Do you feel sick?"

He held up a fluttering hand, gesturing for patience. In a moment he said, "No. No, I'm all right now."

Her wings quit beating, and she sank with relief.

Kevin, closing his eyes again, wondered if he was correct. The world behind his eyelids was blood-red and in constant swirling motion. Every few breaths the redness deepened. Now he was really sweating. Weren't fat people more prone to heart attacks than thinner people? Hadn't he been overdoing it lately? He imagined his parents reading, in a matter of days, a form letter from a remote Highway Patrol office. Their unappreciated son had been discovered dead on some dismal foggy cliff. Cardiac arrest. Serve them right if it broke their hearts.

But suddenly his forehead was cool. He opened his eyes and saw that lovely mirage girl again, now holding a damp cloth. Her face was both worried and comforting, and Kevin's juicy scenario of masochism and self-pity was instant history.

"There, is that better?" the hummingbird wondered. "You shouldn't overdo it in this heat." She had a plastic quart jug half-full of water in her hand, ready to re-saturate the cloth.

"That's okay, I'm fine now. Save your water."

"Are you sure?"

"Positive," he said, pretty sure. "Thanks for cooling me off." He blinked at his surroundings. "What'd you say happened to your bike?"

She dropped her arms. "Oh, it's awful! And what a place for it to happen! There probably isn't a gas station for a zillion miles. I was walking my poor bike when—*bang!*—the tire popped." She placed a hand on her chest and her wide eyes opened wider. "Did I ever jump! I thought someone was shooting a gun."

"But what are you doing all alone out here? This is pretty tough terrain for a chick."

"You're telling me! I was with some friends, you see, and we were all riding up to Monterey on our bikes when Linda (she's kind of square, but she has a darling figure) got ill and had to go home. Then Marcie and Paula and I thought that was pretty much the end of the trip, but we kept going anyway. Then these two *boys* tried to pick us up down the coast a ways, last night on the beach. They were disgusting! They had this pickup truck with one of those little camper houses on the back, and when we were all inside they got drunk and started pinching and grabbing. I guess Marcie and Paula were getting drunk too, because they actually stayed inside. I just crossed my arms and said, 'Well, *you* girls can stay in here if you want to, but *I'm* not going to hang around boys with no manners.' Then one of those boys, *Robert* (he was very rude, and, besides, he wasn't *that* cute), made an obscene noise and started tearing off my clothes. Can you believe it! Well, I just slapped his face (not too hard, he was such a sweetheart when he wasn't drunk) and jumped right out of that old truck and slept by myself on the beach. It wasn't cold at all. All my sleeping bag and stuff was in those *boys'* truck, and when I woke up this morning it was gone, and so were Marcie and Paula and their bikes. Well I hope they have a good time! I can ride up to Monterey by myself."

"You shouldn't try doing that," Kevin said, breathing steadily now. "I mean, there's all kinds of strange people on this road. Look at those guys your friends ran off with." He shook his head. "What a trip. I was riding up to the Haight with a couple friends, and we all got separated too. I'm by myself for the same reasons you are."

"Ooh. That *is* weird. Just like in adventure stories, like when Nancy Drew lost her secret ring just before she met this handsome gynecologist."

"Yeah," Kevin said absently, his mind retreating into gloom. He was sure this girl's standards concerning males were inflexible, never dipping below fantasy handsome nick-of-time do-gooders; brawny toothy yodeling professional men in sleek, gleaming roadsters. By contrast, he saw himself as lowly and foul, ratty and malodorous—the Bad Guy. But, perhaps because the girl seemed so concerned with his present physical condition, he was able to don the white hat of the selfless protector. This girl *was* a damsel in distress, or soon would be. And, he thought, glancing quickly at his expensive customized ten-speed bicycle, he did have quite an impressive steed. Excitedly he asked, "What's your name?"

"Oh, excuse me. I'm Janet. Janet Campbell."

"And I'm Kevin Mikolajczyk."

"Kevin *who?*"

The boy blushed. "Kevin Michaels." He looked away, out of words. "Well," he managed at last, "let's have a look at your bike." He rose painfully, but careful to not let it show. Bending down, he saw repairs would be no problem. The tire itself was unruptured, though very worn. It was just a matter of taking off the wheel, patching the inner tube and replacing the wheel. He had the patch kit in the pouch behind his seat, and the pump to fill the inner tube strapped to his bike's frame.

"Can you fix it?"

"Well," Kevin replied, brow furrowed in apparent deep concentration, "I can give it a go."

She clapped her hands delightedly. "Oh, *could* you?"

As he'd supposed, fixing the flat was a cinch. While he worked—zipping off wing nuts, prying the tire off its rim—he picked up details of the girl's life from her monologue. She lived in Morro Bay, and wondered why he flinched when she told him. He would not go into it. She was seventeen and would be a senior in high school come September. She didn't seem to like her parents very much, and Kevin had a strong suspicion Janet and her friends were runaways. He gleaned from her expressions when she spoke of her parents that they pampered her to a fault. Kevin could understand why. She spoke vaguely of relatives in Seaside, and meant to stop there, hoping the other girls, knowing, might be waiting for her. Yes, she had heard of the big Golden Gate concert, but wasn't San Francisco a pretty dangerous place nowadays, what with the police busts and general unrest, and all that trouble so close by at Berkeley?

Slowly a glorious scheme took form in Kevin's mind. If only his mouth would say the right words, and for once not betray him.

"Look, like I said, you never know what kind of weirdos you'll run into on this road. But tell you what; I'll ride with you as far as Seaside and make sure nothing happens. When we get up there, if you can't find your friends, you think maybe you'd like to keep going, catch the big jam in Frisco? It really should be a happening; lots of dope—Jefferson Airplane...I mean, San Francisco, the Haight, is where it's *at* this summer."

Kevin felt his stomach flutter. She was looking at him quizzically; he was making waves. He should have at least got to know her better first. Make sure nothing happens, indeed. It sounded like he was trying to lure her into his confidence; like he was trying to set her up for the big moonlit rape scene.

"Well..." she said, "I really don't have any plans. I'll figure what to do when I get to Seaside."

"Listen, I know how that sounded, but it's not what I meant to say. I mean it's not how I meant it to sound. I'm really not like that, like how I must have sounded. Anyway...what I mean is you don't have to worry."

"Whatever in the world are you talking about?"

"Oh, nothing. I guess I'm just spaced out." He had the repaired tire back on her bike. A minute later he had pumped it firm. "There."

"Oh, that's wonderful! You really are a wizard."

Kevin stood before her, confused and queasy. It was the make-it or break-it moment. Would she give him her hand to shake, leave him to pedal alone and lonely up the coast? She cleared her throat and looked down.

"Well," he mumbled. "I guess I'd better hit the road. It was really nice meeting you, Janet. I think you're a really nice girl. I hope you find your friends." He straddled his ten-speed.

"You're not going to leave me, are you? After all you said about riding up with me and watching over me—"

"No, no, no," Kevin said quickly, unbelieving. "I was ...like I said, I've been spaced out lately." His heart was pounding. He shook his head. He'd almost blown it again.

So they walked their bikes the fifty yards or so to the top of the grade. They paused to look down.

"It'll be so nice to just coast down this hill," Janet noted. "It must go down for miles."

"Really!" Kevin said. "By the way, um, do you get high?"

"Well, a little bit, sometimes. Doesn't everybody?"

"That's just what I mean. Want to smoke a joint?"

Before she could reply he'd dipped a hand in his shirt pocket, secured a marijuana cigarette and a book of matches. His intention was to get their minds on the same plane, to relate. Already, as he saw it, they had one very bonding appreciation in common. But soon as he fired it up he began second-guessing himself.

And sure enough, after they'd passed the cigarette twice he found his tongue tied again. Lance's weed seemed to have a contrasting effect on the girl, and she rattled on and on about this and that, tirelessly. This standing, however, gave him opportunity to study the girl as an uninvolved observer, and to try to pinpoint his true role in their slowly growing relationship. From the beginning he was jealous and easily hurt. Several times as they covered the miles a painful scene would be repeated: from a passing car would come wolf-whistles and whoops—coarse compliments on Janet's slender sexuality. The girl, annoyingly, was not put off by these vulgar displays. She would always smile in response—a budding young lady accustomed to flattery. Kevin had a real urge to shout something not-so flattering at these fleeting busybodies, but was it really for him to do? Under no circumstances did he feel she was his girl, rather that he was her temporary harlequin; and, if she enjoyed what they were so crudely shouting, was it any of his business to throw a cloud over her pleasure? Kevin felt he wasn't gaining any ground by keeping his mouth shut, but at least he wasn't losing any.

And, shortly after the sun had set, the natural romantic ambience of the summer shorescape began to subtly color the ongoing moment. Odd patterns of crest and swell played dreamily on the Pacific. Not far offshore one could see craggy black islets skirted by swirling eddies and the shallow funnels of sea dervishes. Monster colonies of kelp rose lazily with the waves, settling momentarily to appear as blood-red shoals in the twilight.

But to return to Kevin's status as observer: after several miles of riding alongside he was able to compare his present fortune against his ideals. This haze of warm summer twilight on the gorgeous coast highway, en route to his paradise with a pretty girl riding beside him, seemed the script to any number of his lonesome, hopeless daydreams—he never would have believed it could really happen to him. The fictitious hero he'd created of himself now seemed plausible, and the most vital element of the fantasy was riding at arm's-length. For the first time he could remember, he felt...*right*. And yet a strange pain was riding with him. He knew that each jab of this soft pain was of desperate importance to his being, could not imagine having ever felt otherwise. Home, school, possessions and wants; suddenly these things were all old hat.

The restlessness, the pain were sweet, yet at the same time nearly unbearable. He had a feeling of helplessness so acute he wanted to grab her, hold on tightly and never let her slip away. But all he could do was ride beside her, gawking, letting the sweet flow of idle chatter wash over and suck him in like an undertow.

Thank God she kept talking. Her stream of laughter, of gossip, of stale anecdotes seemed inexhaustible. Kevin had long since lost the thread of her monologue, and was now suffering pangs of anxiety, knowing he was only being talked at, not to. The feeling vaguely reminded him of a recent occurrence, but he couldn't put his finger on it. Something about a girl with a bewitching superstructure...

Out of a fog his vision of the raven-haired girl returned, a Debbie Somebody-or-Other. Only now the vision had no expressiveness, no life. How different was that passionate beauty of his fiery past, compared to this sandy, girlish treasure of the tender present. Love is vertigo. All women are beautiful, and each possesses an allure, and an inscrutable quality, peculiar to their gender.

The sky was rapidly darkening, and in the twilight of his introspection it occurred to Kevin that somehow, apparently, he was going to be sleeping with this girl tonight. The realization excited him, but that excitement quickly gave way to the gnawing presence of doubt. His virginity, so long a burden, might be done away with this very night, his masculinity put to the most crucial and telling test. And it was a test the boy realized he was absolutely afraid to face. Failure seemed so imminent. Then he remembered his earlier statement: *"I'll ride with you as far as Monterey and make sure nothing happens."*

Well, shouldn't something happen? Wasn't it his obligation as a male to be aggressive, and to assert his masculinity in the one manner that would leave, in her eyes, no room for doubt? As if reading his thoughts, the girl began to slow.

"Gee, it's really starting to get dark. I hadn't given a thought about a place to crash tonight."

"Don't worry," Kevin said quickly, way too quickly. "It's still early. Way too early." His nerves were going. "You're not c-cold or anything."

"No, but I am getting a little tired. But listen to you! You sound like you're freezing."

"N-nah!" And suddenly he was shivering out of control. When he closed his mouth his teeth chattered, his flabby jowls jiggled. "Well, l-let's stop for a while," he gasped. "L-let's take a breather."

They pulled to the side of the road. Kevin's hands were shaky enough to jerk the handlebars as he stopped, so instead of dismounting with a semblance of grace he lurched off the bike and rolled, adding a few more contusions to his scores of bumps and bruises. He swiftly found his feet. "Didn't see that rock."

"For goodness sake," the girl cooed, "be *careful*. Did you hurt yourself?" She kicked down her bike's stand and rushed over.

"*No!* I mean, no. I'm—I'm fine. Just fine." This was maddening. He thought: *Get a grip on yourself!* But trying to control his nerves only made the situation worse. The grass, he thought. It must be the grass that was responsible.

"Here. Sit down here. Let's check you for injuries."

Kevin obeyed timidly, slouching on a chalky boulder while she inspected the abrasions on his forehead in the failing light. His nerves took a turn for the worse as she thrust her knee between his. Her soft warm breath brushed his eyelashes. He was conscious of a delicate fragrance; an altogether feminine emanation wafting up his nostrils and flitting through his mind. The urge to rest his head on her bosom was so difficult to control that it set his crass knees knocking against her sweet, insinuated leg.

"Poor cold Kevin," she murmured. "My hero got a scrape on his head." Then she leaned back, one hand on his shoulder for support while the other fanned her pretty face. *"Phew!"* she teased. "Do you ever smell! Haven't they invented soap where you come from?"

Kevin hung his head.

The girl sprang back and ran to her bicycle, fumbled through her purse. In a moment she'd returned with a tiny vial of Mercurochrome and a huge, square, flower-patterned band-age. He clenched his fists, but tears squeezed out at the anti-septic's sting. When the bandage was in place he popped to his feet and looked away.

"Thanks. Look, we'd better get going if we're gonna find a decent place to crash. There's got to be a stop coming up pretty soon, what with all we've been riding. Then we can dig up something to eat."

"I'm not really hungry."

"Well," he stretched, "maybe we can get some cocoa or something." As they remounted he fired another joint, hoping it would open her up again, and spare him the torment of trying to communicate. There were plenty of things he wanted to say, but his mouth just wouldn't respond. Unfortunately, this time the weed seemed to stifle the girl; she kept quiet and rode with her head down, as if embarrassed. The silence soon became intoler-able, and Kevin was reminded of that chilly, soggy night in the garage loft eight months ago—what seemed now like eight years ago. He and Eddie had suffered through this same verbal paralysis, intensely aware of the situation's absurdity. And the rain's meaningless Morse had made them jumpier still, ham-mering away at their nerves until, no longer able to deal, they'd simultaneously jerked their heads to face the warped and rickety loft doors, which after a moment were yanked outward with terrifying abruptness to reveal the mammoth, preposterous bulk of Kevin's father in all his towering wrath. Eddie had paled as his system prepared itself for a torrent of banshee-like scream-ing. And in those breathless pinging seconds Kevin had shrunk into himself while, in steady contrast, Big Joe dilated like a weather balloon, trembling and growing darker and darker, until, just when it seemed the tension would escalate forever, Joe had trumpeted like a wounded bull elephant and torn Kevin out of the loft, thrown him clear across the garage. With Eddie's nightmarish shrieks in his ears, Kevin had crawled away, his scalp afire, his skull and left elbow howling with pain. Big Joe, his face by then a hellish purple, had impaled little Eddie for a moment with great, bulging, sightless eyes, before turning slowly and mechanically to search for his son. Kevin had seen the opacity of his father's eyes change to the bloody glow of anticipation, as Joe thrust out his great meaty hands and began stalking him with ponderous, earthshaking steps, his breath rattling venomously. Before Kevin could successfully crawl out of the garage, Big Joe snatched him off the floor and shook him in the air as if he were a toy, softening him up, bent on squashing him to a writhing pulp. And, giving vent to another mindless roar, he'd hurled him down with all his force, the boy's head again cracking hard on the cold cement floor. Then Joe had just *snapped*; he'd begun stomping on his son, roaring insanely. Kevin had crawled away desperately, and the chase had gone round and round in the garage, Joe trying to stomp him as if he were a scurrying spider, Kevin scrabbling frantically to avoid those huge feet as deadly as pile drivers. Finally Kevin had cornered himself below the loft. Above him Eddie was scrambling like a hamster in a cage, blubbering and whimpering, the doors tightly shut. Kevin had heard a strangled change in Big Joe's stertorous breathing, and, turning with a wail, all set to be exterminated, had seen his father gone completely berserk, stamping his right foot repeatedly on the garage floor as he pivoted on his left foot centripetally, finally losing his balance momentarily, and, recovering, jerking back his head with a bloodcurdling shriek that shook the rafters. Both hands had shot to his chest and he had torn wildly, as if trying to rip out his heart, and suddenly he'd gone deathly pale and fallen slowly, like a mighty sequoia, to crash on his back with an impact so tremendous it had cracked the cement floor. There he'd remained, eyes rolled up in his skull, only his fingertips moving, dancing an erratic, waning jig. The tapping of fingers tapered. Slowly one of the loft doors creaked open and Eddie peeked out tentatively, whining less anxiously now, dropping big tears from his shivering chin onto Kevin's palm. And Kevin began a laborious crawl toward the garage's gaping doorway, for he'd noticed that Big Joe wasn't quite dead. All that revealed this stubborn vitality were the faint sounds of the fingers' tap dance and an occasional guttural gasp—but Joe was a powerful, terrible man; not the sort to leave an aborted murder without a final go. And Kevin's mother had come stumbling in like a headless chicken, prepared by some old presentiment for the scene she would face and therefore already in hysterics. She screeched and tore at her hair, then transferred her throes to big supine Joe, hammering her fists on his chest. If it hadn't been for the trauma of the situation she would have looked supremely comic, with her Medusa hairpile in electric disarray, her spectacles hanging from one ear at an awkward angle, her dumpy body a flurry of spasmodic activity. But then she'd seen her cowering son and a look of satanic rage had darkened her strikingly repulsive face. Having spent countless hours watching daytime soap operas, she had known exactly what to do, and with a truly appalling scream had launched herself atop the boy and pummeled him relentlessly with her pudgy fists, as, safe above all this activity, Eddie slammed shut the loft door and renewed his wailing and scampering. Just then the garage's doorway had miraculously filled with an assortment of dumbfounded neighbors who, supposing Kevin's mother a deranged murderess, ran inside to break up the mess as others scurried off to phone ambulances, the police, the fire department, the Federal Bureau of Investigation, and the local Y.M.C.A.

Now night had settled on Kevin and Janet like a black blanket, awash with stars. Still the uneasy silence persisted. The chattering of Kevin's teeth was the only sound other than the breaking of surf and the soft squeaking of the brake heels wearing away on Janet's bike.

To Kevin's immense relief a cheerful haze of light waxed not far ahead, and in a minute he saw the road sign announcing that Illusion, with GASFOOD and LODGING, was a bare two miles away.

The advent of civilization loosened Janet's tongue right up. With a mile to go she was piping. Half a mile and she was an animated tour guide. By the time they'd reached the first shops she was downright silly. Kevin sighed with relief. This was the strange girl he loved again.

They had hot cocoa and pizza at a tiny diner. Kevin

gallantly purchased several postcards for the girl, and left an enormous tip with the check. It didn't go unnoticed. And as the ancient, papery waitress enthusiastically wished them an extremely good night, the girl linked her arm in his. This novelty—being arm-in-arm with an attractive girl in public—was a complete turn-on for Kevin. But the thrill dissolved once they'd exited. He knew he should be extremely aroused by her touch. He should be champing at the bit. Kevin's hands shook as he and Janet quietly rode around the shops.

The girl patted her lips and yawned. "Hot cocoa always puts me right to sleep. You?"

"Yep," Kevin lied. "Sure does."

"Well, this is all new to me. I've never had to rough it before. I hope you've got some good ideas."

"Don't worry. I've had plenty of experience looking for a place to crash. I used to be a scout."

"Oh?"

Kevin colored. "A Cub Scout. Of course," he said, "that was when I was just a kid."

They pedaled around a while longer. At last Kevin said, "There!" The girl followed him to a nook behind a bowling alley. Beneath a salt-worn plywood overhang were a couple of steel dumpsters. Kevin dismounted and rolled the bins aside. He foraged about until he found a piece of plywood paneling large enough to lean against the wooden overhang, creating a narrow, inconspicuous shelter. The girl kicked down her stand.

"What about our bikes?" she whispered. From behind the wall came the sound of a bowling ball smashing into pins, muffled cheers.

"No sweat," Kevin said. He unstrapped his sleeping roll and set it on the ground. "We hide 'em right here." Kevin leaned his bicycle against the wall, guided the girl's to rest obliquely against his. After dragging the bins back into place he draped wheels and seats with newspaper, scraps of cardboard, miscellaneous bits of trash. As he worked he could feel Janet's eyes on him, and as he bent to unroll his sleeping bag he was hit by a full court-press of desperation.

*She was going to get in the bag with him!*

Kevin knew he should be exultant, but something was

upside-down here, something was inside-out. His mouth tasted like he'd been gargling with vinegar, his legs were rubbery stumps. To clear his thoughts he tried to compose a quick letter in his mind:

> jime
> wl her i am ubowt 2 klim in thu sak with u gorjus chik
> et yr hrt owt
> hr namz janut an shez gawt thez jiunt nawkrz an u as wut wont kwit
> man i kant kep hr hanz awf uv me shez so horne shez in2 chanten an dop an asid rawk an thu moovmnt

And Kevin's mind began to reel. He started whistling shrilly, realized how foolish that was, and stretched out nervously on the open bag, up against the wall. In the ensuing silence came the whack of a bowling ball into pins. The girl slid in beside him, not quite touching. She zipped up the bag, whispering, "I hope we can sleep with all that noise!"

Kevin swallowed. Whispering made it...*wow*. He was beginning to hyperventilate. To cover up he clumsily produced a joint from his shirt pocket and lit it with trembling hands. As he passed it to the girl the back of his hand accidentally brushed her cheek.

"*Sorry*," he whispered. How warm and soft her cheek was, how he longed to have it rest against his hand forever.

Kevin felt a shy stirring in his Levis. His free hand made a fist. He squeezed shut his eyes and ground his teeth, cursing silently. And as he reached for the passed joint his hand grazed her naked shoulder, jangling his nervous system, touching off fireworks in his skull. As if in encore, pins crashed in the bowling lane next to his ear. Getting high, he descended. Inch by inch, into deep and unfamiliar chasms. The roach burned his fingertips. Kevin now used the minor pain of snuffing the cherry to toughen his resolve, to summon the courage to tell her exactly how he felt, if words could explain.

"*Janet!*" he whispered.

Regular, deep breathing. The tiniest snores, so very feminine. Kevin could feel her hair's wispy tendrils fluttering against his face in the warm sea breeze. He sighed, moved his hand across his chest to pocket the butt.

And froze.

The tip of the girl's right breast was grazing the back of his hand with each inhalation. Paralyzed, excited, ashamed, he lay still as the dead. Each small touch jolted his nerves—but so sweetly, so tenderly, that his skull felt like it was stuffed with cotton.

This was *wrong*.

She was asleep.

She didn't know.

Against his will Kevin found himself letting a little of his weight move against her breast, without moving his hand.

Now he could imagine every contour of the sweet, pert fruit…how it sloped upward from the rib cage, how the ruddy peak jutted. In the sweaty miasma of his shame, Kevin felt a real awakening in his loins.

The girl gave a small groan and shifted.

Kevin held his breath.

His hand was no longer making contact.

Deeply troubled, he quietly rolled over to face the wall.

In a world occupied by guilt and lust and cannoning bowling balls, his cannabis-colored thoughts accompanied him into an uneasy sleep.

# Chapter 12

# Louie in the Sty with Dinah

Kevin surfaced, all but drowned. It took a full minute to remember where he was, half a minute more to realize he'd had a wet dream. He stickily groaned to his senses. He was way too old for this; he'd have to do something to the sheet, maybe burn a hole in it so his mother wouldn't catch the stain.

But there was a stranger in his bed. Kevin cautiously opened an eye, saw Janet's lovely sleep-filled face only inches away, felt her straightforward breath on his receding chin. She'd settled heavily, and her chestnut hair smelled of lilies and ferns, of freshly mown grass. Right behind her sweet young face was the full splendor of the waking day.

The boy explored with his senses. Somehow, in the course of the night, they'd become hopelessly entangled. Kevin felt that his right arm, sore below the elbow, was being used for a pillow by the girl, and was glad—glad that he'd helped make her comfortable. But his right leg, pinned hard between both of hers, was absolutely numb. He lay still for a moment, holding his breath. Then, very carefully, eased off his left leg. That part was a snap. It was only when he tried to slip out his right leg that he realized the leg was "asleep." A thousand straight pins ran up his thigh. The girl was mumbling something like "deeper," or "keep her"—something icky-girly; not meant for studs with boogers in their eyes and pins in their thighs. Kevin tried working his leg out little by little, growing desperate at the total lack of feeling from his waist down. His efforts were gently rocking the girl against him, back and forth, back and forth, and from the way she was breathing faster and harder he was certain she was about to waken. He didn't want to be rough, but, damn it, his leg was beginning to burn. If he didn't free it quickly it would atrophy; he'd spend the rest of his life dragging the bloodless limb behind.

He tried jerking it out all at once, but it died on him; the burning ceased. Kevin grabbed and shoved off Janet's leg. She woke with a pretty little gasp, her eyes popping half-open. A fine film of perspiration glistened on her brow.

"G'morning," Kevin grated. And, with that fractured little wham-bam, he was lost for words.

"My *goodness*." She patted a slim brown hand on her lips. "What's the time?"

"Pretty early," Kevin re-grated. "But I…I always get up early. Good for the karma."

She noted the indelicacy of their situation. "We seem— we seem to be a bit tangled up."

"Right. Right. Just let me get this zipper—" He had to lean over her to tug at the zipper, had to roll right on top of her. The zipper was snagged. Kevin grimaced apologetically, still tugging, while she returned the look with a sweet, enigmatic smile. Kevin blushed weenily. When at last the zipper gave he opened the bag in a single quick motion and hopped out on his one working foot.

"Sorry, couldn't be helped, sorry. I'll just make sure the coast is clear; back in a flush." Kevin limped round the building's corner, leaned against a wall, and stamped his foot until some feeling returned.

There was, mercifully, a gas station next to the bowling alley. Kevin snuck into the restroom and soaked a handful of paper towels before sloshing into the only stall. He cleansed his sticky crotch and belly, mashed the towels into a wad, and threw the mess onto the mess below. Then, though there was no one around and a perfectly usable urinal just outside the stall, he fell prey to that confounding impulse that rules every other male in a public restroom. Having ascertained that the stall door was securely locked and the toilet's seat undeniably *down*, Kevin dropped his drawers and peed into the bowl, on the floor and walls, and all over the begging seat. Having thus pheromonally introduced himself to the next creep in line, he absent-mindedly perused some of the filthy partition's cleverer scatalogical scratchings.

Still limping a bit, Kevin stepped to the wash basin, stared glumly at his reflection in the mirror, and peeled off the flowery bandage with a groan of embarrassment. No wonder she'd been smiling. Never, he thought, had he looked so seedy in the morning. His hair, minus the two great clumps, was a wildly tangled jungle, peppered with miscellaneous bits of trash. A sour stench rose from his armpits and crotch.

There was a line of graffiti inked above the mirror. Kevin cleaned his glasses and squinted to make it out. The message read: *If you were as smart as you are ugly, you wouldn't be pissing here.* Kevin sighed and nodded. His eye was caught by one section of a photograph crammed into the full receptacle next to the basin. He plucked it out curiously and found himself gloomily studying the blurry black and white image of a stout Mexican woman dispassionately corrupting the virtue of a frenzied Great Dane. The dreariness of this image crept up his arm. Suddenly he was disgusted with himself.

And just as suddenly he found it necessary to prove to himself and to the girl that he was not a vile restroom gnome. What was he doing here, feeling sorry for himself...surely she was aware, surely she had seen her chance and was even now wholesomely pedaling her rickety bicycle up the coast.

Kevin yanked open the door and rushed out, limped puffing to the back of the bowling alley.

Janet was sitting, head cocked to the side as she brushed her long shiny hair. She had neatly rolled up the bag.

She smiled with secret amusement. "Feeling better?"

"Sure," he replied. "All's well. Well. I guess we survived the night all right." He watched her closely, afraid that in the glare of his nonchalance he stood exposed as a wholly forgettable turkey. But she smiled again—that same strange twisting of the lips and sparkling of the eyes that seemed to say so little, yet imply so very much. Kevin's heart did a belly flop at that smile, and he was hooked for real.

"Thanks," he said.

"Hm?"

"For rolling up the bag. That was really thoughtful. I mean, really."

She laughed musically, said, "Oh, Pooh!" and stood, lifting the bag and tossing it playfully. "Come on, let's go get something to eat. I'm famished."

"Oh sure, sure." Kevin strapped the bag to the rack behind his seat, and before he knew it they were pedaling along.

Then everything was very strange.

She was quiet as she rode, introspective, and for a disturbing moment Kevin could have sworn she gave him, for no apparent reason, a look of almost maniacal hostility. The scary silence was finally broken when they reached a 24-hour diner. Large diesels, coupled to forty-foot trailers, were parked in clusters around this diner. The rigs caught Kevin's eye at once, as nearly all were lovingly maintained, and sported sparkling chromed rims and grilles, flake and pearl paints.

"Looks like a good place," he said, grateful for the break. "Well, let's hurry and find us a booth. Must be crowded inside."

Janet said nothing, walking her bicycle beside him. Kevin locked their bikes to a rail by the entrance. He was aware of a ridiculous intimacy in coupling their machines.

He held the door for her. A barrage of raucous laughter burst out like hot trapped air. Spoons rang on coffee cups.

"Well," Janet purred, smiling again, "you're certainly the gentleman today."

Kevin grinned and bowed his head. "My pleasure," he said with all his heart, and followed her inside.

The place was packed.

The men were of a general sort: massive, T-shirted, roughly sullen or roughly jocular; hairy arms, beardless, hair cut short and without flair. Now and then one would swivel on his counter stool to roughly stare as they passed. A few continued to watch as Kevin and Janet were led to a filthy booth by a shuffling and curlered waitress. A nametag pinned to her blouse provided for the thought-impaired: DINAH. They stood uneasily as she wiped the table clean.

"Back in a sec'," she said, chewing something. "Getcha

ya menus." Dinah winked and lowered her voice conspiratorially. "You kids want coffee?" She looked one to the other, her eyes resting longest on Kevin. "Louie?"

"Sure," Kevin said. Zip, and she was gone. They sat across from each other and were silent. The vibes in this place were razor-edged; it seemed the general hubbub had toned down immediately around their booth. Kevin tentatively appraised the counter. Two men were turned on their stools, staring coldly. The boy looked into their faces and read nothing but contempt. As he turned away he felt their eyes boring into the side of his skull. His appetite had vanished.

The waitress was back, carefully setting down their coffees. "There's yours, honey," she said, handing them menus colored in glossy primaries. "And now here's one for you, Louie. On one bill or two?"

Janet looked up, and when Kevin blushed and said, "On one, of course," she became gay and chirpy, clapped her hands and went over the selections with sparkling eyes.

Dinah turned to Kevin, still chewing, chewing.

"Her first," he said, unpleasantly aware of a regimenting of hostility at the counter. He looked furtively, once. Apparently he was now the center of attention for at least six sneering and insolently seated men. He only had time to see one blow him a kiss before turning away.

"—and an order of English muffins with honey," Janet was saying, "and *ooh*, how about Canadian bacon with those eggs?"

Kevin was considering telling the waitress to cancel their order, to grab Janet's hand and nonchalantly dart out of here. There were two drawbacks to this idea. One, it would be doing just what these hulking truckers wanted: making him run and feeding their Dark Ages egos. Two—and far, far worse—it would be the ultimate cop-out in front of Janet.

"—and a glass of juice, a *tall* glass, please, and one of these little pancake plates like in this picture, with the whipped cream, and—"

"My God," Kevin interjected out of sheer nervousness. "Where do you put it all?"

Janet brought a small hand to her mouth, raised the

menu to cover her face below the eyes.

"Oh…" she said, "I'm sorry; I just get carried away at breakfast sometimes. And you did say I could order what I want—I mean, that's what you meant, isn't it—and I'm simply *starving*, aren't you? It is all right, isn't it?" Her eyes implored.

The waitress turned to Kevin again, still chewing, chewing. He wished, unreasonably, that she would choke on whatever it was she was chewing, chewing, chewing. He threw a hand up irritably, body language for: Oh, just order whatever the hell you want; then realized his irritation was simple release from the hostility hanging like a storm cloud over the counter.

"—and an order of hash browns, and a thing of yogurt, pineapple if you've got it, and a big bowl of Frosty Squares, and—"

"If that ain't just the most God-awful sight I seen all year."

Kevin was sinking; imperceptibly, but steadily.

"So that's the New Generation! Makes you wanna crawl in your coffin and haul down the lid."

Kevin's eyes refocused. Janet was quiet now, her own eyes half-raised in supplication. The waitress was staring very directly, chewing slowly now, considering.

"Nothing for me," he said meekly.

Dinah considered him a moment longer, nodded curtly, and vanished.

Kevin avoided Janet's eyes. It was all he could do to ignore the voices.

"If you're lookin' for dope on the menu, Louie, we're awful dang sorry, but this place ain't used to serving freaks like you."

"Hey, sweetheart, what you see in a fat clown like him?"

"Yeah, darlin'. Why don't you come along and take a ride with a *real* man?"

"Har-har! Why, sure. B'lieve I could ride a sweet little thing like you all night long."

Suddenly Kevin was on his feet, his fists clenched. There were tears on his cheeks and his voice was strained.

"You can't talk about my girlfriend like that!"

He felt Janet's hands at his back. One of the truckers

stood, stomped over, and got right in Kevin's face.

"No goddam pillpopping Louie tells me what I can or can't say!"

Beside himself, Kevin whirled and seized a fork off the table. He made an ineffectual lunging stab at no one in particular. The trucker stepped back.

The rest of the counter trogs roared with laughter. Dinah, rematerializing, wedged herself between Kevin and the standing trucker, shooed everyone to their seats. She was an amazing piece of work; pirouetting in slippers, soothing here, scolding there. Without breaking rhythm, she scooped a dime out of her tips jar, whirled to the jukebox, and made a selection. It was everybody's favorite: that song featured in the gratingly omnipresent Vons commercial where the gomer trucker gleefully pounds the wheel every time the gomer singer belts out, "In the heartland!" The effect on the diner was immediate and magical. The altercation was instantly forgotten. The truckers, mug in one hand and fork in the other, beamed and pounded their fists twice on the counter at every reiteration of that delightful catch phrase. Dinah blew back to their booth. Kevin was wretchedly wiping away his tears.

"Your order's being cooked up, honey," she told Janet, "but I think you kids should run along. Sorry 'bout the trouble. These boys mean well; they just got no manners."

"I think they're terrible, horrible," Janet said, making a face. "And I'm not hungry anymore."

"There, there," said the waitress, placing a hand on Janet's upper thigh and squeezing. "You got a lot of growing up t' do, sweetheart, and a lot of learning, too. Don't let one little bad scene (is that how you Louies say it?) give you the wrong impression."

Now, Kevin had never been able to understand the physical intimacy women so straightforwardly share, but this Dinah person was rubbing and squeezing and stroking and patting and kneading Janet's thigh while she spoke, and the girl appeared to brighten.

"When you get a little older you'll see these boys are the salt of the earth. Like I said, they just ain't got no manners, is all. So you two head north up the highway 'bout half a mile until you see Arnold's Café. Tell Arnie that Dinah sentcha, and he'll fix you up—" she zoned out for two priceless syllables, stomping a slipper and shaking her pad "—with something special, see, 'cause Arnie's seen this kind of thing happen before with kids like you. Arnie *likes* kids, God bless 'im. Got six hisself, Arnie does, loves 'em to death, just doesn't like to see 'em fooling around—Heart-land—with pills, going crazy on that LSB stuff, always protestin' about everything. Can't say as I blames him myself; you Louies got no reason—Heart-land— to be protestin' all the time. Shit, when we was your age times was hard, what with the Depression and the war and all—you kids got it made, let me tell you, things couldn't be better. I just wish to God somebody would of set me down and give me a good long talkin' to when I was your age. Sure, we got into trouble and done some crazy stuff, too; all kids do. Heart-land. But we were *good* kids and we respected our elders, let me tell you, and we listened to *real* music, Heart-land, Sinatra and Crosby and Count Basie, not this nonsense you always hear screaming on the radio all day long nowadays. Yeah, we were good kids, and we were proud to work for ourselves, and we never complained. And at least we had the good sense to mind our own business." She straightened. "Just what is it you Louies see in taking all them drugs?"

"We'd better go," Kevin moaned, eyes red but dry. "Thanks for stepping in and helping." He rose. Janet followed uncertainly.

"Heart-land…" Dinah muttered, chewing thoughtfully.

When they walked out the diner was as loud and rowdy as when they'd entered. It was as if the incident had never occurred. He held the door for the girl and two syllables rang gloriously. A barrage of raucous laughter burst out like hot trapped air. Spoons rang on coffee cups.

# Chapter 13

## A Sur Thing

Arnie's "something special" turned out to be a plate of runny scrambled eggs, bacon so charred it disintegrated when touched, stale toast with jam that was suspiciously bland, and a half-full glass of rancid orange juice. And Arnie did *not* "like kids", at least not the three of his own he badgered around the greasy, dingy café. Breakfast was served by Arnie's filthy sniffling six year-old daughter, on plates that were chipped and unclean.

Arnie was a squat, feverishly balding, gray-whiskered old second generation Italian given to explosive gestures and exclamations, hollering, *"Stupido! Imbecille! Idiota!"* while indiscriminately clouting ears. Arnie appeared to have a select, ungovernable dislike for Kevin and Janet, his only customers. After much shouting and slamming of doors he grimly made his rounds, smearing the grime on the tabletops with a tattered rag of a towel which, from the looks of it, was a multipurpose implement, used to swab floors, scour pots, and grip the pan when Arnie changed the oil in his prehistoric Buick. As he worked he mumbled viciously and incessantly, glaring at them with a spite that kept their eyes on their plates and their conversation at an agitated standstill. And he wheezed horribly, gasping like some ancient janitor attacking stubborn stains in a toilet bowl. He was always right around their table, and when nearest his grumbling would acquire a sharply rising inflection until he was passionately swatting the towel against random chairs and tabletops. At such times he would appear about to break, gripping a chair's backrest with white-knuckled hands, trembling, raising himself to his full four and a half feet while goring them with burning ire.

It was the harrowing tension Arnie generated which made them force down every mouthful of the awful meal, like children at the family table. Kevin paid and they slunk away, swearing off recommended eateries forever. He consulted his wallet, counting the bills with a sinking sensation—where had it all gone? Mostly on goodies. And on treating his friends to meals and snacks. And there was the vest and hat and belt, all much worse for his experiences. And, of course, the pot. For the first time he began to wonder how he would subsist in the magic city, for at this rate he'd be busted shortly after arrival. Poor incarcerated Eddie had often told him that one could survive solely on the love and charity of others, never want for a thing so long as one's head was together, and that one's head was instantly together on arrival. Then again, Eddie was the only person to provide that assessment.

Janet was humming sweetly, watching Kevin affection-ately as he stuffed the bills in his wallet. Kevin smiled back. Love? He was already well-supplied. He was rapt. He was in-toxicated by it. Dizzy, even. A very sharp pain pinched his eyes and passed.

"Are you all right?" Janet was asking, her voice far away. "You just made a face something awful. Kevin...*are you all right?*"

Fine, he tried to say, but nothing happened. He couldn't smile offhandedly, couldn't look puzzled, couldn't move a mus-cle. Kevin swayed, staring at her, wondering at her strange ex-pression. Now she appeared to be speaking urgently, but he heard not a word. Only an angry buzzing in his skull. He willed his arms to move. They wouldn't budge. A novel terror came over him. Was he dead? Disembodied? Why couldn't he speak or move? And what was this freaky numbness creeping up from his extremities, why was the sky dancing with sparks? The air seemed to thicken, to fill with little filamentous bodies. The numbness leapt on his chest. The sun beat down.

The sun beat down. It hurt his eyes to look at it like this, but he couldn't turn his head. Wait. Yes he could. Not too easy, but now something cool was on his forehead, something was trickling down one side of his nose. And a very grim face was right in his. This man was rude to stare so hard and directly, and Kevin felt sure the owner of the face was bent on doing him harm. He had the black moustache and dark eyes of the bully at Perky's house—only he was older, much older, in his thirties at least. Could so much time have passed? Kevin looked away from the face, straight into a navel on a girl's brown belly. There was gentle weeping above him—nothing serious—which obviously came from the owner of this heavenly depression. His head, then, must be on the lap of the brown girl; that made sense. Yep, he could feel the firmness of her sun-baked thighs. That was delightful to know, and certainly exciting to feel, but the dark bully was watching him and that made it not so good. Perhaps that explained what was so disturbing about the face. He must have made a pass at the bully's girl, and been knocked silly for the effort. Kevin sat up slowly and a strong hand gripped his arm. "Sorry," he gasped.

He was at the center of a crowd. Two policemen were crouching next to him. So he'd been right. The owner of the face *was* wicked, for he was surely going to throw Kevin into a pit where Eddie would already be slumped, badly bruised and barely recognizable from malnutrition. Kevin tensed. He tried pulling away from that steely grip.

"Steady there," said the policeman, with a surprisingly gentle voice. "Everything's fine. Just take it easy. You passed out and had some kind of seizure. Do you remember anything about it? Are you all right now?"

Kevin nodded and held out his wrists for the cuffs. Janet took hold of his hands, brought them down to his lap, held them down.

The crowd, disappointed by Kevin's revival, broke up at once.

"Yeah, I'm okay now," Kevin managed. He got to his feet, supported under either arm by a policeman.

"You're sure?"

Kevin grinned lopsidedly. "Yeah."

The mustached officer continued to study him closely.

"Do you remember what happened?"

"The sun," Kevin extemporized. "It was my own fault. I was looking straight at the sun, just to see how long I could stand it. Dumb thing to do. Then I got dizzy and fell over. That's all."

"This young lady says you had some sort of seizure after you fell. Has that happened before?"

Kevin ran a hand over his eyes, careful that the move not appear too sudden. He knew there was something dreadfully wrong with him, and now urgently wanted to see somebody about it. But if he allowed the cops to take him away, or if he went to a clinic on his own, he was sure as sure could be that it would mean losing Janet. And he could deal with anything but that. So he said, "Well, I hit my head when I fell. I remember that. Plus, like I said, I was dizzy, real dizzy. That must have been what caused it. Sure, that's all it was. I'm fine now. I feel great."

"No history of epilepsy, tumor, heart trouble?"

"Uh-uh. No sir, nothing like that."

"Are you taking any medication?"

"No sir. Honest, I'm fine. It was just a freak thing."

The other officer, who was chubby and redheaded, searched his partner with a deeply concerned expression. His cheeks began to tremble, his neck muscles grew taut. He closed his eyes, squinched, and then his mouth burst open with the widest yawn Kevin had ever seen. He shook his head like a wet dog. "Gonna wanna runna shubriety?"

"That's okay," said the mustached officer after a moment. "Shine it on."

The redhead nodded, yawned again. He walked over to clear away the few remaining bystanders.

The policeman looked at Kevin critically. "Come here, son."

Kevin dropped his head and followed him over to the car. So he was going to be taken away after all. The officer hitched up one leg of his trousers and perched casually on the car's front fender. "Have you been taking drugs, son?" he inquired offhandedly.

"Oh, no sir. No, honest to God. I swear. Really."

"Okay, okay. I believe you. You seem like an honest enough kid. But let me warn you, man to man now. If you are, you're just looking for trouble." He held up a hand. "Now, I'm not trying to preach to you. But you'd be surprised at how many kids end up like you were, and then we find out they've been taking reds and acid and God knows what. But they don't learn. They go out and pull the same stunt over and over and over until it kills them. This girl here says you're from Los Angeles, on your way up to San Francisco. There's nothing wrong with that, if you've got your folks' permission, but I guess you know as well as I that San Francisco's the worst place to be if you want to experiment with drugs. So I'm telling you right now...no, let me rephrase that, I'm *asking* you to watch out. I've got every right, and reasonable grounds, to search your effects for drugs, but I'm not going to. You're not holding any drugs, are you?" Kevin shook his head vigorously. "Like I said, you seem a nice enough kid. So just a word of advice. If you *are* holding anything you shouldn't, *throw it away*. Don't take chances with these things. There's so much to live for, so much to look forward to." He patted Kevin's shoulder. "Take care."

Kevin walked back to the girl sagging with relief. Not such a bad cop after all. Janet was all set to go, so he climbed on his bike and they took off immediately, not daring to look back.

"You weren't telling the whole truth," Janet said sharply. "You weren't looking at the sun, buddy, you were looking at me. Now I want the *whole* truth, mister, right *now!* Out with it."

Kevin stared at her, surprised at her change in manner.

"What are you getting all excited about?"

"*I'm* not excited. Don't *tell me* I'm fucking excited. If there's something wrong with you, I want to know about it, that's all, and I don't want you keeping anything from me, either. Why, you had me scared to death back there, flopping around like a big fat fish and saying all kinds of weird shit. And you had everybody staring at *me*, like it was all *my* fault. And what was I supposed to do about it? You didn't tell me what I was supposed to do about it, did you? *You didn't tell me anything!* So I don't want you holding anything back from me, you got that? Or we can go our separate ways right now. Is that *clear?*"

Kevin swallowed. "Wow..." he whispered. "Janet, how can I explain something I don't understand?"

"You can start by being honest, for crying out loud." The girl appeared to mellow as quickly as she'd freaked. She took a deep breath. "Look, Kevin, nobody's ever going to get on your case for not being well. Don't you understand that? It's just the dishonesty, the holding back, that keeps people apart." Her expression was wistful. "And here I thought we had something special between us."

The boy blushed. "Really?"

"*Really*. So tell me, what was that all about?"

"Like I said, Janet, I just don't have a clue. It's only happened a few times now, but—"

"But...*bullshit!*" she screamed. "I ask you to be fucking honest, and all you do is play fucking mind games!"

"I'm not playing games."

"Fucking retard. If you're not going to level with me then just keep your fat trap shut."

Kevin fixed his eyes on his front wheel, his neck bunched into his shoulders. For a moment he saw red, but only for a moment. Janet began humming *Baby Love*, and a soft breeze came whispering off the sea. A caravan of motor homes rolled lazily by. Kevin sighed. At least they were still together. If only these bizarre attacks would cease, or at least become predictable. There had to be a recognizable catalyst, something he could monitor. But the more he thought about it, the farther he seemed from an answer.

They made Big Sur around noon, aided by a lift from a sweet old couple in an ancient, clattering pickup. The man and woman, both in their hale seventies, had sold their Santa Maria farm and were following the coast to belatedly "get out and see the world." Kevin and Janet had accepted the lift only because the couple were so friendly and so insistent. They had secured their bikes in the bed and rode cramped up front in the cab.

The seniors were enchanted with Kevin and Janet, whom they considered model hippies. For Kevin, the experience was as close as he'd ever come to feeling part of a family.

Alongside the road were dozens of bicyclists and hitchhikers in all manner of attire, from the most ragged to the most elaborate and ingenious. Tents could be seen between the pines. As they approached the forest proper the ambience became that of an endless party, for in those days Big Sur was one of the Movement's major stomps.

When they reached Jules Pfeiffer forest they hopped out and said their farewells. There were so many revelers loitering in the road that traffic was at a standstill, so the couples had time for goodbyes that grew redundant. At last the old truck moved away, and Kevin and Janet walked into the throng with stars in their eyes.

There must have been thousands of picnicking, partying, souls present that day, and the ruckus was tremendous. It seemed everybody had an instrument; a guitar, a harmonica, a tambourine. The wood was alive with song. Long-haired satyrs wove melodies with flutes and piccolos and recorders. Somewhere in the thick of it a full drum kit paced an electric piano. And through it all rang countless voices; voices shouting, chanting, laughing, shrieking, reciting, singing.

The moment held a special magic for Kevin. Here was a taste of what he craved, and the first real indication that spots like Haight-Ashbury or Greenwich Village might actually exist as described. He saw Big Sur, via the tutelage of Eddie, as a major oasis in a nation unflinchingly devoted to war, antiquated ideals, corporate gain, stiff associations; a business-suited, arrogant place designed to render life as dull, as mundane, as sober and routine as humanly possible. But this remote and enchanted commune throve upon a philosophy that defied those traditions supposedly responsible for the mortar in all working social structures. Theoretically a society such as this should not be able to endure, since its only requirements were that one be peaceable, use drugs (or at least be tolerant of their use), deny the principles set up by, or approved by, the preceding generation, and have a worshipful sense of identity with rock music and its heroes. Yet this society, and others like it popping up around the world, *could* survive. They persisted partly through the allegiance of the inhabitants and partly through the unsung contributions of benefactors from all walks of life, who, like the straights who so adamantly condemned these docile, carefree outcasts, ached from the bottom of their hearts to be free of their inhibitions, to be bohemians.

But this generation had its own new standards, its own leaders, tenets, heroes, gods. Within this subculture—or counterculture—it was perfectly respectable to be poor and rootless, to run naked or in rags.

And in Big Sur it was always party time. There were characters in turbans and robes offering one odd candies and free incense, long-time residents and newcomers embracing each other like family. You were free to simply look on, or to participate in any music-fest, discussion, or purely social gathering. And of course marijuana was everywhere. Several times total strangers would hand Kevin or Janet a joint without introduction or examination, as if it was the most natural thing in the world to do. But most of all Kevin was blown away by the size and vitality of the crowd. It reminded him of what he'd read about January's Human Be-in on the Polo Fields of Golden Gate Park, when White Lightning tabs had been passed out in a crowd numbering in the tens of thousands, and beaded and feathered freaks had managed to keep it mellow all the while. Now the easygoing affection of the people around him made it possible to believe that, in the near future, he would walk on those very Polo Fields on a date which, he felt, would grow to be of equal historical stature, when, he was pretty sure, this girl Janet here, this beautifully blossoming flower child, would stand beside him and take him seriously, he seriously doubted, when he told her he wanted to be her guru, and she to be his earth mother, throughout the Revolution and beyond. Kevin wasn't sure he could summon the words or the courage, but he was positive her refusal would crush him. Here he was, in the kind of environment where anything seemed possible…and his heart was telling him that without her he was nowhere—that without her happy exclamations and little electrifying nudges and squeezes of the arm he'd might as well be on the moon.

A bit deeper in the woods Kevin and Janet came upon an assemblage interesting enough to bring them to a halt. Perhaps a hundred freaks were gathered in concentric circles around a smaller group of seated persons, each poised with hands raised slightly above the head. After locking their bicycles to a tree trunk, Kevin and Janet made their way down through the crowd to its focus.

In the center a bearded, totally bald blind man sat on an upturned paint can, wiggling his fingers over his head. On his right sat a skinny, leotard-clad middle-aged woman, her eyes rolled up, her arms crooked about her head to form a frame for her face. Members of the inner ring were apparently the blind man's adherents, as they now commenced, almost in unison, wiggling their fingers in rapt mimicry.

It looked like Kevin and Janet had arrived just in time, for even as they sat the blind man ceased wiggling, and his disciples respectfully followed suit.

"Now," the blind man intoned, "we shall demonstrate, for all those who seek inner peace and wisdom, that ancient and most sacred Sri Lankan technique known as *Abu-bu-agubu.* I, having labored a lifetime in search of the Self's ultimate fulfillment, chanced upon this sacrosanct method while a guest in the mountaintop libraries of the Vishbewa holy order.

"It is not mere happenstance that our hands and feet should have precisely five digits apiece. As you shall presently see it is essential that the devotee have a minimum of five fingers upon each hand—although I have personally witnessed certain digitally-challenged elders of the Vishbewa order perform the Abu-bu-agubu using only the toes. Truly an awesome and uplifting experience.

"To demonstrate the technique we have my assistant here, the lovely Moonflower, who has herself transcended the worldly too many times to number, and is the most proficient purveyor of transcension west of Delhi.

"Now, the key to reaching the inner Self is, of course, the severance of the spirit, or *tukhu-khu,* from the senses. You will learn here today that enlightenment resides within each of us, in a dormant state, and that its natural expression is inhibited solely by the barrage of sensory impressions we constantly receive from without. Therefore, you must understand, it is vital that we remove ourselves from sensory stimuli in order to set our spirits free. To this end we employ the five fingers of each hand, our *tukhu-sem,* in the esoteric ballet of Abu-bu-agubu. To prepare ourselves, we engage in *Bawa-khe.* Moonflower?"

The skinny woman now began gracefully wiggling her

fingers above her head. The disciples copied her movements eagerly and with precision.

Kevin and Janet also began warming up. Janet was giggling. "Why do I feel like a jellyfish?" she whispered.

"C'mon, Janet," Kevin said, wiggling away. "Maybe this guy's for real. I mean, look at all he went through just to get inside himself."

She placed a hand on his thigh for support, pushed herself to her feet and looked around. "You go ahead. I'm going to try to get inside myself in a ladies' room somewhere. I'll be right back."

Kevin was about to object when the blind man resumed his monologue. Janet stepped around sitting observers. Kevin heard her asking directions.

"First of all, as Moonflower shall demonstrate, we employ the little finger of each hand, the *tukhu-pe*, and the second finger of each hand, the *tukhu-ba*, in tandem, touching the tips of our tukhu-pes together, and touching the tips of our tukhu-bas together, as Moonflower is doing, to form a temple shape; then bending the first knuckle of each tukhu-ba to create, roughly, a rectangular shape, a *bawa-we*.

"The bawa-we is now placed upon the mouth, or *ama-mi*, and the tukhu-pes and tukhu-bas are brought toward each other, pinching the lips so as to prevent the ingress of any substance polluting to the spirit. At this stage it is vital the follower be breathing only via the nostrils, or *ama-ama*."

Kevin achieved the first step, like everyone else, by copying Moonflower, whose lips protruded obscenely from her cinched bawa-we. The woman was obviously no sloucher.

"And now," the blind man continued, "we employ our middle fingers, or *tukhu-jis*, by thrusting them into the ama-ama, thus further cutting off the profane outer world from the sanctity of the tukhu-khu. It is essential that participants, at this stage, no longer be breathing, and yet remain relaxed and alert. Moonflower?"

Moonflower now rammed the middle finger of each hand up a nostril and rolled her eyes ecstatically, looking like a bulimic gargoyle.

Kevin gently placed his tukhu-jis in his ama-ama, but

found he was cheating, taking occasional shallow whiffs of air.

"Now," said the blind man, "place the index finger of each hand, your *tukhu-mas*, over the eyes, thus shutting out all visual impediments to the liberation of tukhu-khu."

Kevin, Moonflower, and the disciples did so, but Kevin again found himself cheating; peeking this time.

"And finally, place the thumbs, or *tukhu-vas*, in the ears, thus completely blocking sensory stimuli, and allowing the Self its full expression. Moonflower?"

Moonflower jammed her thumbs in her ears and re-mained absolutely still. After a minute or so her face began to turn blue, her ribs to quake, her arms to tremble. One by one audience members gave in to the profane, removing their hands and gasping; embarrassed, ashamed. Moonflower, after quiver-ing a while longer, keeled over at the blind man's feet. Adher-ents rushed to her aid.

"By that sound," the blind man said, "I understand that Moonflower has once again achieved *tukhu-khukhu*, has trans-cended the worldly to commune with her sacred Self in the utmost expression of bliss. Reveal to us, Moonflower, what se-crets your Self has divulged."

Moonflower, supported under the arms by envious fol-lowers, grinned dopily, saliva hanging from one corner of her ama-mi. Suddenly her body jerked forward. She lay on her face, head and legs still, torso thrashing like a landed fish. Moon-flower became absolutely limp, and the crowd went wild.

Kevin wiped his hands on his Levis and got to his feet, looking for Janet. He saw a little cabin-shaped outhouse not more than a hundred yards away amid a cluster of pines, and realized she couldn't possibly be lost. He was just beginning to worry when he saw the unmistakable cascade of chestnut hair only thirty feet to his right.

She wasn't alone. Kevin was surprised to find her en-gaged in animated conversation with a foppish young man who had apparently sidled through the crowd to attempt a pickup. The threat was somewhat diminished in Kevin's untrained eyes, for this intruder was such a phony Janet had to be doing every-thing she could to keep from laughing in his pretty-ass face. With that comically too-neat hair and those embarrassingly too-sharp clothes, and with all those tacky, expensive-looking rings on his fingers and that way-too fancy gold medallion, the gaudy jerk stood out like a sore freaking thumb. He couldn't possibly know what a fool he was making of himself. Yet, perhaps because she was embarrassed for him, Janet appeared to be humoring this phony. Kevin proceeded, not by degrees but by leaps, from wry curiosity to narrow resentment to outright jealousy. He walked right up beside them, as though urgently impelled from behind, and was entirely ignored. A troubled and nondescript bystander, he stood with mouth contorting, hearing portions of their conversation in one ear and a cacophony of partygoers in the other.

"...no really, swear, you remind me of this chick so much you could be her sister."

"...get that medallion? And those rings?"

"...was playing with this group from Blackpool."

"...bet you got all the girls."

"...only the naughty ones."

From Kevin's lungs rose a great bellow of shock and outrage at this betrayal. Somehow the roar got stuck in his larynx, and all that escaped was a croaking sound compromising a belch and a grunt of frustration. Janet and the intruder stopped talking and looked at him curiously; the stranger with mild surprise and she with a touch of irritation. As no further gutturals seemed pending they took up where they'd left off.

Kevin turned his head sharply and clenched his fists, his expression twisting into one only his father could appreciate.

Could she possibly hold his love in such low esteem? Were all his considerate and selfless acts to be dismissed so casually...could anybody really be so cheap and underhanded? Clouds of creeping comprehension passed over his face. Those clouds grew darker and darker still, until Kevin stood alone in deepest shadow. A voice appeared in the middle of his skull, attempting to infuse that skull with wisdom that, to an impulsive male, is only a distraction. And the voice described how women are attracted to the weakest, least masculine end of the male spectrum, and explained that those males are psychologically closer to a teddy bear than to a figure of independence. No self-respecting man, the voice elaborated, would flirt, or allow himself to be babied—genuine men do not pucker; they gag when the maternal instinct rears its gooey head.

This indictment, the intrusive voice went on, is in no wise a celebration of the male marauder, whose profanity is monumental. Yet is there no compromise 'twixt the teddy and grizzly? The dandies dance their darlingest dance, the duet effete permeates our narcissistic, ass-happy land of opportunity. Stress breeds *men*. Lack of same produces...you guessed it. There's just *too much liberty*, that's all—and liberty *does not* bring out the best in people. Seems humankind's heartfelt supposition is that people are basically good, and simply need as much liberty as possible to express their highest potential.

People are animals, both figuratively and literally, and they'll exploit any system as far as they can. It's *so* tough dealing with explosive words such as *evil*, or *immoral*, or *improper*. So the voice coined a noun, one both childish and simplistic, certainly...grammatically awkward, yes—but the only one aptly describing human character. That word was UNGOODNESS. How many truly *good* people, the useless voice inquired, have you encountered? Not people who simply are not bad, and not those who behave positively because they've been proselytized, or reared properly, or scared straight. How many people have you met who live virtuously *because* they are of a virtuous nature, and are instinctively repulsed by worldliness? Don't bother enumerating.

The voice tapered to a murmur even as the sun began to peek through the clouds. Kevin shook his head. Hearing voices was a real bad sign. And Eddie had no damned business fucking with his head right now. There was more at stake than logic. Kevin's eyes refocused. He again became a reactive engine, as nature intended. But though he tried to shut out the broken dialogue beside him another part of his mind eavesdropped intently.

"...beach house in Monterey."

"...just *love* Monterey."

"...going deep sea fishing. Maybe you'd like..."

At this point Kevin turned and asserted himself, every nerve on fire. "*Sorry*, man. But we already had plans. I mean we *have* plans. Look, why don't you just mind your own fucking business and split, okay? Let's, like, let's not, you know, let's *not* lose our heads over this." His hands, forcibly unclenched, were trembling. He was hyperventilating.

The dandy stared in surprise for a moment. His eyes flashed. He looked back at Janet, who seemed grimly absorbed in some godawful noise coming from an amateur band to their right.

"Forgive me," he addressed her gallantly. "I thought you were alone. My apologies. Your brother?"

"*Not* my brother," she grated. "Just a friend I met down the coast."

Kevin flinched. Just a...*friend*. She couldn't...couldn't *possibly* have any idea how those words hurt.

He began blinking rapidly, pain clouding reality.

What was going on here?

She was...*dumping* him.

It was *over*; it was sealed: it could be read in her voice. He was being discarded, traded for this bastard fop as readily as a princess would replace an impudent servant.

"Just a *friend*?" he choked. "Why, I practically saved your *life!* I fed you and protected you and—"

"Don't *you*," Janet said loudly, "shout at *me!*" Several heads turned to look on with interest, bored with love and peace, itching for attitude. "And don't give me all that crap about what you did for me, mister. Nobody forced you to feed me."

The flashy intruder now intruded again, stepping between them while easing a protective arm in front of Janet. "Now look, man, I'm not going to stand here and listen to you badmouth this young lady. Why don't you run along to mama before I forget you're just a big fat kid with a big fat mouth."

Frustration fogged Kevin's vision. The crowd pressed in with greedy faces. The stranger was rolling up his sleeves, and Janet's eyes were gleaming over his shoulder. When that gleam lanced through everything made a savage kind of sense. Clearly, there was only one way to reestablish himself in her heart. Chivalry or insanity, it was convenient this dapper meddler was offering his prissy homo face as an outlet for years of frustration. With a snarl Kevin threw a haymaker, and the power behind that punch was aimed not only at the weasel, but at all the pricks and pussywillows who had conspired from Day One to make this adventure an undeserved kick in the balls; at all the so-called friends who had exploited his trusting nature, at all those pretty pink jock-playgrounds who had taunted him, intentionally or no, with their unbearably desirable bodies— trashing him with a complete lack of sympathy for his honest green susceptibility.

Fortunately the punch was wide; the young man had seen it coming and deftly sidestepped. There was immediate activity all around, as those closest tried to lay on some controlling hands. Kevin's opponent, though easily forty pounds lighter, was a clever and experienced fighter, managing several good jabs with his left fist while feigning with the right, steadily driving Kevin back into the crowd where there was no room to swing. The boy found his hard punches consistently glancing off the stranger's quicker forearm blocks, but he hardly felt the jabs against his nose and chin. He was looking for an opening. When he found it he was going to leap on the pretty-boy thief and thumb out his eyeballs before he strangled him to blazes.

A gesticulating man began pleading for peace and order, but the crowd, deaf to him, gravitated to the action, forming a shouting ring around the fighters, whooping and cheering with each connecting jab.

One of Kevin's random roundhouse punches finally caught his opponent on the temple and sent him stumbling back shaking his head, but the boy was slow to capitalize on his advantage. He threw himself on the dazed stranger clumsily, and the two went rolling in the dust amid a stampede of retreating shoes. The young man, squirming free, leaped right to his feet. He kicked furiously at Kevin's face, drawing ecstatic boos from the onlookers. Kevin rolled away and scrambled upright just as his foe came sailing through the air, delivering a fine judo kick to the side of the fat boy's head.

"Get up," he said, licking his lips.

Kevin's skull was ringing. It wasn't anger that moved him now; most of his rage had passed in that initial swing. The taunts of the bystanders were firing him. Even though he knew the struggle was lost he gamely pulled himself erect. The crowd cheered.

Kevin made a growling rush, somehow coming out of it with a handful of the nimble young man's hair. He held on long as he could, landing three solid hammering slugs to the forehead, until a barrage of desperate kidney-punching caused him to release his grip. They whirled away together, slamming into a group of lounging bikers. These party-crashing thugs immediately reacted by grabbing and trouncing any flower child they could get their greasy felonious hands on.

The domino effect was dazzling.

Hippies showed their fangs, lovers became brawlers. Kevin, struck from behind, was flung hard on his stomach. He rolled over as his enemy pounced, but before the young man could completely straddle Kevin's spread-eagled body a wall of clashing hotheads fell in a line. Kevin had a glimpse of elbows and heads as his opponent was golfed away. Next thing he knew he was desperately fighting to make his feet.

Those interested only in escape were being trampled, falling back into the fray before they could worm out. Kevin scurried underfoot to the melee's edge. He crawled out like a dying man. Park Rangers in jeeps and on horseback were pulling up nearby. With the aid of several huge Hell's Angels members, these men in uniform began wrenching fighters apart. A quickly finished skirmish broke out between two chain-wielding troglodytes and half a dozen efficient Rangers.

A helicopter magically appeared above the trees. As the roar of its rotor hammered down, the fighters pulled apart one by one.

Kevin lay in a heap, too done in to be bothered by running feet. As in a dream, he heard hundreds chanting for peace, with more joining in on each call. The ever-watchful arm of Authority was back in control. The kids were all right.

# Chapter 14

## Love Is For Losers

"...Never *been* so embarrassed," Janet was saying bitterly, her lovely hair flying. *"Never!"* She shook a fist in his face, her expression wild with contempt. "You asshole! You filthy son of a bitch! You fat ugly prick! You...you...*you bastard!"* She buried her face in her hands and sobbed, and when she looked back up she was no longer just a distraught pretty girl. She was a psychotic, raving hellcat. She spat in his face, socked him right in the nose, raked her long nails down his cheek. She called him every insult at her command. Finally she sank against the cab window, breathing heavily, and when she looked at him again she seemed to have regained control. "Why," she panted, "why did you have to bring *me* into it? Just tell me that. It's not enough for you to single-handedly destroy the good vibes in that place, it's not enough for you to just ruin everybody's day with your rowdy shit, but then you have to go connect *me* with all the trouble you caused, and get everybody staring at *me*." Her voice rose, fell, rose again. Then she screamed, *"JesuswasIembarrassed!"* and designer tears tumbled down her cheeks, from an inexhaustible supply. She bit her lip and spat, "I'm getting sick of your shit!" her words and expression nearly identical to those terminating Mike's outburst three days earlier.

Kevin wiped his nose and let his head hang almost to his knees, long past defending himself. It seemed he could do nothing right.

They were in the bed of a Park Ranger's green pickup truck, being banished from the park as troublemakers. The driver, a conscientious Ranger in his late thirties, sat gruffly behind the wheel with shoulders hunched, wearing regulation sunglasses. He never once turned around, though he was no doubt keeping an eye on their reflections in the rearview mirror. The occasional hitchhiker looked after them curiously.

"Sorry," was the only defense Kevin could muster. For the last half hour he'd uttered the word with parrot-like redundancy.

"Well, that's great! That's just fucking peachy! That clears it all up, does it? I was having such a good time, too. At *least* you could tell me why."

Kevin wagged his hands. "I don't know," he whined. "I guess it's a guy thing." He shook his head. "It's just that I...well, I didn't want that phony taking advantage of you."

"I'm a big girl now. I can take care of myself."

"Well, I thought since I was kind of escorting you—"

As Janet leaned forward the glare of her eyes cut him off. She said fiercely and very distinctly, "You don't *own* me, buster. *Nobody* owns me. And for that matter, I don't know where you got this stupid idea you're some sort of chaperone or escort or whatever the hell you think you are, because you're *not*. I'll make my own decisions *when* and *how* I want to make them. Is that perfectly clear? I won't have you playing big brother, either. You're like a child who thinks he can have everything he wants, and when something doesn't go his way he throws a tantrum. But you can't own *me*, mister, so you keep your fat hands out of my personal life. Is that *perfectly* clear? Do we understand each other?"

It was. They did. Kevin, having drawn deeper into himself throughout the scolding, was now peering plaintively between his kneecaps.

"Yes," he whispered. "I said I was—"

"And I *heard* you—for the eight hundred and thirty-seventh time! So just shut up and stay out of my face. You're giving me one hell of a headache. As a matter of fact, you *are* a headache."

Kevin closed his eyes, a ball of remorse. He'd deserved

the scolding, had almost enjoyed it. For, no matter what she said or did, he was still with her, and being near her under any circumstances was infinitely better than being without her. On the back of his eyelids he reviewed her terrible indignation when he'd sheepishly told the infuriated Rangers he was there as her *escort*. Once the Rangers had everything under control, they'd rounded up Kevin's much-dirtied but self-righteous opponent. The crowd was highly in favor of the young man—since he cut a finer figure and had pretty much controlled the fight's tempo—and had unanimously fingered Kevin as the instigator. After damning Janet as roundly as Kevin, the Rangers had confabbed, deciding to not call in the police for fear of a riot, given so many youngsters with their blood up. They had ordered Janet and Kevin into the back of the green pickup, to be forcibly removed from their beautiful and beloved park. Janet had been in tears.

The Ranger drove them all the way to Monterey, although he was not commanded to do so. His orders were to remove them far enough up the coast so as to be out of the county, but he had a girl in Monterey. When he pulled over it was twilight, and Kevin and Janet were shivering.

"All right;" he said curtly as he stepped from the truck, "hand your bikes over the side."

Kevin obeyed, then dropped to the road on aching legs, his shoulders hunched. Janet refused any assistance from the Ranger, who shrugged and gave vent upon Kevin's bowed head the full measure of his fury.

"Now, if I *ever* see either of you in my park again I will personally, repeat *personally*, rout you like rabbits and run you out by the seat of your pants. *You hear me?* We've kept Sur a nice place, even with all you kids up here, even with all the publicity. And let me tell you, most of those kids are really nice guys. Kinky or not, they believe in what they're doing. But there's always some punk who has to throw a wrench in the works. You're damn lucky I'm not dropping you off at Carmel City Jail. The only reason I'm not is because we don't need the bad publicity. And we don't need creeps like *you*."

Kevin took it all wordlessly, by now conditioned to reprimand. The Ranger stormed away, climbed in his truck and threw it in gear. Janet immediately mounted her bike.

"Wait!"

"Wait," she wondered icily, "for *what?*"

"Look, let me make it up to you, Janet. I didn't mean—"

"Yes, you've *told* me and *told* me and *told me!* You're sorry. It was all a mistake. You're a peace loving hippie. A *sorry* peace loving hippie."

"Okay, then I won't say I'm sorry. But please don't run off without me. *Please.* Look, I'm asking you—I'm *begging* you. Janet, I'll make it up to you, I *swear!*"

Something like a smile firmed the girl's soft lips, but it passed as she looked away, up the road at the brightening lights of the city. "I'm almost there;" she said quietly, "that house I told you about. I'm quite sure I can make it the rest of the way without *your* kind of help."

"At least let me get you a cup of cocoa first. It's too cold to ride without something to warm you up. Maybe you'd like something to eat." He was clutching.

"Okay," she said presently. "You can buy me cocoa."

Monterey was cracking and fizzing with fireworks. It was the beginning of the municipally-sponsored Fourth of July celebration, and just the distraction Kevin was praying for. Janet, delighting in the aerial displays, quickly forgot all about the day's unhappy episode. Kevin bought her Smokey Petes to toss, sparklers to wave, an expensive king-size fireworks kit and, later, gratefully bought her cocoa, and then a meal that would have pleased his father. As she led him through the boulevard shops her mood continued to brighten. Janet allowed him to buy her a blouse, a multicolored handbag, a transistor radio, and a poster showing The Beatles romping through several scenes of the movie *Help!* Kevin was relieved to be on something like speaking terms again, although he realized his appeal resided in his wallet. That was all right with him. He would rob banks to keep her.

As they found the coast and began to idly pedal along it was old days again. She rattled on tirelessly about the fireworks and about her friends, while he sucked up beside her, his jaw slack, like a loyal pooch fascinated by the absurdly complicated modulations of his mistress' voice, and impatient to delight in that single command which kept them a unit: *Kevin! Fetch!*

They made slow headway. As they neared the Seaside residence Kevin used every excuse to stall for five minutes here, for ten there. He was, already, visualizing himself being rewarded and dismissed with a perfunctory handshake or peck of lips. Kevin saw it coming—but not as a bad turn. It was another ice-cold rip-off, just like the rest of the crap he'd taken all...oh, years. But this was worse than a loss; it was a calamity. And a guy can take only so much...there comes a time when the victim wears a new face: the face of an animal without compromise. At this stage no compassion remains, no honor. Only the high-gear nervous action of snarling defense. The grip on Kevin's handlebars became viselike. His mind went dark, his pouting expression twisted into a savage grimace. His face grew so contorted Janet immediately braked her bicycle.

"Wow! You've simply *got* to stop and check out your mug!"

Kevin braked hard. He was trembling head to toe. "It's okay," he whispered. "I'm all right."

"Are you *sure*? You look terrible."

"I'm fine. Fine." They were in the residential section of Seaside, on a homey sparkler-lit avenue. "Your friend's house," he managed. "How—how far?"

"We're almost there. It's on the next block. Look, are you *positive* you're all right? If Jamie's home he'll give you a ride to the hospital."

Kevin closed his eyes. "Jamie?" he muttered. He shook his head. The side-to-side movement faltered, became a broadening elliptical progression, and then Kevin was nodding—he'd been right all along. He'd outlived his usefulness. Jamie? He blew out his cheeks. Fucking *Jamie*? "No," he whispered. "No, I'm okay."

"Whew! You had me worried there. I thought you were going to pull another of those stupid numbers like the other— *look*, there's Jamie's house now! The one with all those eucalyptus trees in the front. You can see the porch light."

"Far out," Kevin muttered.

When they reached the house he knew it was over. In the back of his mind he'd been praying that any tenants would not be home, giving him a chance to convince the girl to go elsewhere, if only temporarily. But light filtered through psychedelic posters on the windows. Electric music could be heard. He stood on the walk while Janet rang the doorbell.

A soft yellow haze illuminated her as the porch bulb came to life. The door was opened and a pleasant looking young man of twenty peered out. His light brown hair was cut like the young Prince Valiant's, although longer and fuller, and there was also something of the Hal Foster character's noble bearing and poise about him. He reminded Kevin of somebody else. His eyes were very clear and bright, his figure slim and full of grace. He was dressed casually: Levis and a brown rayon shirt open at the neck, tan hushpuppies.

"Jannie!" he cried, embracing her exuberantly, gently rocking her by swiveling his pelvis. "*Sweet*-heart, how've you been! Why didn't you let us know you were coming? It's been ages."

"Oh, Jamie, I missed you so! I was *so* afraid you wouldn't be home."

On the walk, forgotten, Kevin was wondering who to kill first. As his body coiled and his fingers flexed, a profound sense of alienation transformed the powerful compression of his frame to a cringe. And while he watched their identical shut-eyed expressions during the embrace that went on and on, his mind, curiously, decided to take a stroll; remarking, quite transiently, that one of the window posters was similar to a poster on his own wall in his room at home, or what used to be home; that his bicycle was holding up to the journey well; that San Francisco, according to Eddie, was Spanish for Saint Francis. Just compulsive thinking, the sort any healthy mind resorts to at point of surrender. But then he thought, *Why doesn't he just throw her down and ball her on the spot, for Christ's sake. What's he waiting for?* He was close to vocalizing his thoughts when the two pulled apart, allowing light from the front room to wash over him. His eyes glinted.

Jamie noticed him, said, "Oh."

Janet turned. After echoing Jamie, she said, "*Excuse me.* Jamie, this is Kevin Michaels, a *very good friend* I met way down the coast. He's on his way up to San Francisco, and he was thoughtful enough to *escort* me up here and make sure I didn't have too much fun."

Jamie grinned. "Hi!" He offered his hand, expecting Kevin to approach, but the boy remained hunched and stationary, glaring. "Well!" Jamie said. "Why don't you two come on in and make yourselves at home." He turned and, with another friendly grin, strode inside.

Janet returned Kevin's stare for a long silent moment. She folded her arms across her chest. "Well?"

Kevin's jaw worked spastically before creaking open. "I—I...I've got something to say, Janet."

*"Well?"*

What he had in mind was something along the lines of, *Listen, you skinny fucking bitch, you may not know it, but I'm a human being with feelings too. And I've done everything to prove my love, but you're so self-centered it was all like totally in vain. So this is the big goodbye, honey. I've been hurt, but I'll heal, so save your sobs for the next sucker. I'm not saying it wasn't fun, or that you ain't cute, but there's a whole buncha other funky fish in this funky-ass sea,* etc. What came out belied his thoughts.

"Oh Janet, I'm *so* sorry for all the trouble I've been. For real. I know you're sick of hearing me say I'm sorry, and I know what you must think of me. It's hard to admit this, Janet, but...I can't let go. Oh *please* don't leave me alone now."

"*Jesus*, when are you ever gonna grow up! Didn't you just hear Jamie invite you in?" She turned on her heel and skipped inside, her aloof and disgusted expression changing in the wink of an eye to one of brainless gaiety.

Kevin looked around uncertainly. "Slut," he whispered. He walked his bike to the porch, passed the lock and chain through the rear spokes. Inspired, he stood Janet's bike against his and locked them together to the porch railing. Kevin regarded his Peugeot an extension of his body; to tamper with it was to pinch a nerve and bring him running. He almost felt he had a say in the situation.

He stopped just inside the door, flabbergasted.

Against the far wall were three totally naked persons, perched on cushions in the lotus position, palms turned up on knees, eyes closed.

They appeared to be in trances, entirely unaffected by the hard driving psychedelic music pulsating from flanking stereo speakers. The two males, one old and one young, were both gaunt and starved-looking. The girl sitting between them was a chubby, unclean thing of twenty. What shocked Kevin was not the nakedness of the girl. It was seeing naked men in front of Janet—he wanted to cover her eyes…and for reasons best left interred, his own. Maybe he just wasn't cut out to be a revolutionary after all. What was going on here was, thenadays, perfectly acceptable conduct. The black light, the enormous ceramic water pipe, the musky scent of incense in every corner—these were all standard stimuli. But he couldn't overlook the nudity. No doubt about it, this Jamie guy had to be one righteously sick dude.

Janet was seated right next to him, on a low crushed velvet davenport, her tapering legs curled up comfortably, her slender feet bare. Just in front of the couch, on a glass-topped driftwood coffee table, were several glasses, a bowl of ice, a quart of Pepsi, and a fifth of Cream of Kentucky bourbon. Kevin stood by the door, his mouth shoveling warm air and incense fumes, watching Janet's and Jamie's teeth gleam surrealistically in the black light's glow. He felt such a minor part…he was sure what looked like an orgy in the making could proceed without paying him the least mind. When at last the record was over, and only Janet's musical laughter and the hiss of the stylus broke the silence, Jamie looked up and waved.

"Well don't just *stand* there, man. Have a seat!"

Kevin mumbled something and shuffled over, sat down heavily. The impact of his body would ordinarily have merely rocked Janet in his direction, but Jamie picked that precise moment to get up to change the album, telling the boy to go ahead and fix himself a drink. As a result Janet rocked heavily against Kevin, and, recovering her balance, laid a small hand gently on the sensitive pudding of his inner thigh. Her giggles were like bubbles popping melodiously against his eardrum, as she breathed essence of cola and bourbon in his face, and whispered:

"Well, pour yourself a drink, silly. You don't have to

look so grumpy and uncomfortable. We're all friends. Just make yourself at home; take off your shoes...*relax*. While you've been standing around acting too cool for the room I've been telling Jamie all about what a hero you've been; how you fixed my flat and stood up for me against those big men when we almost had breakfast this morning. That really scored some points with Jamie. He thinks you must be a super high dude to be so inventive and brave. He digs people who have confidence, so don't act so stiff and paranoid. Just sit back and make yourself at home. Take off your shoes and get comfy. *Relax*. Have a drink, why don't you? Why are you so quiet?"

Kevin grunted. He was keenly aware of a juxtaposition of past and present; how this event so strongly paralleled the time at Perky's house when the raven-haired girl had perched so near and likewise placed a hand on his thigh. A chill raced up his back, and with horror he felt his lips leak the words,

"He your boyfriend?"

"Who? Jamie? He's my cousin, but he's like a brother to me. He stays out here with Rod every summer. We used to live only a couple of miles from here; me and Jamie and my family."

"Rod?"

"That older man sitting over there tripping. He's heavily into the Consciousness Movement. He doesn't need acid or anything. Jamie told me that Rod and Linda and Holland—the other couple there—said the Om exercise this afternoon and have been grooving on inner space all day long. Isn't that *heavy*?" She leaned against him.

Kevin kept his big mouth shut. The nudity and Janet's on-again off-again behavior were related in some way, held some special message for him, but right now he didn't know if he was coming or going. Only minutes ago he'd been begging her to come back, and now he was praying she'd move away. Her slim brown hand was alarmingly close to his crotch, and she didn't seem to be worried about Jamie noticing. Or was Jamie part of the plot? And, to aggravate his confusion, Janet's hand, unlike the ivory fingers of the raven-haired girl, was eliciting no response from his body. Kevin looked away.

The chubby girl was the first female (besides his squat

and shapeless mother, and not counting photographed models) he'd ever seen naked. But unlike the nudes Kevin had goggled in adult magazines, this Linda person sagged at every curve. Her skin was the hue of raw potato meat, scored with pimples and brown bruises. Her breasts were collapsed with the slump of her heavy shoulders, and her crotch, that secret land, seemed a foul place, all smelly and kink-wired and clammy and unclean. The huge lumps of her feet were gateposts, their nails chipped and unpainted. And, horror of horrors, her legs and armpits were unshaven, sporting a dark curly growth like that of the Laurel Canyon girls.

Janet kneaded his thigh. "Re-*lax*, will you?"

"I'm not uptight," Kevin maundered, perspiring. "Who said I was uptight? It's just that…well, *you're* not bugged by seeing these guys all bare-ass naked? I mean, it doesn't bother me, of course. After all, I have to take showers at school, don't I? And seeing a chick in the buff is nothing new—like, I'm no prude or anything, you know. Don't get that idea. I just thought you might be offended, or embarrassed, by having to look at these guys."

She laughed. "Is li'l Kevin afwaid Janet might see the boys' nasty ol' pee-pees? Oh, you *are* a child. We used to sit around here naked all the time. There's no hangups. This is the Sixties, remember? Have a drink!" She drained her glass and leaned forward to mix him one as Jamie rejoined them on the couch.

"Janet was telling me what a good job you did of taking care of her on the road, and I'd like to say I really appreciate it, man. The whole world's turning on to love, but there's still some nasty little pockets of uncool out there."

As Kevin drank down the sweet mixed beverage he peeked over the rim of his glass and for the first time noticed subtle similarities in the cousins. There was a rare frankness in the eyes when either smiled, and the same silky tone to their complexions.

"Really!" Janet said. "You never know who or what you're going to meet on the road. It's a terrible place to be alone. Oh! Did I tell you?" She turned back to Kevin. "Jamie says that Marcie and Paula were here yesterday, and took off on their bikes again. They went up to Golden Gate Park to catch the concert. I'm going too, if only to give those girls a piece of my mind for ditching me like that." Her eyes sparkled. "So it looks like I'll be needing an escort." She sipped half her second drink while watching him over the rim of her glass, in a manner that struck Kevin as sultry.

He stared back until his eyes were burning. Fate or Karma or Providence or Whatever had granted him a reprieve. He masked his emotion by draining his glass and leaning forward to pour another. The liquor warmed him and he laughed. And somehow they were all holding hands and singing along as Roger Daltrey artfully stuttered and snarled through *My Generation*. The moment for Kevin was powerful and magical, containing the long-craved elements of friendship and family. He laughed again, loudly, and killed his second drink.

"This is it," Jamie said contentedly. "This is our house, our world, our future. God damn it, this is *our generation*, the dawning of a new world devoted to love and peace and the reformation of a power-hungry society! Just think: in a matter of only a few years, maybe, every lonely or needy person will be united as we are now, holding hands and sharing a common soul, and that soul, that single soul I tell you, will be nothing less than the communal substantiation of God Almighty Himself!"

"Oh, Jamie," Janet cooed, "you have such lovely thoughts in your head."

"I'm hip," Kevin said, and promptly knocked over his third drink. He bent forward to clean the mess.

"No, leave it!" Jamie said. "Fuck it, man, what's that rug anyway. Just the plastic, dyed, prefabricated product of a technology bending over backward to conceal nature with crud. Soon, soon enough, the only carpet we'll see will be the real green of sweet grass itself, and our homes will be teepees, and we'll shit in the woods like bears, the way man is *supposed* to live! To hell with technology and the atom bomb! Man, that's regression. This generation is sick of the stagnant past and the slippery present. Progress! God damn it, we'll show 'em progress!"

Janet hiccoughed. Jamie poured her another drink. She

sipped it, sighed, draped an arm around Kevin and an arm around Jamie, let her head rest against Kevin's shoulder. She yawned and hiccoughed twice more.

"Hooray for the Revolution!" Kevin blurted, in seventh heaven and more than a little tight. He pulled out his baggie of grass and his rolling papers. "Roll us up some joints, brother Jamie. And make 'em bombers!"

"Right on!"

"I'm so sleepy," Janet mumbled, hiccoughing. "I'm so tired."

Jamie rolled and fired up a monstrous doobie. Janet abstained, and by the time the two had finished smoking she was snoring softly on Kevin's shoulder.

"Look," Jamie said, "I'm late for this Fourth of July bash over at my partner's pad. And after the party I'm gonna see about scoring some hash oil. I'm talking quantity here. This kind of deal always takes all night, so you guys can crash in the room I'm using. Is that cool with you?"

"Sure."

"Okay. Feel free to use the pad any way you want. And don't worry about Rod and these people. I've seen them on this trip before. They won't come out of it till sunup."

"Right."

Jamie rose and offered his hand. "Well, it was cool meeting you, Alvin."

"Same to you, Jimmy."

"I'll catch you in the morning." Jamie winked man-to-man. "Take good care of my cousin."

Kevin shook hands tipsily but warmly. "Yeah, be cool, man. Take it easy." Jamie removed his hand with difficulty. Kevin's arm dropped lifelessly to his side. Jamie opened the door.

"Later on, then."

"Keep high, man."

"All right. Don't do anything I wouldn't."

"Easy on."

"Catch ya later." Jamie stepped out.

"Take it easy!" Kevin shouted at the door. "Have a good one!" The house was now quiet, except for the *hiss ca-chuck, hiss ca-chuck* of the needle at record's end. Kevin listened to the sound for a few minutes, half-conscious. Finally he got to his feet and staggered across the room. As he was bending to pick the arm off the record he checked himself. He'd been here before. He took a deep breath and, with the utmost care, lifted the arm at its tip with his thumb. He had it halfway back when it slipped off and tore across the disk. He picked it up hastily, dropped it again. After dropping it twice more he came to his senses and switched off the set. As the turntable slowed, the rasping sound wound down with a noise like a fading air raid siren. He straightened and blinked. The paralleling of past and present again. Perky's house...he'd knocked on the door, almost a week ago, and the music had—

Janet groaned. Kevin turned and walked over unsteadily, roughly shook her shoulder.

She half-opened her eyes. "Whachoo want?"

"Jamie split. He says you crash his bed. I sleep here ...couch."

She yawned, stretched, and held out her arms, hiccoughing. Kevin hauled her to her feet and danced her to the bedroom, apologizing extensively when his hands unintentionally gripped her rear in the awkward shambling embrace. As soon as they'd lurched into the room she kicked shut the door and pulled him down on the mattress. As he tried to rise she held tightly. "When first met you," she hiccoughed, "didn't realize what animal you were."

"Said I was sorry."

"Help me with my clothes." She sat up, belched daintily, and pulled off her pretty new blouse.

Kevin swallowed and turned his head, sobering considerably. He squeezed shut his eyes, as if to obliterate the second's impression of her jiggling breasts. The girl wore no bra— her torso proud, slim, tanned. The nipples were smallish, dark and coarse. He suddenly wanted out of there fast.

"Don't be embarrassed," Janet said. "You're not embarrassed, are you?"

"Of course not. What makes you think I'm embarrassed?"

She reached to unbutton his reeking shirt.

"Because I'm not embarrassed. Why should I be? Cause what's there to be embarrassed about?"

"Of course you're not, darling," she peeled off his shirt. Kevin steeled himself for her laughter. When she didn't laugh he only trembled harder.

"I'm not embarrassed, really. I feel fine, fine."

"*Look* at me." Softly commanding.

He turned his head slowly, forcing himself to look at her face and not at her taunting breasts. Her eyes were unbearably direct. Kevin quailed; his own eyes slunk away. It wasn't supposed to be like this. He willed his gopher to become engorged with blood, to manfully get the job done. But there was no response. None at all.

"Your shoes;" Janet said, "take off your shoes. You don't sleep in your shoes, do you?"

Kevin slowly bent to unlace his boots, his fingers numb chubby sausages. It wasn't fair. There just had to be some kind of credible, wholly acceptable excuse a guy could use under these circumstances to justify an immediate and unavoidable exit. Or at least a damned good reason for not performing. But young men in Kevin's position are expected to be blessing their stars and horny as all get-out, not trying to dodge the culmination of all their wet little fantasies. Maybe, Kevin thought desperately, maybe she would fall for a last-minute stance of chivalry if he could pull it off convincingly enough. He could say the time wasn't ripe, that he respected her too much to engage in carnal shenanigans without a longer, deeper relationship. But that was copping out. And real men don't cop out. He just wanted to make a lasting impression. Yet, according to everything he'd picked up from locker room banter and from pornography, the only thing that *would* impress her was a great throbbing purple erection—an organ so rigid and immense she would be swept to multiple orgasms on sight.

Finally he'd fumbled off his boots and socks. As he sat he felt the bed rock.

Janet was standing in front of him, a hand on his shoulder, gracefully wiggling free of her cutoff jeans and soft blue panties. He closed his eyes, his mouth dry. The pressure in his bowels intensified. In his mind he tore through the girlie books and smutty souvenirs of his old bedroom cache. He visualized massive pendulous breasts, great beseeching buttocks, pouting red lips, long silky legs…all to no avail.

"Lay back," Janet ordered, whispering huskily in his ear. He hesitated, obeying with a whimper. But when he felt her hands at his fly he bounded to his feet.

"I'll take care of that," Kevin said. And…she was still standing in front of him, a knee against his, cupping her breasts with her hands and pouting sensuously. Feeling sick, he faced his frontispiece to the dorsal while fumbling with the snap and zipper of his Levis.

Janet reclined on the bed.

*C'mon, c'mon*, he thought feverishly. *Get up, grow big and fat! Just this once, c'mon!* He dropped his pants and stepped free, felt Janet's warm hand on the back of his thigh, steadying him. *C'mon, you fucker! Come ON! Grow! Grow!* Kevin's mind began to wander, remarking how filthy his underwear was, how badly he needed a shower. *Come on!* He whipped down his shorts and surveyed the crucial area. Nada. He'd might as well have just stepped from freezing water. Kevin sat in a crook, ashamed, his traitorous member covered with fat trembling hands.

Janet's arms encircled his neck. He winced.

"*Look* at me, darling Kevin. Look at me, my sweet, sweet lover."

He looked at her, almost in tears. She just had to be the loveliest piece he'd ever seen, a thing sleek and brown and luscious, curving in all the right places. Why then did he want only to cover this tanned gazelle? She placed her hands on his plump pecs and squeezed and caressed. Tremors shot through him at her touch. She leaned forward and, incredibly, began to suck on his left nipple. But, instead of rising to the occasion, his hapless tool only shriveled further. At last she pulled away. "Now you," she whispered firmly, like a teacher demonstrating for a retarded pupil. She pried his hands from his lap and clamped them on her breasts, dropping back her head and moaning as she maneuvered them roughly. She pulled them down to her waist and, with another moan, looked hard at the place where Kevin's prong was supposed to be.

Dropping his head, Kevin was mortified to find he was weeping softly.

"Shh, *shhhh*," she soothed, slowly passing a hand down to his scrotum and gently squeezing his cringing jewels. He caught his breath mid-groan, let his head fall against a breast. She began squeezing harder, almost to the point of pain, until the miracle occurred. Kevin's shrunken pal poked its head out sleepily, understood, and quickly firmed in her hand.

"There, there," Janet crooned. "That's it, baby. Oh, darling Kevin, oh come on sweetheart."

Kevin ground his teeth. His mind went fuzzy. His machine drew sensation as a bellows draws air, became a vital, demanding, powerful entity. He gasped as she started stroking it. His hands went to her breasts and she pulled him down on top.

"*Yes*," she hissed as he fondled and tweaked her nipples, "Yes, that's it! That's *it*, darling!"

Sweating, grunting like a pig, Kevin mounted and began thrusting away. His aim was wide, but she slid down a hand and eased him in. There was the briefest sensation of dampness.

After a moment he remembered who and where he was. Kevin slid off with a smacking sound as their sweaty bellies pulled apart.

He lay trembling anew, his heart hammering, hearing her fingertips drumming on the sheet. She turned to face him, hiccoughed.

"You were wonderful," she lied enslavingly, a woman at heart. "That was pure heaven." She kissed his forehead.

Kevin tentatively placed a hand on her hip, drawing current and encouragement. He was her puppy now, her grateful fool. His arm moved to girdle her waist.

"No," she said.

Not "not now."

No.

She turned away from him, and from the sound of her breathing was instantly asleep.

# Chapter 15

# Thrasymachus Was Right

How does it feel to have taken that momentous step; to have crossed that seemingly uncrossable chasm separating cocksure manhood from timid boyhood...from a boyhood spilling over with hopeless longing, with botched opportunities, with naivete; with pointedly-replayed scenes of transparent poses, with utterly forgettable episodes of slinking down the avenue of that week's goddess praying she'll appear—yes, and belaboring the bygone, guilty only of innocence; elaborating on smoke and self-deception, knowing yet refusing to believe; fantasizing, wondering how the act will feel, *yes*, and whether you'll faint or go all to pieces with the unbearable, impossible ecstasy of it as you imagine it will be...how does it feel to have experienced carnal knowledge and become, through the feverish gymnastics of your beloved, as different from your inexperienced little buddies as night from day? And how does it feel to know you've come into the closest possible contact with a warm, giving female—one of those hypnotic little creatures equipped with a variety of slopes, curves, peaks and orifices...*oh yes*...strangely fascinating turf your tortured psyche has relentlessly demanded you poke, squeeze, lick, and fondle with every appendage at your frantic body's command until you moped, until you grated, until you nearly howled with the frustration of it all? What's it like to have been, at long last, laid? Kevin, attempting to address this all-important question, was being eaten alive, for he was anything but elated. Multiple orgasms, indeed. He was sure Janet had been barely aroused; certainly not beside herself with panting, snarling passion. One fuckup after another. Mike had been right.

He was curled on his side, feeling sticky and sore, letting the hot morning sun wash over his chest and face. Beside him was only the impression of her body. Kevin had surfaced from another of those heavy slumbers, having recurrently dreamt he was chasing her sheer rippling figure through some vast crowded building. She had not been avoiding him in the dream, yet had somehow managed to elude him, to lead him on. She had drifted like mist; through a ghostly, droning mob, to the building's gigantic entranceway. There she'd become tiny in the yawning night. The portal had expanded, ever outward, at last dissolving in endless space.

Kevin donned his eyeglasses to study the length of his reclining body, flexing comfortably buried muscles. He rolled off the bed and almost collapsed. For some reason his left hip hurt like crazy. It felt like he'd been hit with a sledge hammer. He massaged the hip, and, after determining the house was otherwise unoccupied, took a long and scalding shower, scrubbing until it hurt. Kevin shampooed his hair thoroughly, dried himself, and stood before the hallway's full-length mirror wearing only the towel around his waist, amazed at the number of bruises on his legs and shoulders.

What he saw lacked not only magnetism…his *image* lacked (except for the great incorrigible mane, now inching up into a shapeless wad as each drop transferred its weight to his shoulders) any *personality*. But as he watched himself dress, he saw the ho-hum reflection transformed, bit by bit, into something dynamic and complex. The crusty boots were, in his eyes, symbolic of his generation's flight from the plastic and neon garden. The frayed and faded Levis represented an enlightened, wash-and-wear hardiness; the work wear of a people dedicated to building a new world. The DO YOUR OWN THING belt buckle, he felt, justified his appearance and ideology to all the ulcerous, uptight straights he encountered, without his having to say a word. And Lance's peace medallion was even cooler than a crucifix…like, who's against *peace*? The mangled leather vest, with its Zig-Zag logo and remaining strung beads, showed he was stone carefree; a carouser, a card, a guy at home underground. The floppy felt hat, besides concealing that malicious shearing of Danny Boy's, lent him, in his opinion, an added dimension of transience—made him a restless and face-less sometime hobo; Guthriesque frequenter of boxcars and campfires, known and loved nationwide, a laconic but likeable treasure trove brimming with tales of strange encounters, yet made distant by tender memories of horizon-searching lovers. Metamorphosis complete, he stood erect. Now the picture had composition. In Kevin's eyes the mirror reflected a young man of deep insight and conviction—a wandering soul of conceivably profound intellect, yet certainly of simple means; a hip, happening, tripped-out specimen the Movement could take pride in.

The eyeglasses, though, would have to go. They looked *so* geeky. He removed the damned contraption, and his mirror image became a watery apparition. The solution was, of course, clip-on Polaroid lenses. But he'd never been able to tolerate looking through the things; they made the world appear closed, and the wearer introverted. Kevin wanted to look aloof-cool, not aloof-cold. He decided to check out the house for ideas. In the kitchen, while going through the wide cabinet drawers below the Formica sink counter, he discovered a paper bag containing small glass beads in a variety of shapes and colors. Eleven of these teardrop-shaped beads had tiny clips screwed onto their narrower ends, presumably for fastening the ornaments to lamp-shade bases and such. These he arranged, while squinting at the table, to dangle from the arms of his glasses. Kevin returned to the mirror. The result was a cross between tacky exuberance and a sort of psychedelic aboriginal silliness. He was satisfied. The reflection was of a multifaceted, serious boy who did not take his seriousness at all seriously.

*Where was she?*

Kevin found pen and paper in the kitchen. He sat at the table and stared out the window shaking his head, the beads tinkling against the plastic arms of his spectacles. After a minute he began to write:

jooli 5 1967

jime wuts goen awn prtnr howz yr hed

im ritn this ltr frum csid up pas mawntura csid iz u vaere hv town man to2le 2gthr an kumpletle trnd awn

we wr in big sr ystrda kan yoo blev that didn sta thu nit bcuz thu h8 iz supozd 2 b waer its <u>rele</u> hapunen

i gs bi now yr wundren hoo i men wn i rit we

chk this owt

i mt this litl fawx namd janut down thu kost thu da b4 ystrda we hit it awf lik pnut butr an jam man an <u>i bawld hr</u> las nit in this pad im riten frum

wutd i tl yoo man

didn i sa id b bawpen u bunch uv chix up her

i havn mt ne groopz yt but i thenk il drag ulawng <u>this hune i skrood</u> 4 u yl

wl it loox lik im gunu hav 2 sin awf now jime <u>thu orgz ubowt 2 strt</u> an iv gawt mi i awn this blawn flowr chiul with <u>jigantik boobz</u>

im sndn yoo sum pawt bak 2 kep yoo kumpune sta hi

kevin


He found his pot right where Jamie left it, on the coffee table, by the carpet stain; near the couch now so mocking in its emptiness. Very little remained. Just a pinch. Kevin idly rolled three cigarettes for Jimmy, found an envelope and stamp in the kitchen, and dropped the letter, with the contraband flattened between the folds, into the envelope. He was left with a single joint, which he determined to save for a moment when its heartening effect could best serve him. He walked to the front door, drew it open.

It was going to be another scorcher; another clear, cloudless day, perfect for swimming and riding. Gulls circled like flies beyond the houses he was facing.

He gazed for a long time at their locked bikes. With the smell of the sea and the cries of the gulls, he felt cast adrift. Kevin remembered the letter in his hand, and was about to seek a mailbox when he heard an automobile make a racing change down the block and come tearing in the direction of the house.

He inched the door until it was nearly shut, leaving a crack to peer out.

A primer-gray 1957 Chevy screeched to a halt directly in front of the house. At least seven teenagers were crammed inside. Over the car's blaring radio Kevin could hear feminine shrieks and masculine cheers. An empty beer can dropped out the passenger-side rear window. The door flew open, and a bleached-blond teenage boy wormed out laughing. He crouched with his fingertips gripping the edge of the car's roof, staring inside while cheering. Half a minute later Janet emerged giggling, gracefully sidestepping the boy's grubbing paws. Kevin tightened his grip on the doorknob. The blond boy, laughing lustily, resumed his spot on the back seat. Janet, as gaily pretty as a *Sixteen* cover girl, lifted and kicked shut the door. She bent at the waist and leaned on the door with her elbows, her rump seemingly thrust out for ogre-voyeur Kevin. Her rear revolved lusciously as she bent a knee back and forth to the music's rhythm. Now Janet leaned in laughing, grabbing at the boys in the back, who responded by trying to pull her in. She danced out of reach. The driver honked the horn and Janet waved. The car screeched off in first gear, smoke jetting from the rear tires. The girl watched until the car had whipped round the corner. She turned and skipped up the walk.

Kevin ducked back into the kitchen, where he busied himself lacing his boots. She froze when she saw him, the smile capsizing, as if he were a stranger caught rifling the bureaus. Gradually the smile returned. A little crooked, only half-lighting her face.

"So! So you decided to wake up! I never in my life saw a heavier sleeper. And what a fuss you made!"

"Fuss?"

"Fuss. Disturbance. You know. You whined all night. Every once in a while I'd wake up and you'd be kicking and throwing your arms all around. Then you'd just sort of mumble and start whining again. What a racket!"

"Sorry. Guess I was dreaming."

"Well, at least you didn't snore up a storm like the night before last. What's that hanging on your glasses?"

Kevin reddened. "Oh, I borrowed these, hope you don't

mind. It's…it's what the Indians do, see. It's hip to do it because the Indians are hip, and the Indians do it. It's like a way of showing you're down on the Establishment, and don't dig the trip of ruining nature and fucking with the Indians, who are super cool and just want to groove on nature. It's very hip."

"Weird. Well, are you all ready to go?"

"Go?"

"Yes, *go*. Leave the premises. Get on our bikes. Ride up to the park." She blew out a sigh. "I saw some old friends while you were still in La-la Land. Randy says that Marcie called Ernie's house and told Mikey they were already up there, at the planetarium. They'd *better* stay put! I can't wait to get my hands on them. And Marcie told *Tod* when he was over at Ernie's house with Petey-pie that the place is swarming. It's just like you told me. A real festival of brothers and sisters."

"How about that."

"So let's *go!* And did you eat breakfast?" Not really looking for a reply, the girl jumped on eggs, links, and browns.

Kevin was muted by the endless barrage of her chatter. While he watched her work he wondered if she'd been out satisfying the urges he'd left unanswered. She might have seduced any one of those guys in the car. Hell, she could have taken care of all of them, repeatedly, and in concert, if what he'd heard of the feminine gender's sexual insatiability was true. Whatever, she never brought up last night. Kevin thanked his God, sotto voce. If just thinking about…it…was painful, discussion would surely be torture.

And while he ate she wrote Jamie, thanking him for both of them. Before Kevin knew it he was unlocking their bikes.

It was less than ninety miles to the park now.

If he kept at Janet's pace they'd be there by tomorrow afternoon. And if she found her friends in the park there wasn't a chance in Hell he'd be allowed to tag along. No way. They would whisper in a secret language only girls understand, conspiring. He would be a burden, a downer, a gleep; an embarrassing load to be ditched at the first opportunity. It was crucial Janet never find her friends. With any luck the park would be so crowded she'd give up entirely. Kevin swallowed. Maybe, given that scenario, she'd feel his company was better than nothing, and stick with him until the concert was over. Then what? No telling. Perhaps Fate would work something out; there was still time. Time...Eddie had told him there was no such thing. But then Eddie had never been in love.

Janet blew him back to reality: she gasped and rode away frantically, waving her arms so hard she almost lost control of her bicycle. "Linc!" she cried. "Oh Lincoln, Lincoln, Lincoln!"

Kevin, cursing quietly, followed her to an old flatbed truck stalled off the road. Spouting steam showed above its raised hood. The bed was full of junk—fenders, cardboard, broken-down appliances—everything coated with a thick film of grease. The bed had wood siding leaning dangerously to the right, as though one more shock would send it clattering down the road.

The head of an ancient black man appeared from behind the raised hood. His leathery face broke into a dazzling smile.

"Why, miss Janet—bless mah soul!" He held out his arms as Janet dropped her bike and flung herself against his chest, embracing the stout, crooked old man with squeals of delight. Kevin pulled up unnoticed.

"Oh, Linc, what's it been—three years? And you're still the same. You haven't changed a bit."

Linc looked down. "Tree yeahs? Musta been." He looked back up, and the sun caught the gold of his front caps. "An' tha's mighty flattrin' of ya, sweetheart, tellin' an old fella like m'self Ah hasn't changed. But lookit you! A fine growed woman awready, my, my." And then: "Whups!" The truck's radiator was erupting jets of rusty water. "Same ol' truck, an' she ain't changed none neither." He slapped his knee. "'Member when we was mobin' ya ma's fuhniture dat day, honey? An' dis ol' gal blew right at the innersection of Grace an' Stanley during Chrissmas rush hour?" He held his side as he chuckled. "We backed up traffic so bad it look like a parkin' lot, an' nobody knew what t' do."

Janet was laughing too. "And then when the tow truck came and lifted up your truck's front end all mom's stuff went flying off the back. Boy, was she mad! And they had to back everybody out and close off the street until they could clean up the mess."

Linc looked sober. "Was mighty gracious of your ma not to hold it agin me, though. A mighty fine woman, Missus Campbell." He heaved his shoulders. "Well, guess I best get busy an' get the ol' aich-two-oh outta the back. Though Lord knows she'll jus' go agin." He patted the truck's fender and winked at Janet. "Dat's a woman fer ya, honey. Treat her *jus'* right, or look out!" He began a hobble to the back of the truck for the ten gallon water container he always kept handy. Janet stopped him short.

"Wait, Linc! Let Kevin do it. Don't strain yourself."

"Kebin?" Linc, turning slowly, noticed the boy for the first time. "Well, *bless* me, son! Ah didn' see ya dere. Guess Ah'm slowin' down fuh real." He stuck out his hand. Kevin dismounted and shook it, surprised by the strength in the dry old paw.

"Kevin!" Janet snapped. "Help Linc with the water can!"

He couldn't help giving her a hard, offended stare. She sounded like a harried housewife berating a naughty child. "Don't...*worry* about it," he said slowly. "What kinda guy d'you think I am, anyway?" He climbed onto the bed and found the water container, danced it to the rear, and with Linc's help lowered it to the ground. Then, to show Janet, he refused Linc's aid and carried it balanced against his hip to the front of the truck. Linc flapped after him, his face worried.

"*Nebah* carry it like dat, son! Ya gots t' *roll* it on the bottom, like dis." He demonstrated, then creaked back to his normal stoop, face shining with sweat. "Elsewise," he puffed, "ya gonna end up a bent ol' man like me."

Kevin scoffed good-naturedly and hefted the can to rest on the frame above the caved-in grille. Old Linc seemed about to lecture him further, but since the can was already in place he just loped around the side, hauled himself into the cab and played with the ignition until the hot engine kicked over. Kevin poured slowly, wrestling with the container. When water began bubbling out the radiator's mouth he set the container down, much lighter now, and stood by proudly as Linc forced on the bent radiator cap. Linc lovingly eased shut the hood. He stood grinning and mopping his brow while Kevin carried the container to the rear and heaved it onto the bed. Kevin came back strutting.

"Ah'm obliged, son. An' t' you too, Miss Janet." He took Kevin's hand in his right and Janet's in his left. "But now Ah gots t' be mobin' on b'fo' she blows agin. Ah'm so glad t' see you agin, missy, an' right pleased t' meet *you*, Kebin."

"How far—" Janet burst out, "how far are you going, Linc? Can you give us a ride, oh pleeeease, Linc, we're in *such* a hurry."

"Why sure, honey, if you're goin' dat way. Ah gots t' go clear t' A'bany, 'counta Mista Bruce so kindly offered me two 'frigahraters he don' need no more. If dat'll help ya any, of course you can come."

Janet threw her arms around him. "Oh Linc, that's perfect! We're going to Golden Gate for a big festival. You could let us off downtown." She gripped both Kevin's hands in hers. "What a break! We can be up there in a couple of hours." She embraced him and squeezed, kissed him full on the lips. Tickled and surprised, he climbed into the truck's cab beside her after making room for their bicycles in the bed. It wasn't until they were bouncing up the highway that he began to sweat. The hours were rapidly being shaved off his respite, and, unless the old truck failed to make it, this could very well be the end of the line. Kevin impulsively grabbed Janet's hand. Thinking he was sharing her excitement, she squeezed his sweaty hand and placed it on her lap.

As they bumped along, Janet whispered in Kevin's ear: "So what do you think of Linc? Isn't he just the sweetest?"

Kevin pondered. When he whispered back, it was with complete sincerity. "Well, you gotta admit, Janet, that he *is*, no offense, kind of a stereotype. I mean, to be like totally honest. But he sure does have good manners."

Linc turned his head, and for a moment his eyes bore into Kevin's. "Ah gots good ears, too."

Kevin swallowed. "I didn't mean that. Not the way it sounded."

"Shuh you did. Dat's ex*zackly* what you meant." He shifted his gaze back to the road and shrugged side-to-side.

"Mebbe Ah *am* a stareyatype, son," he said after a moment, "but ya gots t' unnerstan' dat Ah was bohn way back in 1901, an' dey wasn' all dat many oppatunities fo' a young black man growin' up. T'be honest, dey wasn' *no* oppatunities." He heaved a sigh. "But how 'bout you, Kebin? Speakin' of stareyatypes, you jus' gots t' take a good long look at y'self sometime." He laughed, reached over and tugged the brim of Kevin's floppy hat down over the boy's eyes. "My, my," he said. "Now ain't we a pair?"

Some time later, as they passed through Watsonville, Linc observed: "Mus' be a plenny big fes'ibal. Ah nebah seen so many younguns hikin' dis highway b'fo'." The truck's bed was already loaded with over a dozen hitchhikers old Linc had taken pity on, and forty miles per hour was now top speed. Linc hummed in his deep throaty voice, a kind of jazzy gospel; part sustained growling, part formless melody. The humming was tremulous from the old truck's vibrations, as earthy and hopeful as the endless highway.

In Santa Cruz a man completely ignorant of the concert would have known something big was happening farther north, as it looked like ninety percent of all traffic was headed that way, and hitchhikers lined the road, alone and in groups. Linc picked up five more, slowing the truck an equal number of miles per hour.

And so it came to pass that, at one o'clock on the fifth of July, old Linc dropped everybody off at the Harrison Street offramp, just across from the Hall of Justice in downtown San Francisco. Before he drove on to the San Francisco-Oakland Bay Bridge he motioned Kevin to the cab. Linc leaned out wearing an anxious expression.

"Dat's a might fine young lady dere, Kebin, a mighty fine young lady."

Kevin swallowed. "I know it, sir."

"You keep a real good eye on her, hear?"

"Yes sir."

He motioned Kevin closer. "Ah didn' say nothin' t' miss Janet b'fo'," he whispered, "'cause Ah didn' wanna be puttin' the scare into her. But Missus Campbell—dat's miss Janet's mama—she call me up on the telephone t'day, at the crack o' dawn, an' she was powerful worried, Kebin, Ah means t' say. An' she tol' me she was settin' the poe-lice out aftah her." He gripped Kevin's shoulder passionately. "Now, Kebin, Ah don't wanna see missy Janet put in the jail, no how. She too sweet a chil', an' no good would come of it. She wanna have a little fun so she run away from home t' see dis big ol' fes'ibal. Dey's nothin' unusual 'bout dat. All chillun do it once in a while. But poor Missus Campbell is fit t' bust on account of it. So Ah says t' m'self when we was dribin' up here, Ah says, 'Linc, ya ain't good for nothin' but pickin' up othah folks' gahbage, but ya gots to' help out Missus Campbell who's such a fine woman, an' ya can't be takin' miss Janet's fun from her, so jus' what you gonna do? An' what Ah figgers is dis: Ah'll let miss Janet have her fun, an' Ah'll call Missus Campbell from a pay phone an' tell her miss Janet's safe wit' me at mah house. Missus Campbell an' me's always had us a unnerstandin', Kebin. She trust me, an' if Ah tell her missy Janet's safe she won' need t' know no more. Den when Ah comes back down from Richmon' in a coupla days Ah'll pick miss Janet up at the bus station obah on Sebent' Street. She know where it is. Now, Kebin, Ah gots t' count on you t' take care of her an' make sure she be at dat bus station! Ah'll be dere day aftah t'morrah at six in a aftahnoon, an' Ah'll wait all night if Ah has to."

"But Linc," Kevin whined, "how can I do that? I can't force her to stay with me, and I just know when she finds her friends they're all gonna ditch me."

Linc thought and thought, the pleats of his forehead bunched like a monument to worry. "Dey's bad girls miss Janet's runnin' wit', Kebin. Bring her nothin' but trouble." He slapped his hand against the seat. "But Ah nebah lie t' miss Janet, an' Ah can' be startin' now. You jus' tell her the truth, Kebin, like what Ah tol' ya. She a sensible girl, an' she know Ah wouldn' be tellin' her t' do nothin' what wasn' in her own bes' innerest. You tell her Linc say he want her t' stay wit' you, an' t' meet me at the bus station when Ah tol' ya."

"Okay, Linc," Kevin said, his heart singing. "Gotcha."

"Ah'm countin' on ya, Kebin," Linc said, his face still scrunched by concern, "as one stareyatype to anothah." He waved, and steered the old truck down the road.

Kevin almost skipped up to Janet, just emerging from the ladies' room at the corner Chevron station. For two days he was her appointed guardian, and after that who could say? He'd already made up his mind to accompany her back to her Morro Bay home, and there sleep in the bushes outside her window like a watchdog, protecting her from the advances of foppish young suitors with mod haircuts. He still had money, so he still had hopes of inspiring her affection in one way or another. When that was gone he could get a job, maybe, and pursue her from close to home. If she were to go on a date with some smirking dandy, well then, it would just be a matter of following the guy and, when the moment was right, yanking him into an alley and beating the holy crap out of him. A few instances like that and the offender would get the message. Vicious and dirty and against principle, but that couldn't be helped and to hell with the Movement and anybody or anything that got in his way. After seeing her beaus with shattered smiles and their Sears and Roebuck specials torn to ribbons, Janet would pay kinder attention to the faithful young man who simply would not go away. She'd see the light. Eventually. If it took a spotlight.

"Got some bad news for you, Janet," he said as they rode down Harrison Street. "Linc told me your mom's got the pigs looking for you. They don't know you're up here yet, but I think your mom's got the idea, 'cause she called Linc this morning before we ran into him. Linc wants me to look after you for a couple of days. That'll give him time to cool your mom. Then he says he wants us to come back with him to Morro Bay."

"It," Janet said bitterly, "*figures*. Sometimes I think she can read my mind. It's just like that nag to get the cops to do the dirty work for her." Her mood changed abruptly. "Oh, Kevin, I'm sorry I didn't tell you I was running away. I hope you don't think I was trying to keep secrets from you. It's just that I thought you might go off and leave me if you knew."

Kevin goggled her. "Listen, Janet, I don't know how to put this, but you...*never* have to worry about me leaving you. Ever. Janet—I've been trying to say this since I first met you, but I can't get my mouth to work right. What I mean is, what I mean is, I mean…I mean I think you're a really far-out chick. I don't know how else to put it."

She stared. Hard. By common impulse they stopped. They traded looks for a long moment, panting. Janet blushed prettily. "Do you really mean that, what you said about you think I'm a far-out chick?" Her eyes were downcast, the lids softest pink below the suntan.

Kevin tightened the grip on his handbrakes, and when he spoke it was with the heartfelt naivete of those two syllables soldering matrimony. "I *do*," he spewed. "I mean, I did. Mean what I said, I mean. What I said I meant. The first time. Yes."

"That's just because you happened to meet me on the road. You'd say that to anyone." When she fished for compliments she had an endearing, albeit melodramatic, habit of turning her head to one side. Now she looked as far behind as her neck would allow.

"Oh no!" Kevin said quickly, eyes wide in pleading sincerity. "I'd think you were far-out whether I happened to meet you first or not. Really. Honestly."

"You're just being sweet."

"No, *believe* me, I mean it! I think you're just the nicest and the coolest and…the foxiest chick I ever met. I don't mean that dirty-like, when I say foxy, I mean more like pretty…and wholesome—like a real sister of the revolution. *You* know."

"You're just saying that."

Kevin paused for breath, seeking the right word, the apt phrase. "No, really, you should read the mail I write home. It's so flattering, you'd…you'd think I was in love."

She looked up, her stare unbearably direct. Kevin swallowed, realizing he'd put his foot in it again. Why were those three little words so very difficult to say? And was it just all the pot he'd smoked, or had he suddenly become intuitively aware, in the congealing hush of her crosshairs stare, of an ages-old prim bitchiness that had plagued man throughout his occupancy of this planet? But suddenly he saw himself genuflecting at the base of her pedestal, puckering to receive that slender extended foot for the latest in a series of meek offerings. Kevin gnashed air, trying to find the correct digressive response to the prompting of her eyes, though the only assuaging answer hung in the air between them like a spider from its web.

*Well?* Her eyes demanded. *Aren't you?*

A jeep stopping at the light saved him from having to reply. He was spared because an extremely powerful radio on the front seat made an audible reply nearly impossible. A moving popular song by Scott McKenzie now advised millions of restless teenagers over the AM airwaves:

> *If you're going to San Francisco,*
> *Be sure to wear some flowers in your hair.*
> *If you come to San Francisco*
> *Summertime will be a love-in there.*

Kevin and Janet turned with spontaneous feelings of awe and tenderness and fellowship; authentic flower children now, pilgrims in the holiest of holy cities. And the question didn't have to be answered. Of course he was in love with her.

> *If you're going to San Francisco,*
> *You're going to meet some gentle people there.*
> *In the streets of San Francisco,*
> *Gentle people with flowers in their hair.*

In this jeep in the streets of San Francisco were three men barely out of their teens. The young men were obviously Army fodder, for each had hair cut so short he had to be fresh from boot camp. The driver had orchids taped to his scalp, and the guy in the back seat was holding a laundry basket filled to the brim with freshly picked wildflowers. They all waved, and Kevin and Janet waved back. The driver honked the jeep's horn maniacally, made the peace sign with his free hand. The ex-warrior in the back seat laughed and began strewing flowers in all directions. The light changed and the jeep roared off in a shower of petals and stems.

Janet waved after them, delightedly clapping her hands as she skipped into the street. She came back pelting Kevin with flowers.

"Hold still!" she commanded, and reached into her purse. She fished out a saucer-sized badge proclaiming I LOVE

RINGO in black on shocking pink, and used this to fasten a fan of wildflowers to his hat, overriding his frantic objections with equally passionate acclaim.

"No, really," he said desperately, catching his reflection in the glass of a parked car, "I mean, *really*, I can't; it's silly like this. You don't want to ride with a guy who looks like a fool, do you?"

"I just told you," she said sharply, "you *don't* look silly. You look divine. Now hush up and quit complaining. After all you've said about the Revolution, about letting your freak flag fly, now you want to look all stiff and sober."

"No, it's not like that," Kevin corrected her gently. "There's no one more into the Movement than I am. It's just that this badge, well, it's not *me*."

"Why not?" she leapt. "*Don't* you love Ringo? I thought you said you thought the Beatles were practically the greatest thing to ever happen to the whole world."

"I did. I mean I do. The Beatles almost single-handedly shaped the Movement, and I think they're the heaviest group of all time. But it's like I don't *love* them. I mean, they're guys, and I'm a guy. It's just not right."

"And why not? You yourself said that society has perverted the word love to having sex meanings only. Now you seem ashamed of the word."

Kevin dropped his hands. "How can I make you understand…guys have to be careful nowadays with the impression they make. If you're even friendly with another guy, like if you just put your arm around his shoulders for a second, people will think you're a fag."

"Oh, that's just silly. That's all in your mind."

"Sorry," Kevin said firmly. "I wouldn't wear this thing in public for the world."

Janet folded her slender brown arms across her chest and looked at him coolly, from beneath half-closed eyelids. "You wouldn't do it for *me?*" she asked quietly.

He didn't like the sound of that; it was much too like a threat. His mouth fell open in mute rebuttal, and a furious finger came up preparatory to a firm wagging in front of Janet's unflinching face. But he was sensitive enough to fear she might actually just push off and pedal away without him if her childish demand was not met, and the now-you-listen-here gesture wimped out to one of ear-reaming pensive consideration. He removed the finger and absently displayed it as in lecture, its tip shiny with wax.

"Tell you what," he said compromisingly, sensing one of her tantrums just itching to break surface, "I'll wear it a while for your sake—but first person makes fun of it or gives me one strange look…off it comes and back in your purse it goes. Is it a deal?"

"It's a deal!" Janet piped, her face all rosy pretty smile. She stuck out her tiny hand.

Kevin shook hands, a smirk on his face. She thought she had it all over on him, but he could play her game. The first person to see him would laugh uproariously; he'd have made his point and reestablished masculinity as the authoritative force in a relationship. But as he looked around it hit him…*he'd really arrived*: some of the denizens were so freaky-looking he felt his appearance was tame by comparison. There were men with radically bushy beards and hair reaching clear to their waists, their bodies painted and clad in bizarre and colorful garments; a young man naked save a dirty rag wound up like a diaper, sitting lotuswise at the corner of 12$^{th}$ and Folsom and mumbling a garbled pseudo-Hindustani; a filthy-but-happy group of new arrivals, all hair and rags and backpacks and beads, the only female member dragging along two naked screaming children; and of course the inevitable train of shaven, pale, punished-looking Hare Krishna chanters, rattling their tambourines and jabbering to high heaven or wherever, trailing their diaphanous, flesh-colored gowns behind them. As for the conservative populace, sick to tears of the sideshow siege; they were too conditioned to this vivid new wave to pay much attention to Kevin and his I LOVE RINGO badge. They saw nothing remarkable about his getup, and if pressed would probably have said they had taken it for granted that he *did* love Ringo, passionately and unwaveringly, and that that was his business and more power to him. And so Janet came out on top, and Kevin grumblingly admitted his error in prematurely judging these obviously hip inhabitants. In time he grew proud of the badge and searched for other goodies to enhance his appearance. The leather fringing of his vest soon had a punctured bottle cap or nickel washer suspended from every strand; he wore additional flowers on his boots, the stems secured under the laces.

And this was only the threshold; a few more miles and they'd be at the park itself. If only Eddie could be here, Kevin thought remorsefully, instead of rotting away in some dungeon for a crime he had never even committed. It may have been merely an outlet for his own guilt, but suddenly Kevin inflated with rage. What *crime?* For possessing the leaves of a harmless plant in the name of the Revolution? For lovingly offering his energy in the tutoring of his fellow man? For minding his own business and trying to live in peace? For *this* gentle little Eddie was being dragged to the gallows by some mammoth, slavering, porcine degenerate in a funny dark costume, whose occupation was lawful sadism and whose orders were being excreted by grim and savvy black-suited politicians who kept their greed for money and power hidden behind a mask of law and order? Whose law? What order? Officers of the Peace: what *hypocrisy!* Eddie had been kidnapped, Kevin suddenly realized. Forcibly removed by order of those deranged politicians, who, Kevin supposed, had probably kept poor little Eddie under surveillance for years, wiretapping his home and shadowing him to school and back. With a gasp of horror Kevin understood: Eddie had been bagged by those two brutal robots and driven somewhere to be grilled and eliminated. In all probability the sensitive, kind, harmless boy was already long dead; incinerated or fed to starving captured illegal aliens, or whatever the Government did with its victims once they had been milked of all possible information to use against other Innocents. And Kevin's confiscated grass? Used the same way; planted on some preoccupied flower child the Government suspected was guilty of being loving and generous, and of other egregiously intolerable attitudes. Snuffed out by the machine. So Eddie had explained it that cold soggy night last November, when he and Kevin had fled to the garage to escape the bellowing tantrums of Big Joe, who, in his purposeless and directionless rage, had just threatened to mutilate Kevin's

mother, and had instead literally torn the door off the re-
frigerator on finding his beer supply dwindled to a single
twelve-ounce can of Eastside. Like rats the boys had scurried
outside, and, finding it too wet to walk anywhere, had climbed
into the little wooden garage loft. Big Joe had made a
tremendous impression on Eddie, who blamed the Government
without compromise for Joe's erratic behavior. It was The
System itself, Eddie had claimed, which brought on those
violent reactions he described as "terminal sociocultural aggres-
sion," a condition shared to some extent by everyone over
thirty. In excited whispers Eddie had expounded on his theories,
which, he said, were actually ingrained truths revealed under an
LSD trance. It seemed ages ago, when man was at the halfway
stage separating quadruped and full-fledged biped, beings from
another galaxy had decided, for some reason Eddie said had not
been related in his trance, to experiment with the genes of these
dull-witted creatures, using their advanced technology to inspire
in the species a tendency toward unreasonable avarice. Though
of long range, this influence was impermanent and, according to
Eddie, mankind was just now shaking free of it. Hence the new
generation was actually the first generation not dominated by
this extraterrestrial power, the first generation capable of *free
will*. It was obvious, Eddie had explained. The change was
everywhere. Kevin, who had recently seen a movie that was
coincidentally nearly parallel with Eddie's theory, had been
excited by this portentous train of thought. Only the day before
he had been a self-pitying, unpopular, futureless nobody, and all
of a sudden he was a dignified member of an advanced culture
lifting its shaggy head to claim its birthright to a planet gone
mad with industrialism and warlust. And Eddie, becoming more
animated, had described certain communities where this
evolution into the Age of Aquarius was taking place at an
accelerated rate. The names of these communities had had
faintly familiar and exotic flavors: *Greenwich Village, Haight-
Ashbury, Big Sur*. In particular Eddie had raved about Haight-
Ashbury, a district of a few square miles next to a great big
gorgeous park named Golden Gate after the famous waterway
connecting ocean and bays. In Haight-Ashbury, Eddie had
contended, people sprinkled hallucinogens on their morning

cornflakes as liberally as sugar, and as a result everybody was in a state of euphoria around the clock. Public nudity, Eddie had maintained, had the sanction of City Hall, which was decorated with Persian tapestries and gave away magic mushrooms at the Department of Peace. Marijuana, pre-rolled and packaged, was sold in vending machines, profits providing new strobe lights for the community's street lamps. Haight-Ashbury, Eddie had explained, was world headquarters for the revolt against the power pox, the deadly malady of the dollar. And the Flower Children weren't content to let the old age die out naturally, for by then the world might be too corrupt and contaminated to survive. It was touch and go, and those revolutionaries actually present in the Sacred City during the fall of the old social order would go down in history as heroes, and become Grand Gurus on the cabinet of the Great Guru, who, Eddie had pointed out, was presently a tossup between George Harrison, Donovan Leitch, and Dr. Timothy Leary. And the method of revolt, Eddie had concluded, was child's play: a simple formula of passive resistance, indefatigable intoxication, willful poverty, indiscriminate loving, and rock and roll idolization. That had all sounded pretty good to Kevin, and he had been filled with envy of all those lucky souls who were so fortunate to be on that hallowed ground while history was in the making, and wasn't it a drag that he and Eddie had to be in the thick of one of the more industrialized areas in the world while the great carcinoma of greed closed about them, with Haight-Ashbury only four hundred miles away? Eddie had looked up from studying his tightly clasped hands and said, "Three hundred eighty-six and a third miles," and then grown pensive. After a moment of silence he had looked back up and said with pent excitement, "And it's all beautiful coast all the way. I've got a bike." Then he was silent again, having read nothing but a formless enthusiasm in Kevin's face. Finally he'd said, "Do you?" "Do I what?" "Have a bike." "No." Eddie grew increasingly restless, and pretty soon he'd fished a fat marijuana cigarette from his pocket and raised an eyebrow quizzically at Kevin. Uncertain of the procedure, Kevin had imitated Eddie's intense expression, and finally Eddie had said, "Do you?" "Do I what?" "Smoke pot." "When?" "Ever." "No." "Want to try it?" "Right now?" "Sure."

"Wow!" So Eddie had fired up the joint, taken a deep hit, and passed it to his new pal. Again imitating Eddie, Kevin had sucked hard on the joint, and, though the urge to cough the smoke back out had been powerful, he had held it in long as possible to impress little Eddie. After two more deep hits he had become aware of a number of novel and agreeable sensations, such as a physical lightness, a pleasant congestion within the skull, an increased sensitivity to sound and color. There were also quite a few not-so-agreeable sensations. A sort of ululating claustrophobia, an almost panicky urge to be alone, an almost panicky terror of being alone, a stuffiness of the nasal passages, an acute sense of embarrassment. Eddie had apparently been going through this same blunted trauma, for, although there were all kinds of things to talk about, the boy's tongue and brain had simply refused to cooperate. Both he and Kevin had been wary of speaking first, and perhaps saying something that would be misconstrued and need taxing explanation, or, worse, something that would be taken as offensive. The problem was the duration of this silence. The longer either of them waited to speak, the more difficult and less valid the breaking of the silence would be. And so the silence had extended and the animal electricity had arced between them until they had simultaneously turned their heads to face the rectangular panels of the loft's doors, as if each thin piece of wood were a picture window revealing some activity without of interest to both. And suddenly the doors had been whipped outward with insane force to reveal gargantuan Joe in all his senseless, wanton wrath, his beet-red face contorted by a hideous snarl. Yet there had been no look of surprise on that face, only a perverse triumph, and this suggested he'd been standing there, clad only in his foul jockey shorts and sweat-soaked T-shirt, for a good while, listening and waiting for the proper moment to pounce. And pounce he had. He ripped Kevin out of the loft by the hair and hurled him across the garage. He silenced screaming little Eddie with a glassy stare, then turned and stalked his son, stamping furiously until the great heart staggered in its struggle, stalled and sent Big Joe crashing on his back. And Kevin's mother had come barreling in like the demon in a cheap horror film, hurled herself on Joe and then on Kevin, until a nick-of-time rescue by the neighbors. It had taken eight strong firemen to lift, haul, drag and heave elephantine Joe to the ambulance, and then they'd discovered that trying to fit Big Joe into the ambulance was like trying to cram a baby grand piano into a station wagon. While they were sweating over the problem, Joe, who by all rights should have been stone dead, somehow had pulled out of it long enough to embrace two firemen with the reserve of his fury, crushing the pelvis of one and dislocating both arms of the other. Then, swearing profusely, he had slipped back into unconsciousness. The two injured firemen had been taken to hospital in one ambulance, Kevin's hysterical mother in the other, and neighbors, cops, firemen, and Y.M.C.A. members had pooled for a group effort, finally heaving mammoth Joe onto the bed of a neighbor's pickup truck, thereby transporting him to Santa Monica General. Kevin had watched all this activity in hiding, cowering with little Eddie behind the avocado's great trunk. And after all the official vehicles had departed Eddie had run to the loft to get the joint butt, fearing the F.B.I. would respond to all the excitement by sending a special squad to the garage, ferreting out the roach, and somehow getting his fingerprints off it. Then, Eddie was sure, there would be no rest. The Government would track him to the darkest corner of the planet. When Eddie returned he found Kevin sprawled in the dirt, face pale and tongue bleeding badly. Kevin wouldn't respond to Eddie's shaking him by the shoulders, nor to the few gentle slaps Eddie administered. Kevin's eyes had been rolled up and his mouth working strangely, making drowning sounds. Spooked, Eddie had used the garden hose to soak Kevin down. Kevin had choked, flailed his arms about, and come to his senses retching on his knees. The fit, a mystery to both boys, had been attributed to the stress Kevin had undergone. Kevin had spent that night at Eddie's, and the very next day Joe was back and as full of fury as ever, though his skin had taken on a waxy look and his hair grown grayer overnight. But there was a change from then on. Kevin had been allowed to look the way he wanted to look, and Joe had even, perhaps out of some long-suppressed sense of guilt, decided the wretched little family should celebrate Christmas that year and offered to buy Kevin a present of whatever the boy might want. Kevin had passionately specified he wanted to find a ten-speed under, or next to, the tree (Joe had gone on a rampage that Christmas morning, murdered the neighbor's Great Dane and made matchsticks of the Christmas tree, but that's another story), and Joe had complied with one of the finest ten-speeds Peugeot puts on the market. Kevin and Eddie had become riding buddies, which meant that Mike, Eddie's old riding buddy, had to accept Kevin or lose Eddie's friendship, and the three, under Eddie's tutelage, made plans for what Eddie called "The Ultimate Run."

That had all taken place over half a year ago.

And now Eddie was dead and Mike was at large and Kevin was looking for an excuse to get the hell out of San Francisco and down to Morro Bay. A lot of growing up had taken place mighty fast, and this particular ass had already learned to equate the carrot with the stick.

Just so: There's an unbearable, almost unbelievable lesson which *self*-respecting human beings must come to accept in the real world—a lesson which'll be lost on all the shallow, materialistic, hypocritical anybodies out there; fighting, fucking, and finagling away in the carnival, with their silly religions, marriages, careers, and assorted bullshit fronts: the facades they so neatly slip behind to gainsay the very appetites which drive them, crucifix in one hand and genitalia in the other, to transmogrify the natural, healthy outcome of every vital activity…

They are legion.

We must ignore them, for we cannot possibly survive them. They are pumping out impressionable babies, and indoctrinating them into the ways of the herd, even as we, peering aghast, perish. We *must* ignore them, for they can only diminish us. They make us digress. And burn. Through the onslaught of their slimy, overt mundaneity, through their celebration of— nay, through their *worship* of—mediocrity, they *compel* us to ream them intellectually, to speak freely, and to, in moments of stolen quiet, question the worth of our noble ideals. And sometimes they can even drive us to write angry, profane-yet-profound prose. They make us want to go postal, and to desecrate their gaudy altars, and to stand on street corners—erect, indignant, articulate, intense—and cry to the deaf stampede:

*"The Big Camera is whirring, sure enough, and it wants*

*you all to perform for it; just as loudly, just as lewdly, just as publicly as you possibly can. It wants you to strut your stuff. You're right! You're right! You* are *special. You can tap and shuffle and wiggle and pose. You can feign and parry, you can huff and bluff. You* can *and* will *do anything to get what you want, then claim you're doing it for your mate, or your children, or your country, or your deity. The Big Camera has known it all along: you're* stars! *So get yours, you soulless, posturing pigpeople. Go preen. The great lesson is this:* Life, for the individual who doesn't possess the 'brains' to 'make it' as an ass kisser, is over at conception.

*"And yes, the Power of Denial will get you by. But anybody who buys into this game is guilty of collusion, of dumping on his own potential and perpetuating the Pig. Pretentious bastards. You* are *why the world is a sty. You have* social-esteem. How dare you *lay claim to* self-esteem. *You know you're all frauds.*

*"You* know. *"*

Ah, the voices, the *voices!*

Hi, Mom!

Rest In Piss.

# Chapter 16

## People In Motion

"Do you—do you realize where we *are?*" Janet asked.

Kevin looked up, shooing away the naughty voices and unpleasant memories. *"Where?"*

She indicated a west-running street sign. "Look! Haight Street!"

Kevin pulled out his San Francisco street map, scanned it excitedly. "Why, according to my map, we're only about a mile from the center of the universe!"

Janet waltzed her bike next to his. Together they spread Kevin's map over their handlebars. The paper was so crumpled and ridged he had difficulty pinpointing their location. After ripping it down the middle he gave up trying to smooth it.

"Look!" he said. "Here we are, on the corner of Haight and, um, Gough Street. We follow Haight under that overpass, going...*west*; we go west until we hit Ashbury Street. Haight Street and Ashbury Street!"

Janet looked at him sultrily, from between narrowed eyelids. Her nostrils were flared. "Haight-Ashbury," she breathed.

"Can you *believe* it? Aren't you excited?"

"Of *course* I am. I'm excited for *you.*"

"It's...it's like a dream," Kevin mumbled. He grabbed her hand. They looked long and hard at one another. At last Kevin cried, "Let's go!"

So they pedaled down the street, and blent right in; two

more straggling teenagers in the going groove. This asphalt river flowed straight and true to the Holy Corner; to the spot Eddie had described as the terminus of all streets. Already Kevin sensed an exalted change in the denizens about him: their hair appeared to be longer and totally neglected, their clothes downright ragged. They all seemed to be in hallucinogen trances, wandering aimlessly, gathering in lethargic groups along the river's banks. Fascinated, he quickly made his way downstream.

"Wait!" Janet called. "Wait up, Kevin!"

With a start he realized he'd been pedaling hard, neglectful of the girl. It was the first time she'd lost her grip on his heart, and it scared him. He looked back. He'd gained almost a block on her. Kevin, shaking his head, imagined himself spending the rest of his life searching these unfamiliar streets. She looked so pretty and childlike struggling to narrow the distance between them. He felt like kicking himself.

"I'm sorry," she said, breathing hard. "I can't ride that fast."

He stood straddling his bike's frame, his mouth hanging open.

Janet mimicked the look, eyes crossed and tongue lolling. "*Well*? What are we waiting for?"

Kevin's face relit. "Look!" he cried. "There's Webster Street. C'mon. Not too far now." He called off the streets as they were crossed, his heart swelling anew.

And so at long last they'd reached their Mecca, and found themselves. There their selves stood, panting, at the corner of Haight and Ashbury, drinking it all in. The area was crawling with young people in wild dress, and with children in no dress at all. The tenements lining Haight Street were marred by graffiti urging the rapid and indiscriminate consumption of drugs both hard and mild, and the immediate disbanding of all American military forces. Garbage was heaped in the gutters. The air reeked with the smells of sewage and incense and burning marijuana.

But Kevin noticed all this peripherally. His stare was fastened on a single signpost on the intersection's northeast corner. He slowly walked his bike toward this signpost, taking measured, pious steps. When he reached the pole he tenderly wrapped his fingers round its warm, coarse surface, a recently discarded wad of chewing gum adhering to his palm.

Janet spoke close to his ear, "I wish I'd brought my Brownie. This is a moment to always remember."

Kevin regarded her from on high, his eyes translucent, his hair gray.

"Wow!" Janet said. "Do you ever look spaced-out!"

He pulled himself together, took a deep breath and let it out with a long sigh. "I feel like I've lived here all my life. I feel like I belong here."

"You *look* like you belong here."

Kevin lit his last joint. "Let's meet The People!" They sauntered up the sidewalk, steering their bikes carefully, and Kevin, in the grip of his emotions, impulsively wrapped his left arm around Janet's slender waist. She pulled free immediately, then giggled and let her head rest against his shoulder. He squeezed her body against his, and, carried away, planted a sloppy swashbuckling kiss full on her lips. A sudden lancing pain pinched his eyes and passed. She gripped his hand and they skipped along, laughing, flashing the peace sign at everyone they saw. Kevin's heart was hammering like a blown transmission.

The sidewalks were jammed with characters of every possible description, the air tumultuous with their mingled conversations. Street poets spewed their antiauthoritarian doggerel to constantly splintering groups. A chubby girl of twenty, completely naked, sat atop an overturned city trash bin, laughing gaily and pelting pedestrians with begonias. Farther down the street stood two bemused beat policemen, grinning helplessly amid a throng of chanting, pot smoking youngsters. Kevin flashed the peace sign at the officers and they smiled. Silly with the moment, he went so far as to offer a hit off his joint. The officers looked at him uncertainly, then one shook his head and smiled. Kevin shrugged and grinned idiotically, smoke squirting from his nostrils. He and Janet waved goodbye and both officers flashed the peace sign.

"This," Kevin cried, "this is just *too much*. It's just like what Eddie said; greater than I ever imagined."

"What?" Janet laughed. She was having trouble staying by his side and hearing him. The knot of their hands was constantly broken and reformed as they made their way through the crowd. The din of voices was astounding.

"I said I love you!" he shouted, snatching her hand again.

"What? Oh, look, *look*." And he was desperately holding on as she wove her way to a tenement porch cluttered with wine bottles and grinning teenagers. A banner decorated with scribbled hearts and peace symbols announced THIS IS THE SUMMER OF LOVE from above a boarded-over door. On the stoop a stoned girl was holding a frazzled Afghan, its once-beautiful coat choked by filth and mange. The beast stank from six feet away, and the smell was no laughing matter. The intensity of the stench left no doubt about the advanced nature of the animal's condition, and the miasma had infected the unknowing flower children on the porch; it was in their clothing, their hair, in their lungs as they breathed. The dog's tiny yellow eyes were bright and staring, but at a scene the flower children were blind to. The hound was wearing a silly home-made hat hanging low over his long muzzle. Patches reading LOVE and PEACE were sewn into the hat's crown. A sweater had been converted to fit the dog, and he wore it now with sweltering ignominy. There was a pouch sewn on the sweater's chest like a marsupium, and in this pouch an equally mangy alley cat was secured by lengths of colored twine, only its head and forepaws free to languish in the light and confusion. Every now and then the Afghan would give the cat a rasping lick with his tongue, occasionally receiving a lick in return. The poor cat had miniature sunglasses, with peace symbols painted on the lenses, strapped to its head.

"Oh!" Janet cried breathlessly. "Aren't they darling!"

The spaced-out girl looked at them with a warm, hallucinogenic smile. "Peace," she said.

"Peace!" they responded.

"This is proof that animals can live in harmony," the girl said, scratching the quarter-sized ringworm patches practically covering her forearm. She gestured globally, indicating the street to be a working model of humankind in its entirety. "Out here's proof the whole *world* can live in harmony. Can you dig that?"

"*I* can dig it," Kevin said.

Janet was in loving genuflection, holding the dog's head while scratching the cat behind its ears, murmuring affectionate gibberish, kissing the animals as they licked her chin. She looked up with small tears streaking her face, at the several teenagers crowding around her and the dog.

"Isn't it wonderful?" she bubbled. The youngsters all agreed it was simply marvelous, contagious tears popping from their eyes and rolling down their pinched, grinning faces.

The dog's owner wiped her eyes with the back of a scabbed hand. "He's a hip and loving dog because he's a *high* dog." She lit a pipe, its bowl full of hashish, and filled her mouth with smoke. The Afghan appeared to know what was coming, for he lowered his head and closed his eyes. The girl tugged at his scrawny neck, but the animal wouldn't budge. She finally took hold of his muzzle and forcibly turned his head, blowing the smoke directly into his quivering face. She repeated the process three times and released her hold. The beast drooped his head wolfishly, strings of unhealthy-looking saliva hanging from black gums.

"He *likes* it," the girl said. "We stoke his head every time we get high."

"Who *wouldn't* like it," Kevin said.

"There's a word for it, for what's happening here," the girl continued. "It's called *symbiosis*. And he's digging it. It's almost like I can tell what he's thinking. It's like he's tripping on all this heavy scene and wondering why his ancestors ran around scarfing each other up, when they could have been cool and grooved."

"Yeah," Kevin said. He was inspired. "Maybe," he said, "maybe in the future all the wild animals will get hip and become peaceful. Maybe someday they'll all turn into, like, vegetarians, and stop bumming each other's trips."

"Oh, that *would* be heavy," the stoned girl crooned. "And it *can* happen. It's happening here!"

The Afghan abruptly shook from head to tail. He snapped at something imaginary in the air, retched and sneezed convulsively. The cat tried to bail, but only became further entangled in twine. "He's cool!" somebody cried. "He just needs another hit!" As Kevin and Janet proceeded down the sidewalk they watched two of the youngsters on the steps helping the girl hold the dog still while she administered ever-increasing doses of smoke into the creature's grimacing face.

They stopped to admire a group of musicians at the entrance to an alley blocked off by a police car. Lavishly ornamented blacks tapped and palmed conga drums to the abbreviated gyrations of a toothless old woman rattling a tambourine. There were flutists and harmonica players, half a dozen guitarists. A painted young woman wearing only a pair of police hats wiggled her way among the musicians, her arms thrown back, her head lolling. The two hatless policemen sat on the hood of their squad car, nodding and clapping their hands to the reggae-like music.

A battered tin can was displayed on a coffee table just inside the ring of onlookers. A sign taped to this table read: DONATIONS. HELP THE CLAYTON ST. FREE CLINIC HELP OTHERS. GOD BLESS YOU. LOVE AND PEACE. Occasionally a figure would step from the audience to drop in a few coins. Kevin impulsively took a ten dollar bill from his wallet, held it up for the makeshift band to see, let it fall in the can.

"Outtasight, brother!" called a guitarist, quickly echoed by the other musicians. There was scattered applause, a flurry of hooters just for Kevin, a brief ascension in donations.

"Kevin!" Janet said, as they continued along the sidewalk. "How can you just give away so much money?"

"What the hell," he replied. "That was for Eddie." He took her hands. "Janet, money doesn't mean anything anymore. What's money? Money's shit. It's like there's a revolution going on! Everything, I mean *everything's* gonna change! The new world won't be built on money. It's gonna be built on love and sharing."

"Right," said a haggard young ruffian who had witnessed Kevin's charity and followed them. "I can dig what you're saying, man, and the Haight is where it's all happening. You're really beautiful, man, and your girl's beautiful, and the whole fucking world's beautiful. But it's like I got to eat, man, and so does my old lady and our kid. If you can lay a little bread on me, man, I'd sure appreciate it." As he extended his hand Kevin saw a skeletal arm pocked with the telltale scars of hypodermic injections.

Kevin glumly reached into his change pocket and fished out his remaining coins, perhaps two dollars worth. "That was all the bills I had," he lied, "but you can have what change I've got."

The panhandler scraped the coins off Kevin's palm with a rigid claw. "Thanks, man," he said suspiciously, mentally balancing his chances of snatching Kevin's wallet. He looked at Kevin's face out of dark and sunken eyes. "That's *all* you got, man?" When Kevin nodded he whirled and elbowed his way through the crowd to the shadows of a tenement.

"Peace!" Janet called after him. She pressed herself against Kevin. "That was sweet of you. That poor man and his family will be able to eat now. You're so right. Love and sharing are all that matter."

Kevin grunted evasively. "I wasn't telling the truth," he confessed after a moment. "I've still got plenty of cash in my wallet. But we've got to eat, don't we? And how about dope? We've just *got* to stay high. And speaking of dope—"

He was cut off by a wild shriek from another stoop, where a seated group was holding hands in a tight circle round a disheveled woman in her late forties. The woman's makeup was streaked, her blouse torn.

"Oh, my God!" she was screaming. "Help me, it's coming, it's everywhere, *Jesus God* it's beautiful, help me, *help me!*" Her face was a fluid mask, running the emotional gamut from weeping bliss to raving horror. The people around her were a gently bobbing wreath, attempting to console her. "Yes;" they were saying, their voices deep and chilly, "yes, we're friends…help you…yes…you're beautiful…yes."

"*It's the acid!*" the woman screamed. "It's God. IT'S GOD!" Her voice lashed Kevin's nerves. He wanted to pull Janet away, but the sidewalk's human tide had encountered an obstruction somewhere out there. They were forced to remain where they were, helplessly watching the woman thrash about.

Kevin, reminded of his own harsh experiences on LSD, had an idea of what she was going through. *"Help me!"* she shrieked, her head flopping and rolling on a neck suddenly shorn of muscle control. "God, it's beautiful, it's *beau*-tiful—it's the acid, *the acid*." She began raking her long nails down her face. "Somebody help me!"

"Yes..." the circlers sang, "yes...it's fine, you're fine...the acid is God...yes. It's the acid. The acid's fine...you are God...God is fine . . ."

Kevin's face began to melt. He needed to run, and fast. There came a pair of spine-jarring crashes. Without having to look down, he realized that bolts had just been hammered through his feet. A massive member split the sidewalk just in front of him. Kevin seized a man's shoulder and spun him round. "Hey, man, why doesn't somebody help her? Can't you see she's freaking out?"

"Yes..." the man replied eerily, "...don't worry, everything's fine...I'm fine and you're fine...acid is God."

Kevin let go the shoulder as if the man had bubonic plague. He looked into eyes that were glassy whirlpools, tore his feet from the sidewalk. The monster went limp. "Let's get out of here!"

"...Yes..." Janet said. Kevin grabbed her wrist and side-armed a path through the crowd. Much subdued, they walked their bikes along the sidewalk, their eyes downcast, hearing the mumblings of motionless characters loitering in storefronts. It was the sidewalk come-on of dealers. "Mescaline?" the voices would offer, popping into the mind like memories. "Speed? Acid?" Kevin shook his head with gathering urgency. "Crystal, man?" "Hey hey, got some *dynamite* Primo here." "Dust...*hey man*, dust over here." "Barbs?"

Soon Kevin was too depressed to continue. "Sorry," he mumbled, "but my head's getting all bummed out."

"That's okay. I know just how you feel." Janet found a few vacant trash-covered steps in front of a boarded-over door. They sat down wearily.

"Everything's groovy," Kevin said. "It's just that those acid trippers brought me down a little."

"There, there."

"We just need to rest a while."

"Sure," Janet said. "We can watch it all from here."

There was a lot to watch. Colorful paraders bore pickets demanding America leave Viet Nam alone. Homosexual couples, hand in hand, promenaded with smiles of triumph. In the middle of the street a group of protesters was openly burning draft cards. Hell's Angels members rode plowing through the thickest groups, kicking, heedless of cries of protest and pain. Everywhere there were youngsters, some barely into their teens, guzzling beer and wine, popping pills and smoking grass.

And coming down the sidewalk was a constantly halting procession both colorful and familiar. Above the primitive thump-and-clatter of their tambourines Kevin could hear them chanting:

*"Hare Krsna Hare Krsna*
*Krsna Krsna Hare Hare*
*Hare Rama Hare Rama*
*Rama Rama Hare Hare."*

He grabbed Janet's hand. "Time to go."

They walked their bikes across the jammed street and began moving down the opposing sidewalk, still proceeding west. Janet was handed a stick of incense by a devotee who had splintered from the procession. She lit it gaily, sniffed the smoke with simple, childish pleasure. She waved it in front of Kevin's gloomy face. The scent was frankincense. "Oh cheer up," she said sternly, her mood shifting swiftly to the dangerous level. "We come all this way, and I have to listen to a zillion boring lectures all about San Francisco, and about how happy you're going to be, and then you start moping around like a goddamn—"

"Keep your voice down," Kevin begged. "Everybody's starting to stare."

"Don't you fucking tell me what to do, buddy! Who the fuck do you think you are! And get your fat fucking hands off me—" for Kevin had gently gripped her shoulders "—before I start screaming rape."

"Oh no," Kevin said with rising alarm. "Don't do that.

*Please* don't do that! I'm sorry. Really I am. Look at me; I'm smiling, see? I'm smiling. Please don't yell."

"*Rape!*" Janet screamed. "Rape! Rape! rape rape—" She fell against him, beating her fists on his chest, heaving with sobs. At last she gasped, "I wanted so much to have a good time. Why did you have to spoil it for me?"

He put his arm around her, gently patted her shoulder. Women, he thought, sure are funny creatures. Regular yo-yos; up one minute, down the next. But he enjoyed the feel of her in his arms, felt very protective.

Janet ran a hand down to his waist. Then below. Then...Kevin gulped. "Rape," she giggled in his ear.

Kevin pulled away as gently as he could. "Not here!" he whispered. "*Please*. People might—"

Janet shoved him hard, her face wild. "You fat asshole! Don't you fucking tell me what to do!" She took a swing at him, but he caught her tiny fist, pulled her back against his chest. She began to cry again. Quietly now. Faces in the crowd grinned knowingly. "Why did you have to be such a grouch?"

"I'm just...sorry," he whispered. He didn't know how to play it. What would Bogart do? Shake her roughly, tell her to can the kid stuff? "I'm *sorry*, Janet," he repeated. "I don't know what came over me. I need to get my head straight, that's all. I just *wish* we still had some pot."

One sweet pretty beam, and the sun was gone. Kevin, suddenly in a vacuum, clutched her bike to his. As Janet was swallowed by the crowd he searched desperately; raising himself with his toes, catching sight of her as she stopped couples and nuzzled into groups, losing her again. When he caught her at rest, she was engaged in a gesturing conversation with another girl. At last she made her way back, guided by his calls. The relief he felt at hearing her voice was like plunging into cool water on a scorching day.

"Ooh! I did it, I did it! She's a really sweet girl, and she says she knows where we can score a lid for ten dollars. Aren't you proud of me?"

"Sure," Kevin said as they walked their bikes, "only I wish you wouldn't run off like that. I don't want you getting hurt."

The girl Janet had befriended was sitting on a low wall, as unstably as Humpty Dumpty. Although she was only seventeen she appeared about to give birth to quintuplets. Except for the great globe of her lower torso the girl was frightfully skinny; simply an enormous round melon with two stick-arms and two stick-legs, and a dirty, bug-eyed doll face framed by electric strands of grimy blond hair.

"Peace," Kevin said. "I'm Kevin, and I guess you've met Janet."

"Yeah, yeah, peace," the girl responded in a husky voice. "I'm Jennifer. Y'know: 'Jennifer Juniper.' If you guys wanna lid we gotta walk down a coupla blocks to Grattan Street. Just gimme a sec' here, and I'll be right with you." She eased herself off the wall, aided by Janet. Kevin could now see she was very tiny; scarcely four and a half feet tall. He and Janet formed a protective wedge with their front wheels as she waddled down the sidewalk between them, puffing and groaning. She had them turn south on Cole.

Janet's sparkling eyes caught Kevin's dullards. "Do you *live* here, Jenny?"

"Yeah. I been living in the Haight for almost a year. It was really a gas at first, but by parents quit sending me checks a coupla months ago, and the pigs caught up with my old man, Harvey, who was AWOL. Lemme tell you," she swallowed, "I been feeling really shitty since I got knocked up this last time. It's got me thinking about making some serious life changes. All this rap about acid and chromosome damage is screwing with my head. Now I'm determined to just stick with booze and downers." Her expression went deathly pale. "Being pregnant in the Haight," she gasped, "can be a real drag. 'Scuse me a sec'." Jennifer stopped and leaned against a fire hydrant, pressed a hand to her side.

Janet steadied her by the shoulders. "Are you okay?"

"Yeah, yeah," she gasped. "Yeah, I'm fine. Jesus, this kid's gonna be a whopper."

Kevin thought a minute. "It's really like a bummer," he observed, "that your old man got kidnapped by the pigs. If what my friend Eddie told me is true, they never let their victims see the baby."

"Whoa!" Jennifer laughed, wincing. "*He's* not the papa, that's for sure; not Harvey. Ever since I first met the guy he was either too loaded or too paranoid to get a hard-on. I dunno who knocked me up this time, man. Hell, ever since this free love business began I've spent more time on my back than on my feet. I'll just be glad when it's over. Pregnancy's a drag, but labor's a real bitch. And I guess I'll name it Peace if it's a dude, or Love if it's a chick. Here's my pad." They halted facing a lot overgrown with weeds. All that remained of the house was the foundation, but in the rear was a ramshackle, squat, one-story little building built like a bomb shelter. At first glance Kevin saw only the broad double doors of a garage. As they walked up the dirt drive he noticed a cottage porch jutting from the rear. "It's not really *my* pad," Jennifer said. "Me and some other heads share it. You'll like them; they're groovy people. You better stash your bikes behind these bushes; around here de-raillers get ripped off quicker than dealers." It looked like a safe place, but Kevin locked their bikes to a gas line just the same.

The wooden garage doors were old and splintered. Rust-ed hinges groaned as Jennifer tugged. She paused just inside, wincing and holding her ribs. The interior was illuminated by candles placed haphazardly, and by a pencil-thin beam of day-light emanating from the rear, where apparently the wall had been broken through.

The sudden wave of bright daylight must have dazzled the garage's occupants for the moment the doors were open. Perhaps a dozen pairs of eyes gleamed at their entrance like rats, and then Jennifer had closed the doors and Kevin's eyes began adjusting to the darkness. The floor was mostly taken up by mattresses and blankets and rags of clothing. A few back-packs and a single crutch were propped against the left-hand wall. The air was heavy with incense smoke, and the walls were covered, as in Perky's house, with posters of rock stars and multicolored graphics. The rats themselves stuck to the old pattern: long unwashed hair and beards; dressed for the most part in rags and beads. But there were a few hapless souls who helped make the room look like a disaster ward: a white-haired old man either dumped or collapsed in the space between a mattress and the rear wall; a filthy Mexican girl breast-feeding a naked infant; a boy with one arm and one leg in casts; a teen-aged boy, his face in darkness, shivering on one of the yellowed mattresses and staring up fearfully. There was no music, and when the sudden shock of daylight had worn off Kevin could hear their voices begin to stir anew, like wind through leaves.

Jennifer started the introductions. "Hi, guys. This here's Janet and Kevin. And this is Booger and Lalena and Funkho and—oh, hell, you guys just make yourselves at home and get to know each other. Sahib's got the pot; he's probably in the back. You guys wait here. Sahib doesn't dig it when I bring in strangers to score; I guess he likes to check 'em out first." Jennifer waddled into the cottage like a fat mother hen, dis-appearing into the black recesses of what, from the flickering of candlelight on old stainless steel, appeared to be a kitchen con-version. Now, Kevin could bring down the humblest room. He looked to Janet for comfort, but she deserted him for the nursing girl, begging to hold the baby. "Oh, he's so darling!" Kevin heard her cooing, "but the poor dear looks so sick." Soon they were involved in a girlish banter that knows no language bar-rier, and Kevin found himself looking down at the shivering boy. He remembered the name, offered his hand in greeting.

"Um…what's happening, Booger?" He zoned out. "My name's…um…my name's Kevin."

Booger hugged himself, shuddering violently. His eyes seemed to barely reflect the candlelight. "Are you—are you the police?"

"The pig?" Kevin laughed. "No! Of course not." The room, except for the girls' exchange, went deathly quiet at Kevin's bark of laughter. Then the baby screamed and, one by one, the voices pattered anew. Kevin's laugh, even to himself, rang false and harsh. "No, I'm just visiting," he said in a quieter voice. "I only dropped by to try and score some pot."

Booger, gripping himself tighter, dropped his head to his knees. Kevin had to move even closer to hear the boy squeeze out his words. "You're…not the police…God, I'm glad. You're not the…police."

Moved, Kevin sat beside him, placed a comforting hand on the boy's bony shoulder, felt a shudder run up his arm.

"Please…don't touch me."

"Okay, Booger." Kevin removed his hand. "I can see you're sick. Is there anything...anything I can *do?*"

Booger shook his head sharply, once each way. He straightened his back, his neck muscles taut, and stared at a point midway between the top of the garage door and the ceiling. Kevin suddenly saw himself as a huge intruder all in shadow, so he picked up a sputtering green candle set in a coffee can. Booger turned to face him with an agonized tremor. Kevin recoiled at the sight of Booger's face. The wing of one nostril was eaten away, the left side of his forehead terribly distended, his hair spare and brittle-looking. Booger's teeth were in miserable shape, his gums bleeding freely from the act of speaking. His face was little more than a skull mask with a thin covering of gray flesh, the cheeks hollow, the eyes sunken. The boy's left iris was of a much paler hue than the right, and nearly twice as large. Kevin instinctively looked away, just as Jennifer reentered the room and spoke his name.

Sahib was a huge man of forty, sporting an incorrigible beard and dark snakes of hair rapidly going white. Rimless spectacles with lenses thick as Coke bottles perched on the sad bridge of a broken nose with a gleaming bulbous tip. He was heartily overweight and blissfully sanguine, dressed in modified Army fatigues and a bright Mexican serape. Sahib, with his maple complexion and mischievous round eyes, certainly appeared to be of Indian extraction. In the early days of his turning the garage into a sort of hospice, some of the first arrivals, ignorant of the appellation *sahib* as applying respectfully to Europeans of rank in Colonial India, had supposed it meant something more akin to *swami*, and the name had stuck. Sahib liked to spoof sobriety, so the contrasts he displayed suited him fine. Now a small and compactly built man, with hair bleached almost white, stalked into the garage and peered angrily over his shoulder.

Sahib smiled hospitably, but the small man said, "So you're looking for a lid, huh? Who sent you?"

"Nobody sent us," Kevin replied uncertainly. "We're just passing through and need some weed."

"Yeah? Where you from?"

"We rode up from L.A."

"Jesus *Christ!*" the blond man spat. "*Another* one!" He shook his head disgustedly. "Go head, Sahib. Sell him a lid. But this is the last time." And he stormed out, slamming the garage doors behind him.

"*Who*, might I ask," Janet wondered in a cold voice, "was *that*?"

"*That*," said Sahib pleasantly, "was *Spacer*, our high-strung connection." He dismissed the subject with a flick of his wrist. "Booger, me lad," he said soothingly, "you're very tired, son. You can barely keep your eyes open. Don't you think you should sleep now?" He took Booger by the shoulders and gently helped him to his feet. "You come sleep in Sahib's room, where it's quiet and cool."

Booger, shuddering hard, let his head rest on the big man's shoulder as he was led from the room. In a moment Sahib had returned, and in his hand was an ounce bag of marijuana. He sat cross-legged on the floor and rolled a sample joint.

"What's wrong with Booger?" Kevin whispered. "I've never seen anybody so...sick."

Sahib shrugged and said brusquely, "Fuck if I know." He caught himself. "Forgive me. Perhaps effendi Spacer's current bout with paranoia has begun to get under my less than impermeable skin." He looked pensively at the dark opening leading into the mysteries in the rear, and after a moment said, "The boy was like that when we found him. Only not so advanced." He handed the joint to Kevin. "Oh, we tried to get the little guy to the hospital—*believe* me, we tried—but for some reason he's become so conditioned to this marvelous abode that he'll react most violently at the first suspicion of being moved. I have a friend who's a practicing diagnostician at Litteman General. He came by to check Boog' out as a favor and said he was damned if he know what was wrong. Anyway, from what we've learned from the boy, this is the closest he's ever come to having a home. So we just keep him warm and tell him stories, feed him the best we can. If we put him out on the street he'd die like a dog. Oh well, Mr. B has a date with Mr. D soon enough. Even a fool can see that." He smiled broadly, his eyes twinkling behind the thick lenses. "Just another victim of dat heartless ol' wilderness out dere," he said grandly. "They come and they go, the Boogers of this world, and there are plenty more on the way to take the place of those who fall. Though why so many of 'em are turning up in San Francisco beats the hell out of me. Funny. But you should see some of the unfortunates this shoddy little dwelling has entertained. Big kids, little kids, young and old," he sang, "and how many of 'em will be successful? How many will raise healthy families? How many will even be sure of a roof and a hot meal? Ah, well. Ours not to reason why. That's for theologians and psycho-analysts and the doctors of various sciences; all striving to learn what makes Johnny run, or, as in our Booger's case, run down. Bad chemicals, you wonder? Rotten parents, perhaps? No education? Who can say, who can say..." Sahib allowed his voice to trail theatrically. He blinked at the figures around him, wondering if he was losing his audience. When he saw the mesmerized expressions he gleefully hunkered down to become the campfire storyteller, but, perhaps because he'd fallen victim to his own pessimistic turn of patter, his true morbid nature found vent instead. Sahib's soul now discovered gravity; he became the prey of his own "bad chemicals," and ran down. The garage was morgue-quiet. Sahib looked inward, at a gaudy stage in an empty house, and, speaking as much to himself as to his company, brazened out the mess of his dark spirit's debut.

"Every time the adrenaline starts to flow I get this spooky feeling I'm being manipulated. You guys know where I'm coming from? It's like each of us has some gung-ho freak perched on his back, and these freaks just keep fucking with our heads and kicking us in the ribs. We're all half out of our minds with anxiety, but something's got us boxed in, something won't let us breathe. And we wanna go, man, we wanna *go*, because if the tension gets any higher we're all gonna chew right through our bits. But wait a minute. What's in it for us? And if we're so damned afraid of the finish why are we so desperate to break out of our gates? It's almost as if we're being used, y'know? Consumed. It's as if we're being goaded into busting our butts for...what? To keep our silly asses at each other's throats? Ah, the joke's on us all, my intent and starry-eyed little friends. Because all along it's actually the merry-go-round that's been running the riders, and because...because something just ain't kosher in the cosmos, kiddies."

Sahib stopped mid-thought. He was clearly becoming agitated. He'd thought "I suffer" for so long that articulating "We suffer" was not so much about a feeling of relief as helping to define the common quarry. Now he was no longer the prey. He was a man again. He smelled figurative blood, and for a moment imagined the scent was shared by his company. Then just as abruptly he said:

"Fuck it!

"I tell you, life's a gag, man, a joke; a silly little diversion in the endless labor of creation. And I'm not saying it's not a good joke. I bust a gut every time I think about it. But it's like this is a *running* joke, you dig? It just goes *on and on and on*. Okay, so maybe I'm not smart enough to see the glorious purpose of this living hell, and maybe I'm not deep enough to know whether it's a deity or a demon running the show, but before I go, man, *before I go*, I just gotta get my hands on whatever's in charge and say, 'Hey, Sucker! I'm hip to sick jokes, okay? And I'll take the fall as lamely as the next second-billionth banana. But don't leave me hanging! Man oh man oh man, just what the hell's the punch line'?"

Sahib looked down. He absently fingered the hem of his serape, painfully aware he'd exposed his nonchalance to be as much a façade as his attire. He handed Kevin a book of matches, speaking as though he were addressing one of the idle rich, "You would perhaps consent to sharing some of your herb with the poor souls about you?" Upon Kevin's nod Sahib was rejuvenated. He raised his arms like a choirmaster. "Gather round, boys and girls, gather round. Let us join hands and bask in the generosity of a fellow refugee, this blessed young man from L.A., from the Big Machine." Kevin heard the shadows sliding and shuffling closer. He fired up the joint, took a hit and passed it to Sahib, who drew on it deeply and lovingly, savoring every aspect of the experience. The joint lasted twice round the circle. Then they all held hands around Sahib, who looked on them collectively with a jolly and genuinely compassionate expression. "Friends," he began. "...No, that's not entirely fitting. *Brothers* and *sisters*.

"Brothers and sisters, we are linked here at the dawning

of a new age in the history of civilization as we understand it. On the surface things might not appear as hunky-dory as they are, I assure you, in reality. What with all the shit that goes down, it's not easy to perceive what looks like a lousy and useless life as the celebration it really is. We must always remember this is only the surface we see. Forget all that silly dark crap I was saying. Any fool can see that the source of universal light is love, and that your generation is bringing it home. Now I know this is all old hat, but, if you'll excuse my somewhat irritating penchant for long-windedness, I'd like to take this opportunity to make a few predictions, if I may. Firstly, I see before the turn of the century a complete revision of the old standards. Power, which, as we all know, goes hand in hand with money, will lose its flavor, its *relish*, once it is made evident that love and community are beyond price. There will be more power manifested in a small group forming a chain as we are now, than in all the cabinets, police forces, and administrative institutions in the whole wide wonderful world. Money will eventually become obsolete, unfit even to wipe our precious little asses with, for in our new society no amount of cash will buy...*respect*. The pariahs of today are the elite of tomorrow. And you wanna know something? There's no monopoly on light. Love is gently burning in each of us, just waiting to express itself, to penetrate the darkness as the break of day bleeds back the night. Everybody, I mean *everybody*, is just about to *burst* with love and—what the devil?" For there was a revving of motorcycles at the front of the drive.

"I'll see," Kevin said. He grabbed Janet's hand, and together they crept to the double doors and peered out. What he saw froze his heart. Three motorcycles bearing huge Hell's Angels members were storming the garage. Before Kevin could shout a warning the lead cycle crashed straight into the right-hand door, tearing it from its hinges. Chaos ran through the garage like wildfire as the rats scurried squealing and hobbling through the break in the wall. Janet was screaming and screaming and screaming. Kevin clamped a hand over her mouth, the breath whistling between his teeth as she gnawed his fingers. Neither had been hurt by the falling door, which had lost momentum against the garage wall before sliding on top of them.

Through a crack in the wood Kevin now saw an enormous hairy man in sunglasses, spiked helmet, and full Hell's Angels regalia, dismount and heave his bike back on its stand. His partners crunched in behind him, leaving their choppers just outside.

Sahib, still sitting cross-legged, blinked up at them. "Greetings, gents. Don't be bashful. Come right in."

The burly Angel grabbed Sahib by the front of his Army shirt and hauled him to his feet. "Where's Spacer?"

"That," said Sahib, squirming a little, "is anybody's guess. However I can *assure you* he is most certainly not down the front of my shirt, nor is he anywhere on these premises. He left, in fact, scarcely ten minutes ago."

"You're a liar!" the huge biker roared. He shook Sahib like a dusty rug. "We know he's got our skag. Where does he keep it?"

"I never heard anything about it," Sahib gasped. He coughed horribly, but the biker only twisted harder. "He didn't," Sahib choked, "he didn't say—he didn't say anything to me about—*Vishnu*, you're hurting me!"

"You're a lying motherfucker!" the biker roared. He drew back his fist, aimed, and smashed Sahib in the nose so hard the older man's glasses disintegrated. The Angel picked him up and hammered him in the face again, then took him by the hair in both fists and hurled him down. "You're a liar!" the biker hollered. "You're a motherfucking liar, you motherfucking liar!" He began stomping furiously on Sahib's head with his heavy motorcycle boots.

Kevin flinched at every bloody crunch of boots. Being a hero was out of the question. There wasn't a doubt in his mind that he and Janet would also be stomped if they were discovered, and discovery seemed imminent, for Janet was struggling fiercely beneath him. She seemed bent on chewing clear through his hand.

Now the Angel picked Sahib up for the last time, grabbed him by the hair and throat, repeatedly smashed his bloody face into the wall. "You're a liar!" he bellowed. Jennifer, who had swooned, came running up, beating at the biker with her tiny fists, wailing piteously. Without breaking his rhythm the Angel backhanded her across the face as hard as he could. He hurled Sahib down again, stomped him for good measure, and stormed back to his bike. He pulled an enormous chain off the sissy bar, turned around and began flogging Sahib, who was quite insensible, with all his might. At last he finished and got to work on the walls, whipping the chain around like a lariat. He brought it down hard on the thin wooden partition shielding Kevin and Janet from death, wound it back around the sissy bar and kick-started his motorcycle. He deliberately ran over Sahib's legs, then roared out the doorway and down the drive to the street. There was the double kick and roar of his two accomplices' cycles, the sound of garbage cans kicked over, a squeal of pain from a bystander, apparently also kicked over.

Kevin carefully poked out his head, pushed away the door and wiggled free. "Sahib?" he heard himself whisper, unbelieving. There was blood everywhere. He crept over and slumped against the streaked and bespattered wall, cradled Sahib's broken neck in the crook of his arm. Janet crawled out behind him, saw what had happened and promptly went into hysterics.

Kevin ignored her. *"Sahib?"* he repeated.

After a long moment Sahib's bloody eyes opened.

"How do you…" Kevin stammered, "how do you feel?"

Sahib stared. "How do I feel?" he gasped. "How do I *feel?* I…why, just fine, thank you very much. Never better." He blinked, and a long shudder rolled from his thighs to his shoulders, passed through Kevin, made the boy's feet tremble and his toes cramp. Kevin watched Sahib's facial muscles leap and subside erratically. Sahib shook throughout his final exhalation; a long, ghostly moan that was a shivering legato descent from tenor through basso profundo. Then Sahib turned to stone.

And the garage was swarming with properly concerned people off the street. Kevin felt vomit rising, and a fury so great it drove him howling to his feet. As if cued, Spacer stepped back into the picture, pushed his way to Kevin's side and looked down.

"What happened?" he demanded.

Kevin turned on him with eyes ablaze. "Some fucking

bikers killed Sahib," he sputtered, his whole body trembling. "Because of *you*, prick! They wanted their smack, and when Sahib covered for you *they fucking killed him!"*

Spacer grabbed Kevin's shoulders. His eyes looked like they'd blow out of their sockets. He looked down at Sahib's smashed and gory body, then back up at Kevin. "Oh my God!" he cried, and covered his eyes with a hand. He looked back up, desperately. "They didn't find my stash, did they, man? Tell me! DID THEY FIND MY STASH?" He tore himself away, burst into the kitchen area, and returned in a minute with an expression of immense relief. "Listen," he said reasonably, "I think you two better split. The pigs ought to be here in no time, and the less people involved, the better."

Kevin gaped, his mouth working soundlessly. A woman off the street moaned and began retching, just as the distant wailing of a siren underscored Spacer's forecast. Kevin shoved his way to Janet, grabbed a hold of her arm.

"You motherfucker!" she screamed, and cracked him on the side of the head with a heavy glass ashtray. "You son of a bitch!"

There was a sudden outburst from the crowd, a pressing of bodies. An authoritative voice began hollering for the instant dispersal of all persons capable of voluntary locomotion. From outside came the trilling of a beat cop's whistle. The siren seemed closer. Kevin shook his head and brought Janet down with a flying tackle. He threw her over his shoulder and barged around the side of the garage to their bikes, trying to ignore the teeth at his back. When he set her down he was all ready for another barrage. But she was sobbing quietly now. Kevin shook her by the shoulders.

"Get a hold of yourself, dammit! The pigs are coming. Now calm down!"

She caught herself mid-sob and looked at him strangely, her complexion pale.

"Are you all right?" Kevin demanded.

She shook her head yes, her mouth puckered as if she'd just sucked on a lemon.

"Are you sure?"

She shook her head no. Then she was bent at the waist,

vomiting, choking, vomiting some more, and Kevin was holding her up, trying to think of other things.

The moment she was done he bent down and shakily unlocked their bikes. He had to practically lift her and set her on her seat, and then they were pedaling down the drive. They turned onto the street just as a police car pulled up, lights flashing and siren fading. Kevin made Janet ride double time, and soon they had turned the corner back onto Cole Street, where the flower children were dancing without a care in the world, singing of peace and religion, of love and hope. Kevin wanted to scatter them like tenpins.

# Chapter 17

## Ungoodness

Kevin gingerly lifted the cup to his lips. His hands were trembling so hard the coffee appeared to be violently boiling. Deep brown streaks laced the rose patterns on the porcelain. He sucked the hot coffee down as if it were cool, clear water.

"I only *wish* you'd relax," he said for the umpteenth time. Janet just blew into her own cup and glared.

They were in a nearly deserted diner on Clayton.

Kevin had been on tenterhooks for the past ten minutes—Janet's aura was scaring the hell out of him.

It was her second cup, Kevin's third. He didn't really care for coffee all that much, especially black and unsweetened, but little by little the brew was calming him.

"You feel okay now?" he asked after a while.

"Do you have to keep asking me that? Do you *have* to keep telling me to relax? Can you for five stupid minutes mind your own fucking business?"

Kevin groaned. "Sorry." He could feel another tantrum breaking. "What I mean is, I was only being conversational, Janet. I'm glad you're feeling better. Really I am. And I didn't mean to pry."

"Because maybe it never occurred to you that other people, *real* people, might have feelings and thoughts of their own. How would *you* like it if every time you tried to think *for five crummy minutes* some creep stuck in his big fat face— 'How are you *feeling*, dear'?" she spat. "—'Is *everything* all right now?' Calm down, calm down, *calm down!*" She stood up.

"You're right, of course," Kevin gabbled. "Me, I'll shut up for real, this very minute. You won't even know I'm *here*, I promise. I mean, you can just ignore me if I start to get on your nerves, but I won't, 'cause I'm gonna keep a lid on it beginning right *now*; you'll see, you'll see. And really I'm just like so super sor—"

"I'm sick of it!" she shrieked, and smashed her cup on the table. "And I'm sick of *you!*" She stormed past him and out the door.

"I promise!" Kevin called. "Not another word, I mean it!" He gasped, pushed himself to his feet and made after her. The waitress jumped in front of him, her mouth working, pointing at the table. Kevin pulled a five from his wallet and stuffed it in her hand. He raced outside, catching hold of Janet's arm even as she was straddling her bicycle. "I'll shut up!" he wailed. "I won't say anything else. Ever again. You can count on me because—" She launched herself on him furiously, swinging, kicking, biting. The boy wrestled her arms behind her back, wanting desperately to calm her, trying to be gentle.

"Janet, I'm sorry, please…wait, just let me explain."

She spat in his face, stamped on a foot, kneed him right in the groin. "Get your hands off me, you bastard! *Get your fucking hands off me!*"

"*Please*, Janet," he managed. "I'm really sorry. Really. I promise I won't—"

"TAKE YOUR FUCKING HANDS OFF ME!"

Kevin released her and dropped to his knees in slow motion, fighting for air.

The girl immediately pushed off and tore down Page Street, muttering the vilest obscenities she could muster. Kevin watched blearily for half a minute, at last heaving himself on his bike. He chased her down Page all the way to Pierce, where a mob of screaming freaks forced her to stop. Kevin caught up just in time to pull her clear of a sudden rush of flailing bodies. Janet, blown away by the emotional tempest, for the moment forgot her own crazy anger in the protective enclosure of Kevin's strong arms. A dozen longhairs broke from the mob with expressions of outrage. Others were flinging themselves into the thick of it.

Just as Kevin was melting in the embrace there came an explosive surge. Behind that blew a harsh scream, the squeal of rubber on asphalt, the sound of a store's front window being smashed. A girl stumbled from the thrashing bodies with her fists clenched. She whirled and screamed at the top of her lungs, "You fucking pigs! You fucking pigs!" and burst into tears.

A young man leaped out of the melee and pulled an empty beer bottle from a trash container. He hurled it without aim into the mass of waving arms.

Kevin and Janet gaped at one another, and just like that one flank of the crowd burst like a wave. Kevin shoved Janet out of the way. He plunged back in to retrieve their bicycles.

"Wow!" He ducked his head to avoid flying debris. "What's happening?"

Janet pointed at an open space near the crowd's hub. There, adrenaline-crazed policemen in riot gear, just like the soulless berserkers Eddie had once described, were swinging their riot sticks indiscriminately. Kevin saw a Chinese student, bespectacled, confused, come staggering into the gale. Immediately a cop grabbed this young man by his shirt's collar and cracked him across the forehead with his trusty stick. The student's books and papers went flying, the papers showering all around in the manner of snowflakes. Thrilled camera buffs popped up like jacks out of boxes, recorded the event, crouched, and whirled to catch others.

Litter baskets were blazing all along the sidewalks. Kevin saw a middle-aged beatnik-type, morphing out of the smoke, leap atop a battered automobile and heave a cinder block at a busy policeman. The cop spun and plunged into the shrieking crowd in pursuit. In a moment he reappeared with blood trickling down his face, manhandling a different individual than the offender. This man was windmilling his arms in desperate retaliatory punches, but the policeman had him by the shirttail, pulling him face down and forward. Another cop jumped in and tackled the helpless captive. The crowd roared hatefully as the policemen beat their prisoner senseless. He was dragged away by the collar.

There were whistles, shouts, bullhorn commands. At

least a dozen more policemen breached the mob's center.

Kevin and Janet didn't wait to catch the score. They zigzagged the streets, dazed and confused. Every intersection was a pocket of unrest.

"Man!" Kevin gasped. "Was that ever hairy!"

Eventually their luck turned. They chose streets that were calmer, calmer, and calmer still. On Fulton it was nice and peaceful. They dismounted and sat trembling together on the curb, like waifs.

"Listen," Kevin panted, "I think we should head for the park. I don't know what everybody's all uptight about, but my friend Eddie once told me it's always totally together at the park, no matter what."

Janet draped an arm over his knee, rested her head on his shoulder. "You were so brave. Just like Clint Eastwood."

"John Wayne, at least!"

"Okay, okay. John Wayne, then. Kevin, I think it's my turn to apologize. Maybe I shouldn't have been so rude to you. And back there, when you were protecting me, I started feeling really bad about how I've acted lately. I know I've been a bitch, but please don't ask me to explain." She smiled impishly. "It's a chick thing. I guess when you start to really care for somebody you overreact, and you end up hurting that somebody when you don't mean to. Thanks for putting up with me." She gave him a maidenly kiss on the cheek.

For no reason at all they both laughed. The spontaneity struck them as funny and they laughed again, mounted their bicycles and began to idly roll along, not realizing they were, by choosing their turns indiscriminately, gradually describing a rough square and so, bit by bit, heading right back to the hot spot. But Kevin couldn't take his eyes off her.

He almost spilled. Turning his head, he saw he'd collided with a crazy-looking longhaired man, a man reminding him strangely of a speed freak he'd met at Perky's, millennia ago. The man looked at him angrily.

"Gosh," Kevin said. "I'm sorry."

The man grimaced. "Do you know we've got pigs in the White House? They're drafting our brothers to go shoot poor Viet Namese mothers and children right now! For what? Can you tell me that?"

Kevin shook his head.

"To stuff their fat wallets, *that's* why! To stop the Movement, *that's* why! To stamp out peace and love; all we've worked for, slaved for, busted our sweating butts for! Would *you* like to see your kids sent overseas to get shot up? Huh? Is *that* what you want?"

Kevin recoiled, not comprehending or caring. He looked around wildly. Janet was unseen in the crowd. A gargling sound rose in his throat. He pushed off frantically.

The man grabbed him by the arm. *"Huh?"* he shrieked. "Do you wanna see your fucking kids get shot to pieces?"

Kevin jerked his arm away. "I don't *have* any kids," he gasped. "For Pete's sake, I'm only sixteen!"

"Sixteen! Sixteen! Then you'll be seventeen, before you know it eighteen, and the pigs'll snatch you!"

Kevin broke away, the man scrambling after him, still grabbing. And as Kevin penetrated the crowd's perimeter he could hear the anguished screams—

"Go ahead! *Run!* Run, *coward*! Run to mama's skirts! Run and hide behind your Auntie Sam! You traitor, you fiend, you pervert, you faggot!" Then a haunted, bloodcurdling wail, issuing from a familial gap left unsuccored somewhere between infancy and puberty, *"You lousy motherfucking Commie-loving murdering son of a bitch!"*

Ahead a flash flood of faces turned to see who the murderer was. Faces became elbows, became backs, became a whole army of legs and arms as Kevin plunged deeper and deeper. He plowed into people, vaguely registered their curses, but was deaf to their grievances.

She was gone; that was all he knew. A minute ago she'd belonged to him, and now she was aching memory. He began screaming her name, his eyes afire. But his was only one of hundreds of voices now, and he was being shoved and jostled by a nearly impenetrable sea of humanity, all crying out their empty threats and demands, their voices mingling as one universal, youthful plea for guidance.

"Janet!" Kevin croaked. He was bounced from person to person, was rammed and jammed and caromed about. He'd instinctively kept his grip on his bike's handlebars, and the continually hammering frame was badly bruising his legs.

Then he saw, like a beacon in the night, his deliverance. Not thirty feet away the long chestnut hair beckoned, waving with the heaving human sea. He swam hollering through the arms and heads. Suddenly afraid the current would sweep him off, Kevin lifted his bicycle as an offensive weapon and began smashing his way.

Faces looked at him in terror and pain, in disgust and surprise, but he just kept bashing and bashing until he was a few feet from his goal. But she was looking in another direction, was also being swept away.

*"Janet!"* he screamed, in the confusion not even sure he heard himself. Panicking, he made a frantic snarling lunge and grabbed a shoulder. The chestnut hair flashed across his eyes, and he was looking into the angry face of a young man with long chestnut hair and a fine, sweeping chestnut moustache.

"Hey man," the guy demanded, "what the fuck's your trip?" Instantly he was sucked away, and Kevin was again being pummeled by countless young people, people shoving in all directions.

The passion out of him, he numbly allowed himself to be elbowed along, sucked like a bough into a maelstrom. Dozens of faces rushed by him strobewise; shouts and cries came as in a dream. The angry sea claimed him, engulfed him, made him a nondescript drop in a wave.

And all at once the sea parted.

Twenty feet away, in the partial shelter between two parked cars, Janet was leaning against a handsome, blond, athletic young man. Did she know him? Or were they strangers, finding each other in the whirling madness? There was no time to tell, no time. For his great brown arm was around her shoulders, and her eyes were shining in response to his amorous gaze, and now, and now she was looking up into his half-closed eyes as his handsome face came down and their open mouths met…

Lingered.

The fat boy stood gripping his bicycle, paralyzed. An excruciating pain began at the inner corners of his eyes and worked its way up his forehead, feeling like it was cracking his skull in two. Everything went black for a few seconds; the longest few seconds of his life. His jaw dropped to his chest. His eyes glazed over and his heart contracted. Then, in retarded time, the sea closed in and the bodies came crashing down. But he was rooted; he was fixed. He couldn't be budged.

An hour passed, and still the fat boy stood there, paralyzed. Young people plowed into him again and again, bounced away, and gradually the sea shrank until there were only a few people moving by in the mob's wake, and voices were quite far away.

And still the fat boy stood there, paralyzed.

Throughout the barrage he'd clung instinctively, tenaciously, to his bicycle—the only meaningful thing left. As a consequence there was hardly a square inch of flesh between the ankle and hip of his right side that hadn't been deeply bruised. His vest and shirt were now tattered rags; the big felt hillbilly hat, still secured by its choking leather chin strap, was flattened and jammed down around his ears. One curious result of the battering was that the arms of his glasses had become so fouled in this strap that the glasses had not been dislodged; rather, the apparatus had become virtually implanted in his face, creating a raccoon-like visage of pallid cheeks and brow surrounding the broken red flesh about his eyes. Both lenses were veined with fine cracks from direct and indirect concussions. The bridge had cut his nose badly.

A hilly, littered street stretched before him, but he couldn't see it. His mind would admit only one event:

*A handsome young man was moving his head with extreme slowness. A sweetly pretty girl with chestnut hair was, also in slow motion, parting her red, red lips.*

It took ages for the lips of each face to meet, and when they did the picture froze. A perfect snapshot. Adam and Eve. And, beneath the photograph, an inscription containing a word he'd once heard and not fully understood. His mind, unbeknownst, had filed the word for future application, for a time when unbearable pain made precision vocabulary particularly useless. That word made perfect sense now. The inscription beneath the photograph read:

# SO FICKLE

The boy kept repeating it to himself in his mind.

So fickle.

So false.

So fickle and false and fragile.

Somebody was speaking to him. Somebody was shaking him.

The snapshot, fragile, shattered like glass, splintered and spiderwebbed and was replaced by a figure wearing a blue suit and blue cap.

"I said can you *hear* me?" a voice was saying, clearer now. "Jesus, son, what are you high on?"

"So fickle," Kevin mumbled.

"What?"

The blue-suited figure had something bright on his chest which dazzled the boy.

"Here. Look up here at my eyes," said the voice.

Kevin tilted back his head and stared at a similar bright light on the speaker's cap.

"Where are you going, son?" asked the voice kindly, sympathetically.

Kevin dropped his head. "So false," he said.

"Son, you're going to have to move along. There's an awful lot of angry kids roaming around, and you could get hurt standing here. Can you ride?"

"Fickle, fickle, fickle."

"Look, I want you to get on your bike and ride over to that café there. Can you do that? Get yourself a cup of coffee and something to eat. Do you have any money?"

Kevin felt rough paper being pushed into his hand and two gentle-but-firm hands turning him so that he and his bicycle faced east. Obediently he mounted, found himself awkwardly moving forward. His body got into the easy rhythm of pedaling, and for a while he rode up and down the streets in a trance, unfeeling, wondering only how she could be so fickle and false, how love could be so fragile and finite and feeble and finally he coasted to a stop, exhausted, played out.

Along the sides of this street were endless chains of old and colorful shops. On the opposite side, one of the little shops had the word *CAFÉ* snarled on its front window in flaking red paint. Kevin, fulfilling some obligation he did not understand, stumbled over to it, dragging his ten-speed. He leaned the bicycle against the building's side and, one at a time, removed his aching, swollen hands. In his right fist was a sweat-stained dollar bill.

He pitched through the door. Chimes tinkled. He staggered into a counter stool and his body melted onto it.

An exceptionally ugly old woman was scowling in his face. A half-full glass of dark water was smacked down before him, and a greasy rag went through the motion of swabbing the hopelessly filthy counter with one sweep of a deformed hand.

"Well, if yuh jus' come in here t' gawk at me, yuh kin git yer ass back out the door."

"Huh?" Kevin said.

There was a bark of laughter from the back of the café. Somebody said "Shit," and spat.

"What'll it be, guru?" said the exceptionally ugly old woman.

"Coffee," Kevin muttered, "coffee."

"Thet it?"

"Coffee and…and…and something to eat."

The woman slapped the scummy rag on the counter, turned her stumpy body away. *"Hank!"* she bawled. "Coffee an' a hamburger fer the daffydil." She whirled and glared at him suspiciously. "I'm jus' supposin' yuh got money."

"Money," Kevin parroted, unclenching his fist. The tortured bill dropped to the counter, writhed briefly. He heard the woman curse, the ringing of a cash register, the sound of a few coins being slapped down.

At length a rancid smell reached his nostrils, made his stomach turn. Time passed and his food and coffee went cold.

Little by little he became aware of voices across the room. One, the cackling voice, he dimly recognized as belonging to the exceptionally ugly old woman. The others were unfamiliar.

"If any of my kids ever turns out like that fat son of a

bitch I'll whip the shit out of him."

"Aw, leave 'im be, Ernie. Can't yuh see he's flyin' high?"

"Say there, hippie! You meditatin' on Flo's hamburger? Whaddaya see?"

"Yeah, hippie. You're supposed to eat it, not bless it."

"Hyaw-haw."

"Looks to me like he don't appreciate Hank's cooking none. Now I call that just plain bad manners. What do you boys think?"

"Now, Ernie. Don't be startin' no trouble. C'mon now."

"No trouble, Flo. No trouble at all."

It occurred in a matter-of-fact way to Kevin's crippled consciousness that at least a couple of the voices were approaching.

"Okay, loverboy. Just take your dope and your fat ass out of here before I lose my temper—now, look: I'm not playing around. I said I'm *not playing around!* MOVE!"

"Oh, Ernie, don't hurt him overmuch."

Heavy footsteps. "*Now* what's going on?"

"Hank, this groover's giving us trouble."

"What kinda trouble?"

"Look at him. All doped up. Insulted your cooking. Won't leave after we asked him polite."

"Yeah? Listen, kid. You been served, nobody asked you in here. Go on, beat it. Damn you! *Go on!*"

"Hank, yuh think we should call a cop?"

"Hell no." Two pairs of hands now heaved Kevin off his stool. He heard the door chimes ring a merry *ta-ta*, a burst of laughter, and then his face hit the street. The chimes rang again, followed by the slamming of a door.

Kevin lay stunned for the longest while. Somehow he picked himself up. He wasn't aware of any real pain, nor of any sense of humiliation. And he really wasn't surprised to find that his sleek ten-speed Peugeot, his pride and joy, had been stolen—that the last of his treasures was history. Now the world had just about picked Kevin clean.

Yet the web was still becoming.

# Chapter 18

## Man Down

The day was on the wane.

For hours Kevin sleepwalked the city, climbing up and up and up the interminable hills, flowing down down down and climbing again; around corners and across brightly lit streets choked by traffic, drawing off some bottled-up reserve energy that allowed him to run on automatic pilot—effortlessly, endlessly, miraculously unscathed. He never tired. Those pedestrians he actually blundered into tolerated his stupor with mute resignation. And his absurd costume, which in the daytime might have triggered bitter and drastic retaliation, somehow complemented the festive atmosphere of the city's famous nightlife.

It was a mild, gorgeous evening, the sky crisp and marvelously cool. Cheery, tireless window-shoppers were out in droves, laughing and raising hell, noisily killing time while Kevin parted them like a cable car, following a definite, albeit roundabout, route. The current which drove him on and on appeared to be inexhaustible, his private track stuck to the sidewalks, and eventually his bounds narrowed as his center of gravity stabilized. He bobbed along in a fairly straight line and, except for those occasional collisions, went largely unnoticed as the night progressed.

The safety valve that kept him from shattering—by letting energy escape in this walking and walking and walking—was closing by the time he reached the downtown financial district. For a while he followed Pine Street eastward. He turned left at Kearny and, before turning, glimpsed for a second the lights of the Bay Bridge crossing placid inky water, and beyond that water the glow of Oakland. Kearny Street was jewel-lit, blinding, boisterous and confused, and now Kevin's legs were faltering, his arms dangling at his sides. He was winding down. He stumbled through jabbering Chinatown, where the clamor and bustle turned him on his heel, sending him south back down Kearny all the way to Geary. Here his automatic pilot decreed he perform a right-face and pitch westward to Union Square, where the movements of the crowd milling round the monument commemorating Dewey's Manila Bay triumph got him orbiting the slender spire in steadily narrowing circles, tightening the loops until his foot at last struck the pedestal. He rested his forehead on the cool stone for the briefest moment, only to abruptly rebound into an orbit running counter to his original, backpedaling until his dizzy brain objected and turned him about.

He staggered west on Post Street, stubbing his clumsy hooves on curbs, becoming increasingly maladroit while drawn the mile and a half to the color and hysteria of Japantown. He was weaving across Van Ness Avenue when there was a *click* in his skull, and he performed an awkward left-face. He shambled down Van Ness to the maze of Civic Center, circumnavigated City Hall, plowed through the hedges in Fox Plaza and rammed into the flanks of the Civic Auditorium, where the mercilessly jostling crowds sent him off reeling, zigzagging down Grove Street to Market, down Market to Seventh, at last stumbling through the mob outside the Greyhound Bus Depot. Kevin lurched into the great vault of the depot, barking his shins and bashing his elbows, at last collapsing on one of the cushioned benches. Instantly he was back on his feet, wobbling through the crowd. By chance he wandered to the very bench he'd so recently vacated, and when he crumpled down this time he remained crumpled, drained. His face trembled with dry sobs, the remaining junk beads on his eyeglasses clattering along.

And the diaphanous image of a pretty, fickle girl with fine chestnut hair shimmered before his eyes, her lips parting for a silent laugh at his gullibility. Kevin's jaw dropped and a gut-deep moan of utter despair, of groundless apology, passed from his throat like gas. He granted this apparition exclusive possession of his body and soul; to succor, to trash—to do with as it would. And she laughed again, soundlessly, waxed opaque, offered a slender, ethereal hand. He groped to his feet, lunging for the hand. But she teased him, floating away, her body rippling like a banner in the softest breeze. Forever just beyond his reach, she grew wispy, becoming fainter and fainter as she carefully guided him through the crowd. He followed her back out the depot's giant main entrance, where she glowed angelically in multicolored streaks of neon, grew dimmer in the night, laughed silently again, vanished. Kevin cried out and stumbled off the curb, his arms spread wide. There was the harsh blast of a car's horn, a shriek of rubber on asphalt, and something struck him a terrible blow on the left hip, knocked him ten feet to crack his temple against the bumper of a parked car. Searing pain rocketed up his left side and passed. Absolutely numb, he pawed at the car's fender, fighting to stand. His left leg refused to respond.

Frantic voices gathered round. A woman screamed, a man grated "*Jesus, Jesus,*" over and over. A wild pain blasted his hip when he tried to rise, unlike anything he'd ever imagined. Hands strove to hold him down, but he lashed out and lurched screaming alongside the parked car, the lifeless leg dragging behind. Other voices pursued him, more hands seized his shoulders and arms. He whirled snarling, pitched between two parked cars and across the sidewalk, slammed against a brick wall. To his left rose the urgent howl of a siren. Kevin, using the wall for support, scratched and scraped away. The siren stopped half a block back and the wall ended abruptly. Kevin hopped down an alley gripping his leg, made a left turn down a smaller alley, and burst out into the thinner crowds of Mission Street. The pedestrians moved aside and watched him pass; some frowning, others with laughter. Still gripping the paralyzed leg, he zigzagged the streets again, up Ninth to Market, up Market to Page, up Page to Gough, down Gough to Haight, throwing quick glances over his shoulder.

Haight Street.

He stopped and slumped against a storefront, wincing,

gnashing, hammering a fist on his leg. But the leg might as well have been severed at the hip. A sick pain pulsed at his temple.

Haight Street was darker and less crowded, populated only by shuffling shadows. Kevin fell in shuffling, throbbing along darkly until he reached the great green expanse of Golden Gate Park. The park and surrounding area were inundated with people, and the noise was terrific. Powerful emotions conflicted in his heart when he realized where he was, but the racket drove him away. And besides, the thing in command of his actions didn't want him to enter the park—not yet. It wanted him to follow Stanyan, to stumble across the brief verdant loveliness of the Panhandle, to limp all the way to Geary, to reel westward on Geary to Twenty-Sixth Avenue. At Twenty-Sixth the autopilot grew flustered at a flurry of sensations originating somewhere behind Kevin's eyes and racing through his brain, turning out all the lights inside. The autopilot aborted, dumping the boy on some bags of garbage a few yards into an alley.

The seizure rocked Kevin with varying degrees of violence for five long minutes, and during that span at least a dozen people passed by the alley's entrance. Each made a valiant effort to not notice him, moving along hastily, observing their wristwatches. The boy lazily swam back to consciousness. His perception became crystal clear. Where he lay his view was quite limited: only the brick wall he was facing, the sudden harsh double glare of passing headlights, a smattering of frosty-looking stars in the black wedge of sky above. Still, things were amazingly well-defined, from the pocks in the mortar between the old bricks, to the spiked green halos ringing the headlights. The sounds of traffic grew oddly muffled, the noise of approaching and retreating motors made him grow drowsy. And the drowsiness burned his eyes, and the burning grew hotter and hotter until at last a large round tear formed under his eyelid and made its slow rolling way over his cheek. In quick, scalding succession the tears tumbled from his eyes, rolling down his face to draw dark stains on the front of his shirt.

How could she be so heartless, so blind to love?

How could she just use him, lead him on so insensitively? How could she just toss him? So fickle, so manipulating and selfish. As if drowning, as if going down for that last gasp of water, he saw her face flash by in a fat, flapping portfolio. In what may have been minutes or hours he relived their entire story, from his first impression of her sitting alone by the highway, to the final crushing image of her standing engulfed in the arms of Adam.

At last traffic ceased, and with the ominous silence Kevin's whole world froze. His only observation was a projection that seemed to be dancing on the wall: his burned-out God was cruelly replaying the slo-mo film of Adam and Eve over and over for a one-man audience. Kevin could even hear the steady hum of the projector, see its light hitting the wall from somewhere to his right.

No, it wasn't a projector after all. Kevin's lolling self-preservation instinct let him know the light came from headlights, and the hum from the idling engine of a vehicle that had apparently been motionless down the alley for a few minutes, its occupants observing. He thought he heard something like dogs whining nervously, but the sound didn't jibe with the sadistic film on the wall. There came the grinding of a transmission's gears being changed. The vehicle slowly moved away in reverse as the light grew dimmer and dimmer and the film faded and faded and faded until he lay alone in the blackness of space and limbo.

No getting around it—it's better to have never had than to have had and have lost.

Or, better still, it's better to *have* had and still be indifferent. And yet…what *good* is having; what good is love if it *isn't* of desperate importance? But that means being desperately dependent, desperately vulnerable.

> *Old child, young child, feel all right*
> *On a warm San Franciscan night*

Kevin imagined he heard Sahib's voice, saying, "The joke's on us all," but only a masochist could find humor in this pain.

Silence swallowed him whole. He became insensible to the large and minor sounds, the heartbeat of a great city, and some time passed without his blinking an eye. Then the projector's light was once more mysteriously playing on the wall, and Kevin again heard the whining of dogs—what sounded like big dogs.

*I wasn't born there. Perhaps I'll die there—*
*There's no place left to go...San Francisco.*

A truck door slammed, Another. In the frozen, eerie night, just above the background sounds of kennels and movie houses, Kevin numbly made out the voices of approaching intruders.

*Shee-it! What Ah tell ya. Dat hippie ain't dead. He jes' shammin'.*

A second voice, closer: *"Hey! Homeboy! What ya doin' in da gahbage?"*

*Hee-hee.*

*Git yo' ass up when Ah'm talkin' at ya, foo'. C'mon. Git up!*

Kevin was vaguely aware that his foot had just been kicked, but his whole body was numb, and the kick was no more concrete than a nudge in a dream. He was kicked again, harder, and now there was excited yammering above him.

*Le's check 'im out. Mebbe he gots some dope.*

*He sho' look like he be trippin' on sumpn!*

Hands yanked him roughly to his feet. Kevin found himself looking into the faces of three black toughs.

*Say,* boy. *You gots any dope? You gots any money?* Kevin stared blankly. A sudden fist to the middle doubled him over. Hands began going through his clothes. At their touch something finally penetrated his stupor, and he began to half-heartedly struggle. Fists and feet tore into him, clubbing his skull and ribs as he fell sprawling on his face.

The toe of a boot found his chin, heels came stomping down on his head, and all he could do was throw his arms over his face and take it. In the glare of the headlights he had a quick, blurry impression of a young black holding back two huge frantic Doberman Pinschers, and then he was kicked hard and deliberately in the teeth. There was a splintering of bone. That one act of brutality was a trumpet call. The fists and feet came down in a psychotic hail.

Kevin was now treated to a strange out-of-body vision—he was watching a separate self lying motionless as six eager black hands ran over its broken splayed form.

*Ah gots his wallet. Shee-it! 'most a hunned dollahs!*

Still! Remain absolutely still! Kevin passively examined the hands scurrying over his dead-looking double, tearing open its shirt, yanking down its pants. He very clearly heard the assailants' lusty breathing.

*Nuthin!*

*Le's git da fuck outta heah b 'fo' da poe-lice come!*

*Check out dis belt!*

Kevin's gorgeous snakeskin belt was ripped from his pants. The buckle slashed his face wildly, over and over, until the letters GNIHT NWO were plainly dug across his temple and cheek. A boot slammed into his nose. Arms of radiant light shot from his eyes and passed. Blood began to pool around his head.

*He gonna git da license numbah!*

*No he ain't.*

Where his glasses lay six inches from his gushing nose Kevin saw a shoe come stomping down. His glasses disintegrated with a crunching, kaleidoscopic explosion.

*Le's split!*

The oddly muffled sound of doors slamming shut. The piercing *raw-raw-raw* of Pinschers. The pickup tearing by, narrowly missing crushing his leg. An elongated screech of brakes, then a howl of tires burning as the truck roared away. The sound of the truck's engine became a growl, a hum, a whisper, a memory. And the night caved in, claiming one more statistic for the city.

# Chapter 19

# Be Stupid And Multiply

Kevin's eyes burned. Though very nearly blind without his glasses, he was alert enough to realize it was no longer night, and that he was no longer alone. He was still collapsed on his side, and could dimly make out a figure sitting in a slump beside him. His nostrils relayed to his brain the presence of a nauseating stench.

The figure made a sound somewhere between a belch and a sigh, thrust a bottle of cheap wine in front of Kevin's livid, terribly swollen face.

"'ere, par'ner," a voice slurred. "Nothin' like wakin' up to a good snort o' vino." The figure began to hack repetitively—*ack-a, ack-a, ack-a*; little coughs that were so weak they were almost dainty. Finally he moaned, *"Oh, mama! Oh, please! Oh, Jesus!"* and closed his eyes. A thin stream of vomit rolled out his mouth and down his arm.

The terrible smell and this vague impression of a sick form lasted a while. It grew dark again, light again. Dark once more. Eventually Kevin became aware of a very loud, very scornful voice. Hands hauled him to a sitting position. Bit by bit he was yanked to his knees, to a half-standing slump, and finally upright. The outline of a thin woman's face, laden with huge black-rimmed spectacles, was all he could make out.

"Shame!" her voice rang out; undulant, overwrought, and disgusted. He saw a jaw drop. "Look at you!" She slammed his back against the wall to keep him propped while she pulled up and snapped his Levis. "Just *look* at you! Laying in the gutter drinking wine! Just. Look. At. *You!* And look at that *man.* Do you want to end up like *him*?"

Kevin gaped at the sprawled and unconscious blur.

The hands, locked on the front of his shirt, rocked him with hopeless urgency as their owner strove to get her point across.

"Oh, *why* do you kids *do* it to yourselves? *Why?* What is it you *want*? Do you want us to *listen* to you? Well all *right,* we're *listening!* Do you want us to see it *your* way? *Okay,* then, we'll give it a *try.* But why do you have to *do* this to yourselves? *Look* at you! You're all *filthy* and *sloppy.* You're *drunk* and on *dope.* You just don't *give* a damn, *do* you? And you've been fighting, fighting, *fighting!* All this high-horsing about *love,*" she mocked, "and *peace,*" she spat, "and then you go out and *street fight and drink wine!* Oh, you kids aren't fooling *anybody!* Only yourselves, *only yourselves!*"

She shook him and shook him until his head rolled like a dashboard toy with a spring neck.

"Jesus God! *Why won't you kids listen!*"

The hands shoved him away with failure and disdain, with wasted appeal. Kevin, staggering from the alley, went reeling down the sidewalk under the impetus of that shove, his head bobbing and weaving. He ricocheted off lampposts, wobbled into buildings, careened among quickly parting, cursing morning pedestrians.

A bus bench checked him. Stumbling into it from behind, he was doubled at the waist like a switchblade. Kevin very nearly did a complete flip over the thing, and remained in check: weight supported by the wood backing, knees slightly buckled, torso bunched on the other side, arms splayed, head pressed back against his neck at an awkward and painful angle on the bench seat.

The picture of Adam and Eve mugged him; quick-punched his unblinking eyes, pinned his head with a vicious iron heel. His brain turned on a spit as memories seared it like tongues of flame...her sleeping face, inches away, framed by the powdery dawn. Her silly tears as she soothed the Afghan on Haight Street. Her eyes wide on the side of the coast highway, forehead pale from resting on her arms.

And the ugly truth burst like a wave: He'd been tricked, suckered.

Played for a fool.

She'd never cared for him, the bitch; she'd been leading him on. Played for a fool—*the whoring cunt had played him for a fool!*

Kevin, his wasted face purple with fury, summoned the strength to rise with savage images: he slapped her silly, he beat her senseless, he hurled her into her grave.

He buckled in remorse.

A bus rolled up with a fart of pneumatic doors and immediately roared away. A cloud of black diesel drove him choking to his feet.

Kevin whirled along, his arms before his face, doing a mad pirouette in a world that was a fluid blur; a world teeming with cursing and dodging shadow people, swimming with vague lumbering machines that honked and screeched as he danced among them.

And a blue field was filling his vision, darker than the sky and nearly as immense. This body of water was impossibly placid, shimmering with fuzzy sunshine. Something resembling a serpent spanned the water in roller coaster swoops and climbs. Tiny jewels of bugs swarmed to and fro along a belt running just below the serpent. Toward this gleaming display Kevin was irresistibly drawn, as an infant is drawn to trinkets.

The metal-and-rubber boxes and the shouting flesh dolls grew more numerous as he neared. He shouted back, waving his arms, and somehow they parted. The waving of his arms deteriorated to a spiraling: Kevin whirled round and round, round and round. In this manner he proceeded across the bridge, twirling and dipping until his hand struck a cable and clamped a firm hold. His body was jerked to a halt, but his brain kept spinning; slowing, slowing, at last coming to a smooth merry-go-round rest.

Kevin climbed over the railing.

Everything was cool.

By simply placing one foot before the other and hanging onto these sweetly vibrating strings he found himself perched on a gilded platform, a cotton-soft catwalk. Far below lay the luscious bed of the bluer-than-blue bay. Kevin saw its warm heart concavely, so that the water seemed to reach up round the rim of his vision. He felt that if he let go he would not plunge— he would drift lazily like a dead, disengaged leaf…down down down to the blue water's forgiving, all-encompassing bosom. Like such a leaf, the chorus to a popular song by Donovan Leitch floated into his thoughts, the lyrics contorting his lips:

> *Way down below the ocean*
> *Is where I want to be*
> *She may be…*

A strong hand seizing his forearm aborted his graceful planing descent. The hand jerked him so roughly he almost pitched back over the railing. Inches from his nose Kevin made out the pale, worried face of a middle-aged man in need of a shave. This man's eyes were dark and sunken under oblique brows, as watery and illustrative of pathos as the drooping eyes of an aged bloodhound. The pinched mouth was formed into a perfect O of dismay, and emitted a rhythmic garlicky blast.

"Whoa, son. I said a-*whoa there!* That's no way to solve your problems. That way lies nothin' but sorrow and the for-sakin' of your immortal soul." He hauled Kevin completely over the rail. Gripping the boy's shoulder with one hand, he brandished a ratty copy of a familiar book in the other. "The Bible says you're God's temple, son; it says so right here in this glorious book in glorious black and white, and I can see it wrote in your eyes. And it goes on to say that if anyone destroys God's temple then God's gonna get mighty unhappy and de-stroy that sinner, just as sure as I'm standin' before you now. And to that I say Hallelujah! I say Hallelujah, son! And mighty is the hand of God!" Kevin groaned and let his chin fall to his chest. Another one! Was the world really so full of them…could this dynamic, star-bound species—could this incredible animal that had produced everything from poetry to philosophy to telecommunications—really be, at heart, so intellectually infant-ile? The intruder looked on Kevin's bowed head with keen concentration. "So you repent, do you? And just in time, I'd say. Glory in the wisdom of God! And Hallelujah! All thanks be rendered unto God Almighty, who in Christ always leads us in triumph!"

A number of pedestrians had been drawn to the commotion. The soulsucker whirled on them, holding Kevin's shoulder like a slave auctioneer. "Do ye all come to witness the salvation of a sinner in God's eyes? Do ye see in this child's pain sins native only to his own miserable soil? Well then let me tell you something, my friends, and that something's that there ain't a man amongst you any less guilty of sinnin' before God. Oh, I know you may take the kiddies to church on Sundays, I know for the most part you many be decent enough folk, but I can see it in your eyes—you been fornicatin' and covetin' and carryin' on and hopin' the good Lord's been lookin' the other way. But let me tell you this: Even Satan disguises himself as an angel of light!" He released Kevin and pounded a fist in the air for emphasis. "I can see you snickerin' an' all, but I'm tellin' you, if you don't accept Christ as your healer your soul ain't gonna be worth a damn. Not a damn! You'll rot in Hell, just as sure as I'm standin' before you now." The groaning audience broke up and began to drift away. The street preacher took off after those making the long trek across the bridge, as the duration of his soul-baiting would be extended, unless his victims decided to toss him the two hundred and fifty feet down to the water, by well over a mile. "Hear my prayer, O Lord! Let my cry come unto thee! That's all you got to do: jus' get down on your ever-lovin' knees and ask the Blessed Lord to accept your sinful soul. Is that so hard? Are you all *that* busy? Well, don't be! Don't let Satan get away with it no more! Let 'im know they ain't no fun in fornicatin', they ain't no hope in covetin', and they ain't no time for philanderin'. And," he railed, his own worst enemy, "*they ain't no sense in carryin' on!*"

Kevin limped off the bridge the way he'd come.

The sun imploded, the sky went black, a dizzy rain lashed his hide and passed.

Something oblong cast a stark shadow upon him. He raised his heavy head, peered through blackened eyes.

A yellow sign on a slender pole looked down on him

sternly.

*State Highway 1* said the sign.

Kevin trembled all over, his breath rattling in and out. In a trance, he began taking faltering, rusty steps; the tin man following the yellow brick road to Emerald City, but with no sweet smiling girl to hold his big rigid hand.

It was a long walk.

He reeled through a dark tunnel, groped along a darker wall as traffic whizzed by, passed the Presidio golf course, and so came to the city streets. Far ahead he could see a green expanse capped by the tops of sycamores standing like sentries. As he drew nearer he made out the blurry figures of policemen. These policemen meant to prevent access to the park, but Kevin's automatic pilot, by now a master of timing and obstacle skirting, took over in time to prevent his blundering into their clutches. When they moved down Fulton Street the boy stumbled into a wonderland of cherry trees peppering an endless spread of rolling lawn. He stepped through dainty Tea Garden streams with clumsy brontosaur feet, plodded mechanically over sunny flower gardens, kicked a meandering swath through the John McLaren Rhododendron Dell. Everywhere was a foreboding stillness, a nightmare world of silence punctuated only by the cooing wind and the redundant quacking of ducks at Quarry Lake.

Kevin stopped. Where were all the people? There was only the dimly seen, unending panorama of the park, and this silence heavy as water. The hillocks and roads were littered with every imaginable form of debris, from beer cans to cellophane wrappers to abandoned sleeping bags to used condoms. It was as if a city had stood here, lived and breathed and fought and fornicated, and then suddenly been wiped from the face of the planet with only its waste for an obituary. Kevin stood hearing his stumbling heart, and taking deep gulps of that silence. Now the silence was breathing with him. He stood watching over the mounds of garbage for what seemed hours, waiting with the silence, waiting for Death to step onstage.

And from deep in the quiet came muffled rumbling, a tap dance of vibrations underfoot. The rumbling became the ominous clopping of a horse's hooves, with the chill implication of carriages and headless riders. From the foggy corners of his vision the gloom condensed into a central shadow, the shadow into a huge dark form galloping up on a black steed.

"All right, clear out," the rider called with an unconcealed nuance of menace. "The concert's over, so beat it. The concert's over."

Kevin threw his hands over his head as the rider approached. Just before the stick came cracking across his knuckles he saw a cop dressed in riot gear on horseback. Mounties! Saddlepigs! Real fear rattled him right out of his trance.

"Out of the park, fucker!" the cop was spitting, swatting at Kevin's shoulders and hands. The boy could only protect his head with his arms and gallop Quasimodo-wise as the cop whacked him and the horse's hot foul breath lashed the back of his neck.

"Move it, fucker, *move* it! And don't kick all the shit you left behind. Have a good party, prick? Huh? Whose cock did you suck? I said move it, fucker, *move it!*"

Kevin moved it, screaming, hobbling along like a bike with one training wheel. He felt his face raked by branches, felt his right foot encounter only space, felt concussions on his knees and elbows as he tumbled head over heels down a rocky grade, screaming bloody murder all the way. At the bottom he picked himself up and staggered down a rose-bordered walk. He brought a hand close to his streaming eyes. The hand was swollen and throbbing, discolored in half a dozen spots. He tried to flex his fingers but could manage only the pinky and thumb. He tried to swivel his head, but his neck was bruised and stiff.

He shuffled along, a creature articulate in limps, stumbles, heaves, and spasms. The park, as far as he could tell, was still deserted, but occasionally he heard the cries of wild humans, whooping, shouting, upending trash cans. There was a hint of smoke in the air; the burning of scrub far away in the park. To Kevin's left rose the sound of humans stampeding in terror. A moment later there came a quick-flight clopping of hooves. A small explosion to his right was followed by the distant scream of an automobile's engine at high revolution.

One by one the noises sorted themselves out and left him alone with the silence.

Kevin strained his neck. Several bulges decorated his misty world, but nothing presented itself as a possible mounted policeman. After a minute he leaned against a tree, slid slowly to the ground.

He was undoubtedly still in the park, for all this green could only be trees and grass. Ahead, a flat stretch of blue pond reflected the sun. Kevin was sedated by a feeling of completion, of finality. The peace and this green expanse reminded him of cemeteries he had explored on happier occasions, when the world's deceitfulness had been veiled by his simple trust and basic decency. And suddenly he knew why Fate had aspired, from the beginning, to lead him here, and prevented his meeting his end in a hundred less creditable places. There was a real beauty to abandoning the flesh in such a garden of truth and human awakening. Eddie would gladly have chosen this very spot, but poor Eddie had most likely met his demise in an appalling barred pit under the gloating scrutiny of the Government. Kevin was ready, then. He knew he was ready to die.

No. Not all was sickness and perversion. Somewhere out in the thick of that warped serpentarium we call society there walked a slender goddess who had taught him love, although she had, almost casually, also taught him despair. Everything was in apple pie order. There's no mystery to it at all. Love is fool's gold.

And he was a fool.

But *love* is all gossamer illusion—according to Eddie it didn't exist at all. Then what, Kevin found himself wondering, was this special feeling he was experiencing? What was the name of the emotion that had crippled him? He felt cheated. Betrayed. Abandoned. And coupled with these pains was the awful knowledge that he would still risk even greater pain for the one who had abandoned him.

Just to touch her face, or smell her hair.

For these little things Kevin knew he would willingly, would gladly allow himself to be wounded anew.

"Hello?"

The voice sounded strange, hollow. Kevin slowly, expectantly raised his head. Distinct within the blur, he saw that his angel had come for him.

"Hello," he replied. "I'm ready."

The angel had very pale skin. Her figure had a Renaissance chubbiness, her face a rosy-cheeked fullness, and she turned her head a little in confusion at the boy's reply. Then she beamed.

"I'm glad," she said. "I wish the whole world was ready."

Kevin sighed, saying with difficulty through swollen lips and missing teeth, "Why not? I lost the only thing that really mattered. There's nothing left to live for."

Now the angel came down on one knee, moving her face close enough for Kevin to see her concern.

"Oh, you mustn't think that! There's just *so* much to live for. Why, I don't think a day goes by that I don't laugh, or thank God how lucky I am to be alive on His wonderful Earth."

Kevin sighed again, a deep, autumnal sigh of resignation. "Then you *are* lucky. You must be the only one in the world who thinks like that."

Kevin felt a hand clutch his. The angel said, very softly, "Would you like to meet some more lucky people?"

He couldn't answer, baffled by the no-nonsense reality of her grip, paralyzed by her nearness.

She tugged gently, but persuasively. "Come on. And don't be afraid. Salvation is waiting for you with open arms."

The boy stood and hobbled along beside her, allowing himself to be led. Now he was limping closer, and could hear she was humming an oddly familiar tune in a carefree young manner.

He said gropingly, "I—I don't even know your name."

"Rose," she said, beaming again. "My friends call me Rosy."

"I like Rose better...pretty name. I'm Kevin."

They stopped. A huge yellow school bus blocked their way. Religious graffiti seemed to take up every inch of the old vehicle, and the two words—JESUS SAVES—nearly an entire side. The angel led him up steps into the bus.

"Hi Jerry, hi Mark, hi Brenda. I want you to meet

Calvin."

The guy sitting in the driver's seat spun around and pumped Kevin's hand exuberantly, presenting him with the most psychopathic smile the boy had ever seen.

"Calvin, the man! I love you, brother. I love you!"

"You *do?"* Kevin turned to the angel. "I—I don't understand."

He felt another soft hand placed gently on his arm, and a different girl's voice ask, "What don't you understand, Calvin?"

"He said—he said he *loves* me."

"We *all* love you, Calvin."

Kevin's confusion was so great his first instinct was to flee. Before he could do anything to prevent it, he felt tear after tear roll saltily down his cheeks. He swayed. Hands helped him to a place in the back of the bus. Kevin sat heavily.

"I'm—I'm sorry to act like this," he bubbled.

The angel patted his hand. "You don't have to be ashamed to cry, Calvin. Jesus wasn't ashamed to weep for our sins, and, bad and wicked as we all are, he loves us anyway."

Kevin shook his head slowly. "I don't see how you can talk about love like that. I was in love, and I gave, and she just chewed me up and spitted me out, and love is phony and she was fickle and—and…" his rambling words ended in a gasp of exhaustion. Amazed, he felt his head eased to rest against the angel's warm bosom. He heard her pure heart beat regularly against his ear.

"There's a bit of Judas in us all," she whispered. "But the only way to show them is to love them, and to turn the other cheek." She paused. "What was her name?"

Kevin sank deeper into the fleshy warmth. "Rose," he mumbled, "oh, Rose."

The angel giggled. "Not *me*, silly. What was your girl-friend's name?"

"Name? Her name was—was…gosh, now I can't even remember."

"See?" said Rose. "See how silly it is to worry?"

A close scraping sound. A quiet voice asked, "Is he ready?"

Rose tested Kevin's temple with a forefinger. "Nice and

soft."

He heard the old engine kick over and die. There was laughter up front, the sound of a cheap guitar being tuned. The driver tried twice more. The engine turned over wearily.

"Hallelujah!" came a chorus from all around. "Praise Jesus!"

"Praise Jesus," Rose echoed.

"Where're we going?" Kevin asked.

"We're going to heaven, all of us."

Kevin sighed and let himself lay full-out, his head on the angel's lap. She very gently eased the hat's chin strap about his jaw until it was limp in her hand, then carefully removed the hat. Slowly a smile grew on his battered face. He closed his eyes.

One of the girls gasped. "Look! Look! Look at Rosy and Calvin! It's the Pieta. The *La Pieta!*"

There were several gasps of awe. Kevin sighed again and nestled even deeper in the warmth, unashamed.

"Praise Jesus!"

The guitarist strummed a wobbly chord, but it was the sweetest sound Kevin had ever heard. Then the whole busload was singing:

> *That's the way God planned it.*
> *That's the way God wants it to be.*

The angel's warmth became his universe, her heartbeat his, and Kevin was unaware that the gears of the bus had changed, that they were slowly rolling along.

> *That's the way God planned it.*
> *That's the way God wants it to be.*

Jerry steered the bus over Golden Gate Bridge, up Highway 101 to Mill Valley, then caught Highway 1 to the coast.

On one side of the road a couple of Highway Patrolmen were sitting on their parked motorcycles, sharing a thermos of lukewarm coffee in the shade of a billboard. They both saw the bus coming, and their groans were simultaneous. Over the gargling sound of the engine they could hear laughter and voices ringing:

> *That's the way God planned it.*
> *That's the way God wants it to be.*

"Well, well," said one of the officers in a resigned undertone. "The carnival's in town."

Jerry, grinning insanely, noticed the patrolmen and leaned out the driver's window, flashed the peace sign with his left hand.

The other officer cupped his hands round his mouth and shouted, "*Jesus saves S&H Green Stamps!*"

Jerry honked and waved.

The officers laughed and waved back.

The bus continued lumbering up the road, seemingly dwindling in size. The laughter and singing grew fainter. The bus rounded a bend and vanished.

awgus 18 1967
jime
praz thu lord
i jus wish yoo kood b her 2 fin gzus lik me
i no now i wuz supozd 2 rid up her
i misd thu big kawnsrt in thu prk but i joend thu bigr kawnsrt uv gawd
insid iz ~~litruchr~~ ~~literusher~~ stuf frum owr chrch
i hop yoo wil red it jime in tim 2 sav yr sinfol sol bi taken thu lord gzus az yr savyr
i pra 4 yoo ech minut uv thu da jime
frst i pra 4 yr lag an thn i pra 4 yr hrt an thn i pra yool sa yr u sinr an lt gzus tuch yoo
plez jime plez dont mak gawd go an gt mad at yoo or yoo mit az wl fas it yr u gawnr
thaerz stil tim 2 repnt an remmbr that at owr chrch we r awl polen 4 yoo jime
ps

im kawld bruthr kalvn up her but yoo kan snd yr mune 2

<u>krist r us chrch</u>
<u>pos awfis bawx 10095</u>
<u>yooreku kalu4nyu</u>

sa halulooya jime
bls awl gawdz childrun hoo r awl bruthrz an sistrz in gzus wich
iz wut thu bibl sz an thu bibl iz thu wrd uv gawd awlmit hoo
luvz yoo jime an hoo kan fix yr lag if yoo wil onle sa yr u siner
so jime plez praz gzus thu fawthr thu sun an thu hole gos
amn
bruthr kalvn